A SHOT

WORTH

TAKING

SAMANTHA GUDGER

Books by Samantha Gudger

A Game Worth Watching (Worth Series Book 1)

A Shot Worth Taking (Worth Series Book 2)

Dedication

For Families.

Table of Contents

One

The floorboards groaned as Emma tiptoed across the kitchen floor. She froze, balancing on the balls of her feet, listening. The drip-drop from the kitchen faucet. The growl of a car engine down the street. The whoosh of heat from the vents. No sound of her dad or brothers. Relief flooded through her.

Opening the refrigerator door, the bulb illuminated the dark kitchen. She grabbed what she needed for her breakfast of toast and water.

Her stomach grumbled as she dropped stale bread into the toaster. When the toast jumped from the heat a couple minutes later, Emma scraped the edges of the empty peanut butter jar with a mostly clean knife, extracting barely enough to cover the bread.

Water pipes groaned as a faucet turned on. Emma gasped. Either she was up late or someone else was up early. Her half-eaten toast forgotten, she grabbed her basketball from the floor and headed for the front door.

Outside, the day overtook the night, while inside the shadows refused to give up their hold. The heavy curtains on the front windows prevented light from reaching the interior of the house, so Emma took caution in navigating her path to the front door so she didn't slam into furniture or step on any Transformers or piles of books.

Movement caught her eye from the shadows. A silhouette appeared at the edge of the hallway, causing her to freeze. Lenny. Her younger brother took a step back into the darkness, but didn't retreat any farther. He watched her watching him, neither of them speaking. When the seconds ticked into a minute, Emma took a cautionary step toward the front door. Since her movement didn't elicit any reaction from Lenny, she proceeded on her course, trying not to feel guilty for sneaking out of the house. Not that anyone cared anyway.

Two steps from the exit—two steps from freedom—the door flew open, casting her in daylight, and she found herself face-to-face with Lance. The smell of pot and auto grease made her cringe.

A sneer formed on Lance's face. "What are you looking at?"

Her eyes narrowed as she looked up at him, but she didn't answer.

His eyes fell to her hands. "Nice ball. Where'd you get it?"

Knowing any response on her part would only encourage him, she remained silent. Apparently, he was in the mood to fight because he snatched the ball from her hands. She lunged toward him, reaching for the ball, but he held it out of her reach.

"Give it back, Lance," she growled. She would have sacrificed any other ball for freedom, but this ball had been a gift from Riley. Giving her no reason or explanation for the gift, Riley had placed it in her hands a couple weeks ago with a kiss on her cheek. Only later did she see the message he'd inscribed with a Sharpie. "To Emma. With love, Riley." No way would she let Lance take it from her.

She immediately regretted showing any emotional attachment to the ball, because Lance wasn't stupid. He

2

knew as long as he possessed it, he controlled the situation. He tossed the ball between his hands as she watched him contemplate his next move. Fear crept up her throat. Dropping his eyes to the ball, his hands smoothed over the leather. His sneer dropped for a second, before returning with a vengeance. "It's sad how you still think you have a future in this stupid sport." His hateful eyes met hers. "Let me help you with that."

He reached into his back pocket and, in one quick motion, brought his arm between them and flicked his wrist. She hardly had time to register the exposed blade before he plunged it into the skin of her ball. The air whooshed out as Lance extracted the knife and squeezed the ball between his palms. Her mouth open in a silent scream, she watched the ball flatten in her brother's hands. Fury built within her. Her eyes burned, her throat constricted, her hands formed fists at her sides.

Lance held up the carcass of her ball between them and shrugged. "Oops." He dropped it into her hands and stepped forward, a laugh dying on his lips as he stopped shoulder-to-shoulder with her.

Sensing movement behind her, she turned her head to identify the source. Their dad had stepped out of the hallway, his hand rested on Lenny's shoulder. She didn't know if her dad had witnessed what had happened, but she was convinced Lenny had seen everything, despite the blank stare he gave her.

Lance turned toward her, their faces inches apart and both filled with repulsion for each other. "When you leave today, don't feel like you have to come back." She looked to her dad and younger brother, wondering if they had heard Lance's words. No recognition appeared on their faces. "No one wants you here." Lance's whispered words vibrated through her. She didn't have to question the truth behind them; she knew her dad and brothers felt the same way.

With the deflated ball tucked under her arm, she fled the house, slamming the door behind her.

Her entire body shook as she fought to calm the hatred wreaking havoc inside her. She looked down at her beloved ball. The blade had sliced through Riley's message. If her brother had intended to puncture her heart, he sure had perfect aim. No way could she take the dead ball to Riley's.

Tossing it into the bushes so she could retrieve it later, she squeezed her eyes shut, focusing on slowing her breathing to an acceptable rate.

It didn't work.

Even with the anger coursing through her, she was smart enough not to punch the side of the house, but the forgotten tire swing dangling from the maple tree on the corner of their property promised to be more forgiving. Her fist slammed against the rubber, causing the tire to spin as it rocked backward. Her fist connected with it again as it swung back toward her, the friction tearing open the skin on her knuckles. One more hit exhausted her strength, and she caught the frayed rope of the swing to stop its momentum.

She glanced toward her dilapidated house as if she could see her brother through the walls. Why did every interaction with Lance have to be this way? Yes, they'd had their share of differences over the years, like most brothers and sisters did, but his hatred of her seemed to stem from something much deeper than mere sibling rivalry.

Pushing away from the swing, she examined her knuckles. Fresh blood oozed from the patches of broken skin, but it looked worse than it felt. Grateful she'd worn a black sweatshirt that would hide the blood, she pressed her knuckles against the fabric, hoping the bleeding would stop by the time she arrived at the Ledgers'.

Shoving her fist into the front pocket of her sweatshirt, she started down the street toward Riley's house, taking deep breaths and readying her fake smile to hide the evidence of her morning. Yes, Riley was her best friend.

Yes, he knew about the hardships she faced with her family, but he didn't always need to hear about her latest altercation. She didn't use him to vent about her family, nor did she use her family as a way to milk attention from him. He was her escape from it all, the one shining light she had to help her through it. She wouldn't give him any more reason to worry about her.

Brushing hair away from her face, she shook out the last of her adrenaline and approached the Ledgers' front door. Mr. Ledger greeted her with a smile and ushered her toward the kitchen as he headed for his study. All she had to do was follow the smell of homemade muffins to find Riley's mom pulling out a warm batch from the oven. This is what heaven and home smelled like for Emma.

Mrs. Ledger turned when she heard Emma's footsteps. Her face erupted into a smile, and she threw her arms wide as she pulled Emma in for a hug. "I'm afraid my son didn't share your enthusiasm about getting up with the birds this morning."

"Typical." So much for his promise to be up early.

Mrs. Ledger laughed. "Feel free to go wake him."

Emma crossed the kitchen, heading for the stairs.

"Oh, and Emma?" She turned at the sound of Mrs. Ledger's voice. "Keep the door open, please."

No matter how thrilled Mrs. L was about the developing relationship between her son and his best friend, she was above all, a mom.

"We always do, Mrs. L," Emma muttered.

"And keep both feet on the floor."

Cheeks burning, Emma took the stairs two at a time.

She reached the landing and stopped at the bathroom. The cold water stung her knuckles. Sucking in a breath, she washed the dried blood from her hand, cleaning the wounds as best she could before dabbing them dry with toilet paper so she wouldn't leave traces of her blood on the hand towel.

She tiptoed to Riley's door. Cracking it open, she peered inside and saw him sprawled on his back across his bed. One hand rested on his bare chest, while the other outstretched arm hung over the edge of the mattress. Following Mrs. Ledger's orders, Emma left the door halfway open and crept to the side of his bed. Tousled brown hair, strong jawline, blue eyes at rest behind closed eyelids. He looked younger than seventeen, reminding her of the boy he was when he befriended her eight years ago. What would she have done without him by her side all these years?

Despite her intent, she couldn't bring herself to wake him. She turned back to the door, leaving him to sleep, but an arm wrapped around her waist and tugged her backward. Her scream cut off as she crashed down on top of Riley. He laughed and rolled her over so she was sandwiched between him and the mattress. He smiled down at her. "Stalker."

She smacked him on the chest and tried to shove him off her. "I'm not a stalker. Your mom told me to come wake you."

"Uh-huh. Sure, she did."

"She did." When his weight proved to be too much for her to push off, she attempted to remind him of his mom's words so he'd let her free. "She also told me to keep both feet on the floor."

Riley looked at her feet dangling off the end of his bed. "Uh-oh. You broke the rules. I'm going to have to report this."

"I didn't—"

"Mom!"

"What are you doing?" she hissed, her eyes flicking toward the open door. She tried to scramble off the bed, but Riley kept her pinned to the mattress.

"Moooom!"

"You're going to get me in trouble—"

Catching movement out of the corner of her eye, Emma turned to find Riley's mom standing in the doorway.

"What is going on?" Mrs. L asked.

Riley pointed to Emma's feet. "Emma broke the rules."

"I didn't—"

He clamped his hand over her mouth, while at the same time managing to pin her arms beneath him. "And then she tried to get me to close the door."

Emma managed to thrash around enough to free part of her mouth. "No, I—"

His hand found her mouth again, stealing her opportunity to defend herself.

"She's becoming a bad influence on me," he shout-whispered.

Forcing back a smile, Mrs. Ledger shook her head and tsked. "What should we do about her?"

"House arrest. Ours, not hers. For a month."

Emma stopped struggling. House arrest at the Ledgers' for a month? She raised her eyebrows at Riley's mom, silently communicating the need for punishment. She did break the rules after all.

Mrs. Ledger laughed. "I'll think about it and let you know." She disappeared down the hall, her voice floating back to them. "Breakfast is ready when you are."

"Ooh, breakfast." Riley kissed Emma on the forehead and jumped off the bed. He disappeared into his walk-in closet and reappeared a couple minutes later in a pair of basketball shorts and a sweatshirt. "You coming?"

She remained on the bed, making no move to get up. "I don't know. Now that your mom thinks I'm a bad influence on you, am I even welcome at the table anymore?"

He grabbed her hand and tugged her up. "Hmmm, good question. I'll have my dad talk to her; he's a pro at getting back into her good graces."

Emma laughed, knowing she was more likely to get kicked out of her own house than the Ledgers'.

◆◆◆

After scarfing down a couple muffins and fruit salad, Emma and Riley waved goodbye to his mom and headed down the hallway toward the front door. When they passed the study, they heard Mr. Ledger on the phone.

"Today?" A pause, as if Mr. Ledger took time to exhale. "No, of course not."

Despite his words, Mr. Ledger's tone seemed unsure as he reassured the person on the other side of the conversation.

"Sounds serious," Emma whispered to Riley, who nodded in agreement. Although Mr. Ledger often took phone calls from his fellow engineers, he didn't often do business on Saturday mornings.

"It's fine. I promise," Mr. Ledger continued. "I understand."

"Come on." Riley grabbed her hand and pulled her away from the door. "I'm sure everything is fine. He's probably consulting one of his clients about a project or something."

As they laced up their shoes, Riley asked the question she'd been dreading.

"Where's your ball?"

Ordinarily, it wouldn't have been an issue, but ever since he had given it to her a few weeks ago, she had carried the ball with her everywhere. She couldn't meet his eyes; she couldn't tell him that her brother had stabbed it. "I forgot it."

Riley grabbed his ball and followed her outside, pulling the door closed behind him. "How about you try the truth this time."

She pulled up the hood and pulled down the sleeves of her sweatshirt to hide from Riley's penetrating stare. "I didn't feel like bringing it today."

He turned his focus to the ball in his hands. "Must be quite the story if you're still feeding me lies." With a sigh, he set the ball down and crossed his arms, showing he would wait it out until she could muster up the truth.

She bowed her head, her fingers working the sleeves of her sweatshirt. "It was flat."

"Is that all?" He picked up his ball and descended the porch steps. "Let's go get it. We can pump it up before we go to the park."

When she didn't move to follow him, he stopped and turned around.

"We can't pump it up," she said.

"Why not?"

"Because it got a hole in it."

"How?" Walking back to where she stood, his eyes scanned her as if she had the answer written on her body somewhere.

"It doesn't matter." She hoped he took the hint that not only did she not want to talk about it, but she refused.

"Emma—"

His tone alone put her in defense mode. "Riley, stop." She shook her head, meeting his determined look with one of her own. "Let it go."

"Emma—"

"Let. It. Go."

The muscle in his jaw twitched and his nostrils flared as he put two and two together. He always knew something had happened with her family when she put up her wall. When he spoke, his voice was low, barely controlled. "What about your hand?" He picked it up and looked at the raw skin, some of which had started to bleed again. "Are you going to tell me to let this go too?"

"Yeah," she bit out. "I am."

He opened his mouth to protest, but she yanked her hand from his and walked away, heading to the park. She didn't need to turn around to know he was taking deep breaths and swallowing his pride. He couldn't force her to talk, and he knew it. It took him a couple minutes to catch up to her. When he did, his fingers snuck their way back between hers. He brought the back of her injured hand up to his mouth and kissed it. When she stopped and looked up at him, surprised by his change of behavior, he flashed her a Cheshire cat grin. "This is our first fight as a couple."

"And you're happy about that because?"

He shrugged. "It feels like us. We've survived years of fighting with each other, and I was worried it would be different now that we're together, but it's not."

She laughed. Only Riley would turn their first fight into something to be happy about.

They arrived at the park hours ahead of the others so they could shoot around and play some one-on-one before everyone else arrived. She usually relished in their time together, but today, more than anything, she needed a game of basketball with the guys to blow off steam.

Two

E mma braced for the collision. The new guy, Tyler, charged straight for her, driving toward the basket with no intention of stopping. Pushing off the ground, he took flight, the basketball secured between his hands as he slammed into her. His momentum carried him up toward the basket as gravity claimed her as its own. The dunk, followed by the five-second hang off the rim, would've been impressive if the guy hadn't executed it a half-dozen times already over the past two hours.

Riley glared at Tyler's back and reached out a hand to Emma to haul her body off the ground for the fourth time that day.

"I really wish you'd stop putting yourself in his path," Riley grumbled.

"I wouldn't have to if anyone else stepped up to guard him."

Shiloh clamped a hand on Emma's shoulder. "Our girl's right. The guys are letting Tyler dominate the court; they're not even trying."

Riley wiped the sweat from his forehead. "This game is getting old."

Saturday morning basketball games with the guys, including Shiloh and Ashley, were usually the highlight of the week, where everyone congregated to play the game they loved until obligations pulled them away, but today was different. Unlike other new guys who had joined them in the past, Tyler made everyone look for a reason to quit early. While the guys had pretty much given up, Emma was determined to shut him down, or break a bone trying. She didn't care that Tyler's six-three frame towered over her, that his bulging muscles could have flattened her with one swipe, or that his permanent scowl fixated on anyone who dared get in his way. All she saw was a competitor, one who helped her keep her thoughts away from her family.

Riley's forehead pinched in concern. "You sure you're okay?"

"Yeah, I'm fine."

His concern gave way to a scowl as he snatched her hands and turned them over. She winced as his thumbs rubbed against her newly torn palms.

"You call this fine?"

"Yeah, I do. Simple flesh wounds." Tugging her hands out of his grasp, she blotted them on her sweatshirt. "See?" She held her palms out for his inspection, hoping they looked better without the fresh drops of crimson. "Hardly enough blood to stain."

Before he could respond, the guys shuffled into position for the next play. With a sigh of disapproval, Riley kissed her cheek. "Please be careful."

"Always."

He rolled his eyes. "Hardly."

At the top of the key, Tyler offered the ball to Tom to initiate the offense, but when Tom reached for the ball, Tyler lobbed it to his other hand. They stared at each other before Tyler offered him the ball again. Tom hesitantly reached for it when Tyler dropped it and dribbled between his legs, enjoying his game of keep-away. Tom wasn't amused. Foregoing the ball, he shoved Tyler, causing the new guy to stumble backwards.

"What the hell, man?" Tyler's playfulness turned to anger as he regained his balance and lunged toward Tom.

Emma flung herself between them, a hand on each of their chests, before the punches started. "Guys, come on. It's just a game. We're all here to have a little fun."

Yeah right, like anyone on the court believed that. Saturday morning games were more than mere recreation for their group. Knowing it wouldn't take much for Tom and Tyler to start pounding on each other, Emma figured a change was in order. "Tom, go guard Cy; I've got Tyler."

No one moved. She felt the tension in both of their bodies, her hands humming from their anger, as they glared at each other.

"Go," she growled, shoving them in opposite directions.

"No way am I letting you guard that guy," Riley muttered in her ear, his arm slipping around her waist. "That guy has been looking for a fight all day; I don't want you to get hurt."

Rising on her toes, she kissed his cheek, an act that had become natural lately. "I'll be fine. It's not like the guy is going to hit a girl." Right?

"Let me guard him instead."

"Riley," she said firmly. "I got this." No way was she going to play the damsel in distress and let Riley spare her from facing the beast.

They stared at each other, waiting to see who would relent first. Riley broke eye contact and tugged her into a hug. He pulled back and placed his hands on the sides of her face. "For the record, I don't like this."

"I know," she whispered. "But you've got my back, right?"

"Always." He kissed her briefly before turning his attention to the rest of the guys to try and diffuse the lingering tension. Emma walked over to the sideline to get a drink of water and talk with Shiloh and Ashley, giving the guys a chance to cool down. Ever since that fateful day when Emma's two worlds collided in a game of basketball, girls from the team still showed up. With playoffs looming in the near future, Emma advised the girls to take a break from Saturday games with the guys; Shiloh and Ashley were the only ones who refused.

"Your boyfriend isn't too keen on you taking on the new guy, is he?" Shiloh said, coming up behind her.

"Do you blame him? Tyler's a monster."

"Yeah, that's why Riley doesn't want you guarding him." Shiloh laughed before guzzling water from her water bottle.

"What is that supposed to mean?"

Shiloh pointed across the court. "Look at Tyler. He is the epitome of tall, dark, and handsome. If you were a normal girl, you'd know he's the kind of guy girls drool over and the kind of guy boyfriends despise."

Emma squinted to try and see Tyler more than a guy with an attitude problem. "I'm not seeing it."

Shiloh and Ashley laughed.

The break ended, and the three girls headed back to the game. The freshman was supposed to sub in for one of the guys, but Emma stopped her. "Hey, Ashley, do me a favor."

Even after three months, the kid still followed Emma around like a loyal sidekick. When the freshman had asked Emma for help with basketball at the beginning of the season, Emma never thought the kid would make it on the basketball court, let alone as Emma's friend, but Ashley had proved her wrong on both accounts.

"What's up?" the freshman asked.

"Sit this one out."

Ashley opened her mouth to protest, but Emma cut her off. "Please. I don't want you getting hurt." It didn't escape her attention that these were almost the exact words Riley used on her minutes ago, but unlike Riley, when it came to

Ashley's safety, Emma wasn't going to take no for an answer.

"You don't think I can take Tyler, do you?"

Emma laughed. "I don't know if *I* can take Tyler, and things are getting pretty intense out there. Please. Just this once."

"Okay, Coach."

Emma squeezed her shoulder before turning back to the court and finding herself face-to-face with Shiloh. Emma opened her mouth to reiterate her request to her friend, but her teammate didn't let her get that far.

"Don't even think about it. You know your commands don't work on me."

Emma rolled her eyes. "Fine. Just be careful. We really can't afford you to get hurt before playoffs."

Playoffs. It was hard to believe the Bradshaw High School girls' basketball team had secured enough league and district victories to qualify for regionals. Their win against Evergreen High School three weeks ago had fueled the team with enough momentum to make them unbeatable. One more week and Bradshaw would be playing their regional game, which would determine if they'd get to go to the state tournament.

"We can't afford you to get hurt before playoffs either," Shiloh said.

"I'll be fine," Emma reassured her.

Shiloh plastered on a smile. "Me too. Besides, we both know us girls are the only ones who can maintain any sort of peace around here."

Emma smiled. "You know it."

The two girls bumped knuckles and returned to the court.

Emma matched up opposite Tyler, her game face securely in place.

"Oh, yay." Tyler closed the distance between them so they were practically chest-to-chest. "I get the beauty queen."

"If you're looking for a beauty queen, you've got the wrong girl," she growled, pushing off his chest. She sprinted toward the three-point line, her hands held out to Jerry, asking for the ball. He passed it to her, and she turned toward her defender.

She wasn't a stranger to tight defense, but Tyler's closeness made her want to hit him. The hand he placed on her hip to better track her movements slid lower, and a chill of disgust and anger swept through her. She rammed her shoulder into him to gain some space, but that only seemed to encourage him.

"Hey!" Riley flew across the court and shoved Tyler. The new guy stumbled backward, laughing. "Keep your hands off her," Riley growled.

Tyler smirked. "Jealous?"

Riley charged ahead, and once again, Emma found herself in the middle of a battle. She knew Riley would do whatever it took to protect her, but she really didn't want to explain to his parents how she let their son get beat up over her.

"Riley." His eyes never strayed from Tyler. "Riley, look at me." She put her hands on his face, guiding his focus to her. His shoulders were tense, his hands fisted and ready in case a fight broke out. Reluctantly, he dragged his eyes away from Tyler and focused on her. Hatred swirled in the depths of his eyes.

"It's fine," she said.

"It's not fine," he yelled. "His hands were all over you."

"What's the matter?" Tyler taunted. "You afraid of a little competition?"

Emma laughed and spun around. "You're not competition." She grabbed Riley's arm and pulled him away as Tyler's arrogance cracked a bit, his smirk sliding into a sneer.

She opened her mouth to try and calm Riley down, but he spun on her and cut her off. "Don't, Emma." His eyes burned into hers. "Don't tell me to let this go. I'm not going grin and bear it as some other guy puts his hands on my girlfriend."

She held up her hands in surrender. "I'm not asking you to. The guy is trying to prove to everyone that he's in control. Rather than fight with him, we need to beat him at his own game by playing ours."

Riley seemed to consider her words. Jaw set, eyes tight, he dropped Emma's hand and took his position across the court, somehow remaining calm when Tyler resumed his tight defense strategy.

A few plays later, they got their opportunity to knock Tyler off his pedestal. Emma intercepted a pass and dribbled downcourt with Tyler as her only defender. She knew he would block any shot she put up, but Riley and her hadn't played together for years for nothing. She knew he was a few steps behind her on the left side, so as she approached the basket, she tossed the ball into the air. Riley snatched the ball from its descent, and with a 180 spin, he executed the perfect backward dunk. He didn't hang from the rim or emit a growl of victory, instead, as Tyler recoiled in surprise, Riley landed on the ground smooth as a cat. Mr. Ledger had taught his son how to play the game, not how to steal the spotlight by showing off. Just because Riley didn't usually dunk, didn't mean he couldn't.

Tyler was all power and aggression, whereas, Riley was all grace and finesse. Every move Riley made on the court was intentional and flawless. It was hard to believe he was the same ten-year-old boy who could barely muscle the ball up to the basket. His once scrawny arms and legs had become toned and muscled, giving him the strength he needed to excel on the court. Confidence and love of the game held any potential cockiness in check.

"How was that for playing our game?" Riley asked her.

She shrugged a shoulder. "It was okay. Your timing was a little off."

"That was to be expected since I had to deal with your lousy pass."

Her laughter joined his as he wrapped her in his arms.

As they passed an awestruck Tyler on their way to the opposing basket, she couldn't help herself. "What's the matter? You afraid of a little...competition?"

He didn't say anything, but the aura around him darkened a few shades.

On the next play, Tyler tried barreling his way to the basket to dunk, but Carson and Alex blocked his way, so he pulled up to shoot instead. Emma saw the opportunity to sneak up behind him. As he raised the ball over his head to shoot, she slammed her hand into the top of the ball, forcing Tyler, his momentum, and the ball back to the ground.

"Foul!" Tyler yelled.

The guys laughed.

"Sorry, man," Jerry said. "That was all ball."

"Ouch." Tom sucked in a breath. "I bet that hurt. Getting stuffed by a girl and all." The guys chuckled, silently giving Tom props for his comment.

No one offered a hand to help Tyler up. On their court, that sort of gesture had to be earned not given.

As they set up for the next play, Tyler stepped in front of her, his signature sneer in place as he looked down on her. "You may act like you're all that, but all I see is a pathetic loser."

He brushed by her, giving no indication he'd said anything at all, but his words reminded her too much of her brother, and she lost it. Spinning around to follow him, she shoved him from behind. Hard. He flew forward, regaining his balance in time to spare himself a face-plant with the concrete. He whirled back in her direction. When he lunged at her, she didn't move; she didn't even flinch. She had years of pent-up anger that she was more than willing to take out on this jerk. The guys erupted around her, a few of them grabbing Tyler before he reached her.

18

A chest and shoulders impeded her vision of Tyler, and she looked up at Riley. Pinched eyes, open mouth, hands out in the attempt to calm her down. All signs questioning her behavior.

She turned away from him.

"Whoa," he said, grabbing her arm to prevent an escape and stepping in front of her, searching her face. "What happened?"

"*Nothing*. The guy is a jerk; he had it coming."

Riley shook his head, not taking his eyes off her. "You and I both know that's not it."

"Come on, Riley. Let's just play." She gestured to the court where Shiloh and the guys were setting up for the next play, not in the mood for a lecture. "The guys—"

"The guys can wait." He waved away her protest. "I know you don't want to tell me about whatever happened this morning, but this?" he pointed to the court, referring to her outburst. "Between this, your ball, and your hand…" He pressed his lips together and shook his head. "I'm asking you as your best friend to tell me what's going on. Please."

Oh, no. Not the best friend card. He only played it as a last-ditch effort before doing something drastic like getting their parents involved or questioning her brothers. She searched her thoughts for a believable story that didn't divulge the entire truth. "Riley—"

"Don't lie to me, Em. I'm serious." The intensity of his eyes and the energy surging through his rigid body affirmed his words. "When I see you with a bruised and bloodied hand and listen to you try and feed me lies to cover it up, and then the words of some jerk cause you to start a fight you can't win, it doesn't exactly make me feel like I can trust you to keep yourself safe. I can't stand around and watch your family hurt you again and again. I won't. So I'm asking you. What happened?"

She turned her head away, noticing Shiloh, Ashley, and the guys watching them. With a look as hard as stone, but with a touch as soft as a bird's feather, Riley's finger guided her chin back to him. His eyes asked her to trust him, and she couldn't say no. Having no other choice, she recounted the incident with Lance, including her attack on the tire swing.

When she was done, she expected him to yell or for anger to flash in his eyes. What she didn't expect was for him to place a hand on the back of her head and draw her against him. His other arm circled her waist and his lips rested against her forehead. "Emma."

"I didn't want you to know that I ruined your present," she confessed.

"Like I care about a stupid present." After two deep breaths and a shake of his head, Riley pulled back from her. "You want another ball? I'll get you one. You want ten? Done."

"You're missing the point."

He raised his hands to capture her face between them. "The point is, I'd rather your brother take out his issues on a ball than on you, and I'll replace as many presents as he destroys without complaint as long as he keeps his hands off you." He pulled her against him again, squeezing her harder than before. "Geez, Em, he had a knife."

She shook her head, knowing the direction of Riley's thoughts. Yes, her brother's words sometimes sliced her like a million paper cuts, but they were just words. Aside from a few scuffles growing up, he'd never laid a hand on her. "I know Lance is mean, but he would never hurt me."

Riley didn't have to say anything to indicate he wasn't as trusting. Wanting desperately to move past the drama, she rummaged up a smile. "Can we get back to the game now?"

He breathed out a laugh. "Yeah, just don't try and take on Tyler again, okay?"

"I'll be on my best behavior."

Not wanting to break her promise, she resolved to let Tyler's words go and focus on basketball. Tyler held the ball on his hip in triple-threat position, watching her. She waited for him to pass the ball to one of his teammates, but he didn't seem to be in the sharing mood. A crack in his sneer, the ghost of a smile directed at her. It caught her off guard and she wondered what it meant, but he didn't give her the chance to think on it. He drove to the basket like a freight train. She stuck with him, determined not to give him an easy basket. When he pushed off the ground, she matched his jump. With her arm outstretched, her hand attempting to block the ball, she saw Tyler's elbow too late as it swung toward her, connecting with her face. Her head snapped back, her momentum lost, as she crashed to the ground.

Tyler's smile made so much more sense now.

Three

E mma's head exploded in pain. She was vaguely aware
of the guys charging Tyler, of Riley's voice calling to
her, and the warmth of his hand on her cheek.

"Emma?" Riley's voice shook with concern. "Em, talk to
me. Come on. Open those beautiful green eyes and tell me
I'm an overprotective boyfriend who has no basketball
skills."

"Finally, you admit the truth."

His laugh included a sigh of relief at hearing her voice.

Her eyes fluttered open, and Riley's face filled her
vision. "Did he make it?" she asked. Riley's face pinched in
confusion. "The shot. Did he make the shot?"

"No," Riley said. "He missed."

She pushed herself into a sitting position. "Good."
Taking a deep breath, she assessed the damage. Aside from
a throbbing in her eye and cheek from Tyler's point of
impact, and a pounding in her head from where it had
smacked against the pavement, she figured she'd survive.
When Riley touched her hand with the sleeve of his
sweatshirt, she hissed and knocked his hand away. "Ow."

"Sorry." He held up his blood-splotched sleeve for her to
see. "You got another cut on your hand."

Now that he had said something, she felt the pain and numbness fighting for dominance on her marred hands. "Great," she muttered.

Shouts echoed around them, and she looked over to see the guys ganging up on Tyler. Ashley once told her the guys would've taken a bullet for her. Judging by their current facial expressions and threats, she believed they would.

"It's not my fault she couldn't defend herself." Tyler swept his arm in her direction. "This only proves that girls shouldn't play basketball with the big boys."

"Is that why you took a cheap shot at my face?" Emma called out as she pushed off the ground to stand.

Tyler rolled his eyes. "It was an accident. Just because you've got no game doesn't mean you need to blame me for your incompetence."

"Incompetence?" She took a step toward him, her arms flinging wide to challenge him, despite the throbbing in her face and head. "You want a rematch? Let's go."

Emma nodded to Jerry. "Pass me the ball."

Jerry's eyes flicked to Riley, as if asking for permission.

Riley slid a restraining arm around her waist. She tried to shove him off, but he held on.

She whirled around to face him. "Riley Aaron Ledger, if you don't let me go—"

"What are you going to do?" Riley challenged her.

Her threats didn't hold any power over him, but he knew she'd never backed down from these jerks before, so he should understand her need to prove herself now. "Tell Jerry to give me the ball."

He shook his head. "No, we're done here." She barely registered his words before she found herself hanging upside down over his shoulder. "C'mon, tiger."

"Riley," she yelled. "Put me down."

Ignoring her, he waved to everyone. "Guys, we'll see you later. Shiloh and Ashley, make sure they don't kill each other."

"Riley," Emma snapped.

Everyone laughed as he carried her off the court. Good to know her humiliation could defuse tension.

Flailing her arms and legs, she tried to break free, but Riley knew how to restrain her to avoid harm. When did he get so strong? "Do you enjoy humiliating me in front of our friends?"

Riley chuckled. "The last thing I was going to do was let you go head-to-head with the guy who almost knocked you out. So yes, a little humiliation for you is fine with me."

"He didn't almost knock me out; he took me by surprise. I could've taken him." She gave up fighting and hung limp over his shoulder.

"Hey, Riley?"

"Yeah?"

"Do you think your mom will ground you for letting some guy hit me?"

Before she had time to laugh, her world righted itself as Riley placed her on the ground in front of him. His eyes widened with fear.

"Only if she doesn't kill me first."

If they had wanted to keep what happened at the court a secret, they should've steered clear of Riley's house, considering the parental figures of the Ledger household were a force to be reckoned with. Riley and Emma weren't three steps in the door before Mr. Ledger turned the corner into the entryway, his eyes zeroing in on the two of them.

"What happened?" Mr. Ledger asked. He caught Emma's chin in his hand, turning her face to inspect her swollen eye.

"Some jerk at the park punched her," Riley said.

"He didn't punch me," Emma said, twisting out of Mr. Ledger's grip. "I just happened to be guarding him when he went up for a shot and let his elbow do the talking. It's not a big deal."

"Riley," his mom scolded, joining them from the living room. "How could you let this happen? You're supposed to look out for her."

"Mom I—"

Emma laughed and put her hand on Riley's arm. "Don't blame him, Mrs. L. He tried. If it makes you feel better, instead of attacking the guy, Riley stayed with me like a perfect gentleman to make sure I was still alive and breathing."

Mrs. Ledger tossed her son a disapproving mom look. "I guess I can't be completely disappointed in him then."

"I should've seen it coming." Riley growled. "Especially since the guy hit her on purpose."

"Do you know that for a fact or are you merely pointing fingers?" his dad questioned. Emma sensed he was on the verge of his "innocent until proven guilty" lecture that they had heard a million times.

"It could've been an accident," Emma said, knowing for a fact it wasn't, especially not after the smile Tyler had given her right before it happened.

"Trust me, it was intentional," Riley assured his dad. "The guy wasn't exactly a saint when he stepped onto the court, and considering Emma stuffed the ball in his face on the previous play, the guy elbowed her on purpose."

"Oh."

Emma laughed. "Oh? What's that supposed to mean Mr. L?"

"It means I'm going to have to agree with Riley on this one."

"And why is that?"

"Because whenever a guy gets his shot blocked it's humiliating, but when a girl does it, well, most guys just aren't that strong."

Mrs. Ledger's fingers gently caressed Emma's cheek as if trying to suck the pain out. Was it wrong for Emma to enjoy having a mom express concern for her? Emma's mom had abandoned her family five years ago, but Mrs. L had become a welcome replacement in Emma's heart over the years.

"I'm glad you two are here earlier than usual," Mr. Ledger said, his tone turning businesslike and suggesting bad news was to follow. He exchanged a look with his wife that neither Riley nor Emma missed.

Riley reached for Emma's hand and they shared a look of their own, trying to reassure one another that whatever had happened they would face it together. "What is it?" Riley asked.

Mr. Ledger ushered them into the living room. "There's been a change of plans."

Riley and Emma sat on the couch, their sides pressing against each other as they braced for whatever Mr. Ledger was building toward.

"Remember when we told you the son of one of your dad's old friends would be staying with us for a while?" Mrs. Ledger asked.

"Yeah," Riley drawled out, his eyes skipping from one parent to the other. "He's coming next month, right?"

"I got a call from my friend this morning." Another one of those shared parent looks. "His son actually came—"

The front door swung open, and they all spun around to face the person entering the house. It took Emma and Riley only a second to recognize him. "What are you doing here?" Riley growled, launching off the couch and stepping in front of Emma as if he expected the guy to hit her again.

Tyler groaned and his head fell back. "You have got to be kidding me."

"Get out of my house," Riley roared. "Now!"

Riley's anger did nothing to deter Tyler from stepping forward, his face breaking into a malicious grin as he looked between Riley and Emma. "This should be fun."

Riley's hands clenched into fists, but before he could do anything, Mr. Ledger stepped between them. "Riley," he scolded. "What in the world is wrong with you?"

Emma had never seen Mr. Ledger's eyes burn when they

looked at his son. The look of disappointment emanating from them made her look away.

"This is the guy who hit Emma," Riley said through clenched teeth, ignoring the look from his dad.

Mrs. Ledger gasped, her hand darting forward to grab Emma. Mr. Ledger spun toward Tyler.

"Is this true?"

Tyler shrugged a shoulder. "Sometimes things happen."

Riley charged him, but this time Mr. Ledger intervened rather than Emma. "That's enough. Both of you," Mr. Ledger snapped, his eyes darting between the boys before settling on Tyler. "Your parents sent you here because they said you needed some time away, but if I hear of you hurting my son or Emma or anyone else, accident or not, you'll be on the first plane back to California, and from what I hear that means military school for you. Am I right?"

Tyler pushed off the wall and matched Mr. Ledger's glare, but he didn't say anything, which was confirmation enough for Emma.

"Do I make myself clear?" Mr. Ledger yelled, causing Emma and Riley to flinch.

Tyler's eyes hardened as he puffed out his chest. "Yeah. Sure."

"Good." Mr. Ledger turned to Riley. "May I please speak to you and Emma in my study?"

They followed his determined strides silently down the hall where he ushered them behind closed doors.

"Dad." The edge in Riley's voice suggested he didn't care about exchanging a few heated words with his dad in order to be heard. "There's no way I can live with that guy in our house. I don't trust him, and I—"

Mr. Ledger spun toward his son. "Enough!" Mr. Ledger's harsh tone left no room for argument. "That boy is a guest in our home, and you *will* treat him as such."

Riley bowed his head and took a step back. Through all the years Emma had known him, she'd never witnessed him and his dad argue. As far as she knew, they hardly ever disagreed. Watching them now, she didn't know whether she should stay or leave, whether she should defend Riley or remain silent. If she hadn't embarrassed Tyler on the court, none of this would've happened—Riley and his dad wouldn't be fighting.

"Sorry, Mr. L," Emma said, trying to apologize for Riley's behavior, while letting him know that his son had reasonable cause to be upset. "It's been a rough day."

Mr. Ledger walked across the room, one arm crossed over his chest while his other hand dragged down his face. "Tyler is here because his parents are out of options. He got caught up in a bad crowd and needed some separation from them, so I offered to let him stay here while he finishes his senior year." Mr. Ledger paused and took a deep breath before continuing. "I know it may be difficult, but I need you two to be his friend."

"What?" Riley shouted.

Emma gripped his hand, trying to calm him.

Mr. Ledger studied his son. "Riley, please."

Riley released a slow breath and looked at Emma, his focus on her bruised cheek. Pain flickered in his eyes, as if he thought going along with his dad's request would mean he was betraying her. She didn't know what he needed. Reassurance from her, maybe? She nodded her head a millimeter to let him know she would stand by him. He wrapped his arm around her neck and pulled her against his chest, while she wound her arms around his waist.

"I won't stand by and let him hurt Emma." Riley addressed his dad over her shoulder. "I won't alienate him, but I can't be best friends with the guy either. I'll show him around and introduce him to people, but the rest is up to him."

"I understand," his dad said.

Emma felt Riley's head nod before he turned her toward the door.

"Emma." Mr. Ledger's voice stopped her, and she forced herself to turn and face him, hoping he didn't shift his anger to her. Mr. Ledger picked up an envelope from his desk and held it out to her. "This came for you."

She was almost afraid to touch it. The envelope had her name typed on the front with the Oregon State University logo and address in the top left corner.

Riley peered over her shoulder. "What is it?"

She looked to Mr. Ledger for an explanation.

"I didn't open it," he said. "But if I had to guess, I'd say they may be interested in a certain basketball player, considering this is the third letter they've sent you in the past couple weeks."

A month ago, she had accepted Mr. Ledger's offer to help her look into college options, not really thinking anything would come of it. He had compiled footage of her greatest moments on the court and sent them to a dozen colleges, helped her write letters to college coaches to inquire about their basketball programs, and spread the word about her as a player. It seemed he was almost as invested in getting her to college as his son. Rather than have information mailed to her house, she was using the Ledgers' address so her dad and brothers didn't get involved.

Mr. Ledger perched on the edge of his desk. "Emma, I know you're reserved about the possibility of going to college, but if your team makes it to the state playoffs, college scouts might come see you play."

She nodded absently. College scouts. Prestigious individuals Emma had only seen in movies and heard about from rich kids whose parents had paid for years of private coaching so their child could excel in a sport. Despite her efforts with Mr. Ledger to get on college coaches' radar, she never thought college scouts would take an interest in her. Riley and his dad had guilted her into playing on the Bradshaw girls' basketball team for one season. One season! Play a few games with a bunch of girls and call it good. She wasn't supposed to be recruited by colleges or thinking about life after high school at some university. That kind of life wasn't meant for her, was it?

Needing a moment to collect her thoughts, she turned the focus on Riley. "Have you decided where you're going yet?"

He shared a look with his dad before shaking his head. "Not yet."

"Why not?" He had been recruited by colleges since his sophomore year, and he'd never been a procrastinator, so his indecision about colleges confused her. "You've gotten a ton of offers and you've been thinking about college for years. What's the problem?"

He shrugged. "I'm taking time to think and to make sure I make the right decision."

She rolled her eyes but allowed him to take her hand and lead her toward the hallway. As she reached the door, she stopped and turned. "Mr. Ledger?"

His eyes softened as he looked at her. "Yes?"

She looked at the man who was so much more than her best friend's dad, the man who had become a second, and sometimes even a first, dad to her. "Do you think I'm ready for college ball?"

His opinion meant so much to her, but he put it back in her court. "Do *you* think you're ready for college ball?"

She shook her head. "Definitely not."

He chuckled. "We are all capable of more than we think."

"But I'm a nobody."

"You are certainly not a nobody. Word has been getting around about you, and if colleges are still looking for a point guard or a shooting guard, you're the one to watch."

Hearing his words solidified her desire to at least see what might happen if she bought into the idea of going to college. "What do I have to do to make them notice me?"

He crossed the room and put a hand on her shoulder.

"Nothing. You just need to play the game you know and love. It'll speak for itself."

Emma always wished she could talk to her own dad about all this—that it would be his face filled with love and support looking down on her as she thought about life after high school—but that wasn't a possibility. He'd made it clear he wasn't interested in her or her life. So, yeah, Emma had to admit, it felt nice having someone besides Riley on her side as she navigated foreign waters.

She clutched the letter from OSU in her hand, afraid to open it. Folding it into quarters, she stuffed the letter in her pocket as she dismissed herself from Mr. Ledger's study.

◆◆◆

Seating arrangements for dinner had always been the same at the Ledgers'. Emma and Riley sat across from each other, as did his parents. With the added guest, the table felt unbalanced. Riley and Emma sat side by side facing Tyler. Wise move on Mrs. L's part considering the three of them had yet to establish a truce.

Not one to give up an opportunity for affection, Riley's hand sought hers under the table. It was an innocent gesture, but it still brought a blush to Emma's face as she tried not to draw attention to herself. She glanced over at Riley and almost laughed out loud as his left hand fumbled with the fork. The boy could dribble like a pro with his left hand, but eating left-handed proved to be more than he could handle. The fork fell from his hand and clattered against his plate, drawing the eyes of his parents.

"Sorry," Riley mumbled, his face growing red.

"Mmhmm," his mom responded.

Emma snuck a glance at Mrs. L only to discover her eyes locked onto the table as if she had x-ray vision and could see their clasped hands under the wood. Based on her smile, she didn't object to her son holding his girlfriend's hand

31

during dinner, but Emma still felt weird. She tried to pull her hand away so Riley could eat dinner with some grace, but he wouldn't let go. He smiled his goofy grin at her. When Emma's focus shifted back to his mom, Mrs. Ledger winked. Yeah, this whole girlfriend-boyfriend thing was awkward.

"So, Emma." Her name coming from Mr. Ledger's mouth snapped her attention in his direction. "Are you ready for Friday?"

Basketball. Although it was her favorite topic to discuss at length, it was tainted now that the girls had made the playoffs and the boys' team had failed to advance due to a heartbreaking loss in the deciding game. She didn't want Riley to feel bad considering everyone thought the Bradshaw boys' team was a shoo-in. However, by the way his thumb traced circles on the top of her hand, he didn't really care about basketball at the moment, and Mr. Ledger seemed oblivious to the secret handholding.

"What's Friday?" Tyler grunted between mouthfuls of food.

"Regional playoff game for the girls' basketball team."

Tyler snorted as if he found the idea of female competition funny.

Mr. Ledger leveled his eyes at Tyler. "And we will all be going to support them as a family."

"Have fun," Tyler said.

Mr. Ledger sat back in his chair to study his guest. "Since you are currently part of our family, you will be joining us."

Tyler's head snapped up, his jaw dropping open. "What?" His eyes frantically searched for the loophole. "I'm no part of this family, and there's no way I'm going to watch a bunch of girls try and play basketball."

For this being his first meal with the Ledgers, Tyler sure wasn't shy about voicing his opinion, nor was Mr. Ledger shy about setting rules and expectations.

Probably sensing the helplessness of the situation, Tyler grumbled to himself. Something about girls' basketball being a waste of time. He sulked through the rest of dinner while Mr. and Mrs. Ledger carried the conversation, and Riley distracted Emma by caressing her hand.

After dinner, Riley and Emma found refuge in Riley's room from the Ledgers' houseguest. Riley fell onto his bed and covered his face with his hands.

"How long do you think you'll be able to keep your promise to your dad and be BFFs with Tyler?" Emma asked, sitting beside him on the edge of the mattress.

"Based on how today went? Less than a week." He pulled his hands away from his face and let his arms flop to his sides. "I mean what kind of guy gets kicked out of his house and moves in with a family he doesn't know to finish his senior year of high school with only half the year left?"

"Who knows? But maybe Tyler will be good for you. Maybe he'll help you build character," she teased.

"You think this is funny?"

She opened her mouth to say something, but he pounced on her, pinning her arms to the bed as he sat on her. Laughing, she tried to buck him off, but he didn't budge. She attempted to roll and knock him sideways, and when that failed she tried to wiggle an arm or leg free so she could increase her chances of winning the wrestling match. His strained laughter made her think she wasn't making it easy for him to maintain the upper hand.

"Please tell me I don't have to listen to this for the next six months."

Riley jerked his head toward the door where Tyler stood watching them.

"Get out," Riley growled, crawling off the bed and advancing toward Tyler.

Tyler pushed off the wall and matched Riley's step with one of his own. "You gonna make me?"

Riley squared his shoulders, intent on rising to the

challenge. Emma scrambled off the bed and threw herself between them.

"Okay, guys, chill out."

"Move." Tyler's hands formed fists at his sides. "Your boyfriend and I have business to discuss."

"Is there a problem here?" Thank goodness for the wrath of moms everywhere. Mrs. Ledger's voice sounded almost lighthearted, but everyone could hear the threat beneath it. Start a fight in her house and military school would start to look like heaven.

"No problem." Tyler spoke to Mrs. Ledger but his eyes remained locked on Riley. "Just thanking your *son* for allowing me to be part of his family."

"If you expect me to fall for that, you're in for a rude awakening." Mrs. Ledger grabbed Tyler's arm and guided him out of the room. She reappeared a minute later to find Riley and Emma in the exact same positions.

"I'm sorry, Mom."

She waved away her son's apology before walking over and kissing him on the cheek. "I guess we'd better prepare ourselves for some interesting times."

Four

Night settled into place as Emma walked home. Overgrown bushes and trees concealed her house behind them, which was probably for the best since the house itself was more of an eyesore than a neglected yard.

The brown and black colors of the house, along with the dim yellow porch light, made the structure appear more like a shadow than a dwelling place. Cracked and faded paint clung to the sides of the house, waiting for strong winds and rain to set it free. The front yard was a sorry patch of lawn with more weeds than grass. These same weeds infested the gravel driveway and thrived among the rusting wheelbarrow and garden tools that sat forgotten along the side of the garage. Ferns and ivy crawled up the front of the house as if trying to find their way inside or swallow the structure whole. Emma hated them the most. Something about their presence caused her to shrink away from them, afraid they would succeed in fully capturing the house and the family inside. She gave them a wide birth as she ascended the front steps.

She paused before entering the house. This morning's incident with her brother only reminded her of the long history they shared. It had been over a month since she'd stood in the kitchen opposite Lance as he flung hate-filled words at her and accused her of wanting to follow in their mom's footsteps and abandon the family. His words from that day echoed in her head: *You're just like Mom. She left because she wanted something more, something better. Better than Dad, better than us. You remind Dad too much of Mom. He hates having you around as a constant reminder of her.*

Squeezing her eyes closed, she tried to force Lance's voice out of her head and calm her escalated breathing, but it didn't work. His words were still so clear and hurt just as much.

Dad hates you...You'll never amount to anything...You're worthless.

You're worthless.

You're worthless.

Dad hates you.

Dad.

Hates.

You.

Those were the words that hurt the most.

The front door groaned as she pushed her way inside. At Riley's, home smelled like fabric softener and fresh-baked cookies and the kind of fresh air that swept through open windows during the first warm days of spring; at Emma's, home smelled like dirty feet and muddy boots and hints of rotting food. The smell assaulted her nostrils every time she stepped into the entryway, but she didn't cringe at it. No matter how bad it may have been, it was the smell she associated with her family.

She latched the door behind her and turned to assess the situation. Newspapers were strewn across the coffee table and piled haphazardly next to the brown recliner. Dirty dishes resembled Leaning Towers of Pisa on the remaining surfaces with a couple of Logan's books thrown in for good measure. Lucas's action figures littered the floor, and who knew what other items lurked in the corners?

Meandering through the mess, she made her way toward her garage-bedroom, but her brothers congregating at the kitchen table didn't allow her safe passage through the house.

They looked up when she stepped from carpet to linoleum. Silence took over. They looked at her, but they didn't speak to her. They never did. Lucas and Lenny, the youngest of the group, sat at the kitchen table spooning SpaghettiOs into their mouths while Logan, the oldest, sat across from them reading a book. Lance leaned against the counter, a half empty glass of root beer in his hand. Even though she had endured this sort of behavior from them for years, it still made her feel like an intruder.

Her eyes flickered from one brother to the next before settling on Lance. His mouth spread into an evil grin and he laughed. "Nice eye."

She couldn't remember the last time she'd seen him smile.

"What happened? Did Riley finally get sick of you and put you in your place?"

She flinched. His words induced more pain than Tyler's elbow ever could. Yes, she had endured years of her family's ridicule and rejection, but never had any of her brothers expressed happiness at the idea of her getting hurt. Did their hatred of her really run that deep? Hurt and anger surged in her veins as she narrowed her eyes at Lance. "That's what brings a smile to your face? *That's* what makes you laugh? The thought that your sister is getting pounded on by her boyfriend?"

Considering she knew of her brother's viciousness, maybe his comment shouldn't have elicited such a response from her, but she couldn't help it. The morning's encounter, plus the fact that her pain brought her brother such happiness, killed her. She could either cry or fight, and there was no way she'd ever let Lance see her cry.

Lance's grin faltered into a smirk. "I'm sure you deserved it."

"Emma." Logan put his book on the table, his eyes flickering between her and Lance. "He didn't mean—"

She whirled on him. "Don't," she growled. "Don't you dare defend him."

Four sets of eyes stared at her. Lucas's innocent ones widened in fear, Logan's sagged with pity, and Lenny's, pinched with loathing, looked so much like Lance's that Emma had to look away. No way could her world have more than one Lance in it. Despite the fact she looked like her brothers with curly blond hair, green eyes, and soft features, that was where their similarities ended. She had hoped their silence over the past few weeks was merely a truce, that maybe their walls against her had cracked, but they were thicker than ever.

Unable to stay in their presence, she stumbled backward. "You can all go to hell."

Another shade of darkness dropped over Lance's face. "What did you say?"

She probably should've remained quiet and left. "You heard me."

Lance dropped his glass in the sink. Pieces of broken glass trickled down between the piled dishes as he stepped toward her. She stood her ground.

"Lance—"

Lance jabbed a finger at Logan. "Stay out of this." Of course Logan obeyed. He always did. Even though he was the oldest, Logan always let Lance dominate. Emma didn't know what Lance would do next, so she waited as he crept toward her step by step. No way would she let him come within three feet of her, not when his entire body looked poised to fight and his eyes swirled with black.

Hands gripped her shoulders when she stepped backward, readying her body for flight. She looked up to see her dad standing behind her, his eyes scanning the faces of his children. "What's going on?" The fact he dropped his hands from her shoulders as soon as he knew she wouldn't run into him didn't escape her attention. It was like merely touching her caused his skin to burn.

Taking a step away from him, she looked at her dad's face. No matter how much she tried, she couldn't see past the man who had let his daughter be the target of their family's hatred for so many years. "Like you care," she bit out.

Not waiting for anyone else's next move, she dodged past her dad, flung open the garage door, and slammed it behind her. She maneuvered between the boxes and family throwaways and dropped onto her bed. Burying her face in her hands, she tried to shut out the rest of the world and stop her body from shaking. If college didn't work in her favor, she'd have to find a way to get out of this house, because if she had to endure another year with her family, she'd be nothing but a shell of a person.

Five

Unable to face her dad and brothers the following morning, Emma decided to skip breakfast and leave the house early. She slipped out the side door of the garage and walked to Riley's house.

As she approached the Ledgers' driveway, she saw Tyler climb into the passenger seat of Riley's jeep as Riley tossed his backpack into the backseat.

Not wanting to let her family ruin her entire day, she brushed aside the morning's incident and mustered up a smile. "What's a girl gotta do to get a ride around here?"

At the sound of her voice, both boys turned, Riley smiling and Tyler scowling.

Riley retrieved something from his bag before jogging toward her and throwing his arms around her waist. "Hi."

"You're happy this morning," she said, returning his hug.

"I'm always happy when I see you."

As cheesy as it sounded, Emma couldn't help but find comfort in his words.

"Kill me now," Tyler moaned, slamming the passenger door shut.

Emma and Riley shared a laugh, neither of them making a move to join Tyler in the car.

Riley pulled out of the hug. Something in her face must have hinted at the morning she'd had, because his eyebrows scrunched in concern. "Uh-oh. Do I want to know?"

She shook her head. "It's nothing."

"I think I know what might cheer you up." He presented her with a brown paper bag.

"What is it?"

"Open it and find out."

She placed her hand on the bottom of the bag and felt heat on her palm. The smell of sausage and eggs wafted up from the bag as she opened it. Her eyes snapped to Riley's. "You brought me a breakfast sandwich?"

He shrugged one shoulder and gave her a lopsided grin.

She didn't waste time plunging her hand into the bag and snatching the sandwich. "Tell your mom I said thank you."

He slapped a hand to his chest, insulted. "I'll have you know I woke up early this morning just to make you that."

"Uh-huh," she said.

"I did."

She knew he was probably telling the truth since the egg, sausage, cheese combo on a toasted English muffin was Riley's signature breakfast meal, not his mom's, but she couldn't help but tease him. "You probably made it last night and stuck it in the microwave this morning."

"And risk soggy bread? I think not."

Emma took a huge bite, stuffing her cheeks full of the steaming goodness and resisting letting out a moan of content. And to think she almost had to go without breakfast this morning.

"How is it?"

She shrugged, her mouth still full of food. "I've had better."

"Oh, really? No problem." Riley swiped the sandwich from her hand. "More for me." He turned away from her as he guided the sandwich to his mouth.

"No!" she shouted before launching onto his back and

wrapping her arms around his neck to reclaim her breakfast. "I'm sorry. I take it back. It's the best sandwich I've ever had."

He looked over his shoulder at her, his eyebrows raised as if to question her sincerity. "Really? Best sandwich you've ever had?"

She nodded like a bobblehead going over potholes. "Absolutely. Without question." Anything to get her sandwich back, not that it was that far from the truth.

He straightened, and she dropped off his back. Clasping her hands together as if she was ready to drop to her knees in prayer, she plastered on an innocent smile, or at least as innocent as she could muster.

Releasing a fake sigh, he pointed to his cheek. As she rose onto her toes to connect her lips to his cheek, he turned his head at the last second so she kissed his mouth instead.

He wrapped an arm around her waist and squeezed her against him. "You know, if you wanted a kiss, you could've just said so."

She laughed. "I didn't want you to feel obligated."

Tyler pounded on the side of the car and groaned. Riley and Emma shared another laugh before pulling apart to join Tyler in the car.

◆◆◆

If Tyler felt any nervousness over his first day at a new school, he didn't show it. As soon as Riley pulled into a parking spot, Tyler bolted from the jeep without a word and disappeared.

Riley glanced in her direction and gave her smile. "Here we go," he said, as if needing to motivate himself to face the school day and hoping Tyler didn't make his life miserable.

She slid out of the car and joined Riley on the other side, her fingers slipping through his as they crossed the parking lot and headed toward the two-story gray building of

Bradshaw High School.

At her locker, Riley watched as she swapped books for her morning classes. He could have waved to people passing by or played a game on his phone or done a million other things, but he chose to watch her execute the most boring task in the world.

"Stop staring at me," she said.

He wrapped his arms around her waist and whispered in her ear, "Can't help it. It's part of the boyfriend job description."

"What boyfriend job description?"

"In the boyfriend handbook. Rule number 27 says, 'Stare at your girlfriend.' Not in a creepy stalker way, but more like a she's-the-only-girl-for-me kind of way."

"I think I need to see this boyfriend handbook."

"You can't. It's for boyfriends only." He leaned closer until his face was inches from hers. "If I showed you, I'd have to kill you. It's that confidential."

She tried, but she couldn't resist him when he conjured up that charming smile of his and leaned in for a kiss.

Before their lips touched, someone slammed into them from behind, sending them crashing into the lockers.

"What's up, Wrangton?"

Riley groaned, his moment with her ruined. He kept his arms around her as he slouched against the wall.

"Sorry," Emma mouthed to him. She looked over her shoulder at their intruder. "Hey, Shiloh."

"How's the eye?" Shiloh asked, leaning against the wall beside them and stripping them of any privacy.

Emma twisted around to face her so Shiloh could see the black and blue combo for herself. "You tell me."

"It makes you look tough," another voice said. Emma would know that voice anywhere.

"Thanks, freshman," she said as Ashley popped up next to Shiloh.

Tom's head appeared over Ashley's shoulder. "I think it

makes you look like you got your butt kicked."

Riley let go of Emma and punched Tom in the arm. "Don't talk about her like that."

"Or what?" Tom asked.

Riley grabbed Tom in a headlock. "Or I'll hold you down while she beats you up."

Tom held up his hands in mock surrender and they all laughed.

The smile slid from Shiloh's face, her attention diverted from the group. "So it's true."

"What's true?" Ashley asked.

Shiloh nodded down the hallway and all of them turned to find Tyler walking in their direction. "The jerk from the court is sticking around."

Five pairs of eyes locked on Tyler, but his focus never wavered from Emma. "Nice eye," he said with a smirk as he walked by.

Riley's fingers found hers. "I'm really starting to hate that guy."

"What's the deal with him?" Shiloh asked.

Tom clamped his hand down on Riley's shoulder. "He's Riley's new house pet."

"Meaning?"

Riley glared in Tyler's direction as he tightened his hold on Emma's hand. "Meaning my parents have graciously welcomed him into our house, and from the sound of it, he'll be staying awhile."

Ashley's eyes flickered back and forth between Riley and Emma.

Shiloh let out a low whistle. "This will be interesting."

♦♦♦

First period Calculus classes should be banned from school. No one should be forced to tackle complicated math problems so early in the morning.

Emma slid into her seat and glanced at the whiteboard for the daily warm-up routine of three equations based on yesterday's lesson. Caught up in working through the problems, she didn't realize the empty seat behind her was occupied until a voice whispered in her ear. "I'm surprised to see you without your boyfriend attached at your hip."

Her eyelids slid closed. *Please tell me Calculus did not just go from bad to horrendous.* She turned in her chair and confirmed the presence behind her with her eyes. "You."

Tyler's face broke into a grin. "Miss me?"

"Hardly," she grumbled. "What are you doing in here? Don't tell me *you* know Calculus."

"What can I say? I'm a guy of many talents."

"Really? Because I have yet to see one."

Turning sideways in his chair so he could lean against the wall and drape his arm over the back of his seat, he chuckled. "Feisty, aren't you?"

The guy seemed to be in better spirits than he had been two days ago on the basketball court. He'd replaced his sneer with a smirk of cocky playfulness that had probably claimed a half-dozen female victims already this morning.

She returned to her math problems as Mr. Williams's shadow fell across her desk.

"Emma," he said with a smile fueled with way too much enthusiasm for someone who had devoted his life to math. "I see you've met our new student. Good, good. I'm sure you won't mind showing him the ropes and making him feel right at home."

She shook her head and waved her hands in front of her to ward off the craziness voiced by her teacher. "No, no, no. That's not a good idea."

"That's a great idea," Tyler's dulcet-toned voice exclaimed, overshadowing Emma's words by matching Mr. Williams's enthusiasm and smile. "Emma's been such a huge help to me already. We're getting along great."

She glared at Tyler. "That's not—"

45

Mr. Williams clapped his hands together. "Great."

"But—" Emma's protest died on her lips as her teacher sauntered away to address the class. She whipped around to face Tyler. "What was that?"

"What was what?"

"You know what. The last thing I want to do is help you."

"Why? I'm a nice guy."

She pointed to her eye. "Nice guys don't give girls black eyes."

He sighed. "It was an accident."

"You and I both know that's a lie."

"Relax, Princess. I'm not out to destroy your life." The corner of his mouth tipped up. "Just maybe make it a bit more interesting."

Her eyes narrowed. "Stay away from me. And don't call me princess." She almost gagged on the p-word. The princess nickname was reserved for little girls in sparkly dresses and tiaras who had their dads wrapped around their little fingers. Emma had never been one of those girls. In addition to the word grinding against her ears like fingernails on a chalkboard, it stood as a reminder to the nonexistent relationship she had with her dad. Tyler using the word to mock her only made her hatred of the nickname stronger.

He chuckled. "You're cute when you're mad. Your nostrils flare and your eyes get all crinkly." He reached out to touch her face, but she slapped his hand away.

If the conversation continued, Emma would have shown him what her elbow could do to his face. She glanced at the clock, silently groaning when she saw only ten minutes had passed. Another 40 minutes with Tyler sitting behind her. The guy had been here less than three days, and she was already doubting whether she would survive the week being Tyler's "friend."

Six

Sounds of basketball echoed throughout the gym—the squeak of shoes against the hardwood, the thunder of dribbling basketballs, the voices of girls calling out instructions to their teammates.

The Bradshaw High School team was not the same one it had been at the start of the season. Three months ago, eight girls showed up for the first day of basketball practice expecting to continue the school tradition of being the worst team in the league, but their hard work had paid off. Three weeks ago they beat Evergreen High School. It had been Bradshaw's first victory against their cross-town rival in over ten years. Despite Bradshaw's coach, Jen Knowles, disappearing at halftime and the team guilting Emma into coaching them for the second half of the game, the girls had united as a team and proven their worth on the court. They had won their final four league games and taken first place at the district playoffs the previous weekend.

Now, as Emma stood on the sideline watching her teammates take some last-minute shots before their regional game started, nervousness like none she'd ever felt, coursed through her. If Bradshaw lost, their season would be over; if they won, they would go on to the Washington state tournament at the Tacoma Dome for the first time in their school's history.

She'd spent the week trying to prevent Riley and Tyler from killing each other and helping her teammates perfect their skills that she'd hardly had time to think about the actual regional game, but now the weight of the game slammed into her. The tension in her arms and legs wouldn't leave, no matter how much she tried to relax. Emma and her teammates had worked so hard all season, but what if they lost this game? Would everyone think their string of wins was merely luck? Would they think Emma was a failure?

The buzzer sounded and her teammates joined her on the sidelines. Shaking out the tension from her shoulders, Emma took her place in the huddle and half-heartedly listened to Jen's instructions. Shiloh made funny faces at Emma from over Jen's shoulder and Emma had to admit, it helped break through the fog...a little. Jen stopped talking, and after a team cheer, the starting players took to the court.

Shiloh wrapped an arm around Emma's neck. "What's up with you, Wrangton? You look—"

"Scared," Lauren cut in as she tightened her blonde ponytail and brushed bangs away from her forehead. "You look scared. Whatever it is, suck it up. We need to win tonight to move on, and we can't have you freaking out on us."

Shiloh made a fist with her hand and held it in front of her face like it was a microphone. "And the award for world's worst motivational speech goes to—" a pause and gasp for dramatic effect, "Lauren Thompson! What do you have to say for yourself?" Shiloh shoved her microphone fist into Lauren's face.

Rolling her eyes, Lauren tossed her ponytail over her shoulder and headed toward center court without comment as Shiloh laughed at her.

Despite her teammate's lack of tact, Emma had to admit

that Lauren's words rang true. "She's right."

Shiloh stepped in front of Emma. "Forget her. You've worked hard to get here, we all have, and we win and lose as a team. So whatever is going on, use this game to fight through it. Let's prove to everyone that we belong here and that this game is ours. We got this."

In true Shiloh fashion, she held up her fist. "Pound it, you know you want to."

Emma couldn't disappoint. She tapped her teammate's knuckles with her own, took a deep breath, and faked confidence as the ref blew the whistle for tip-off.

Apparently, the game of pretend only went so far. Despite her best efforts, Emma couldn't focus. Her shots weren't falling, the team wasn't gelling, and Jen's meltdown on the sidelines wasn't helping anything.

"Move the ball!"

"Watch for the open player!"

"Block out!"

"Get your heads in the game!"

Jen's behavior did nothing to settle the team down. Ever since she'd abandoned them during the second half of the Evergreen game, due to some family emergency she never explained, Coach had taken a more active role on the sidelines, as if trying to make up for leaving them. Sometimes it worked to inspire the team, other times not so much. One loss and Bradshaw was done. No more games, no state playoffs. Enough pressure threatened to flatten them; they didn't need their coach making the task of winning more difficult. Anytime the basketball passed in front of Bradshaw's bench, Jen sprinted along the sideline screaming instructions and jabbing her finger in the air like she was popping bubbles.

"Is it just me or has Knowles gone crazy?" Shiloh panted as she matched Emma's stride down the court.

Emma glanced toward the sideline. Jen flapped her arms like a bird before throwing down her clipboard. "She's definitely losing it."

"I say we quit the game, grab some popcorn, and watch her self-destruct."

Emma laughed but before she could respond, the guards from Krenshaw High School crossed midcourt on offense, and Emma and Shiloh split up to defend the basket.

Even as the game progressed, Emma still couldn't block out distractions and focus on basketball. The crowd's cheers deafened her senses. The scoreboard mocked her from above. The other team taunted her every move. It took all of her focus to set up and run each offensive play without getting the ball stripped from her hands.

Ashley kept getting beat on defense, Steph and Shiloh spent the first half getting boxed out beneath the basket, Lauren kept forcing shots and missing, and Emma couldn't beat the defense to get off any decent shots.

Swiping the back of her hand across her forehead to catch beads of sweat before they dripped down her face, Emma tried to figure out a game plan. She had to give Krenshaw credit, they were good, really good, but Emma knew Bradshaw could win if only they could find a way to pull themselves together.

Emma and her teammates filed into the locker room at halftime, down by seventeen. Jen took front and center, pacing back and forth in front of them until the extra chatter died down.

"This team is bigger and stronger than us, and they're beating us with their offense eight times out of ten."

Emma nodded in agreement. Everyone knew this already.

"What we need to do is gain control of this game. Krenshaw is good, better than any team we've faced this season, but they aren't invincible. We need to stop being afraid of them and start playing our own game." Coach Knowles pointed out the weaknesses in offense and defense and talked strategy for the second half of the game. "We can win this game as long as we don't give up. We fought our way here, so let's fight our way to a win."

The girls rose from the bench and peeled themselves off the wall to huddle up. With hands and arms stretched forth into the center of the circle, they shouted their school name before dispersing and exiting the locker room.

As her teammates turned left to return to the court for the remaining minutes of halftime, Emma steered right. She knew their ability to win depended on more than just words, and she needed a minute alone to pull herself together.

Emma shook the tension out of her shoulders, walked to the end of the hallway and visualized Saturday morning games at the park with her friends when they captured the essence of teamwork and fun and support of each other. She knew how to play basketball, she knew how to work with her teammates' strengths and weaknesses, she knew how to see the court and read the other team's defense. Coach Knowles was right. She needed to stop being afraid of the other team and play her game.

Feeling a renewed sense of confidence, she spun around to return to the gym, and her body slammed into a pole that hadn't been there before.

Hands reached out to steady her, and she looked up into one of the last faces she wanted to see. Tyler. His face split into his infamous grin. "Hey, Princess. Nice playing."

Mockery dripped from his words. She held up her hand to stop him. "Not now, Tyler."

"Why not? You think you're too good for me now because some college scout is here watching you?"

"What are you talking about? College scouts don't come to these games." She didn't know much about the recruiting process, but she knew college coaches rarely attended any game prior to the state tournament.

Tyler laughed at her. "Keep telling yourself that, Princess, because with the way you're playing the recruiter won't be here long. That display of cockiness you've got going on is a huge turnoff for college coaches."

She hated how his words mattered to her.

He reached up and caught a stray piece of her hair, attempting to tuck it behind her ear, but she slapped his hand away.

He laughed. "You know, you told me how you and your bunch of girls could teach me something this weekend, and you were right. You've taught me that girls really don't belong on the court because all they do is embarrass themselves."

Emma's mouth dropped open. Did he seriously just say that? Insults lined up in her thoughts like bullets ready to be fired, but before she could formulate them into words, he trailed a finger along her cheek and retreated down the hallway toward the gym, leaving her to fume alone.

She glared at his back and rubbed her palm against her cheek, trying to remove the feel of his touch. It felt less like a caress and more like a slug leaving a trail of slime on her skin.

By the time she made it back to the gym, the final seconds of halftime were clicking off the clock. She plunged into the team huddle with fire in her eyes. "We are not losing this game."

Shiloh laughed and slapped Emma on the back. "There she is. Our basketball warrior has returned."

Lauren blew out a puff of breath. "It's about time."

It was Bradshaw's ball at half-court, and Emma lined up between her teammates. Madison slapped the ball from out of bounds, spurring them into action. Breaking away from her defender, Emma popped out to the side and caught the pass from Madison.

Bradshaw's newfound momentum started slow. A jump shot here, a block there, but for every shot Krenshaw made, Bradshaw sank one of their own until they broke the routine four minutes into the third quarter. Krenshaw's shooting guard put up one of her infamous three-pointers. The ball arced in the air, but instead of swishing the net, it made a resounding thud as it bounced off the rim. Securing the inside spot, Shiloh pulled the ball out of the air and fired it to Ashley at the sideline. The kid looked downcourt to Lauren who had broken free from the other players. Lauren's hands welcomed the ball, and she dribbled toward Bradshaw's basket. With a two-step lead, Lauren encompassed the grace of a ballerina and took the ball all the way to the hoop where she bounced it off the backboard and sent it through the hoop for two points.

With half the fourth quarter left to play and only a couple points separating the teams, Krenshaw brought the ball downcourt looking to score from close range. Their point guard tried to dump the ball inside when Shiloh's hand punched out, knocking the ball out of its trajectory. The ball took off down the court on its own. It rolled across the floor, and Emma knew they couldn't let the other team gain possession if Bradshaw wanted to take the lead. She pushed off her defender, sprinting toward the loose ball. Her defender didn't waste any time either. Both girls raced downcourt, but Emma dove first. She caught the ball and curled her body around it as her defender fell on top of her. Frantic hands tried to steal the ball, but Emma held on until Ashley appeared beside her. Emma thrust the ball at the kid. One-on-one, Ashley charged toward Bradshaw's basket as Emma hopped off the floor and flew down the other side of the court. Ashley's defender lunged in the kid's direction, causing the freshman to pass to Emma. Catching the ball on a run, it was Emma's turn to charge to the basket, her only obstacle being the lone girl from Krenshaw. With some fancy footwork and shifting hips, Emma didn't commit to either direction until the last second. She put her head down, driving down the right side. Her defender braced herself against the charge, staying low and anticipating the layup. Emma took advantage of her position and pulled up, shooting the ball five feet from the basket. Nothing but net.

The shot tied the game at 45 with three minutes left on the clock.

It was anyone's game.

Krenshaw changed to a 3-2 zone defense as Bradshaw set up on offense. Needing to know how the defenders would shift as the ball transferred hands, Emma called for a passing offense. She threw the ball across the top of the key to Ashley, who passed it to Shiloh popping out on the same side at the baseline. Lauren shifted down to fill Shiloh's vacated position at the bottom of the key. The defense shifted accordingly, but since Bradshaw's offense overloaded on one side, Krenshaw's forward was slow to determine who she should defend since two people were in her zone. The girl was big, but her feet were slow. Instead of guarding Steph, the girl shifted toward the overloaded side, leaving Steph wide open. Of course, everyone knew passing across the court was a high-risk move considering the number of arms that could snatch it out of the air, but it wasn't impossible to pull off if done right.

Shiloh passed the ball back to Ashley, but before Shiloh resumed her position at the bottom of the key, she caught Emma's eye. The two girls stared at each other in silent communication. Shiloh's eyes shifted to the spot where Emma had identified the hole in the defense, and with a quick nod of her head, they agreed on the plan. Emma received the pass from Ashley as Lauren popped out on the baseline. Lauren snapped the ball back to Emma immediately, but instead of passing it back to Ashley, Emma threw an overhand bullet pass to Shiloh underneath the basket before the defense could adjust. Without a defender, Shiloh shot the ball off the backboard for two points, and Bradshaw took the lead.

"Nice one," Emma said as Shiloh ran by her.

Shiloh smiled. "I know."

Emma shook her head and laughed. She was going to miss her teammates when the season ended.

Krenshaw set up their offense, but they rushed the shot. The ball bounced off the rim and Steph secured the rebound. Unlike Krenshaw, Bradshaw seemed to grow more focused as the final minutes clicked down on the clock. With patience and clean passing, Bradshaw grew their lead by another two points when Lauren sunk a jump shot.

Krenshaw answered with another missed shot, and Emma hit a three-pointer in response. By the time the clock ticked down to 30 seconds, Bradshaw was up by seven and the Krenshaw players were frantic to get the ball. Their desperation caused a turnover, and Ashley broke free from the herd and made a layup. The buzzer sounded, confirming Bradshaw's win: 54-45.

Tacoma Dome, here we come!

Seven

Only five days separated the regional game from the start of the state tournament. With barely enough time to celebrate their win, Bradshaw faced their first game at the state tournament. Tip-off was in seven hours. Emma's bag was packed with everything she needed for the day, so all she had to do was sit around and wait.

And wait.

And...wait.

Slipping into the kitchen for breakfast earlier than usual, she dropped her bag on the kitchen floor and plopped bread into the toaster. Outside, slices of orange split the sky overhead as the darkness shook off the last traces of night.

"Today's the big day, isn't it?"

Gasping, she spun around, her heart racing. Her dad sat at the table with his hands folded around a cup of coffee. How had she not noticed him when she entered?

She blinked, trying to make sense out of his words.

A chuckle bubbled up from her dad's throat, a sound she rarely heard from him. "Sorry," he said. "I didn't mean to startle you." His eyes locked on hers. As in they didn't look away, they weren't cast downward, they weren't focused on her shoulder. They looked right at her, and they weren't filled with hatred or disgust. She stopped breathing.

"The state tournament is today, right?"

His words snapped her out of her trance, and she sucked in a breath. "Oh. Um, yeah."

Her dad nodded, but didn't say anything else, which left them with a huge gap of screaming silence because Emma couldn't think of a single thing to say. No one in her family had said anything about their regional victory. With the way they drooled over the daily sports section of the newspaper, no way would they all have missed the article listing the teams that would compete in the state tournament. As much as it hurt, Emma knew they hadn't said anything because none of them cared. But now, her dad had thrown it out there like he'd known all along. Maybe she could ask him to come see her play. He'd always avoided it in the past, but maybe this time would be different. He had, after all, mentioned the tournament. Confidence built within her, and she took a step in his direction to close the gap between them, but he stood at the same time.

"Well, good luck," he said.

He turned to leave, but Emma couldn't let him go. "Dad, wait."

Pausing, he turned around to face her. With a few hurried steps she stood before him.

"Will you come?" Time would only allow him to come up with an excuse of why he couldn't make it, and she couldn't bear hearing the words from his mouth, so she covered the ground for him. "I know you have work, I know you're busy, I know girls' basketball isn't your favorite sport, and I know you may not be able to stay for the entire game, but will you come see me play today? Even just for a minute?"

He covered his mouth with his hand as if considering her request.

"Please?" she whispered, desperate to have her dad in the stands cheering her on. Heck, she didn't even need a solid answer. Even an, "I'll try," would let her know he wasn't totally opposed to the idea—opposed to her.

He reached out to her, and she let him grip her shoulders, relishing in the feel of it. She took it all in, his strong supportive grip, the gentleness in his eyes, the feeling of hope swelling in her chest. "Emma, I—"

"Dad has better things to do than come to your stupid game."

Her eyes closed at the sound of Lance's voice, knowing the moment with her dad was dead. Her dad's hands loosened on her shoulders, his arms dropping to his sides as he took a step back. She immediately missed the feel of him.

She opened her eyes, pleading with her dad to stay, but it was a lost cause. "I'll see you guys later." He retreated into the living room as Lance opened and shut cabinets behind her.

"Hey, loser, is this your bread in the toaster?"

The sound of her brother's voice only made her shoulders sag further. She didn't have an answer for him. As he tried and failed to get her attention with threats of what would happen if she didn't clean up her mess—like their house wasn't already a disaster—she grabbed her backpack from the floor and left, heading to the Ledgers'.

Riley's dad greeted Emma at the front door, and then proceeded to his study. Voices pulled Emma through the house to the kitchen. She stood in the doorway watching Riley and his mom at the counter. Mrs. Ledger added ingredients to a bowl, stirring its contents as Riley stood beside her and dipped his finger into her concoction. She slapped his hand away and Riley laughed before reaching around her and copying his taste-testing technique from the other side. The sound of Emma's laughter alerted the mother and son to her presence.

"Hey!" Riley pushed away from the counter as Mrs. Ledger sighed in relief.

"Oh, Emma. Perfect timing. If my son eats anymore of this batter, breakfast is cancelled." She pointed at Riley with the spatula in silent warning as she glared at him.

He shrugged. "I had to make sure it was edible."

His mom muttered something about how he would eat whatever she cooked, whether it was edible or not.

Riley greeted Emma with a kiss on the cheek. "Have you eaten?"

"I had something before I left." Technically her *intent* to eat something counted, right?

He raised an eyebrow, not believing her. Probably because he had seen the bare cupboards in her house too many times and knew breakfast at the Wrangtons' paled in comparison to breakfast at the Ledgers' any day of the week.

He leaned toward her, and she thought he was going to kiss her on the cheek again, but his mouth stopped next to her ear. "Liar."

"I'm not a liar," she hissed back, not wanting his mom to hear. "I had toast." Almost.

His eyes narrowed at her. "Oh, there's a breakfast for champions. How many bites of toast?"

How did he know? "Doesn't matter. Besides, I'm not hungry."

And that's when her stomach decided to protest her lie.

Riley laughed at the grumbling sounds as he turned away from her and headed for the cabinets. He pulled dishes from the shelves to set another place at the table. "My mom is going to make way too many pancakes, so you have to help me eat them. Besides, I'm not letting you step onto the court today without eating something more than toast."

Mrs. Ledger turned from the stove and smiled at her. "There might even be chocolate chips in them."

Oh, sure. Mrs. L knew Emma could never resist

chocolate chip pancakes, even if her nerves would protest. "Fine," she sighed dramatically, knowing Riley and his mom would never take no for an answer.

She dropped into a chair as Riley sauntered back over to the stove to "help" his mom finish cooking breakfast. Emma caught sight of the time: 6:23 a.m. Six and a half hours until tip-off. She tried to take a deep breath, but it caught in her throat. No way would she be able to survive two hours at school before the team was dismissed.

"There's no reason to be nervous, Em. You're going to be great today."

Riley's voice broke her out of her trance, and she looked up to find him standing across from her.

"Not if she plays like she did in the first half of the game last weekend." Tyler plopped down beside her and propped his arm across the back of her chair like their relationship had evolved to that level. It was still weird to see him saunter through the Ledgers' house like he owned the place.

"Gee, thanks for the support," she muttered, elbowing his arm off her chair.

His face split into a grin. "Welcome."

Riley took a seat and reached across the table for her hands. "Don't listen to him. You've been playing great. Just keep it up and you'll be fine."

Tyler snorted. "Do you always fill her head with lies before a big game?"

"Tyler—" she tried to scold him, but he cut her off.

"I'm serious." Tyler leaned forward to rest his elbows on the table. "You babying her isn't doing her any good. She doesn't need you to tell her how good she is; she knows it— everyone knows it. You need to tell her to focus on the game and not the drama like she did last week. You need to tell her she's going to have to rely on her team more than she ever has before. She can't be a ball hog, not if she wants a chance at winning today. You want to do what's best for her? Tell her the truth, because she's not weak. She can take it."

Riley's hands tightened around hers as his body tensed. "I know she's not weak."

"Do you?" Tyler challenged him. "Because every time I turn around you're telling her what to do or what not to feel, like you don't trust her to make her own decisions. And why are you always in her face? Give your girl some space from you for a change."

Tyler's words did nothing for Emma except reassure her of his lack of tact and his love of stirring up trouble, especially when it concerned her and Riley. "Are you done yet?"

Tyler shrugged. "Depends on if your boy, here, needs me to give him some pointers on keeping you happy."

"Like you know anything about keeping me or anyone else happy. All you do is scowl and brood and cause trouble for everyone." The words were out of Emma's mouth before she could think about whether or not to say them.

None of the tension left Riley, but Tyler leaned back to his original position and placed his arm across the back of her chair again. He spoke to Riley even though his amused smile was meant for Emma. "Sounds to me like your girl has been spending a lot of time watching me, Riley. You better watch out before I snatch her right out of your arms."

Emma almost spit out the milk she just drank. After ensuring the liquid was safely down her throat she turned to Tyler. "Are you insane? Number one, so not true. Number two, never gonna happen."

Tyler shrugged. "We'll see. Either way, your boyfriend—"

"Tyler," Mrs. Ledger called from the stove, her sweet high-pitched voice dripping with warning. "Why don't you come help me carry this food to the table."

Tyler's chair groaned against the floor as he pushed away from the table. "Don't miss me too much while I'm gone, Princess."

She ignored him and turned her focus back to Riley. In part she expected him to be shaking with anger, two steps away from tackling his houseguest and solving their differences with punches. Instead, he sat with his head bowed, fingers wringing his napkin.

She reached across the table for his hand. "Hey, you okay?"

He looked up at her, but she saw through his fake smile. "Sure." Then he shrugged. "You know Tyler, always knows how to push people's buttons." He raised her hand to his lips and kissed it, but she wasn't convinced all was well. Before she could question him further, Mrs. Ledger and Tyler arrived at the table with a stack of pancakes and bowls full of eggs and fruit. Aside from their muttered words of gratitude to Mrs. L for the food, they ate in silence.

She watched Riley through breakfast and during the rest of the morning when she saw him at school, and although he put on a good front, she sensed something odd swirling beneath the surface. She didn't know whether to question him about it or give him space, but as time stole away the minutes, her thoughts gradually shifted to basketball.

Game strategy, shot technique, opposing teams. Ready or not, Emma and her team had a game to win.

◆◆◆

The people who thought girls were nice and sweet, prim and proper, had probably never stepped foot in a girls' basketball tournament. Sure there were ribbons and curls, face paint and tube socks, sporting school colors and mascots, but the underlying current surged with a competitive spirit Emma had never felt before.

Top teams from across the State of Washington staked out sections of the floor and bleachers at the Tacoma Dome, their gear piled high as they camped out between games. Having just arrived, Emma and her teammates huddled by the door to the gym, watching the game in session. Feet thudding against the hardwood floor, fans cheering, teammates and coaches shouting instructions at each other. The intensity swirled in the air, and Emma couldn't help the smile building on her face. She could get used to this level of competition.

Someone slammed into her from behind. The momentum sent her flying into the nearest pair of arms: Lauren's. Instead of pushing her away, Lauren grabbed her shoulders and prevented Emma from a face-plant into the wall.

"What's your problem?" Madison yelled at the offender.

The girl with the high ponytail and red ribbons threw Emma a smirk as she pivoted and kept walking backwards. "We're trying to find our competition." Her eyes scanned over Emma and the rest of Bradshaw's team. "We'll let you know if we find any." Without breaking her stride, the girl spun back around and kept walking with several of her teammates.

"You okay?" Lauren asked.

Emma stepped out of Lauren's grip, straightening her sweatshirt. "Yeah, I'm fine. I just didn't know people here were so friendly." The two of them shared a look and laughed.

"That was Morgan Quinn."

The freshman's voice said the name with awe and stared after the girl who'd slammed into Emma like she was a celebrity.

"Do you know her?" Emma asked.

Ashley looked up at her with wide eyes. "You don't?"

"Should I?"

A familiar elbow plopped down on Emma's shoulder. "What the freshman is trying to say is that Morgan Quinn is one of the top prospects in the state."

"One of the top?" Ashley asked Shiloh in disbelief. "Colleges have been recruiting her since her freshman year. I bet she has a million letters from every school in the country. She's led her team to an undefeated season for the past two years. They're returning state champions."

Lauren shrugged a shoulder and examined her fingernails. "She sounds lame."

"Yeah," Madison agreed. "Besides, Emma can totally take her."

Emma held up her hands and backed away from their circle. "Don't bring me into this. I have enough to worry about without taking on that girl."

"You don't have a choice," Ashley said. "She plays for Kennedy High School."

"So?"

"So, they're our first game, which means you'll be the one guarding her. No one else has been able to touch her."

Emma looked at her three other friends for a sign that the kid was exaggerating and that Morgan Quinn wasn't as good as Ashley made her out to be. Instead of reassurance, she saw doubt in their eyes. Even Lauren, who had been seemingly unimpressed by the girl seconds ago, seemed to have lost some of her conviction. Great. Just what Emma needed, to play against some basketball superstar.

Eight

A half hour later, Emma stood on the sidelines watching the remaining minutes of the game in session as she waited for the court to clear before Bradshaw's first game. Where in the world did these teams come from, and what had they been feeding their players? A straight diet of steroids? They looked like fully-grown women on a mission for blood, not gangly high school girls who merely played out of a love of the game. Emma thought Shiloh and Steph were big at six feet, but they were skin and bones compared to the tallest girls on opposing teams who hovered more around the six-foot-three-inch height. And the muscle! Had these teams grown up in a weight room? What some girls lacked in height they made up for in girth, outweighing Bradshaw's players by a good 20 to 50 pounds. Poor Ashley. The freshman looked like a sixth grader compared to every other girl on the court, even the shorter ones.

Not only were the other teams bigger, but their knowledge and execution of the game far exceeded all the teams Bradshaw had played against so far. They smoothly transitioned from defense to offense, finding the open player and moving the ball around the court without taking the time to think. When a shot opened up, there was no hesitation to take it, and the majority of their shots dropped through the hoop.

Shiloh rested her elbow on Emma's shoulder and assessed the game. "You think we have a shot at this?"

Emma had never heard her friend's voice waver in nervousness before. She shrugged. "We'll soon find out." Her role as the team captain was to inspire her teammates with vague answers, not divulge the truth and crush their hopes of winning before their game even started.

Shiloh nodded into the stands. "College scouts."

"Where?"

"Middle section. Halfway up."

"How can you tell?"

"How can you not?"

Emma had never seen a college scout in action before, especially since she never did spot the one at their regional game. Maybe she expected them to be accompanied by the fanfare, for their presence to be announced and revered by girls fighting for a scholarship. The individuals Shiloh pointed out looked so...normal. Men and women recruiters were scattered in the bleachers. Some wore slacks and collared shirts while others wore athletic sweat suits. They all had a clipboard and stopwatch in their hands, their eyes plastered on the action.

"Great," Emma muttered. "One more thing to make me nervous."

◆◆◆

Morgan Quinn. While everyone had kept a close eye on the girl, Emma was about to compete against her firsthand. The girl exuded confidence, and Emma wondered if Quinn's skills would measure up to her attitude.

Players from both Bradshaw and Kennedy High School sauntered onto the court as the referees consulted the scorekeepers and timekeepers before the start of the game.

"You certainly don't look like much."

The words danced across Emma's neck and slid down her spine. Turning around, she stepped back as Morgan Quinn attempted to ram into her again. The high ponytail, glittering red ribbons, and fake tan would be a sight Emma would have to get used to over the next couple of hours.

Morgan assessed Emma with a look of forced pity. "If it isn't the underdog and her pack."

Lauren stepped beside Emma with a cocked hip and raised eyebrow. "If it isn't Barbie wannabe and her groupies."

Quinn ignored Lauren's comment. "I have to say, I'm surprised you managed to pull off a win at regionals. I figured a ragtag team led by a motherless no-name would've been crushed."

Morgan's reference to Emma made the insult personal. When words failed and emotions ran high, she liked to solve things the confrontational way. The deep breath she took to voice her rebuttal cut short when Shiloh stepped in front of her and blocked Morgan from view.

"Out of my way, Shiloh," Emma bit out.

"Although I'd love to watch you take this girl down, you need to suck up your pride and think about where you are." Her eyes nonchalantly scanned the crowd. "I don't think college recruiters would like to see a potential prospect start out this game with a fistfight, if you know what I mean."

Emma glared up at Shiloh as she let her friend's words sink in. She had to remember that this wasn't some pickup game at the park where anything goes, but a school tournament with plenty of witnesses that would probably love the dramatic effect of a brawl. "I hate it when you're right."

"It happens so often that even I get annoyed with myself."

As much as Emma would've liked to stay mad, Shiloh's cockiness cracked her resolve. Even Shiloh knew the effect she had. "Good girl, Wrangton. Now, deep breath and show me your pearly whites."

"Don't push it."

Shiloh held up her hands in innocence. "Fair enough."

"How did she even know about my mom?"

Shiloh shrugged. "Seems like Morgan's approach to dominating the court is to weaken her prey before tipoff by digging up dirt on her opponents. You should feel honored that she sees you as a threat. Now all you have to do is stand strong mentally and not let her get to you."

It sounded like Tyler wasn't the only one who loved to push buttons to gain an edge over his opponent. "Easier said than done."

"Yeah, well, you better suck it up and do it, otherwise, you can kiss any chance of a scholarship goodbye."

Shiloh was right. There were more important things riding on this game than one girl's insults. "Fine."

The buzzer sounded and the refs called both teams to center court.

"Let's play our game or none at all. Sound good, Wrangton?"

For once Shiloh didn't raise her fist, so Emma did it instead. "Sounds good. Now go get us the ball."

Shiloh laughed her approval and pounded her knuckles against Emma's. "Coming right up."

Despite Emma's attempt to focus on the game, Morgan wasn't finished with her. They matched up outside the center circle in anticipation for the jump ball.

Morgan licked her hands and then swiped them across the bottom of her shoes to clear the dirt and help with traction. "I hope people don't get bored watching us slaughter you."

Bite tongue, taste blood, and focus on the game. Emma scanned her teammates on the court, making sure they were all in position. She gave Ashley a nod of encouragement like she did before every game and then crouched down, her eyes on the ball in the referee's hand.

Time stood still.

Everything fell silent.

Emma's world consisted only of the ball and the players around her.

With a black whistle bobbing from his lips, the referee bent his legs and then popped up, releasing the ball into the air halfway between the opposing players at mid court.

Emma anticipated the tip coming from Shiloh, like it had so many times before, but instead of the ball sailing in Emma's direction, it dropped into Morgan's hands. Apparently, Kennedy's jumper had height and hops.

The ball snapped from one set of hands to the next, making its way downcourt to the hoop. Before Emma and her teammates could set up on defense, the ball soared through the hoop and Bradshaw was down 0 to 2.

Morgan brushed by Emma, her red ribbons bouncing as she ran. "Beat that."

All Emma could do was laugh. It was time to play some basketball.

◆◆◆

Kennedy may have scored first, and with ease, but Bradshaw made them fight for every shot after that. Shiloh and Steph, though seemingly outmatched under the basket, held their own as they blocked out their defenders and fought for the inside position. They rarely let Kennedy rebound a missed shot to put it up for a second and third chance to score. Lauren and her defender were fairly evenly matched on both offense and defense, but Lauren won the edge in determination. The girl may appear to be focused on boys and makeup and gossip most of the time, but Emma wasn't fooled. Her blonde teammate loved competition and stepped up when someone threatened to dominate her space on the court. Lauren put on the pressure, which often resulted in her defender passing the ball to a teammate or turning it over to Bradshaw. Ashley and Emma teamed up to shut down the outside shooters, one being Morgan Quinn. This was easier to do when the opposing guards weren't shooting with ninety percent accuracy from the three-point line, but Ashley and Emma didn't exactly play like amateurs in the sport.

Although Kennedy led the scoring throughout the first two quarters of the game, Bradshaw stayed within striking distance. When the buzzer announced the end of the first half, Bradshaw only trailed by three.

During halftime, Coach ran through Kennedy's strengths and weaknesses and explained through whiteboard drawings how Bradshaw should approach the second half, but Emma's thoughts shifted to her opponent.

Over the years, Emma had faced players who were bigger, stronger, and more aggressive than her, and she had always found a way to dominate them on the court, but even Emma had to admit that Morgan Quinn could have been her best competitor yet. Riley was amazing, but he was familiar. She knew he favored head fakes and hesitation moves, and she could often anticipate his next steps. Morgan was a stranger, and Emma had to be ready for anything. The girl matched Emma in every aspect of the game, offensively and defensively, and Emma found herself being challenged in new ways. In all honesty, she thought Morgan Quinn just might even be better than her. Maybe Emma should've been scared or threatened or a million other things, and in part she was all those, but another part of her was excited. Excited that girls' basketball just might help her become an even better player.

With a few final words of encouragement, Coach freed them from the stuffy team room to return to the court.

Emma glanced at the scoreboard as she chose a ball from the rack to shoot around before the second half started. The score was close, too close for Emma's liking. Exhaling a deep breath, Emma turned her focus to the hoop. Just her and the ball, her and the hoop. She knew how to play this game; she knew how to choose her shots and make them count, how to find the backdoor path to the hoop when every obstacle made it seem impossible, how to rely on her teammates to overtake an opposing team and claim a victory. She could hold her own against Morgan, all she had to do was prove it.

As the last minute of halftime fell from the clock, Emma's eyes drifted into the stands, searching for a face she knew wasn't there, a face she so desperately wanted to see. For some reason, she felt that his presence would bring her a sense of hope, that no matter how this game ended, everything would be okay. But she searched in vain for her dad's face. Even though she knew she wouldn't find him in the crowd, his confirmed absence weighed heavily on her. It would probably be the last time he could watch her play, unless he came to any of her college games, but that was highly unlikely. A few times she saw someone with a similar build and hair color, but upon closer inspection the individual disappeared into the crowd or turned out to be a stranger.

Her eyes drifted to Riley, knowing exactly where to find him. His parents sat beside him, deep in conversation, while Tyler stretched out on Riley's other side, looking bored.

As if he could feel her attention shift to him, Riley blew her a kiss and waved at her. His wave brought a smile to her face, bringing her much needed comfort.

Of course, Tyler tried to ruin the moment by mimicking Riley and blowing her kisses as well, only in more of a dramatic fashion. His attempt to mock Riley only made her laugh, especially when Riley turned around and caught Tyler in the act and punched him in the leg.

The buzzer sounded, and she joined her teammates on the court.

Both teams picked up where they left off before the half: same intensity, same pace of play. Here, everyone came to win. Every step had a purpose, every move had a mission. The game was a contest of which team could better execute offensive plays and defensive strategies. Defense couldn't consist of waving arms and shuffling feet in the hopes of distracting the other team, it needed to be deliberate, focused, intentional.

Kennedy whipped the ball around the perimeter a few times before dumping it inside. Lauren crouched down in triple-threat position, her hands and feet spread wide as her opponent protected the ball, trying to determine her next move.

Catching movement from across the key, Emma shouted, "Screen," too late. Lauren slammed into the solid body as the girl with the ball brushed past her firm-footed teammate and drove to the basket. Shiloh hesitated as she gauged whether or not Steph would help out. With one last look at the girl posted at the baseline, Shiloh collapsed into the key, blocking the drive. But Kennedy planned for everything, and the girl flipped the ball to her teammate, the one Shiloh left open so she could help Lauren.

Kennedy's fans erupted as the ball fell through the net. Emma glanced at the scoreboard. Bradshaw had only been down by three points at halftime, but now they trailed by ten.

Ashley passed the ball to Emma from out of bounds before sprinting down the court to set up on offense. For once, Kennedy didn't pressure them full court, giving Bradshaw a moment to put things in perspective before they retaliated for their own shot. Shiloh bent over, hands on her knees as she caught her breath. "They're beating us under the basket," she panted.

Emma nodded in agreement. "Yes, but your person's tiring. Her legs are weakening, and her left side is getting lazy. Play to her weaknesses."

Shiloh tapped Emma's shoulder with a fist in gratitude before racing ahead.

Emma passed the ball to Ashley, and as the rest of their team shifted to the right side, Emma paused before sprinting down the left side of the key and taking a sharp right at the baseline. Shiloh set a screen, causing Morgan to veer out of her intended path as Emma popped out the side. Hands up and ready for the ball, Emma caught Ashley's pass at the three-point line. Taking just enough time to set her feet, Emma released the ball into the air as Morgan caught up with her. Morgan's heavy footfalls did nothing to distract Emma from her shot.

"Wrangtoooon with a three!" Shiloh imitated an announcer's voice as she celebrated Bradshaw's addition to the scoreboard. Down by seven, with a little more than a quarter left of play.

Lance may have said it was a girls' game, but even Emma could contest that girls had the potential of giving boys a run for their money on the basketball court. No, there were no slam dunks or other displays of awesome power, but the ability to play a game based on the execution of fundamental skills and intelligence kept fans invested on the game unfolding before them. Quick feet, able hands, not waiting for a play to unfold, but having the foresight to know what would happen before it did. All the components of great competition were in operation. Now, it was just a matter of which team would claim the victory.

♦♦♦

Current score: Bradshaw 60, Kennedy 61. One minute left to play.

Facing Quinn, Emma protected the ball at her hip as she watched her teammates shift and fight for position under the basket. Everyone seemed to move in slow motion as Emma assessed the court, her senses hyperaware.

A barely there path opened up through the key. Based on the defensive coverage, Emma would have one shot to make her move count. Lauren and her defender shifted half a foot at the foul line, leaving Emma just enough of a hole to slip through. It wasn't much, but she'd take it. Thankfully, her route wouldn't accommodate a plus one. *Sorry, Quinn.*

One dribble to the left brought Quinn close enough for Emma to switch directions with a spin move, followed by a crossover to catch Quinn off guard. Keeping the ball close, Emma entered the key. Like a game of Tetris, players shifted like geometrical shapes. A foot down below, an arm up above, a jutted hip in the middle, Emma slid between them, slicing her way toward the basket. Taking care to strategically place her feet in vacant spaces, Emma pushed off from the floor, every limb of her body working in harmony with each other. Dropping the ball to her hip to avoid a reaching arm, she circled it around and up to her shoulder to avoid a block. Part layup, part hook shot, she offered the ball to the basket. The rim accepted it readily, the net swishing in gratitude.

Cheers erupted around her, but she barely heard them, knowing the game wasn't over. Ahead by one as the final seconds ticked down on the clock, Bradshaw raced back on defense as Kennedy looked for an opportunity to score.

Emma stuck to Quinn, determined not to let her get open, but when Quinn's teammate brushed by and handed her the ball, there wasn't much Emma could do. She sensed the other eight players on the court shift behind her, but Emma knew their efforts to get open or steal the ball were in vain. The final seconds would be a showdown between Emma and Morgan.

She matched Quinn step for step. The girl was quick, so Emma knew not to guard her too close, but she also knew her opponent had a wicked three-pointer that required a hand in her face. It was a tough balance. How much space did she need to put the pressure on, but not be so close to give her the opportunity to drive to the basket or take a free shot?

Regardless of Emma's defensive coverage, Morgan put up a mercy shot with twenty seconds on the clock, and everything went slow motion from there. Emma caught a glimpse of Morgan's face, expecting to see fear and hope and desperation as she watched the ball journey to the basket. But all Emma saw was faith and trust and confidence reflected on her opponent's features. Emma whipped around to watch the ball. It arced in the air, reaching its peak before starting its final descent.

It could be short.

It could be long.

It could catch the tip of the rim or the back corner near the backboard and bounce out.

The basket could decide, for whatever reason, to reject the ball.

A million things could've happened, but only one thing did. The ball sailed through the net, meeting no resistance.

Not taking time to acknowledge the bad fortune, Ashley hopped out of bounds and grabbed the ball from the ref's hands. She snapped the ball inbounds to Emma as the rest of their team sprinted to the opposite basket. All but two of the Kennedy players followed. Emma saw them share a look before they each took a step toward her. She had played enough basketball to recognize the threat of the double-team. Glancing down the court to see her teammates covered by defenders and not wanting to play the pass-and-go game with Ashley to make it past half-court since it would waste too much time, Emma pushed the ball forward, heading straight for the middle of the double-team. A couple steps before the two defenders could trap her, she reversed, pulling the ball back with her before switching the ball to her left hand and changing directions. The two Kennedy players faltered a step before readjusting their coverage, but they weren't fast enough. Seeing the slight gap between them, Emma sprinted forward, forcing the ball up the court. She broke through the double-team, crossing half court with seven seconds left on the clock. Her teammates fought to get open while Emma tried to foresee the remaining seconds of the game before they happened. What were her options? Who was in the best position to take the last shot? Where was the weakness in defense?

Shiloh broke free from her defender. She sprinted toward Emma with her hands in the air. Emma didn't hesitate. She snapped the ball to Shiloh before slicing through the key to the baseline. Shiloh faked a shot before pivoting toward the sideline where Emma popped out, one step ahead of Quinn. Shiloh passed her the ball. Emma caught it mid-flight as Quinn planted her feet on defense. With two seconds remaining, Emma jabbed right, swung the ball left, and squared up to the basket, before releasing the ball on its final journey to the hoop.

Nine

Time stopped.
Sound vanished.
Feelings numbed.

With her arm extended in the air, her wrist still snapped in follow-through, Emma watched the ball's descent. It headed straight to the hoop, good arc, good backspin. All it needed to do was drop through the net. The ball bounced off the rim with a resounding thud. It popped straight up in the air once, hit the rim again and bounced across to the other side of the hoop before hitting off the backboard. It stood motionless on the edge of the rim, balancing...steady...before gravity forced it over the side...the wrong side.

The final buzzer echoed through the dome, announcing Bradshaw's loss.

The Kennedy players threw up their hands and tackled each other in celebration as their fans went wild; the Bradshaw players and fans sagged in defeat.

Emma looked at the scoreboard, trying to make sense of the score: Bradshaw 62, Kennedy 63.

Ashley looked lost. Lauren stood frozen with tears dripping from her eyes. Steph slapped her hands over her face as if the sight of their loss was too much to bear. And Shiloh. She looked to Emma as if she needed someone to share her heartbreak, someone who would understand and help her make sense of things.

Emma looked at the downtrodden faces of her teammates, and her heart bore the burden of their loss. As heartbreaking as the game turned out to be, Emma couldn't fault her teammates. They had all played their best, but that didn't prevent Emma from questioning what she should've done differently to prevent Morgan's final shot and to make her own.

No matter how much pressure Emma had put on Morgan, the girl had put up a shot with nothing but faith in her ability to propel it through the hoop, and Emma couldn't mimic Morgan's perfect shot at the buzzer. Not this time. That's when the realization came, *She's better than me.* Maybe Emma should've felt threatened by her opponent, impelled to prove herself superior, but she didn't. As much as it pained her, Emma had to admit, Morgan Quinn was better than her. The realization didn't bring a surge of anger or resentment toward her opponent, but a sense of respect.

Shiloh engulfed Emma in a hug. She smashed Emma's face into her shoulder, hardly giving Emma room to breathe, before whispering, "You did good. No shame or blame, you got it? You were awesome."

Unable to speak unless she wanted a mouthful of Shiloh's sweat drenched jersey, Emma nodded and patted her teammate on the back, touched by Shiloh's reassurance.

Both teams huddled up, chanted their appreciation for each other, and formed single lines to slap hands. Like her teammates, Emma murmured, "Good game," to every Kennedy player she passed. However, when she found herself face-to-face with Morgan, Emma clasped her hand.

"You played an awesome game." She hoped Morgan could feel the sincerity of her words.

Morgan's lips turned up in a smirk. "Told you we'd

win."

Just because Emma respected Morgan as a basketball player didn't mean she had to like the girl. Without playing into Morgan's taunts, she continued down the line. When she got to the end and made to circle her way back to the bench to collect her things, she heard her name called and turned to find the source.

Morgan seemed to swallow her pride as she extended her hand to Emma. "You didn't play too bad yourself."

Emma shook Morgan's offered hand, questioning what had caused her opponent to make the effort. "Thanks."

"You may even be the best competition I've faced all season," Morgan said with a smile.

Two strong arms wrapped around Emma from behind, breaking her moment with Morgan. "Tough loss," Riley whispered in her ear.

She turned and hid her face in his chest, feeling the weight of the loss, before mumbling her agreement. "Tell me about it."

"Hey," he said, tipping up her chin. "You played awesome. You have nothing to be ashamed about."

"No matter how good I played, losing still sucks."

Riley's face broke into a smile. "It does, doesn't it? At least now you know what losing a heartbreaker feels like."

She slumped against him and let his arms support her weight. If this was what losing a heartbreaker game felt like, Emma didn't want to face too many of them. She was exhausted.

"Don't look now," Riley whispered, "but someone is on her way over to talk with you."

"What?" She broke free from his embrace, regaining her strength from curiosity. A woman Emma had never seen before extended her hand as she closed the distance between them. Without thinking Emma reached out and grabbed it.

"Hi, Emma. I'm Lisa Krola, the head basketball coach for Oregon State University."

Emma couldn't prevent her gasp of surprise. Until now, she'd only ever see Lisa Krola's name in print. "It's nice to finally meet you."

"I've heard a lot about you these past couple months, and I liked what I saw on the court."

"Thank you." Was that the right response? Did she sound conceited?

Coach Krola smiled as if she heard Emma's internal struggles. "Emma, I'd like to talk to you about your future."

Emma stared at the darkened ceiling of the garage. No way would she sleep tonight. She needed to move, to run, to challenge someone in basketball just to get her energy out, but instead, she waited. Waited beneath the covers on her bed for Riley to unlock the door and creep through the garage in search for her.

She counted to a hundred...twice. She named all 50 states from west coast to east coast, and when he still hadn't shown up, she named them east coast to west coast.

Despite her efforts to let the disappointment of the state tournament roll off her shoulders, she couldn't help the ache in her chest thinking about how their season ended. After their loss to Kennedy High School, Bradshaw faced another heartbreaking defeat against Montgomery High, losing by five in the final minutes. Bradshaw had played well, but faced with teams that had spent more than a year building their skills and team unity, Bradshaw couldn't pull off a win to continue in the tournament. It didn't help that they had to play both of their games against the best teams in the state. Kennedy and Montgomery faced off in the championship game, Montgomery securing the title as State Champions.

Emma replayed both games, assessing what she did right, what she did wrong, what she should've done differently until...

The sound of a key sliding through the lock rang like church bells on Sunday morning. She threw off the covers, already dressed with her shoes laced, and crept across the concrete floor to the door leading outside.

Riley inched the door open.

"It took you long enough," she whispered.

He slammed back against the door frame, the sound of body against wood echoing in the night. Reaching one hand out to grab hers while he slapped the other one to his chest, he sucked air into his lungs. "Geez, Em, you scared me."

"Sorry," she said, bouncing on the balls of her feet like a boxer preparing for a fight.

He looked at the smile lighting up her face and glared at her. "No, you're not."

"You're right, I'm not. Can we go?"

Laughing, he grabbed her hand and took the lead as lookout before they snuck through the trees of her front yard, crept across the neighbors' lawns, and found freedom to sprint down the street. Three blocks later, they slipped between the outstretched arms of two Evergreen trees and disappeared into the woods. The familiar path felt different now that they had moved out of the friend zone and into boyfriend/girlfriend status. Riley still hummed, their feet still maneuvered around the tree roots poking out of the ground, and his hand still held hers, but the air buzzed around them. Maybe it was because she knew pretty much all there was about Riley the friend, but Riley the boyfriend? It was unchartered waters and added a new level of excitement to their rendezvous at Puget Sound's lapping shore, or maybe it was the news they had yet to discuss.

Their dirt path gave way to the rocky shore and the sight of reflected lights on the rushing water coerced a smile from her. The smell of seaweed and saltwater swirled in the air.

Riley steered them toward their fallen tree, but instead of climbing up to sit on the trunk like they usually did, they jumped over it and walked another ten feet. On the brink of asking where they were going, Riley dropped onto a patch of sand and rested his back against a piece of driftwood. He spread his arms and legs and tugged her hand to bring her down in front of him. She scooted backward until her back rested against his chest and his arms enveloped her in their warmth.

"This okay?" he asked.

She nodded, settling into the warmth of his body. Definitely more comfortable than sitting side by side on their fallen tree like friends.

"You know, I would've suggested we cuddle up like this long before now," he tightened his arms around her, "but I figured you'd be against it."

She took in their current position: her back against his chest, his arms wrapped around her waist, and his face hovering inches from hers. A bit too intimate for just friends. "Wouldn't you be?"

"Heck no. I've been waiting for this since fourth grade."

"You have not."

His voice turned soft as he said, "Yeah, I have." He leaned his head against hers. "Em, you're all I've ever wanted."

She remained quiet, not knowing what to say. It wasn't like she'd ever been good at voicing her true feelings.

"Don't worry," he said. "I know the only reason you want to be with me is for my body heat."

She laughed and snuggled in closer. "And yet you go along with it."

He tightened his arms around her and rested his chin on her shoulder. "I'd be crazy not to."

"Do you think we're doing the right thing?" The words escaped her before she could determine if she wanted to voice the one concern she had about their newfound relationship.

"About what?"

"Us. Risking our friendship to be something more."

He leaned around her, but she wouldn't meet his eyes. "Don't tell me you're breaking up with me already."

"Of course not, I'm just wondering what happens when we do break up."

"We won't."

He couldn't guarantee their future any more than she could, and she was under no illusion that they would miraculously wind up with a happily ever after. "But what if we do. Then what? Our relationship and our friendship would just be gone."

"That's never going to happen, Em."

She turned her head to look at him, figuring the conversation was one that required eye contact. "Humor me for a second. What would happen?"

He took a defeated breath as he collected his thoughts. "I don't know. I guess we'd just figure it out."

"How?"

"I don't know. We just will. Like we always do."

He didn't sound as worried as she felt. To her, this entire scenario was too good to be true, which meant the end was just around the corner. Sooner or later they would be forced to figure it out, and she had more to lose than Riley did.

"Em, I've waited too long for us to be together. I'm not giving us up for anything. I promise." He kissed her temple. "We're forever."

How many teen boys and girls promised that? How many of them delivered? She settled back against Riley's chest, not at all reassured, and tried not to think about what she would do if she ever lost him.

Riley shifted behind her. "I have something for you."

She leaned forward as he dug something out of his pocket. It didn't take longer than a few seconds, but those seconds were long enough to allow a cold wind to sweep between them, making her shiver.

"Here."

Pinched between his thumb and forefinger was a piece of paper that consisted of multiple folds and points. Now she knew what parents of kindergarteners felt like when presented with their child's indecipherable masterpiece. "Thank you for the...prism?" Prism was a loose term, right? General but not offensive.

"What?" he exclaimed, looking closer at the folded mass in her hand. "It's not a prism; it's a crane."

"Oh," Emma said, trying not to laugh. "That was my next guess."

"Liar," he accused, jabbing her in the ribs and causing her to drop the pri—crane.

Picking up the paper from the sand, she tried tapping into her imagination to see any sort of resemblance to a bird in the folded mess. The poor thing was smashed beyond recognition, resembling a two-dimensional victim of road kill, rather than a three-dimensional creature of flight. She twisted it between her fingers, trying to determine if any of the pointed triangles could pass for a head.

Riley's laughter surprised her. "It doesn't look anything like a crane, does it?"

She couldn't contain the laughter bubbling inside her, which only made Riley laugh harder.

Once their laughter died down, Emma realized she'd never seen Riley attempt folded art before. "Since when do you do origami?"

He shrugged. "I figured it would be a fun way to pass my girlfriend secret messages."

His comment made her pause as she tried to determine if he was serious. Since she couldn't find a message on the crane's exterior, she unfolded the creases and used the flashlight from Riley's phone to search for one inside the folds. In the center of the flattened paper she read, *I'm so proud of you.*

She didn't have to ask the reason behind the words. After all, it was what brought them out to the water in the first place, and she felt her excitement recharge. "Proud of me for what? Coach Krola is only *considering* me for her team, not signing my name on the dotted line for a scholarship."

"You've got to start somewhere."

When Coach Krola told her Oregon State was interested in possibly having her join their team, especially after Bradshaw's loss, Emma had to ask her to repeat it. Twice.

"And to think three months ago you were trying everything you could to not be part of the girls' team. Imagine where you'd be if your," Riley cleared his throat in an I'm-awesome sort of way, "stellar boyfriend hadn't suggested it."

"Yeah, yeah, yeah, you were right. And now my life has changed forever, and I owe it all to you." In some ways he had a point. No matter how much she had resisted joining the girls' team at the start of the season, no matter how many times she'd wanted to quit in the beginning, he had always found a way to encourage her to stick with it. Now, she might have a future in the sport she loved, one that would allow her to move out of her garage bedroom and not be defined by her family.

Riley's body shook as he laughed. "Is that a thank you?"

"No."

"Oh, come on, you know you want to." His next words came out in a horrible imitation of a high-pitched girl voice. "Oh, Riley, thank you so much for making me play on the girls' team. You're the best boyfriend ever, and I'll never doubt you again and—"

Her elbow smacked him in the ribs. "In your dreams, buddy. No way would I ever feed your ego. Besides, I don't talk like that."

She didn't have to look at him to know he was smiling.

"Seriously though, Em, I'm so proud of you. You deserve this; you earned it."

"Thanks."

"Have you told your dad yet?"

She shook her head. "I don't even know what to say to him."

"How about, 'Dad, I might have a chance to play college ball'?"

"Yeah, right. Easier said than done."

"So what are you going to do?"

Fear took hold of her when she thought about telling her dad. Would he be supportive? Would he sigh with relief that he'd finally be rid of her? Would he think she was following in her mom's footsteps and leaving? She knew once she told her dad she would second-guess everything, and she wasn't ready for that.

"You mean besides putting it off for as long as possible?"

"Yeah, besides that."

She leaned her head back against his shoulder, searching the sky for answers and confidence. "I don't know. I'm scared."

He kissed her head. "I know."

Not wanting to talk about it anymore, she raised the paper. "Why a crane?"

He took the paper from her and attempted to refold it to its original shape. He folded the last piece and then held it out to her. It looked more like smashed roadkill than ever.

"I read somewhere that cranes serve as a sort of sentinel over their loved ones. They take turns guarding each other at night so they can detect danger and keep their family safe. They made me think of us. Ever since we were little, we've looked out for each other, and we've never left each other behind." He turned the crane as if looking at it from a new perspective. "I also learned that cranes remain faithful and loyal to one partner for life. Even though my crane looks nothing like it should, that's what it's supposed to represent—my promise of commitment to you. You're my one. I'll always be here for you, keeping watch over you and remaining faithful to you—to us—because...I love you, Em."

His words brought tears to her eyes. She pinched the crane in her fingers and rotated it to look at it from all sides. How could a badly folded piece of paper mean so much? She used to think she was nothing more than Riley's charity case, but they'd been friends for a long time, and she could finally accept that Riley loved her. He'd proven it time and time again throughout their friendship. But this was the first time he'd said it out loud since they'd become more than friends, and she'd be lying if she said it didn't affect her. In the months she'd spent playing ball with the girls, she had heard more than her fair share of stories about boyfriends and betrayal and a lack of respect and appreciation between couples. Enough to make her leery of relationships in general, but then Riley declared his commitment to her and shattered her fears. How could she even respond with how much his words meant to her?

Riley didn't grow nervous with her silence; he hadn't declared his love for her with an expectation of a similar response from her. He sought nothing in return except her. Maybe that was why she felt confident enough to admit her feelings to him. "I love you too," she whispered as if trying the words on to see if they fit. They did.

He rested his open hand on her cheek, his thumb caressing her cheekbone as he guided her face to his, and kissed her. "I know."

Ten

A week later, after playing a pickup game with the girls, Emma walked through the front door of her house. Her state of peace wilted at the sight of Riley and her dad sitting across from each other in the living room. Her dad lounged in the recliner, but his posture was stiff. Perched on the edge of the couch with his elbows on his knees, Riley's head was bowed, almost as if he was asking for forgiveness as his leg jiggled in nervousness.

When Riley looked up at her, she froze. His face tightened as if her presence caused him pain, and his eyes pleaded for her to understand. Her breath hitched in her throat. Understand what?

She had stopped just inside the door, her hand still lingered on the doorknob. "What's going on?" she forced herself to ask, afraid to find out what she had interrupted between her dad and boyfriend. When neither one of them answered, she glanced at Riley. "What are you doing here?"

But it wasn't Riley who answered; it was her dad. "Riley told me Oregon State is recruiting you for a potential scholarship."

Sound whooshed out of Emma's ears, and she stared numbly at the floor. This wasn't how it was supposed to go.

This wasn't how her dad was supposed to find out about her potential post high school plans.

"Is it true?" her dad asked before she could muster up a response.

His voice sounded like it was at the end of a long windy tunnel. She felt his eyes on her—for once she wasn't invisible to him—and she cowered under his gaze. She nodded.

"How long have they been scouting you?" She didn't have an answer for him; she hadn't prepped for this conversation.

Riley stood and took a step toward her, reaching for her hand. "Since January."

Her dad nodded once, as if he expected as much, then rose from his chair and walked out of the room.

Emma watched his back retreat—the sight of him she was most familiar with. It was almost as bad as the look in his eyes the night Lance told her their dad hated her because of Mom's abandonment. Her dad had confirmed his hatred simply by the way he had looked at her, with eyes full of guilt, as he let the truth settle on the stretched out silence. Now, with his back to her, she had another image of his hatred burned into her memory.

She expected Riley to stay, to stand by her side and figure this out, but he didn't. With a quick kiss on her cheek, he whispered, "I'll see you later," and then he was gone. He didn't give her an explanation of why he had told her dad the one thing she'd been keeping from him, the thing she'd been trying to protect him from. The front door clicked closed, and she was left alone.

Swallowing the baseball in her throat, she took a deep breath and stepped into the kitchen. Her dad sat hunched over the kitchen table, his hands wrapped around a mug of coffee, his eyes staring blankly at the steam rising from the cup.

"Dad?" Her voice sounded strange, shy, timid. "Dad, say

something." Her hands squeezed the back of the wooden chair across from him, desperate. "Please."

Quiet filled the space between them until he decided to fulfill her request. "It's late, and I'm tired." He stood from the table, white knuckles gripping the coffee cup. "Goodnight."

Emma squeezed her eyes shut, partly to block out his retreating form and partly to keep her tears from falling. Nine o'clock on a Friday night wasn't late, but she heard his message loud and clear.

She only pounded on the Ledgers' door once before it opened, framing Riley in front of her. He held up his hands in defense. "I know you're mad."

"Do you?" She took a step back, questioning his loyalty to her. "Because I don't know why my *boyfriend*, my *best* friend, would go behind my back on something like this."

"I didn't go behind your back." His words rushed out, desperate to be heard. "I went to your house looking for you, and your dad answered the door. He invited me in and asked me questions about you. He asked if I thought you had a shot at a scholarship." Riley held out his hands, begging for her to understand. "What was I supposed to say?"

"Nothing!" she shouted. "You should've said nothing."

"You weren't there, Em," he said, his tone becoming defensive. "He looked happy when I told him. He looked—"

"What? Like he was happy to not have me around for much longer?"

"No." He took a deep breath and exhaled. "He looked like...like he was proud of you."

She shook her head refusing to believe it. She had spent years trying to gain her dad's approval, trying to win his attention, but he had made it clear he wanted nothing to do with her.

Riley bowed his head and looked at her with upturned eyes. "He's your dad, Em. Maybe he had a right to know."

"And I was going to tell him," she said firmly. "In my own time. And in my own way."

"When? The day you leave?" He shook his head. "That wouldn't have been fair to him."

"Fair to him? Fair to *him!*" Was Riley actually defending her dad? In all the years they had known each other, Riley had always stood beside her when things went awry with her family. Sure, he had somewhat of a relationship with her dad. Her dad did, after all, prefer Riley to her any day of the week, but Riley had never betrayed her like this. He had never defended her dad before, and it hurt. A lot. "That *man* treats me like I'm nothing but a burden. He looks at me with hatred and resentment and has never taken an interest in me. All I ever wanted was for him to come see me play. One game. *One* game was all I ever wanted from him, but he never had time for me. Tell me, was that fair to me?"

"Em—"

"Was it fair!"

Riley looked down. "No."

Her hands balled into fists. "Then don't tell me what's fair to him. That is *not* your call to make. I don't need him. I've never needed him." Even Emma heard the falsity of her words, but maybe if she said them out loud enough times they'd start to be true. She looked at her best friend standing before her, but the hurt and fear she felt made her see him as the enemy. "You had no right to tell my dad anything."

"Emma." He stepped forward and gripped her shoulders. "I'm sorry, I am, but maybe this is a good thing. After all, you were afraid to tell him, so maybe this—"

She shoved his hands off of her. "I'm not a child, Riley. I don't need you to fix my problems."

"You're right." He held his hands up in a gesture of surrender, nodding his head. "I'm sorry."

She spun around, unable to look at him or acknowledge his apology. All she could think about was how her dad had taken his leave of her moments before with a lame excuse and headed to bed without saying anything. She dragged her hands down her face as she peered into the shadows of the neighborhood. She didn't need another reason for him to hate her.

"I thought he'd be happy for you," Riley said, his tone apologetic and disappointed.

"Well, he's not," she spit out.

"But why? This is great news."

After all the years Riley had known her, after everything he knew about her family, he still didn't get it. She spun around to face him. "Is it? Or is it just a reminder for him about what it felt like when my mom left to find a life better than the one he could provide?"

Riley stepped closer to her and studied her face. "Em," he said softly. "What happened?"

Tears blurred her eyes. Riley, her best friend, her boyfriend, the person she trusted with everything, yet she couldn't get the words out to tell him of her dad's rejection of her. She couldn't voice her embarrassment that the one parent she had left wanted nothing to do with her.

She stepped out of Riley's reach and shook her head. "You had no right."

"Em, wait."

She didn't. She brushed past him and descended the porch steps.

"Emma," he shouted, chasing after her. He jumped in front of her, blocking her escape route. "Don't leave. Please," he begged. "Tell me what happened. Maybe I can help."

His words reignited the hot coil in her stomach. "I don't want your help!" He flinched at the force of her words. "This is *my* life, Riley. Mine! You had no right to talk to my dad. You may disagree with me, you may think I'm making the biggest mistake of my life, but it's my mistake to make, and it's none of your business. And if you can't respect my decisions—if you can't respect *me*—then we're done."

Fear flashed in his eyes. "Em—"

This time Emma wouldn't let him prevent her from leaving. She shoved past him, her hurt and anger and fear propelling her home.

Being new at the whole relationship thing, Emma didn't know if a fight of this magnitude meant an automatic breakup or if it would elicit a groveling session from one of them later. All she knew was that she didn't want to be anywhere near Riley at the moment, so she hid in her garage/bedroom, imagining the repercussions of Riley's confession to her dad. Would her dad kick her out? Disown her? Treat her like she didn't exist?

A knock on the door. Emma's body jerked upright as her eyes snapped toward the sound. She gulped down a breath, trying not to choke. *Please don't be Dad.* Not that he frequented her domain often, but the only other person it could be was Riley and he would've used the exterior door.

Before she could decide what to do—open the door or run and hide—the door from the house squeaked open in protest. She couldn't see who entered since the boxes and junk in the garage obstructed her view, but she heard footsteps shuffling closer.

Between the aisle of boxes and broken equipment, her dad emerged. Her breath caught in her throat. So much for the late hour and him wanting to go to sleep.

Her dad stood before her, about as out of place as every family artifact surrounding him. She waited, but the silence built between them. Flashes of his fights with Lance flickered in her head. Fighting, yelling, throwing things. She didn't know her dad well enough to know what a confrontation between the two of them would look like. Would it follow the same path as his fights with Lance? Or would he remain quiet and emotionless as he avoided eye contact and told her to leave? She didn't know what would be worse. The yelling and anger or the quiet and uncaring.

Her dad didn't look at her when he stuffed his hands in

his pockets and asked, "Why didn't you tell me?"

The unexpected question caused her to blurt out the first words that came to thought. "I don't know." Stupid. Weak.

Her dad glanced up, meeting her eyes, then bowed his head once more. He turned to leave.

This action, the one her dad always resorted to when it came to her, made Emma jump up from her bed. "Why do you even care?" She didn't bother to strip her tone of hurt or anger.

He stopped and turned back to face her, but he didn't say anything, so she let her words tumble forth without a filter.

"You've never cared about me before, so why now? Why this?" She didn't give him the opportunity to respond. "You want to know the real reason I didn't tell you? Because I thought me packing up and going to college would remind you of Mom leaving, and I didn't want to hurt you. I didn't want to hurt you the way you've hurt me every day since she left." Emma tried to gauge him, but his face remained blank. "Mom left you. She left all of us. But you left me too. You kicked me out to the garage, you can't look me in the eye, and you've never even tried to see me play basketball. I asked you so many times to come to one of my games, to come watch me play, but you never did. Do you know how that made me feel? Do you know what it's like to have my brothers treat me like the enemy and speak to me with disgust while you stand by and do nothing? You make me feel like I'm worthless. And now, colleges are interested in me. *Me*! Because they think I'm good enough; they think I'm worth it. I may have this wonderful opportunity to go to college and play basketball and do something with my life, but I didn't want to tell you because I didn't want to give you another reason to *hate* me."

Her final words echoed around them. There. The truth was out and she couldn't take it back; she didn't want to take it back. She was tired of being silent and ignored; she was tired of holding everything inside and maintaining her silence, letting her family treat her however they wanted.

Her dad cleared his throat and a few seconds later he cleared it again. When he looked up at her and spoke, his words came out loose and scratchy, like they didn't have a foundation to stand on. "Emma, I'm sorry. I didn't know."

She shook her head from side to side, trying to blur the image of her dad standing before her sagging with defeat and guilt and sorrow. She didn't want to feel sorry for him, so she held her breath, trying to prevent her heart from shattering over the pain screaming from her dad's eyes, pain she didn't know he could feel. Yet, his one moment of emotion couldn't erase years of hurtful incidents between them. Unable to forgive him, her next words were filled with accusation and choked with tears. "How could you not know?"

Unable to continue looking at the man who stood before her, she stumbled for the door leading outside. Slamming the door behind her, she collapsed against the side of the house, gasping for breath and clutching her chest to ease the pain within.

All she'd ever wanted was for her dad to see her and care about her. Even though a large part of her had given up hope on him, another part of her wanted nothing more than to rekindle some sort of relationship with him. She wanted to see the man as her dad, not as a stranger or an enemy, but he'd never given her a reason to trust him.

Looking to the night sky, she tried to pace her breathing and gain control of her emotions. After a few minutes, she pushed away from the house and let her feet steer her into the night.

Whether she was conscious of the decision or not, she shouldn't have been surprised at where she ended up. Still cast in shadows, she looked at the Ledgers' house from the sidewalk. Riley sat on the porch swing, illuminated by the porch light. With his head bowed and his shoulders slumped forward, he looked sad, and she knew she was the cause of it. Loneliness weighed down on her, suffocating, crushing, and despite what she had yelled at him earlier, she needed him. They'd had their share of fights over the years, but they were always able to put aside their differences when something else overshadowed them.

She took a step forward, her feet scraping along the concrete.

Riley's head snapped up, his eyes squinting to see into the darkness. "Emma?"

Not knowing the status of their relationship after their fight, she remained quiet, not trusting herself to speak.

He stood from the swing and descended the steps. "Hey," he said softly. When she didn't respond, he stepped closer. "You okay?"

"Everything with my dad is so complicated," she choked out. "I don't know what he wants from me, and I don't know how much I'm willing to give him at this point, but I need you to trust me. I know I may have overreacted before, but when you have secret conversations with my dad, even if you don't mean to, it makes me feel like I can't trust you. And if I can't trust you, I can't trust anyone."

"I know," he said quietly. "I'm sorry. I never meant to imply I was taking your dad's side or defending him. He just caught me off guard, and I didn't know how to respond, but you're always my number one." He reached out his hand, his fingers lightly brushing hers as if asking for permission to touch her.

Her defenses weakened, and she walked into him, wrapping her arms around his waist and holding on. She tried not to cry, but shudders wracked her body anyway.

"Hey, it's okay," he whispered, running his fingers through her loose hair. For once, Riley didn't try and pry answers from her. He just squeezed her against him, easing the pain in her chest, until she was able and ready to recount what happened with her dad.

When she finished, one question balanced on the end of

her tongue. "Do you think my dad and brothers are bad people?"

Riley glanced at her as if trying to decide whether to be honest or tell her what he thought she'd want to hear. "I don't know," he finally said. "I've known them for years, but..."

"But what?"

His fingertip led a stray hair from her forehead to behind her ear, light as a bird's feather. "But I see how they treat you, and how they hurt you."

"Maybe I deserve it," she mumbled.

"Don't say that." He didn't snap at her, but the firmness in his voice was unmistakable. He held her at arm's length, his eyes capturing hers. "You only deserve what's good. Don't allow their demons to pull you down; don't allow their problems to be your problems. Okay?"

Easier said than done.

"The world needs you for who you are, Em—your courage, your strength, your perseverance. Don't let anyone make you think differently, not even me. Ever."

Stupid tears huddled in her eyes, waiting to be freed, but she refused to let them go. Instead, she slumped against him. "And here I thought you were going to break up with me."

He kissed her head and squeezed her against him. "Never."

◆◆◆

After her night of drama, Emma needed Saturday basketball games with the guys more than ever. Staring into the eyes of her defender, she readied herself for the drive to the basket, smelling victory. From the second she took her first step toward the basket, she was ahead of her defender, and she refused to let him catch up. Her underhanded layup went in smooth and easy.

Arms wrapped around her waist and picked her up off the ground, twirling her in circles before setting her back down.

"What's the matter, tough guy," she said, turning in his arms, "losing your touch?"

It wasn't often that she beat Riley so easily. He gave her a smirk. "You wish."

"If you keep playing like that, I may have to replace you."

"As a boyfriend or a basketball partner?"

"Both."

His mouth dropped open, feigning offense. "I'll show you who's boss on this court."

"I'm pretty sure I just proved it's me."

"I demand a do-over." He lunged for the ball, but she held it out of his way.

"Sorry, buddy, not gonna happen."

One side of his mouth tipped up. "Oh, it's gonna happen."

He lunged at her again, catching her off guard. She managed to wrap her arms around the ball to prevent him from stealing it, but his weight crashing against her threw her off balance.

Maybe she would've had a better chance of standing without his support if his maul-you-like-a-teddy-bear technique didn't make her laugh so hard. She was two seconds away from begging for mercy when Riley stilled, the smile on his face wilting.

"What's wrong?" she wheezed, trying to catch her breath.

He stared past her and nodded. She turned to follow his gaze, wiping her face clean of the stray hairs that had become dislodged during Riley's maul session.

In the past six months, the neighborhood basketball court had had its fair share of visitors. First Coach Knowles then Ashley and the rest of the girls' team. And now...her dad.

Emma froze. If Riley's arms hadn't been wrapped around

her waist, holding her up, she would have sunk to the ground.

"What is he doing here?" Riley asked.

She shook her head. "I don't know."

"Are you going to go talk to him?"

"I don't know. Our last conversation didn't exactly go well."

"Em." Riley squeezed her around the waist. "Go. It'll be okay."

She highly doubted that, but she knew she'd probably have to face her dad sooner or later, so there was no point in delaying the inevitable. Summoning strength she didn't have, she turned to Riley. "Hey, Riley?"

"Yeah?"

She hated asking him for anything, but she couldn't face her dad without knowing. "If my dad, if he..." she took a deep breath, "if he kicks me out of the house, do you think—"

His hands braced her face. "He's not going to kick you out, Em. But if he does?" He glanced over her shoulder toward her dad. "If he does, I'll take care of you. I promise."

She exhaled a laugh. "I don't need you to take care of me, I just may need somewhere to crash for a night or two."

He kissed her forehead. "We'll take it as it comes."

Hoping for the best, but fearing the worst, Emma took a deep breath and walked toward her dad.

Eleven

"You look good out there," her dad said, nodding toward the court and avoiding her gaze as usual.

She responded with a noncommittal, "Thanks."

He bowed his head and rubbed the back of his neck. "You, uh, wanna take a walk?"

She glanced over her shoulder, and Riley met her gaze. The moment reminded her of the white crane, and she saw what Riley meant when he had given her the folded bird at the water's edge. He was her sentinel, standing watch over her to make sure she was safe, even if it was her dad who posed the threat.

Gaining courage from Riley's unconditional support, she turned back to her dad and nodded. "Sure."

He ushered her toward the paved loop that circled the park, and she fell into step beside him. "When your mom left, I didn't know what to do." It sounded like a confession, words laced with guilt, spoken to a priest when seeking forgiveness. Emma had to strain to hear him. "I didn't know the first thing about raising five kids on my own, especially not a daughter."

She held her breath, not knowing where the conversation was headed but not wanting to miss a single word.

"Everything I touched fell apart, and the last thing I wanted was to mess up your life."

He paused as if thinking through his next words.

"I thought if I left you alone, you'd do a better job of raising yourself than I ever could." His eyes never strayed from the ground, and the volume of his words never exceeded a librarian's 12-inch rule.

Could his words be true? Could the past five years have been a compilation of misunderstandings and a scared dad's attempt to give his daughter the best life? She shook her head. No, it couldn't be. "I was only twelve. I could hardly raise myself."

The ghost of a smile flickered across his face. "You may have only been twelve, but even then you were a fighter. You knew what you needed and what you wanted, and you went for it. You had Riley by your side, and together you two could figure out anything. I knew as long as he was your friend, you'd always be looked after by someone who was so much better than me."

It was difficult to hear the same self-doubt and self-condemnation she suffered from be voiced by her dad. Weren't parents supposed to have all the answers? Weren't they supposed to be the epitome of strength and confidence and wisdom? Five years ago when her mom left, Riley had been a skinny boy with knobby knees and feet too big for his body. It would be another three years before he stopped begging her to rescue him from spiders and mustered up the courage to handle his own creepy crawlers. "But I didn't need him. I needed *you*."

Her dad glanced her way, nodding as if contemplating her words. "Maybe, but I didn't know how to be there for you the way you needed. I know I probably went about it all wrong, but at the time, it was the best I could do for you. At least I thought it was." He cleared his throat. "More than anything I didn't want you to grow up hating me, but it looks like that happened anyway."

She'd gotten so used to her dad being a silent, nonexistent part of her life that his words made her slow to a stop to process what he'd said and the truth behind his confession.

It took him a few steps to realize she wasn't beside him. He glanced over his shoulder, looking for her, and stopped when he noticed her staring at him.

"I don't hate you," she admitted.

A weight seemed to lift off his shoulders, and the hope in his eyes caught her off guard.

Her eyes flickered to the ground and then back up. "I thought *you* hated *me*."

He took a step toward her, the tension in his face easing into a smile. "I could never hate you. Not for a single second. I've only ever wanted what's best for you and your brothers, but I never know how to make that happen. Your mom left because I wasn't enough for her. I couldn't give her what she wanted, even though I tried." He took a deep breath, as if his next words needed extra preparation. "I didn't want to not be enough for you too." He closed his eyes and dragged his hands down his face. "I sure have made a mess of things, haven't I?"

For years she'd only been met by silence and what she'd interpreted as hatred from the man who stood before her. She'd never thought there were other reasons behind her dad's behavior.

"Why did you wait so long to tell me this?"

He started walking again, and she hurried to catch up. "When I was a kid, my dad never had time for anything but work, and he didn't value family. Every time I needed him, he would either tell me it wasn't a good time or ignore me. It hurt so bad that I eventually stopped asking him for anything. Even after I moved out, we never talked. I thought one day he'd eventually come around, but when he died, I hadn't talked to him in almost ten years. I often wonder if he cared that he had a nonexistent relationship with his only child. I promised myself I would never be that kind of dad, that I would love my kids and make sure they knew it, but when I look at you, I can't help but think I'm exactly the same." He took a deep, shaky breath. "When Riley told me about colleges recruiting you, and then when you called me out on everything last night, I realized I've been treating you exactly how my dad treated me, and that if I don't do something to break down the wall between us, we're going to end up exactly like me and my dad. Emma, I don't want that for us. I want us to be able to talk and laugh and trust each other."

A part of her wanted to forgive him on the spot and move forward, but the other part wouldn't let her forget the last five years and the pain he'd caused her. What if these were all just words? What if they weren't? She didn't know him well enough to know the difference.

She walked alongside him in silence, debating her next move when her dad broke the silence again.

"I attended your first game," he said nonchalantly.

Emma's eyes snapped to him at his admission. "What?"

"Your first basketball game this season. I was there."

"You were?"

He stopped walking again and nodded. "There was no way in the world I'd miss it." He looked out across the park, lost in thought. "I figured you could play. I mean you can't play years of basketball with Riley and your friends and not pick up a thing or two. Besides that, you come from a basketball family, but I wasn't prepared for what I saw." He shook his head. "I saw the fear in your eyes the first time you got your hands on the ball, and I was afraid you might freeze, but you surprised me. You were amazing. And then your game against Evergreen. You were so strong, so confident. I was so proud of you for stepping up and leading your team." He smiled. "Not to mention the fact that Evergreen needed to be taken down."

A ball of fire burned in Emma's throat. "Why didn't you

tell me you were there?" she choked out.

He shrugged. "I don't know. I guess I didn't want to distract you or make you feel like I was judging you." He paused. "Or maybe it was because I didn't feel like I deserved to be there, cheering you on, when I'd done everything I could to push you away."

She squeezed her eyes shut, thinking when they opened she would be in her bed at home, having dreamed this entire conversation. But no, when her eyelids peeled apart, the park still surrounded her and her dad still stood beside her.

"Emma, I'm sorry." His eyes glistened with unshed tears, and her heart clenched. "I'm so sorry. You deserved so much better, and I know I don't deserve your forgiveness—I know I've given you a million reasons to turn your back on me—but I'd like one more chance to be a part of your life."

The sincerity behind his words made her legs weak. Was she a fool to believe him? Was she an idiot if she didn't want an estranged relationship with him like he'd had with his own dad?

If she didn't start walking, she would either fall to the ground under the intensity of her dad's gaze or start crying like a baby. Her feet carried her forward, and her dad remained silent beside her as she replayed his words in her head. Memories of his rejections and neglect flashed through her thoughts, every one as painful as the last. Could she find it in her heart to put the past behind them and start again?

She paused in front of him and looked up into his face. Lines of worry and fear etched across his features as he watched her, and she knew she had the power to walk away and break him right then for all the pain he'd caused her over the years.

Raising her chin, she stood firm and confident in her decision, hoping she wouldn't regret it later. "Okay," she whispered.

♦♦♦

The conversation with her dad sat heavy on her thoughts as she walked back to the court where the guys and girls were deep in a game. For once, playing basketball didn't interest her, so she sat on the sidelines to watch the rest of the game and digest the conversation with her dad.

The Wrangtons had never been the picture perfect family, but before her mom left, they'd been somewhat civilized to each other. They laughed and fought like all families, and being the only girl, Emma had always had a difficult time figuring out her place among brothers who'd never taken her under their wings. But when her mom left, walls were built and hatred festered, and it seemed like her entire family turned on her. Five years. Just because her dad wanted a do-over didn't mean Emma knew how to make it work.

Riley wasn't subtle in his desire to know what had transpired between her and her dad. She felt his eyes on her as they walked back to his house, and he dropped question after question that she didn't answer because she didn't know how to formulate her thoughts into words.

It wasn't until they were back at his house that Emma pulled Riley into a hug. "My dad wants a second chance."

Although he returned her hug, his body tensed. "At what?"

She pulled back to look at him. "At being my dad."

"How do you feel about that?"

"I don't know." In truth, she didn't know whether to be excited or scared.

"So what does this mean, Em?"

What did it mean? In three months she would graduate high school, and if she went to college, it meant she would have less than six months to build a meaningful and sustainable relationship with her dad. Was that enough time? If not, if she had to choose between a future in basketball or her dad...

Her breath caught in her throat. Basketball had always been a lifeline for her and the idea of going to college gave her purpose in life, but nothing should be more important than family, right? College lasted four years, family lasted a lifetime. Would she be able to make the selfless choice and give up on her dream?

She looked at her best friend, trying to find words to explain her thoughts, but he didn't need to hear them. He saw the doubt clouding her judgment. Shaking his head, he took a step toward her. "Emma." The word came out filled with warning.

"What am I supposed to do, Riley? After all these years, I finally accepted the fact that my family didn't love me, that they wanted me gone. I thought maybe college would be the perfect escape from my life, but what if I was wrong? What if my dad does change? What if it's right for me to stay?"

"Just because your dad says he wants a second chance doesn't mean anything has changed." Irritation built in his tone, but she barely heard him.

On the court she felt strong. She knew when to shoot, when to pass, when to drive to the hoop. On the court she had the intuition of how to play, but in life? She'd had enough experiences over the past five years to walk away, to bid her family farewell and start living her own life, but deep down she knew she'd never be able to live with herself if she refused to give them another chance. If she did leave for college without reconciling things with her dad and brothers, they might never let her back in the door.

"My family needs me."

"Do they?" Riley sounded accusatory. "Or do you just want them to need you?"

She flinched, her brows pulling together at the harshness of his tone. "What is that supposed to mean?"

"It means they've had seventeen years to show you they

need you, but they've done nothing. For the past five years, they've treated you like you don't exist or blamed you for all their problems, and now that you have this great opportunity they suddenly care what happens to you?" He shook his head. "I'm not buying it."

It wasn't supposed to be this way. Riley wasn't supposed to stand in opposition to her fixing things with her family. He was supposed to understand.

Crunch.

The sound broke Emma's focus from Riley. She turned and saw Tyler's steps stutter as he entered the living room and realized he'd stumbled into their argument. He got over the surprise encounter pretty quickly and shoved another chip into his mouth. *Crunch.*

Riley put a hand on her arm, asking for her attention again. Maybe if she started over and tried to explain what her dad had said, Riley would understand better. "Riley, my family—"

"This isn't about them!" Riley shouted, undeterred from Tyler's intrusion. "This is about *you.* Em, I know you're scared. I'm scared too. But don't use your family as an excuse not to go to college."

"I'm not using them as an excuse. And why are you mad? You're the one who told my dad about the college recruiters. You said I needed to be fair to him."

"And you said I was wrong."

"Maybe you weren't."

"I was if your dad prevents you from going to college."

"He's not."

Riley crossed his arms over his chest in a challenge. "So throwing away your shot at a possible scholarship you've worked so hard for is your idea?"

"Like you're one to talk," she yelled, her frustration building. "You have scholarship offers from dozens of colleges, but you can't even decide where to go. If you don't choose soon, you're going to throw your dreams away too."

"This isn't about me."

"Of course not, because I don't get a say in your life, do I?"

"Em—"

"No," she said, cutting him off. "It's true. You're never shy about telling me what's best for me or what decisions to make, disappointed if I make a decision you don't agree with, but you never let me be a part of your decisions. How is that fair?"

"Because unlike you, I'm not trying to talk myself out of things that are right for me because I feel like I don't deserve them."

"In other words, you don't trust me to live my own life, so you have to dictate it for me?"

"That's not what I meant." He shoved his hands in his hair and growled.

Crunch.

"You can still build a relationship with your dad while you're at college. It's called weekends and holidays and phone conversations. In terms of your brothers, they've never done anything to show you they care."

"So what? Like you said, this isn't about them. This is about me." She slapped a hand to her chest to emphasize her point. "I care, Riley. *I* care. No matter how far I try to run away, no matter how much I try to pretend I don't care, something always brings me back to them. They're my family, and if there's a chance that we can overcome our differences then I want to try."

"Even if it means they'll hurt you again?"

She took a deep breath and tried to think what would happen if she failed. Would she be able to live with that? "Yes."

"Well, I can't, Em. Every time Lance lashes out at you, every time Logan ignores you, every time your dad rejects you, it kills me. I can't stand by and watch it happen again and again. I won't."

She wanted to feel compassion for Riley, knowing he'd witnessed a lot with her over the years, but she couldn't. Fear and anger boiled within her at his words. "So what are you saying? Are you telling me to choose between you and my family?" The mere thought sliced her heart in two; she'd never survive. "You want me to turn my back on them because they're not as perfect as *your* family?"

Crunch.

Riley shook his head and pointed at her, his voice coming out low and angry. "My parents and I have been here for you every day since we moved in. Every fight, every disagreement, every time your family hurt you, we've been here to pick up the pieces and put you back together. So *don't* talk about my family like they're the enemy here."

The weight of what she indicated slammed into her, and she bowed her head. She would be eternally grateful for everything Riley and his parents had done for her over the years, and she never meant to disrespect them. Why did fights bring out the worst in people and make them say things they didn't mean? She took a deep breath and tried again. "You're right; I'm sorry. It's just that my dad is talking to me and wants to start over. How can I go away to college and turn my back on that?"

"Don't do this, Em. It hasn't even been a full day since you and your dad talked. You have no idea what will happen tomorrow."

Crunch.

"You don't get it, Riley. The most important thing in your life right now is college. It's not like that for me."

"How can you say that?" Riley demanded. "The most important thing in my life is you. It will always be you. And the only reason college isn't important to you is because you're trying so hard to convince yourself that you don't deserve it. But college *is* your right next step, Em. I know it."

Riley's lack of understanding and Tyler's consistent chip

crunching only escalated Emma's frustration. "Are you listening to me at all? I'm trying to tell you that it might not be my next step. If I have to choose between college and my family, I'm going to choose my family."

"Why?"

Crunch.

"Because my family is broken and it's my duty to try and fix it."

"No, it's not."

"Then whose duty is it? My dad's? My brothers'?"

"Yes!"

"Why is it their duty but not mine? Why should I wait for someone else to make the first move?" Riley didn't have an answer for her. "Maybe I'm the only person in my family who cares or maybe I'm not, but how will I know for sure unless I try?"

Crunch.

Emma spun toward Tyler. "Will you stop with the chip crunching already?" she growled.

With a chip in hand, Tyler paused before sending it into his mouth, his teeth pausing for dramatic effect before they chomped down for an exaggerated crunch. Then he shrugged and dove his hand back in the bag for another one. "I'm hungry. Besides, entertainment like this requires snacks."

"C'mon, man, seriously?" Riley raised his voice, and Emma knew Tyler was getting on his nerves as well. "Can you give us a minute of privacy?"

"You want privacy? Don't dish out your drama in the living room. Everyone can hear you."

Emma exhaled a sigh. Most normal people would've backed out of the room when they stumbled upon two people arguing, or at least divert their eyes and pretend they weren't a witness. But Tyler? He leaned against the doorway, crossed his legs at the ankles, and whipped out the munchies.

"You shouldn't have to choose. There's a way for you to have both, and if your family makes you feel guilty about that, then they're not worth it," Riley said, bringing the conversation back on topic.

"Says the guy who has no idea what it's like to have a dysfunctional family," Tyler muttered. They turned to find Tyler searching the bag for the perfect chip like he hadn't just invaded their conversation.

"What did you say?" Riley asked, his anger spouting.

Tyler looked up. "You heard me. Whether she decides to go to college or live with her daddy forever, it's none of your business."

"Shut up, Tyler," Riley and Emma said at the same time.

"Emma," Riley said, his voice softening. "Put yourself in my shoes—"

"Your shoes?" She shook her head. "This has nothing to do with you, Riley. This is my choice."

"The girl's got a point," Tyler said.

"Thank you," she said, pointing at Tyler to acknowledge his support without taking her focus off Riley. "At least someone understands. Too bad that someone isn't you."

Riley groaned, dragging his hands down his face. "Emma."

"No." She held her hand up to stop him. "You know what? Forget about it. I don't need your permission to live my life."

"I'm not saying you do!" Riley yelled. "But I can't sit here and watch you make what could be the biggest mistake of your life because your dad decided to acknowledge you for a day. Where has he been for the past five years? What happens in a week when he decides to check out on you again? Then what?"

His words hit her hard, and she didn't have a response.

"Geez, man," Tyler interjected. "That's a bit harsh, don't you think?"

"Stay out of this, Tyler," Riley said through clenched

teeth.

"I'd love to, but someone has to side with your girl. You treat her like she's incapable of making her own decisions."

"No, I don't."

"Have you ever listened to yourself?" Tyler's eyebrows pinched together like a commanding officer. "'If your family prevents you from doing the right thing then they're not worth it.' 'I can't sit here and watch you make what could be the biggest mistake of your life.' 'College *is* your right next step.'"

Emma had to admit, the way Tyler repeated Riley's words did sound authoritative and demanding even though they hadn't sounded that way when Riley spoke them to her.

Tyler shrugged off the wall. "You should stop acting all high and mighty and trust your girl to make the right decisions, those that are right for her."

"Stay out of this."

"Suit yourself." Tyler shrugged and shoved an arm into the bag of chips again, like he didn't care one way or another what Riley decided to do. "But if you don't give the girl some breathing room, don't expect your relationship to last very long."

Emma couldn't take it anymore. The fact the guys were fighting and it was Tyler who was sticking up for her only made things worse. "Tyler, shut up. No one asked you to get involved."

"You know I'd do anything for you, Princess." And then Tyler had the audacity to wink at her. Ugh!!

Her hands curled into fists as she tried to contain some of her anger. "Tyler, I swear, if you don't stop—"

"What in the world is going on out here?" Mr. Ledger's booming voice cut her off as he rounded the corner into the living room, his eyes shifting between the three of them.

"Nothing," Emma and Riley said at the same time. The last thing they wanted was more people involved in what was supposed to be a private conversation.

"From what I understand," Tyler said from his perch against the entryway, "Emma wants to blow off college because her nonexistent daddy finally got a clue that she exists." Emma glared at him, but he continued, unfazed. "And Riley's trying to control her life and treat her like a three-year-old who can't make her own decisions."

Riley took a step in Tyler's direction. Without giving it much thought, Emma raised her hand to Riley's chest, keeping the distance between him and Tyler as she shot death glares in Tyler's direction.

Mr. Ledger looked between them, silence building until, "Emma, my study."

She lifted her gaze to Mr. Ledger, her hand lingering on Riley's chest. "What?" she asked, confused.

"My study. Now."

"But—"

Riley slapped his hand over hers, his thoughts probably aligning with hers. Mr. Ledger never called her into his study. His role was to talk to Riley, not Emma. She was always assigned to Mrs. Ledger while the boys talked.

"Riley," his mom said, appearing from out of nowhere. "You're with me."

"But Mom," Riley protested, wrapping his fingers around Emma's hand. Despite their face-off, Riley and Emma were still a united front, and this change in parental jurisdiction shocked them both.

The Ledger parental units both held an arm out in the direction of their individual sanctuaries—the study for Mr. L and the kitchen for Mrs. L—and waited for Emma and Riley to follow orders. Emma and Riley gave each other one last look, second-guessing their fight if it threw the Ledger household out of whack. Riley squeezed her hand in reassurance before letting go, and they both ventured into unknown territory.

Twelve

Mr. Ledger placed his hand on Emma's back, propelling her forward and out of Riley's sight. As she passed Tyler in the hallway, he held out the bag of chips to her. "Chip?" he offered.

She snagged the bag out of his hand, glaring at him as she passed. If she had to listen to him crunch one more chip she would punch him.

Mr. Ledger guided her down the hall and into his study to the soundtrack of Tyler's laughter. When Mr. L shut the door, she breathed a sigh of relief when it shut off Tyler's laughter too.

"Mr. Ledger, I'm sorry. I didn't mean to disrespect y—"

He held up his hand, cutting her off. "You're not in trouble, Emma."

"I'm not?"

He chuckled. "No. Why don't you have a seat and tell me what's going on?"

She sat on the armchair as Mr. Ledger took a seat on the black leather chair behind his desk. He wasn't kept in the dark when it came to her dad and brothers, so it wasn't like she had to divulge any family secrets to get him up to speed. Instead, she relayed the details of her conversation with

Riley without hesitation.

When she admitted that she might possibly choose her family over college, if it came down to that, Mr. Ledger leaned back in his chair and studied her.

"Riley doesn't agree with you, does he?"

She shook her head. "I don't know what the right choice for me is, but he's convinced he does. He won't even try to understand where I'm coming from."

Mr. L took a deep breath. "When you two were in sixth grade, Riley came home from the park one afternoon with the goofiest grin on his face. When I asked him what happened, he told me how you proved yourself to all the boys on the court and how awesome you were. Riley looked up at me and said, 'I'm going to marry that girl someday.' He was so proud of you."

Laughter bubbled up inside her at the thought of an eleven-year-old Riley talking about marrying her because of some basketball stunt she'd pulled. "He did not."

"Oh, yes, he did, and he still looks at you the same way."

Okay, way too serious and way too awkward for the marriage talk with Riley's dad.

"Emma, I know my son can be overbearing and stubborn sometimes, but all he's ever wanted is to love and protect you. Nothing's different now. He doesn't know what it's like to be you or to be in your position, and you can't *make* him understand. All you can ask is for him to respect your decisions. You know as well as I do that his motives are never malicious; he just wants what's best for you. Yes, he still has a lot to learn, but he loves you. He's just scared."

"I'm scared too," she admitted. "I don't want to make the wrong decision. What if I give my dad another chance, but it backfires? What if I don't give him another chance and I ruin everything?"

"Emma, there is no right or wrong decision. Whatever you decide, will be what is right for you."

"I wish I could be so sure," she mumbled.

Mr. Ledger stood and walked around his desk, perching on the edge as he looked down on her. "Think of it in terms of basketball."

She glanced up, silently asking him to continue.

"In basketball, during a close game, everything you do matters. When you have the ball with five seconds on the clock, down by one, you have to decide whether you have a shot worth taking. Yes, there are a lot of factors involved— are you within range, does someone else have a better shot, is your defender going to block you, is it worth taking when your shots aren't falling? Ultimately, it comes down to, win or lose, do you feel like the shot is worth the risk even if you could potentially lose everything?"

His words reminded her of the final seconds of the game against Kennedy High School. Not a day passed that Emma hadn't thought about her final shot. She had missed. The most important shot she had ever taken, and she had missed it. Guilt still consumed her, and she blamed herself for the loss, but what other option did she have? No one else had a shot, there hadn't been time to set up a play, and sometimes, no matter how good she was, she missed. Had the shot been worth the risk even though it had bounced out? Yes. She had given that game everything she'd had, and if there had been the slightest chance she could've made the shot, she would take it again and again.

"What if I'm the only one who thinks the shot is worth taking?"

Riley's dad shrugged. "What if you are?"

Life would be so much easier if answers were just given to her. Not knowing what decision to make, but knowing she'd crumble if Mr. L kept staring at her, she threw her hands in the air and fell back in her chair. "I don't even know why I care. No matter what I do, it's always wrong and my family will always hate me." Of course she liked the idea of trying to bring her family back together, but Riley was right. It hadn't even been an entire day since her dad talked to her. Tomorrow, things could go back to the way they had always been. Self-doubt loomed like a dragon before her.

"Just because all the signs tell you to turn and run doesn't mean you should. Don't give in to fear."

Was that him telling her the right answer? "So you're saying I should give my family another chance?"

"I can't make that decision for you. I'm saying just because the shot is hard, doesn't mean it's impossible; just because everyone tells you not to take the shot, doesn't mean you shouldn't. You don't have to stick with the easy shots. Besides, sometimes it's more about the courage and strength it takes to attempt the shot, than it is about whether or not you make it. That being said it is up to you whether you should take the shot or not."

He bowed his head and gave her one of his infamous dad looks—raised eyebrows, serious eyes, pursed lips. "You understand me?"

She nodded. "Yes."

"Good. Now, while I respect you for wanting to work things out with your family, I have to ask, do you even want to go to college?"

His unexpected question caught her off guard. He thought she didn't want to go to college? "Of course I do."

"To the extent that you're willing to fight for it?"

How could she explain that her decision about college wasn't about her fighting for what she wanted?

Mr. Ledger saw her hesitation and came to sit in the seat beside her, his eyes never wavered from her even though her gaze dropped to the floor.

"What aren't you saying?" he asked gently.

How did he always know when she was holding something back? She glanced up at him, hoping she had the words to convey her feelings.

"I want to go to college more than anything. I want to see if I have what it takes to play at that level and earn a degree and be the first one in my family to graduate from college, but..."

He placed his hand on hers when she struggled to continue. "But what?"

Tears pricked at her eyes as she readied herself to admit the truth to herself and to Mr. L. "But I feel so guilty and selfish and ashamed."

"Why?"

She took a deep breath to calm her shaking body. "Because who am I to want a better life than the one my dad provides? What have I ever done to deserve it? When my mom left, she caused so much pain for my dad and brothers and me. I don't think any of us have recovered. At first I thought college would be perfect because my dad wouldn't care one way or the other if I left, but if he does want a second chance, then I can't help but think what it will do to him if I leave like she did. If I think about what *I* want and what *I* need rather than putting my family first, what kind of person does that make me?" She looked up at Mr. Ledger with glistening eyes. "I don't want to be like her. I don't want to be selfish; I don't want to choose the better life over my family, no matter how bad they've treated me. I won't. Not when they've suffered so much already. So even though I want to go to college more than anything, I won't put my family through that again."

"Oh, sweetheart." Mr. Ledger squeezed her hand. "I understand, I do, but you have no reason to feel guilty or selfish for wanting to pursue an education and do something you love. Your dad will understand."

How would her dad understand when a part of him still resented Emma for her mom leaving?

"Have you talked to him about this?"

She shook her head, knowing she'd never be able to find the words to talk to her own dad like she could with Mr. L. "I wouldn't even know what to say."

"Just tell him what you told me, and if your dad loves

you, which I know he does, then he won't hate you for being honest. He won't want you to sacrifice college for him or your brothers. And Riley was right, you can have both."

His words struck her hard. "You think so?"

"Yes, Emma, I do."

She hadn't realized how much she needed someone she trusted, someone other than Riley, to confirm that she didn't have to make a choice. That everything would work out and she could pursue her dreams while building a relationship with her dad.

Perhaps sensing she'd had enough, Mr. Ledger pushed out of his chair and reached for an envelope on his desk. "This came for you."

The OSU logo was in the corner, but the envelope was different than all the other ones she'd received from them. She lifted her eyes from the package, questioning Mr. Ledger about its contents.

He laughed. "You'll have to open it to see what's inside."

Swallowing, she reached out an unsteady hand to grasp the envelope. She didn't know why she was so nervous. It was probably an informational brochure or something. Breaking the seal, she pulled out the contents and skimmed the cover letter. "The coach wants to set up a face-to-face meeting with me."

Mr. Ledger's face broke into a smile. "That's great."

"It is? I mean, yeah, it is, but what am I supposed to say?"

He reached out to grasp her shoulder. "Relax, Emma, you'll do fine. If you want, we can go over some questions and answers before you go so you'll feel more confident before you talk to her."

Yeah, that would be a good idea considering the moment she sat down across from Coach Krola Emma would probably forget how to speak.

Mr. L stood and returned to the chair behind his desk.

"You should probably get back out there before my son thinks I've taken you hostage."

Emma laughed as she made her way toward the door with the information from OSU in her hand, picturing Riley pacing the hallway in front of the den and trying to listen in on their conversation. As she reached for the doorknob, she turned back to Mr. Ledger. "What if they're not?" Mr. Ledger tilted his head to the side, confused at her question. "What if my family isn't a shot worth taking?"

He leaned back in his chair, bringing his hands together in a steeple beneath his chin. "Then you have to ask yourself if you can live with that."

Thirteen

E mma sat on her bed, trying to make sense of her homework. Her thoughts were everywhere except on the numbers and equations staring at her from her Physics textbook, mostly because Mr. L had given her a lot to think about. After she had given Riley the overview of her conversation with his dad, he'd calmed down about the whole college thing. Of course, Riley's mom probably had something to do with knocking some sense into him as well.

It had been a couple days since she'd had any real interaction with her dad. He acknowledged her in passing and sometimes almost smiled, but other than that nothing much had changed. For a man who wanted a second chance at being her dad, he certainly wasn't showing it, and despite both Mr. Ledger and his son encouraging her to talk to her dad, she couldn't. At least not yet. What would she say?

When the sound of feet shuffling against the garage floor echoed around her, she jumped at the distraction. Even if it was one of her brothers coming to pick a fight, she was all in. Anything to give her an excuse not to study or be consumed by her thoughts.

The face that appeared over the stack of boxes caused her breath to hitch in her throat. "Hey," she managed to croak out. Her cheeks burned with guilt that she'd been thinking about him seconds before he appeared.

"Hi," her dad replied, stepping out from the shadows. "How are you?"

Such simple words, but they held so much meaning. They meant her dad was taking time out of his day to acknowledge her.

"Um," Emma searched for an appropriate response, "good." Lame! Her answer could have been monumental, it could've brought new meaning to their relationship, and she went with good?

Her dad gave a short nod in response. "Good." He took a step closer. "How's homework?"

"Uh." Geez! Of all the actual words in the English language, why did she keep starting sentences with unintelligible utterances? She glanced at her Physics book. "Good."

"Good," her dad mumbled again.

Between the two of them they wouldn't win any effective communication contests. Silence enveloped them, and their eyes skittered in every direction except at each other. Emma tried to think of something to say, anything to say, but the past seventeen years hadn't prepared her for this moment.

After a full minute, her dad gestured to the foot of her bed. "Mind if I sit?"

Startled, she snatched her notebook off the bedspread to clear a space for him. "Yes! I mean no! I mean..." Words failed her so she pointed to the bed instead. "Please."

The corners of her dad's mouth tipped up. He probably regretted coming in here, or even wanting to attempt this whole dad thing again. She couldn't blame him since she was proving to be a blubbering idiot. Why was she so nervous?

He leaned forward, resting his elbows on his knees to stare at the floor. "I drove by your school today and saw a notice about the father-daughter, mother-son dance.

Growing up, I always thought it would be fun to take my daughter to one of those dances."

Good to know. Too bad she wasn't the kind of daughter who wanted to go. She nodded, not sure where the conversation was heading.

He glanced up at her, his body straightening and turning toward her. "I know it's probably going to be cheesy, and it's not really your scene and it may be too girlie and it is kind of last minute, but I thought—"

Realization struck. He was asking her to go? His invitation proved how much he did *not* know about her. "I'm not into dances."

He nodded in understanding, but she saw the disappointment in his eyes.

"No problem," he said. "I just thought I'd ask." He stood from her bed. "I'll let you get back to your homework."

She kicked herself, and scolded herself, and wanted to rip the hair from her head. So what if it was a stupid dance and she would hate every minute of it? Her dad wanted to go; her dad had asked her to go! She couldn't sit here and think about how he wasn't trying very hard and then reject him when he did. If they were going to mend their relationship, she had to be willing to make sacrifices. A stupid dance for a night out with her dad?

"Wait!"

Her dad turned back around to face her.

"I'm in."

"What?"

"The dance." She tried not to roll her eyes at the thought. "I'll go.

"Emma, you don't have to—"

"No," she cut him off. "I want to. Dances may not be my thing, but I haven't been to many, and who knows? It could be fun."

Her dad chuckled. "Even if it means dancing with your dad in public?"

"Yeah." She matched his smile. "Even then."

"What if I'm a horrible dancer who's not up with the latest dance moves?"

If he only knew. "You couldn't be any worse than me. Trust me, I'll be the one to embarrass you."

"So it's a date?"

She took a deep breath and nodded. "It's a date."

◆◆◆

The next day, it wasn't difficult to find the girl she needed. Lauren, Madison, Shiloh, and Ashley huddled together in front of the cafeteria, and Emma weaved through the crowded hallways toward them, her eyes never straying from her target.

Taking a deep breath, Emma emerged from the crowd and nodded a greeting at Lauren. "You got a minute?"

Tilting her head, Lauren placed a hand on her hip and took a moment of silence to assess Emma. "Depends on what you want."

Madison smacked her friend on the arm. "Lauren, be nice."

"I am," Lauren said. "This is me being nice."

"I sort of have a favor to ask." Her throat dry, Emma took a deep breath. She couldn't believe she was doing this. "Well, see, um..." The words wouldn't come, so she resorted to the language of the mimes, clear as swamp water hand motions, to communicate her request.

Lauren rolled her eyes. "Spit it out, Poverty Child."

Maybe it would be better if she didn't have to watch everyone's reaction when she "spit it out." Squeezing her eyes shut and smacking her palm against her forehead, Emma blurted, "Willyouhelpmegetreadyforthefatherdaughterdancenextweek?" When there was no response, Emma cracked open an eye. "Please?"

Shiloh and Ashley mirrored huge grins, Madison's

forehead bunched in confusion, and Lauren stood frozen until high-pitched shrieks of laughter erupted from her mouth. "I'm sorry." Clutching her stomach, Lauren attempted to wave away her laughter. "I think I'm hearing things. I thought you asked me to help you get ready for the father-daughter dance."

"I did," Emma said.

All traces of laughter left Lauren's face. "You've got to be kidding. You're going to that stupid thing?"

Emma nodded.

"Why?" Lauren's look of horror was almost comical. "I would never be caught dead at one of those things."

"Lauren, leave her alone," Shiloh said.

"Relax," Lauren said, rolling her eyes again. "I'm not criticizing her, I'm just wondering." She turned her attention back to Emma. "Why are you going? Aren't you afraid your dad will embarrass you or something? I mean, how do you know he doesn't have two left feet or dance like an ostrich or something?"

Emma shrugged, the hint of a smile flickering on her face. "I don't, but my dad asked me, and for me that's enough." When Lauren continued to look at Emma like she was crazy, Emma forced herself to continue in the hopes Lauren would submit to helping her. "My dad and I haven't had the best relationship over the years. I guess at this point I'd take embarrassment over silence. I'd rather have a good memory of me and my dad than worry about embarrassing myself. Besides, he seemed to really want to go."

After an eternity of her gawking at Emma, Lauren caved with a sigh of irritation. "Fine. Just consider me your own fairy godmother."

Emma breathed a sigh of relief. Attending the dance would be hard enough, she didn't want to go looking like a hunchback with crazy hair. "And one more thing?" Emma looked at each of her friends. "Does anyone have a dress I can borrow?"

Fourteen

A week ago she had said yes to her dad's invitation to the father-daughter dance. What had she been thinking? Sure, she wanted to spend time with him, but a dance? Really? A night of dresses and fancy shoes and (gulp) dancing.

Even though Lauren had more or less become a friend, Emma didn't want to give the girl a glimpse into a poverty child's life, so she arranged to get ready at Riley's house. Her dad didn't seem to mind. He seemed relieved that she wouldn't have to get ready in the garage.

By the time Lauren rang the Ledgers' doorbell, Emma was filled with nerves and fears and nightmarish scenarios of all that could go wrong with the night. She had pretty much talked herself out of going and made her way down the stairs to break the news to her friend. Lauren would probably be relieved to have her Saturday night back.

Mrs. Ledger opened the door as Emma neared the bottom of the stairs, and after a brief introduction, Lauren sauntered in. Her eyes swept across the entryway, hesitating on a picture that hung on the wall just inside the door. The blown up picture captured Riley giving Emma a piggyback ride at the park a couple summers ago. Mrs. L had caught the moment when Riley looked over his shoulder at Emma and she stared back at him, both of them caught smiling at each other as they laughed at some joke Riley had told. Emma loved that picture. The fact Mrs. Ledger had hung it in the entryway made Emma feel like part of the family, as it was oftentimes the first thing people saw when they entered the house.

Emma opened her mouth to tell Lauren about the change in plans when Ashley stumbled over the threshold, followed by Shiloh and Madison.

"Whoa." Emma jumped off the remaining two steps and landed in front of the girls. "What are you all doing here?"

They ignored her to exchange greetings with Riley and his parents.

Emma elbowed her way through the crowd. The Ledgers' was a second, and sometimes first, home for her, and she didn't want Riley's parents to think she was overstepping her bounds and inviting people over without permission. "Mrs. Ledger, I'm so sorry about this. Aside from Lauren, none of them were invited." Emma cast her friends a glare, but they returned it with smiles.

Mrs. Ledger laughed, placing a hand on Emma's arm. "It's fine, sweetheart. Friends of yours are always welcome."

She would say that, which made Emma cringe. Now, it would be impossible to get rid of them.

Shiloh gave her a look of triumph, while Madison answered Emma's question. "We came to help."

Knowing Lauren didn't need any help, Emma turned to confront her. "And you let them?"

Lauren shrugged like she didn't care one way or the other.

The last thing Emma wanted was an audience for her makeover session.

Mrs. Ledger ushered them up the stairs with a "have fun."

When they reached the top of the stairs, Emma threw her hands up, halting the girls in the hallway before they could meander deeper into the house. Knowing none of them would let her back out of the dance now that they outnumbered her, Emma internally admitted defeat. "Before we do this, I have to say, I know you guys want to dress me up like some Barbie doll heading to the prom, but I just need something simple."

Lauren grabbed Emma's shoulders and spun her around, pushing her toward the bathroom. Madison conjured up a stool from thin air, and Shiloh unpacked their bags of girlie supplies while Ashley organized it all on the counter.

Lauren pointed to the stool. "Sit."

"Lauren, please." Emma knew none of the girls listened to her outside of basketball, but this dance was important. "I'm begging you. This is for my dad, and I don't want to be all gussied up to the point where he doesn't recognize me. I want to look nice, but I still want to look like me. Do you understand?"

Lauren's eyes softened, barely, but the tone of her next words were filled with her usual sense of superiority. "Relax, Poverty Child. I know what I'm doing."

Not knowing what else to do, Emma sat. She felt a hand grasp her shoulder and looked up into Madison's eyes. "Don't worry, Emma. You can trust her."

Easy for her to say. Yes, Emma and Lauren could tolerate each other on friendly terms now, but it wasn't always that way, and Emma still didn't trust her completely. Besides, this whole scenario reminded Emma of a time not too long ago when Lauren fixed her up for a school dance and ended up making Emma feel like the ugliest duck in the world. Not wanting a repeat of that experience, she squeezed her eyes shut. Whatever happened, it would be best if Emma didn't see it.

Almost an hour later, Emma stepped into the hallway as the girls huddled behind her. She could hear voices below and hoped the Ledgers and her dad weren't in the entryway waiting on her to descend the stairs. She peeked around the corner of the wall. Mrs. Ledger was working a boutonniere into Riley's collared shirt when he looked up and saw Emma spying on them.

"It's about time, Em," Riley said. "I was two seconds away from coming up there and rescuing you."

Pulling back, out of sight, she took a deep breath, knowing she couldn't escape the inevitable. She forced her right foot forward and her left one followed behind. Gripping the banister so she wouldn't plummet headfirst down the stairs, Emma connected her eyes with her witnesses. Mr. and Mrs. Ledger smiled up at her; Riley's jaw dropped; and her dad cleared his throat and adjusted his tie, never taking his eyes off her. She reached the bottom of the stairs, but nobody moved. It was as if time had frozen, and Emma wasn't about to be the first one to test that theory. From the corner of her eye, she saw Tyler approaching from the kitchen. With a bowl in one hand and a heaping spoon of ice cream in the other, he shoved his dessert into his mouth and looked up. When his eyes connected with her, he started choking. No one rushed to his aid, but since Mr. L stood within striking range, he nonchalantly smacked Tyler on the back to get him to breathe again. Tyler's fight for survival broke the spell, so Emma had to be at least a little grateful to him.

Riley took a step toward her, but her dad dropped a hand on his shoulder. "Sorry, Riley, but I believe she's my date for the night." Riley chuckled and reluctantly stepped back. Her dad met her at the bottom of the stairs and gently took her hand as she stepped off the last step. "You look beautiful, sweetheart."

Her face heated. She would've preferred something black, but Lauren had brought her a blue dress that faded from midnight blue at the neckline to sky blue at the hem of the skirt, which hit her just below the knees. The modest halter top spared Emma from an embarrassing plunging neckline like she knew so many other girls wore to school dances. The dress, although entirely girlie, was surprisingly comfortable and modest. Of all the dresses Lauren could've picked for her, this one was pretty near perfect. In addition to the dress, the girls had swept the sides of her hair back into a bun, and arranged the rest of her normally untamed waves into an elegant cascade of curls down her back. Aside from some light eyeliner and lip gloss they left her face without makeup, for which Emma was grateful. She had to give the girls credit, when it came to makeovers they knew how to capture character without sacrificing identity.

Despite how impressed she was with the girls, Emma knew she looked different from her usual messy bun and basketball shorts and felt the need to provide her dad with a disclaimer. "Sorry if this is too much. The girls tend to go a bit overboard when it comes to this kind of thing."

Her dad reached for her hand and slid a corsage onto her wrist. "You look perfect."

She couldn't help the smile forming on her lips.

"Although I have to admit," he leaned toward her to whisper, "I'm a little surprised you didn't wear basketball shorts and a t-shirt."

Her face burned. Checking to make sure she was no longer the focus of everyone's attention, she reached down and lifted up the bottom of her dress to reveal her favorite pair of mesh basketball shorts.

Her dad's laughter melted her heart. "That's my girl."

She glanced over her shoulder, knowing the girls would be at the top of the stairs, spying on them from above. Shiloh, Ashley, and Madison gave her two thumbs up, while Lauren crossed her arms over her chest in a way that oozed smugness. Emma didn't know what she'd do without them. She met their eyes and mouthed, "Thank you."

Returning her attention back to her dad, she tried to ignore the fact that Riley had his eyes glued to her. She gave him a small wave and linked her hand through her dad's offered elbow.

As Riley turned to his mom and offered his own arm, her dad led them by Tyler. Although he seemed to have survived his coughing fit, Tyler's face had yet to return to its normal color, but that didn't stop him from acknowledging her. "Damn, Princess." Before he could continue, Mr. Ledger smacked him on the back of the head.

"Ow." Tyler ducked out of the way of Mr. Ledger's arm, rubbing his head. "What was that for?"

"Manners," Mr. Ledger barked.

"It was a compliment."

"Then find a better way to express your compliment to a young woman."

"Sorry," Tyler muttered. "I didn't realize I was in finishing school."

Riley chuckled, and Emma laughed into her dad's shoulder as they walked to the car.

Emma stood next to her dad as they watched everyone else dance. The ages of kids ranged from those barely able to walk to those on the brink of graduating high school, and Emma was surprised to see many of her classmates in attendance with their parents. However, while her classmates spun their parents around on the dance floor, Emma and her dad had yet to venture beyond the sidelines, nor had they exchanged more than a few words with each other since entering the school gym. Talk about feeling like a socially awkward wallflower. Even though Emma and her dad were giving each other a second chance to build their relationship, it didn't seem like either of them knew how. Every once in a while, her dad's eyes skittered in her direction, only to fly away when she looked at him. He cleared his throat a few times, like words were trying to escape, but he never said anything.

"So..." Emma said, deciding to give speaking a try. She frantically searched for something, anything, to say. "Did you go to a lot of school dances when you were my age?" Lame topic for a discussion with her dad, especially considering all the conversations they'd missed over the years, but Emma didn't know what else to talk about and the silence was killing her.

Her dad looked over the sea of bodies swaying together, and his face captured a glimmer of happiness. "I went to my fair share."

She stared at his profile, trying to see her dad in his younger years. Her heart tightened as she tried to see past the years of regret and pain etched into his features. She cleared her throat. "Did you dance or were you the brooding wallflower type?"

Her dad chuckled. "Oh, I could definitely bust a move."

Laughter erupted from Emma at the sound of her dad's use of such an old term.

"It was one of the ways I managed to capture your mom's attention."

The mention of her mom, a woman no one in her family ever talked about, caused Emma to divert her eyes from her dad. How was she supposed to respond? Did him mentioning her mom give Emma the right to talk about her too or was it a mistake on his part? She said nothing and they returned to their silence.

As she scanned the crowd, Emma tried to understand the complex relationship between fathers and daughters. Many of the younger girls smiled and laughed, their eyes full of wonder as their knight in shining armor guided them around the dance floor. While some of the older girls looked bored or irritated on the outside, Emma noticed a gentleness to their features, as if their entire behavior was merely a facade, like they were acting how they thought they should rather than how they truly felt. The love these girls had for their dads, though more difficult to detect, burned like an ember beneath the surface. Then there were some who looked as if the world would end because their dads were let out in public. The girl who had captured Emma's attention reflected such horror in her face that Emma couldn't help but feel sorry for her. Her dad's eyes were bright, his smile even brighter, as he bobbed his head to the backbeat of the song playing over the speakers and danced to the rhythm of his own drum. So caught up in his own delight, he didn't see his daughter try to hide her face and put distance between them. It took Emma a moment to recognize the girl: Lauren. The sight of her friend brought a smile to her face. Lauren had said she wouldn't be caught dead at a dance with her dad, and Emma wondered if their conversation the other day had changed Lauren's mind.

Poor Lauren. Her dad had two left feet and no sense of rhythm. For a girl who always worried about appearances, it probably took her a lot of courage to suffer through the dance with her dad.

"Dad." Emma hesitated before stating her request. She wasn't exactly a person who enjoyed public humiliation, but when she thought about her teammates and all they had done for her, Emma couldn't just look the other way without trying to help Lauren.

Taking a deep breath and hoping she wouldn't regret her decision, Emma let the words tumble out of her mouth before she chickened out. "What's the craziest, stupidest, wackiest dance move you know?"

Her dad slapped a hand over his chest as he got a faraway look in his eye. "There are so many."

She turned to look at him, and for the first time all evening they met and held each other's gaze. "Will you show them to me?"

He laughed. "I wouldn't want to embarrass you."

Emma looked back at Lauren. "What if I didn't care about that?"

Her dad followed her line of sight. Lauren's humiliation was written all over her face; there was no way he could miss it. His lips formed a slight smile as he held out his hand to her. "Then I would say this is the perfect song."

Her dad led them to a clear spot on the floor where they had room to move but were still within sight distance of Lauren and her dad.

He dropped her hand and spun around to face her. Music pounded from the speakers, fathers and daughters, mothers and sons, danced around them, and yet Emma's dad stood still as a statue staring at her.

Was this a dance move or stage fright? "Uh..." Seriously, what other verbal utterance could encompass her confusion. Maybe this was a mistake. Emma had no idea what to do.

Then, out of nowhere, her dad lunged forward as he swept his arms up and to the side like he had suddenly sprouted bird wings. His arms flapped and his body shot up straight again. Up and down he moved, his arms sweeping to the sides. And people? Yeah, they stared like her dad had just escaped from the loony bin.

Emma's jaw dropped. Whoa. He bird-danced around her in time to the music, seeming oblivious to the fathers and daughters who stepped back to either give him more room or just move away...far far away.

Her dad popped up in front of her again, breathing heavy. His eyes never left her face as he said, "Was that crazy and stupid enough or do I need to continue, because I could go all night."

He did it. He drew every eye in the room and made Lauren's dad look like a dancing professional. She couldn't help the laughter as it erupted from her. "That was awesome."

Her dad shook as he chuckled along with her. "You want me to teach you my moves, don't you?"

"Absolutely."

Over the next hour, they danced like birds, walked like Egyptians, twitched like sprinklers, moonwalked, and created their own wacky moves. One by one others joined in until almost half the people competed for the title of weirdest dance move. Some dads even attempted breakdancing. Those who didn't bust a move stood on the sidelines cheering for their favorites. Emma expected to see Lauren and her dad in the spectator section, but no, they had their own group on the dance floor. Rather than the horrified look from before, Lauren laughed and cheered on her dad who definitely had his own unique style.

The craziness eventually died down and the DJ put on a slow dance. Emma figured her dad would lead her off the dance floor for a much needed rest, but he put his right hand on her waist and took her right hand in his left, swaying back and forth to the new tempo. "You know," he said nonchalantly, nodding over Emma's shoulder, "that boy hasn't taken his eyes off you all night."

She turned in the direction of her dad's nod. Across the floor, Riley danced with his mom, but his eyes were on Emma. They shared a smile before she turned back to her dad.

"Sometimes it looks like he's awestruck by you and other times it looks like he's examining me."

She laughed. "That's Riley for you. Always my protector."

"He loves you, doesn't he?" her dad asked softly.

His words surprised her, and she took a minute to gauge the intent behind them. It didn't take long for her to nod, confident in her answer. "Yeah, he does."

"And you love him?"

Emma blushed and hid her face against her dad's shoulder.

Her dad chuckled. "I'll take that as a yes."

It was weird talking to her dad about her love life when he'd basically ignored her for the past five years. She figured they should start with topics like school and the weather. Safe topics that didn't lead to embarrassment.

"As your dad, I think I'm supposed to ask," he took a deep breath, "does he treat you right?"

She glanced up at her dad, surprised by his question. She'd spent way too long thinking he didn't care about her, and now, when he questioned the one person she trusted most in the world, it caused her to question his motive. In part, she thought he was just making conversation, but when she caught the genuine concern in his eyes, she swallowed down a retort and answered honestly. "Yeah, Dad, he treats me right."

"He hasn't…uh…you know," he cleared his throat and looked down at the floor, "taken advantage of you or anything, has he?"

"Dad!" she exclaimed. "This is Riley we're talking about." A boy her dad had known for years.

Her dad's eyebrows went up in warning. "This is a teenage boy we're talking about."

She didn't answer, she just stared at him.

"So, you didn't answer my question. Has he—?"

Could this conversation be any more awkward? "No, Dad, he hasn't."

"Good, because if he has or tries—"

Emma got the message. "Riley's one of the good guys. Trust me. He breaks all those stereotypes."

She felt her dad tense as if trying to decide whether or not he could trust his daughter and her boyfriend.

Reminding herself that they had yet to develop that dad-daughter trust, she tried not to be too offended. "When I say Riley's a good guy, I'm not saying it like a naive puppy who overlooks his faults. He's the real deal."

She felt her dad listening, taking it all in.

Glancing over at Riley, eight years of friendship flashed through her mind. "When Mom left, it was hard on all of us, I know that, but when I needed you the most you all pulled away. I know now why you did it, and in some ways I can understand, but I didn't know it then. Riley was the only person I could go to—he was the only person I could trust. He helped me laugh again, he kicked my butt in basketball because he knew it was the only thing that could take my mind off everything, he took care of me when you—"

"Didn't," her dad finished, when she couldn't.

Emma nodded.

He spun them in a circle, pondering her words. "You know, as a father, I'm not supposed to like my daughter's boyfriends." When she raised her eyebrows to question him, he shrugged in defense. "Seriously, it's in the dad code."

What was with guys and their codes?

Her dad looked down at her and then over at Riley, dancing and laughing with his mom. "But in this case, I might consider making an exception."

"Thank you," she said, meaning it. "But don't let Riley know that."

"Of course not. This little tidbit is just between you and me. Whether I approve of him or not, I take great pride in watching him squirm."

The song ended and he stepped backward. "If you'll excuse me, I need to find the restroom."

Before she could reply, he squeezed her hand and left her to stare after him. The sight wasn't supposed to be foreign to her. She'd watched his back retreat from her dozens of times with sagging shoulders and dragging feet, but this time was different. Never before had she seen his confident stride, free of the burden he usually harbored. As she weaved through the dancers to find a resting spot along the sidelines, she couldn't help but wonder if she had anything to do with the change.

It didn't take long for Riley to appear beside her. He bowed and offered her one of the two drinks in his hand. "Drink milady?"

She bit back a smile and bowed her head, playing along.

"Why thank you, sir."

"How's everything going with your dad?" he asked.

"Good."

"Are you sure? Because it looked like you two were having a serious conversation."

"Oh, that. Well, my dad thinks my boyfriend is...you know," she leaned toward him as he raised his cup to his mouth and took a drink, "taking advantage of me."

She probably should have waited to tell him until after he had swallowed, because pink punch sprayed out of his mouth, nearly drenching a couple of bystanders. Riley held up his hand in apology as the people glared at him and walked away.

"He thinks I'm what?" Riley choked out.

"You heard me."

His eyes grew as big as golf balls as he searched her face. "Em, I would never—"

She smiled. "I know."

Catching sight of her dad making his way across the floor toward them, Riley spun around, gripping handfuls of his hair. "Aw, geez. I don't want your dad thinking that about me."

Her dad was right. Watching Riley squirm was highly amusing, and she couldn't help but laugh. As his best friend, she had to take pity on him. "Riley, calm down. My dad doesn't really think that about you."

She reached up to loosen his grip on his hair and pull his arms down by his sides. "You have to remember, he's new at this."

"New at what? Accusing me of," Riley leaned toward her and panic-whispered, "taking advantage of his daughter?"

Emma laughed and looked across the floor at her dad who now stood talking to Riley's mom. "No...at being my dad."

"No offense, but for my sake, I think I liked it better when he didn't act like your dad and look at me as your boyfriend."

"You're right." She dropped her hands from his arms and backed away. "We should go back to being just friends."

"What?" His surprise switched to amusement when he realized she was joking. "Not a chance. You're not going to get rid of me that easily."

"I don't want you to live in fear of my dad."

His arms slipped around her waist and pulled her against him. "I can handle him."

"You sure?" She squinted her eyes at him, trying to appear skeptical. "Because you seemed uncertain before."

A smile grew on his lips as he leaned toward her. "Oh, I'm sure."

The music transitioned to another song as they stole a moment together. The rest of the gym fell away as Emma lost herself in his kiss. True happiness had eluded her over the years and she'd become accustomed to its absence, but being with Riley reminded her that light could always shine through the darkest nights.

A throat cleared beside them, cutting their moment short. "All right, you two. I think it's time I intervene and reclaim possession of my daughter."

Riley jerked away from her as if he'd been zapped. "Sorry, sir."

"Mm-hmm," her dad said, not hiding his disapproving tone. "If I didn't know better, I'd think you were trying to steal my date."

Riley wiped lip gloss off his lips as his cheeks burned red. "I'd be lying if I said that wasn't true."

Her dad chuckled and shook his head. "Beat it."

"Yes, sir." Riley winked at Emma and brushed his fingertips against her forearm before returning to his mom.

Fifteen

The Wrangtons and Ledgers were among the last to leave the dance. The night had flown by, and Emma couldn't wipe the smile from her face. Who knew dances could be so much fun? Who knew a date with her dad could be so memorable for all the right reasons?

It was almost midnight when Emma and her dad returned home. Her dad drove into the driveway and turned the key, killing the ignition. They stared out the windshield, looking at the house, neither one making a move to get out.

"Thank you for tonight, Dad." She smiled as she thought about the night. "I had fun."

"Me too."

"And you were right."

"About what?"

"You can bust a move."

His laughter joined hers, and she relished in the sound. When the last of their laughs settled like morning dew on the truck's interiors, Emma reached for the door.

"Wait a minute." Her dad whipped the keys out of the ignition and jumped from the car. He readjusted his tie as he made his way across the front of their beat-up Chevy. He opened the passenger car door and reached for her. She slipped her hand into his and smiled as he helped her out of the car.

"What's this for?"

"I may be your dad, but I still know how to treat a young woman."

She laughed at the idea of being called a young woman. Sure, she was a girl, but everyone treated her like one of the guys, certainly not like a woman.

As soon as they stepped over the threshold into the house it was like the magical spell for the night broke, and they returned to their sense of normal. Logan, Lenny, and Lucas sprawled across furniture in the living room. An action movie played on the screen, captivating Lucas and Lenny's attention, while Logan read a book. They all looked up as Emma and their dad walked through the door. Logan stared at her like he didn't recognize her, nor did he even have a desire to know her, while Lenny broke out in laughter. "Nice dress. You look like a girl." Lucas, remained silent, but his eyes widened as if surprised by her appearance.

Wanting to escape before her brothers said anything else, she turned toward her dad. "Thank you again for tonight."

"You're welcome."

She didn't know if she should hug him or not. She felt that it might be an appropriate move, but they'd never been a hugging family and she didn't want to make things any more awkward than they already were, especially in front of her brothers.

When her dad didn't make a move in her direction, she gave a limp wave and half a smile and headed toward the kitchen. She took a glass from the cupboard and filled it with water. Staring at her reflection in the window above the sink, she took her time drinking the water. She set her glass on the counter, since the sink overflowed with dishes, and turned toward the door leading out to the garage.

The sight of her littlest brother standing behind her caused her to stumble to a stop. "Hey," she said.

Lucas stared at her. She didn't know the last time she'd had any real interaction with him on a one-on-one basis. She had no idea what he was thinking, and he kind of freaked her out by staring and not saying anything. Considering he was the youngest of the bunch, Emma had no idea what their brothers had brainwashed him to think about her.

"Did you need something?" she tried.

He searched her face before whispering, "I think you look pretty," before scampering off to rejoin the boys in the living room, leaving her speechless.

A couple hours later, Emma stared at the darkened ceiling of the garage, forcing her eyes to stay open. She could've been asleep in two seconds, but she didn't want the night to end; she didn't want another day to come. A new day would make the night merely a memory, and she wasn't ready for that to happen yet.

The image of her dad and his funky dances brought laughter bubbling up from her heart. Who knew he had a sense of humor and would sacrifice his dignity to embarrass himself in front of hundreds of people just because she'd asked him to? She wondered what kind of person he was beneath the single dad exterior.

Shouting erupted from the other side of the wall. What sounded like a chair slammed against the floor. They were sounds that were all too familiar. For a nineteen-year-old, Lance sure did throw a lot of temper tantrums. Nasty ones. She hated listening to the fights between him and their dad. Squeezing her eyes shut, she flinched at the sound of glass breaking.

"I hate you," Lance screamed. "You're a sorry excuse for a father. No wonder Mom left you."

Emma flung the covers off her body and sprinted for the door leading into the kitchen. For years she'd hid in the shadows doing nothing as her dad and brother fought. No more. Her dad didn't deserve to end such a great evening like this, especially when he was trying to be a better dad.

She inched open the door. Standing in the doorway, she watched Lance flee as her dad's shoulders wilted and his head dropped into his hands. It would've been easy to sneak away and give her dad the privacy he probably preferred, but she knew what it was like to be on the receiving end of Lance's tirades. She knew what it was like to have his words echo in her thoughts for days and years to come and break on the inside because of them. She didn't want that for her dad. Not anymore. She didn't want demons of doubt and anger and hatred to take root in his thoughts. Too many times she had watched his head fall while she remained in the shadows. This time she took a step forward, avoiding the broken glass on the floor.

"Dad?"

His head jerked up, but he didn't turn around.

"You okay?" she asked.

"I'm fine," he bit out. "Go back to your room."

Maybe she should have followed his orders, but she found herself taking another step forward. Then another and another until she stood just behind him.

"Dad?" she said again, quieter this time.

He spun around, his face etched with anger, his hands clenched into fists. "Damn it, Emma," he yelled, slamming his hand against the wall. "I told you to get out!"

She flinched at the tone of his voice and the words he shouted at her, especially after seeing another, softer side of him tonight at the dance. It would've been too easy to turn and run before his words slapped her again. But she didn't. For the first time, she saw past the anger and hatred and saw the desperation, the helplessness, the need for reassurance. She'd never seen his face up close after one of his fights with Lance. Jaw muscles tight, teeth grinding together, one more hard etched line forming over his brow, but it was the depth of sadness that contradicted his anger that squeezed at her heart. He had helped her tonight at the dance, now it was her turn to help him.

Before she chickened out, Emma stepped into him, her arms wrapping around his waist and her head resting on his chest, wanting him to know he wasn't alone.

It was the first real hug they'd shared in over five years.

His arms encircled her, slowly, tentatively, as if unsure how he should respond.

"You're a good dad," she whispered. No, he wasn't perfect, but over the last few days, he'd helped her to see there was more to him than the burned out single dad trying to raise five kids on a limited salary. He didn't have all the answers, but he tried to do what he thought was best, even if it seemed misguided at times. She realized he didn't have to be perfect in order to be good.

He sucked in a breath and his body tensed before his arms tightened around her, all stiffness leaving him as he pulled her closer. His body shuddered. She didn't know if he was crying or if it was just an emotional reaction to his fight with Lance, but she held on without judgment.

Emma didn't know how long they stood there, nor did she care. Over the years, when things got tough, Mr. and Mrs. Ledger always reassured her and Riley. They would offer hugs, words of encouragement, and a steadfast conviction that everything would be okay. She supposed that was part of the role as parents, but who was there to reassure parents when storm clouds rolled in? Her dad's parents had passed on years ago, his wife had left him, he never mentioned close friends, so who did he have?

When her dad stepped out of their embrace, his firm hands gripped her shoulders. A smile never fully formed on his lips, but the softness of his eyes spoke loud enough. Without a word, he kissed her forehead and exited the kitchen. She watched him go, her feet inadvertently carrying her in his path. Stepping into the dimly lit living room as he retreated down the dark hall, she noticed that the weight from his shoulders had lessened and his head was raised higher than usual after one of his fights with Lance. As he turned toward the doorway of his room and switched the light on, he glanced back at her. Not expecting to get caught watching him, she froze. The corners of his mouth lifted into smile, and his whispered words danced their way down the hall into her ears, "Goodnight, Ems."

Goodnight, Ems. She'd never heard her dad use the nickname before. It did funny things to her chest and throat and eyes. She returned his smile and raised her hand in response before he closed the door and the hallway returned to black.

She bowed her head, committing the moment to memory. The night had been full of surprises, and when she turned back to the kitchen she got one more.

Her breath caught in her throat as her eyes adjusted to the shadows. On the other side of the wall that led from the living room into the kitchen, the shadow of another figure stood, waiting, watching. Lenny. How long had he been there? Had he witnessed the fight between their dad and Lance? Had he seen the hug she'd shared with their dad? He didn't say anything; he didn't need to. Emma knew he'd seen everything.

Before she could figure out what, if anything, to say, he stepped into the light from the kitchen. His face blank, he stared up at her with curious eyes. When he didn't say anything, she gave him a half smile. "Goodnight, Lenny." She crossed the kitchen floor, and as she reached for the doorknob of the garage, she turned back, expecting to see him watching her, but he was gone.

◆◆◆

Riley was finishing his chores, so Emma took up residence in the living room at the Ledgers' to stare out the window. Part of her had always thought the wind would whisk her mom away from whatever life she chose over her family and bring her home. That maybe Emma would wake up one morning to the smell of bacon and eggs and enter the kitchen to find her mom with an apron and a spatula making up for time lost with her sons. After all, didn't her dad deserve his wife, didn't her brothers deserve a mom? But waiting for days and months and years for a woman who left and probably had no intention of returning was a waste. Emma didn't want to live her life thinking her and her brothers were missing something—someone—and had no hope of being whole without her.

At one time, she had thought her dad was too far gone to reach, that his hatred of her ran too deep to be purified, but he'd proved her wrong. Thinking about the dance, her little brother's compliment, and the fight between her dad and Lance, she knew there was a way to reach her family. There had to be. If she ended up going to college, now was her chance to reconcile things with her family. All Emma had to do was figure out how.

Mrs. Ledger appeared in the living room with a plate of warm chocolate chip cookies. "I thought you could use a snack."

"Thanks, Mrs. L." Emma slid a cookie from the plate, broke off a bite, and stuck it in her mouth.

"What's captivating your thoughts today?"

Emma's eyes flickered up to Mrs. Ledger's. The eyes of a true mother looking back at her broke Emma's wall. "It's stupid, but I was trying to think of something I could do to let my family know I care about them.

"Why is that stupid? I think it's a great idea."

Emma sought reassurance within Mrs. Ledger's eyes. "Really?"

She reached over and covered Emma's hand with her own. "Really."

"But I don't even know what to do."

"Sounds to me like you need to play to their weaknesses." Mrs. Ledger patted her on the leg and stood. "Come on. I've got just the thing."

♦♦♦

The Wrangtons didn't have home-cooked meals. They had pizza, frozen dinners, and fast food. Emma couldn't remember the last time anyone had prepared a decent meal at home, and grilled burgers didn't count.

Taking a deep breath, she read through Mrs. Ledger's instructions for the millionth time, trying to make sure she'd done everything right and hadn't skipped any steps. She didn't know if browning beef and emptying a bunch of cans into a pot to cook was considered a home-cooked meal, but at least it didn't come in a fast-food bag.

The taco soup bubbled on the stove, filling the house with the aroma of dinner. Butterflies launched into action in her stomach. What if her dad and brothers didn't like it? What if they refused to eat it? What if everyone had other plans for dinner? Despite Mrs. L's conviction, Emma knew this stupid plan would fail. She dipped the wooden spoon into the pot and tasted it one more time. Okay, so if her brothers didn't like it, she could eat the entire thing herself in one sitting.

"What is that smell?"

Emma spun around to see Lucas shuffle into the kitchen. The house had been so quiet she hadn't known that anyone was home. The appearance of faces confirmed she wasn't alone.

Apparently, the smell had pulled all the guys from every corner of the house.

"What's this?" her dad asked, leaning around her to look in the pot.

She glanced at the stove, knowing her last ditch efforts weren't a possibility anymore. "Um, nothing."

Logan tilted his nose in the air and took another big whiff. "It sure smells like something."

"Do we get to eat that for dinner?" Lenny asked, his eyes

widening as he sniffed the air.

"Um, yeah. I mean if you want. I made a salad too."

Lance sauntered into the kitchen behind everyone else, took one look at her in front of the stove with a wooden spoon in her hand and laughed. "About time you learned your place is in the kitchen."

"Get out," their dad growled.

All chatter stopped as Emma and her brothers stared at their dad.

"What?" Lance asked in disbelief. After all, it wasn't often that their dad spoke up about anything.

"I said get out!" their dad bellowed, causing Emma to flinch. He pointed toward the front door as he crossed the kitchen toward Lance.

The smile slipped from Lance's face. "Why?"

Their dad stopped in front of Lance, the three inches he had over his son screaming authority. "Don't you *ever* talk to your sister that way, or any girl for that matter. If you don't have respect for your sister, who went out of her way to fix dinner, then you don't deserve to eat with us."

"Dad, come on."

"Out!"

Despite all the horrible things Lance had said to her over the years, her dad had never defended her. Even now, after all his promises to be a better dad, she expected him to remain silent and let Lance ridicule her. But he hadn't. In that moment, her dad's words became so much more than an open-ended promise, and for the first time she felt her trust for him grow.

Mirror images of each other, Lance and their dad remained in a standoff, each one waiting for the other to back down, but neither one did...until Lance took a step back. He threw his arms up with a smile that ridiculed them all. "You know what? Fine. I don't care. I don't want to eat that crap anyway."

Lance cast her a glare and left the kitchen. A few seconds

later the front door slammed shut, rattling the windows. No one moved.

Maybe she should've been grateful that Lance wouldn't be joining them, but all she could think about were the potential repercussions. Would Lance blame her? Would he take out his anger on their dad? Either way, there was nothing she could do about it now.

Her eyes flickered between her dad, brothers, and the food, before she found the courage to speak. "I don't even know if what I made will be edible, but it's done if anyone wants to eat."

"Lucas, help Lenny set the table. Logan get the drinks." Her brothers set to work at their dad's commands even though their dad's voice no longer held the anger he'd expressed to Lance. "Let's eat." Her dad stepped closer to her. He put his hand on her shoulder and looked into her eyes. "It smells great. Thank you for doing this."

"Don't say that. You haven't tasted it yet. It could be disgusting." What if it was disgusting? What if she had missed an ingredient or something? Maybe she should dump it out before they could consume it.

Her dad chuckled and kissed the top of her head. "Doesn't matter."

The boys filled their bowls with soup and piled on the toppings of their choice. Her dad and Lucas dug in without hesitation. Logan took one bite and then examined the soup like he was trying to figure out what was in it. Lenny, on the other hand, scooped up a spoonful before tilting his spoon to the side and watching the soup slop back into his bowl. He poked at it for a few minutes before bringing another spoonful to his face and sniffing it. When he had gathered enough courage to take a bite, his eyes met Emma's and he scowled, like he thought she'd poisoned it or something. She turned her eyes away, not wanting to see him spit it out. The kid was like a mini Lance.

Lenny took another bite, followed by a few more, until

he scraped the bottom of his empty bowl. Emma didn't miss the glare he sent her way before he reached for another helping. She bit her tongue to prevent a smile.

Mrs. Ledger was right. Her recipe could feed an army of men. Even after five full bellies, there were still leftovers. The boys even ate some of the salad she fixed. Turns out food really does soften them up. Well, most of them anyway. If Lance's weakness wasn't food, she wondered what she had to do to crack his wall.

"That was soooo good," Lucas said, leaning back in his chair and rubbing his stomach. "Can you fix it again tomorrow?"

Emma laughed. "I'm sure there's enough leftovers for tomorrow too."

Neither Lucas nor her dad were shy about voicing their thanks over the meal. Even though Logan hadn't said anything, the way he had attacked the food made her feel like the meal had softened him up a bit too.

The boys cleared the table while Emma poured the leftovers into a plastic container. She knew the first boys who got ahold of it would probably finish it off and as she scraped the last bowl full out of the pan, Emma hesitated. Going against her better judgment, she poured some of the remaining soup into a bowl and covered it in plastic wrap. Before placing it in the refrigerator she taped a note on it: *Lance*

Emma sat cross-legged in the middle of her bed, hunching over her notepad and scribbling notes in preparation for her Calculus test the following day. She heard footsteps approaching and looked up to see blond curls and green eyes peering out from behind a pile of boxes.

"What are you doing?" Lucas whispered as if asking for

a secret.

She eyed him closely, wondering what propelled him to venture into her domain uninvited when he never had before. The garage was more like a tomb of broken and forsaken family possessions than a hangout, especially with her bedroom tucked into the corner. "Studying. What are you doing?"

He shrugged and shuffled closer.

"You, uh, wanna sit?" Emma asked, not sure what to expect. Was he here on behalf of their brothers or of his own free will?

Lucas's curls bounced as he nodded.

She collected a few books and stray papers, clearing room for him to sit beside her. He didn't say anything so she returned her focus to her homework, occasionally peering at him for clues as to what he wanted.

He leaned over her arm to see her paper covered in equations. "What are you studying?" he asked.

"Calculus."

"Wow. You must be smart."

"No, I just study. A lot."

"I wish I could be as smart as you."

Emma looked up from her books. "You can."

Lucas shook his head. "Everyone says I'm stupid."

That was all it took for her to shift her entire attention to her brother. "Who said that?"

Lucas shrugged. "Kids at school. And my teacher sometimes."

She clenched her teeth. "Lucas, listen to me. You are *not* stupid. Don't you dare let anyone tell you that you are."

His face tilted to the side, examining her. "But what if they're right?"

"They're not."

"How do you know?"

"Because I'm your sister, and I know you better than they do."

Lucas hung his head. "But I fail all my tests."

"Then it sounds to me like you need to study more."

He frowned, and she could tell that the last thing her brother wanted was to do homework. "We could, you know, do our homework together. If you wanted?" It was funny how talking to her youngest brother could make her feel nervous. She waited for him to protest. To look at her in disgust or laugh in her face. Instead, he jumped off the bed and sprinted out of the garage and into the house.

She sighed and turned her attention back to her own homework, feeling her brother's rejection weigh on her. Her one attempt to be a better sister for him and he ran from the room. Great.

She didn't even have time to write down an entire equation before she heard feet running toward her. Lucas threw his backpack on her bed, scattering her books, and his little body followed. When he twisted his body around to look at her, he was smiling.

Emma laughed. "Where should we start?"

Lucas pulled a pile of ripped and crumpled papers out of his bag. "I've got math homework too." He grinned like the prospect of them having something in common was a good thing.

"Okay, then math it is."

Over the next two hours, Emma taught Lucas math skills he should've already learned. The kid wasn't stupid, he just needed some extra help learning the skills he'd missed during class. She showed him how to do various problems, worked through a couple with him, and gave him the rest to do on his own.

By the time Emma finished her homework, her eyelids fought to stay open. She turned to her brother who'd been quiet for almost a half hour, expecting to see him gnawing on the end of his pencil in deep concentration. She was surprised to find him sound asleep beside her. Blond curls rested on his forehead, and freckles splattered the bridge of his nose. Her heart swelled with emotion. Was this what having a little brother who didn't hate her felt like? She had done her best to push her brothers away over the years, convinced she didn't care about them either, but was it possible that she could miss her brothers when she didn't even know any of them? But she wanted to. So badly. She wanted to know what made them laugh, what made them ball their fists in anger, and what caused the darkened clouds to form over their heads. Was it possible she could bridge the gap with them like her dad was doing with her?

Worksheets were sprawled across his chest and a pencil dangled from his fingers. Her bed wasn't big enough for the both of them, but she didn't have the heart to wake him up and kick him out. She gently peeled the papers and pencil from his hand and set them on top of her own pile of books beside the bed.

Pulling up the quilt on her bed to cover them both, Emma settled beside her brother. The trace of a smile remained on her lips as she fell asleep thinking maybe she did have a place in this family after all.

Sixteen

Her internal clock woke her early the next morning. A heavy weight trapped her arm in the space beside her. Another unfamiliar weight rested across her stomach. Peeling her eyes open, the first thing she saw was a mass of blond curls near her shoulder. She couldn't help but release a silent laugh at the sight of Lucas's deadweight body cuddled next to her, his body trapping her arm, with one of his arms draped across her stomach. Apparently, he hadn't woken up during the night and felt the need to return to his own bed.

"Lucas," she whispered. "Lucas, it's time to get up for school."

When he didn't respond, she attempted to inch her way to the edge of the bed, but her movement caused his arm to clamp down on her stomach.

"Nooo," he groaned.

"I thought you were excited to turn in your homework today."

At the mention of homework his head snapped up and his eyes met hers. "Why am I in your bed?"

She scooted out from beneath his arm. "Because you fell asleep last night sometime between math problems and vocabulary words.

"Oh." He rubbed sleep from his eyes as his head fell back on the mattress. "Your bed's comfy."

He thought her stiff lumpy bed was comfy? "If you say so."

Crawling into a sitting position, he collected his books and papers while she loaded hers into her backpack. They joined the rest of their family for breakfast, but aside from a few questionable glances, no one asked why Lucas emerged from the garage, and the morning proceeded as usual until Logan spoke.

He slapped his book closed, stood from the table, and pointed at Emma. "I'll pick you up from school at 8:30. Don't be late or I *will* leave you."

Emma gulped down the last of her cereal. The college site visit. She almost forgot. She had to go to school to take her Calculus test, but then she'd been excused for the rest of the day to visit Oregon State's campus. Her cereal lost its taste when she thought about meeting with Coach Krola.

Verbal communication wasn't exactly her forte, especially when talking to important people like college coaches. In less than five minutes she could say something stupid and ruin her chances of ever playing ball.

She tried to remember what Mr. Ledger had told her about college visits and talking with coaches.

Just be yourself. What if she wasn't good enough?

Talk to your strengths. Did she even have any?

Know you belong there. What if she couldn't convince herself enough to pretend?

Coaches wouldn't invite you to their schools if they weren't interested in you. Yeah, well they could become uninterested based on anything she said.

Throughout the morning, every time she tried to relax and breathe, her heart sped up and her throat went dry. When it came time to leave school and meet Logan, she wondered if she could squeeze into her locker and hide for the rest of the day. She spun her locker combination and opened the door to assess her future dwelling place when she saw the paper crane perched on top of her Physics book. Compared to the last one she'd received, this one actually resembled a crane. Riley had been practicing.

She smiled as she reached for it, her fingers gently pinching the tail. Part of her didn't want to disassemble the bird because she knew when she did it would become a flat piece of paper with folding scars, but her curiosity over the potential message won out, especially now when she felt everything unraveling. Unfolding the creases, she tried to remember each one so she could return the bird to its original form when she was done, but she was never any good at Origami. Undoing the last fold, she saw the single word scrawled in Riley's handwriting: *Hi.*

Such a simple word, but it carried so much weight. The fact he went out of his way to give her such a simple note caused her cheeks to burn, and the fact he didn't try and pump her up for the interview calmed her.

"Is there a reason you're as red as a tomato right now?"

Emma jumped at the intruding voice, her back slamming against the locker as the paper slipped from her fingers. It floated to the ground but before she could get to it, Shiloh's hand snatched it off the floor. Without hesitating, she opened the paper to reveal its message before Emma could protest.

"Hi." Shiloh raised an eyebrow at Emma. "That's it? Just hi?"

Emma couldn't stop the smile from growing on her face. "Yeah, just hi."

"No I love you, I miss you, my universe isn't complete without you?"

Could her face burn any hotter? "Nope."

Shiloh rolled her eyes and handed Emma the paper. "You two are ridiculously cute."

Tyler appeared beside Shiloh and frowned at Emma.

"What are you so happy about?"

"What do you mean?" Emma asked. "I'm always happy."

"No you're not. You're always mad."

"No, I'm not—" Emma started to respond, but Shiloh shook her head. "No, she's not…just most of the time."

"No, I—" With the two of them staring at her like they were waiting to see what kind of lie she could come up with, Emma knew defending herself was futile. She slammed her locker shut and headed to the front of school, trying to focus more on Riley's note than on Shiloh and Tyler laughing behind her.

"Hey, Wrangton!"

Emma didn't turn around at Shiloh's voice shouting at her from down the hall, thinking her friend had another insult to throw her way. "Good luck at the college visit!"

The fact Shiloh remembered and cared enough to say something caused Emma to pause in her escape. She turned, searching for Shiloh among the sea of faces. Too many students filtered between them for her to see Shiloh, but then she saw a fist shoot into the air from down the hall. Considering how many times she had pounded those knuckles over the past few months, she could recognize that fist from any distance. The act struck Emma as a sign of solidarity, as if Shiloh knew how much Emma could use a bit of encouragement before her meeting. As she made her way through the front doors of the school and toward her brother's truck idling alongside the curb, Emma's footsteps seemed stronger and more purposeful. Now all she had to do was convince Coach Krola she had what it took to play college ball.

◆◆◆

When her dad had told her he couldn't get off work to drive her and offered Logan as an alternative, Emma thought it would be a great time to bridge the divide in their relationship but, obviously, Logan didn't feel the same way. The car ride to the Oregon State campus was almost four hours, but with Logan driving it felt like thirty. Not only did he drive slow, but any attempt she made to engage him in conversation failed. Big time. The guy didn't even acknowledge her when she spoke. So much for some brother-sister bonding to help her overcome fear of her first official meeting with a college coach. She resorted to propping her feet up on the dash and staring out the window, hoping boredom and fear weren't a lethal combination.

When they arrived at the campus, fear struck like a baseball bat between the eyes. Half tempted to tell Logan to turn the truck around and hightail it home, she gulped at the size of the brick buildings towering above her and at the masses of people flooding the sidewalks and grass patches as they headed toward classes or whatever else college kids did during school hours. Sure, Emma had thought about playing basketball for the school, but she hadn't considered life outside the gym. From the looks of it, she would need to leave bread crumbs from her dorm to the gym so she'd be able to find her way between the two buildings, much less classes. Maybe as part of the registration packet students received a flare gun so they could send up a distress signal and be rescued before they died of starvation from being lost on campus due to a wrong turn on the way to class. She gulped down the lump in her throat to return it to the pit of despair in her stomach and reached for the door handle as Logan parked the car.

When the passenger door groaned open, Logan decided to break his vow of silence. "Don't get your hopes up."

She turned her head to look at him, confused about what the words meant. "Excuse me?"

His hands gripped the steering wheel as he took in the sea of people around them, his eyes squinting as if holding them in judgment. "You may be good at basketball, maybe even good enough to play in college, but…"

"But what?" she asked when he ended his sentence with a shake of his head.

He shifted his eyes to look at her. "But college isn't for people like us. No matter how good you are, you don't belong on the college scene. None of us do."

"Why is that?"

"Because it's true."

"Maybe it doesn't have to be. Maybe college is right for me. Maybe it's right for you too."

His face pinched in what could only be pity. "If you want to delude yourself, fine. When you get your rejection letter, I'll spare you from an 'I told you so.'"

He didn't give her more than that. He broke eye contact and waited for her to exit the car. Of all the times he could've said something, he had to choose moments before she met with Coach Krola to tell her she was destined to fail. Thanks, *brother*.

She snatched her bag from the floor, jumped out onto the pavement, and slammed the door shut. Looking at the brick pavilion in front of her, she knew she had two choices. She could come to the realization that her brothers were right and jump back in the truck, or she could meet with the coach and talk about a potential future playing the game she loved. Securing her bag over her shoulder, she left her brother behind and went in search of her future.

◆◆◆

Coach Krola greeted Emma with a smile and started the meeting with an overview of the afternoon's agenda: talk with the coaches, tour the campus, meet with a few players on the team. Too afraid to speak, Emma focused on listening and nodding at the right moments.

Coach seemed friendly enough, but Emma could tell the

woman stood on a platform of principle and ethics. She expected her players to be disciplined, committed, and hardworking, and she didn't play games. What a difference from Jen Knowles. Emma didn't have much experience with coaches, but she could already tell Coach Krola was someone who exuded confidence and earned respect from her players, she didn't demand it. Emma liked her already. As she began to breathe easy and convince herself that college visits weren't that big of a deal, the winds changed.

Coach Krola's relaxed posture turned serious when she leaned forward and placed her arms on her desk, her hands clasped together in front of her as she met Emma's eye with a fixed stare. "Emma, you're a solid player, but I'm not going to lie to you. You're not the only girl we have our eye on. We are a Division I team, and we take our sports here very seriously, which means only the very best have a shot at playing basketball for us. For us, the best includes more than just physical talent. We look for players who know how to lead, know how to be part of a team, and who have the mental toughness to face extreme pressure and come out on top. The fact that we are looking at you when you've only played one year of high school ball is practically unheard of."

Emma knew a scholarship was a long shot, but the way Coach Krola put it, Emma had no right to be sitting across the desk from a college coach, much less a coach for a Division I school. She prepared herself for an inevitable dismissal, knowing it was coming.

"But," Coach looked down at her hands folded in front of her, "desperate times call for unconventional measures."

"Meaning?" Emma dared to ask.

"Meaning, two of our players will no longer be continuing with us next year, both of whom are guards. Ordinarily, we would have filled their positions long ago, but their timing didn't leave me with many options."

"In other words, you're scraping the bottom of the

barrel."

Coach raised an eyebrow and stared at Emma straight on. "I'd hardly call you the bottom of the barrel." She reclined in her black leather chair and folded her arms across her chest. "For someone who's only played one year of school ball and has had basically no formal instruction, I'm surprised you're not riddled with bad habits. Your technique is perfect, you're quick and tenacious, and you have a knack for seeing the court and identifying the strengths and weaknesses of your opponents. I've seen a lot of players over the years, and you've got skills some girls work their entire careers to obtain. So no, you are certainly not the bottom of the barrel, but I am curious as to how you learned to play and why you decided to play for your school team this year for the first time. Why have you never played in leagues outside of school that would've gotten you on the radar of college recruiters long before now?"

The woman was probably expecting some life altering answer, which Emma didn't have. She diverted her eyes from Coach's penetrating gaze and forced herself to be honest. "I could never afford to play sports outside of school."

"I see."

When Coach inclined her head for Emma to continue, Emma took a deep breath to try and steady her nerves before launching into her story. "My best friend and his dad taught me how to play when I was in fourth grade. I spent every weekend playing with the guys; I never had a desire to play for the school team."

"Why not?"

Emma shrugged. "It was the girls' team."

"I don't follow."

"I grew up around boys. Girls and I have never gotten along, and the school team had a ten-year losing streak. I didn't want to play on a girls' team, much less a losing one."

"Until this year."

"Yeah," Emma agreed. "Until this year. Bradshaw's coach showed up at my neighborhood park one weekend begging for me to play for the school, and my best friend thought it would be good for me. He wouldn't take no for an answer."

Coach Krola laughed. "You can tell your friend I'm grateful he talked you into it."

The last thing Riley needed was for Emma to tell him he was right. He'd more than love that.

"And how has it been playing with the girls?"

"As much as I hate to admit it, it's probably been one of the best things I've ever done."

Coach nodded like she understood. "Good." She leaned forward again to place her arms on the desk in front of her. "Now, before we continue, there's a few things we need to discuss so that you understand where I'm coming from. I was intrigued by your letter and highlights video; it was the reason I decided to take a closer look at you. You obviously have the talent to play at this level. At the state tournament, I saw how your teammates respected you and how you took the lead and set the standards for the rest of your team. You impressed me. That being said, you have only one year of experience playing on a team, whereas, the other girls I'm looking at have significantly more team experience than you do. Aside from what I've read about you in the papers, I know practically nothing about you, which makes it difficult for me to predict your commitment and dedication in the long run. For all I know, you'll give me part of a season and leave."

"No, I—"

She held up her hand, silencing Emma's words. "So you'll have to understand that at this point you've impressed me enough to talk with you. If I decide to offer you a scholarship, it will be for one year. If in that one year I like what I see and you prove to me that you have what it takes to continue with my team, I will renew your scholarship. In a normal recruitment, we have time to develop relationships with the young women we are interested in, but the situation is different with you."

"How likely is it that you will renew a scholarship for my second year?" Emma couldn't help but ask.

"That depends on you. If you show up every day and give me 150 percent, keep your grades up, and stay out of trouble, it's very likely."

Despite Coach's words, Emma wasn't reassured.

"Emma." She waited until Emma met her eyes again. "You have an amazing talent; you wouldn't be here if you didn't. I just wanted to be upfront and honest with you. While I believe you could be a tremendous asset to this team, *you* have to want it and *you* have to fight for it. If I invite you to be part of my team, you will have to work harder than the other girls to prove yourself. Being a collegiate athlete is hard enough, especially with juggling academics and other aspects of college life, but basketball has to be your number one priority. The only question is, are you willing to work that hard?"

The rest of Emma's time with Coach Krola consisted of a Q&A where Emma felt like she talked too much to make up for her lack of basketball experience. She second-guessed her answers, and her stream of babble made her sound like an idiot. By the time Coach stood and shook Emma's hand to dismiss her, Emma knew the other candidates were better choices than her, both on and off the court.

As she reached for the doorknob to leave, Emma turned back with nothing left to lose. "Coach?"

"Yes?"

"Thank you."

"For what?"

"For seeing something in me that most people don't. I know you would be taking a huge risk if you invited me to be part of your team, but I want to say that basketball is more than a game for me. It's my mode of survival. When my mom left, when my family turned their back on me, when I couldn't rely on anyone, basketball saved me. It comforted me, it challenged me, it gave me purpose and value." Logan's parting words came back to her, along with all the insults Lance had thrown her way over the years. "People have told me my entire life that I'm not good enough and that I don't deserve to go to college, much less play college ball."

Coach's eyes softened a bit as she listened to Emma's every word.

"I don't know if they're right, but I do know that I'm tired of buying into it. If you offer me a scholarship, I promise I won't let you down."

Leaning back in her chair, Coach rested her elbows on the armrests and laced her hands together across her stomach. Emma didn't know if that meant she had convinced the woman to give her a chance, or if Coach had heard this type of speech a million times.

Emma had always seen college as a luxury she couldn't afford and didn't deserve, but now, standing opposite Coach Krola, she knew college meant so much more. It wasn't merely going to school and playing a game, it was about proving she had what it took to overcome everything she'd faced and make a better life for herself than she'd ever thought possible. She didn't know if Riley and his dad were right, if she could have both her family and college, but she did know that in the end, if she had to make a choice, it would be one of the toughest choices she'd ever have to make.

Coach gave a smile. "We'll be in touch."

Seventeen

A couple days later, Emma and Riley were sprawled across Riley's bed studying. Even though they only shared one class, it seemed as if half the teachers had organized tests for the same week. Both Riley and Emma had several classes to study for and there was no better place to study than the Ledgers' when Riley's mom was on a baking marathon. The smell of banana bread and homemade cinnamon rolls wafted through the house, making Emma's stomach yearn for more than the gingersnap cookies she'd already devoured.

She flipped the page on her notepad and realized she'd just used the last piece of paper. "Do you have any paper?"

Without looking up from his notes, Riley nodded. "Top drawer of my desk."

She slid from the bed and crossed the room to pull open his desk drawer. The letter on top of his blank notepads caught her attention. The orange OSU logo stood out against the white paper. She scanned the contents of the letter, but it didn't make sense. "What is this?"

Riley glanced up and froze. Shaking his head, he hopped off the bed. "It's nothing."

She held the paper out of reach when he grabbed for it.

"I wouldn't call an acceptance letter from OSU nothing."

Rather than try to joke his way out of the situation, he held out his hand to her. "Em, can I please have the letter?"

"Not until you tell me what's going on. Why didn't you tell me you applied?"

"Because it's not a big deal. I applied to a lot of colleges, you know that."

"Yeah, to play basketball, but the guards on the OSU mens' team are freshmen and sophomores, so it doesn't make sense that you'd apply."

Riley laughed. "Sometimes you are so clueless." When her forehead scrunched in confusion, he took pity on her and clarified. "You seriously can't think of a single reason why I would apply to OSU?"

Without basketball, the only reason he would want to attend Oregon State was...

The reason he had yet to make a decision about what college to attend, despite the dozens of offers he'd received, finally made sense. Maybe she should've been grateful that her boyfriend was willing to sacrifice his dream of playing college ball to be with her, but she couldn't help the anger bubbling to the surface. "Riley, no. I'm not going to let you do this. I'm not going to let you waste three years of college sitting on the bench just so we can go to the same school."

His head snapped back in her direction. "I wouldn't be wasting anything. I'd be going to a top university with my girlfriend so I can get a good education and we can have a future together."

"Riley, your dream has always been to play college ball—"

"And I will," he said, grasping her shoulders with a look of determination. She raised her eyebrows and tilted her head, not agreeing with him. "Don't give me that look," he said. "I'll still get to play ball, it's just not as soon as I thought. Besides, dreams can change."

"And yours have?"

"Well, yeah." He gave her a smile. "My best friend finally became my girlfriend, and there's no way I'm letting her go. If I have to sacrifice a little basketball for you, then so be it."

"Riley," she whispered, his words not enticing her to support his decision. She knew how important playing college ball meant to him, how much it had always meant to him, and she refused to be the reason he altered his life. "It's not the best opportunity for you."

"Says who?"

"Says me."

"Then it's a good thing I'm the one deciding what is or is not best for me." His tone took on an edge of bitterness. "So what, you can decide my future for me but I don't even get a say in yours?"

"Not with this."

She bowed her head, disappointed that he wouldn't even listen to her. "You can't throw away your dream just to be with me."

"Why not?" he challenged her. "What's wrong with me thinking about the kind of future I want to have and who I want to share it with? You're more important to me than basketball, and if I have to sacrifice a few years of college basketball to be with you, then so what? At least we'd be together."

"There's more to our lives than our relationship!" Why couldn't he see that? Of course she wanted to go to the same college as him, but that didn't mean it was right. There were so many other factors to consider.

Some sort of growl emitted from his throat as he turned away from her, only to spin back around with hurt and anger reflected in his eyes. "Why do I get the feeling that I care more about you than you care about me, that I'm more invested in *us* than you are?"

Her mouth popped open in surprise. "How can you say that?"

"Because I'm willing to give up everything for you, for us, and all you're doing is pushing me away."

"I'm not trying to push you away; I'm trying to be realistic. We've been best friends forever—"

"Yeah, *friends*," he said like he resented the word. "*Friends* come and go, especially now that we're headed to college. We may never see each other again."

Over the past few months he'd made promises to her about their relationship and how much she meant to him. What happened to his conviction, to his promise of commitment to her? "I thought you said that wouldn't happen to us; that we were forever."

"Yeah, well, you're starting to make me question that." He looked at her like she was a stranger. "Do you even want to be my girlfriend?"

"Of course I do!" A lump built in her throat. There was a time she'd never thought of herself as girlfriend material, and she'd had plenty of doubts about having a relationship with Riley at first, but things changed. Being with Riley meant everything to her. How could he doubt that? "I'm just trying to do what's right," she said in a quiet, timid voice that was so unlike her.

"Are you?" he shouted. "Or are you trying to sabotage the one positive relationship you actually have so you can convince yourself, yet again, that good things never work out for you?"

The impact of his words felt like a slap across the face; the harshness of his tone like a knife in the back. He implied so much in that one sentence: that he was the only one who cared about her, that she intentionally ruined everything good in her life and she enjoyed it, that not even her family wanted anything to do with her. "Is that what you think of me? That I enjoy living in misery and that I bring it on myself?" She shook her head, hurt and disgusted by his words. "Tell me, Riley, what did I do to make my mom leave me? What did I do to make my dad push me away for so many years and how did I make brothers hate me? Why would I want to build that kind of life for myself?"

Riley's eyes squeezed closed, and he pinched the bridge of his nose in what appeared to be regret. He closed the distance between them and wrapped his arms around her neck. "I'm sorry," he exhaled. "I didn't mean what I said."

With her fisted hands lodged between them, she pushed him back, ignoring his apology and trying to push down the emotions welling inside her. "If I'm so horrible, why have you stayed my friend for so long?"

He grasped her face between his hands, forcing her to look him in the eye. "I'm sorry."

She closed her eyes, not ready to forgive him.

"Hey," he whispered, waiting until she gave him her attention again. "I'm being a jerk, and I don't mean to be. I just—I thought we both wanted this, but I guess I was wrong." His shoulders sagged like all hope had left him, but his hands continued to hold her face steady.

Anytime she caused Riley pain, Emma felt it through her entire being. It made it difficult to put her needs before his, and as she looked at the void in his eyes and his drooping shoulders, she pushed her hurt feelings to the side and attempted to explain herself better. "I would love to go to college with you, but what if it doesn't work out for me? I may not even get a scholarship to go, and if I do, it's only good for one year. I could flunk out in the first quarter. The coach may decide I'm not good enough to play for her team and decide to end my scholarship after the first season. If OSU doesn't work out for me, I don't want you to be stuck there alone. If things don't work out, if you aren't happy, I don't want you to end up hating me."

"Em," he said softly. His finger nudged her chin upward until she looked at him. "Hey, I could never hate you. No matter what."

"You've done so much for me over the years, Riley," her voice shook with emotion, "and I only want what's best for you."

He pulled her against him and squeezed her in his arms, but it felt different than usual, like he was holding a part of himself back. "I know you do," he whispered. "Just like I only want what's best for you."

"So what do we do?"

"I don't know, but we'll figure it out. Okay?"

She nodded, not wanting to fight any longer, but it left a bitter taste in her mouth. Their exchange of words had done nothing to solve the problems between them. Despite that he'd implied that they would work it out together, she knew he would do what he wanted in the end, regardless of her protests. She just hoped they survived, and that they wouldn't end up hating each other in the end.

Eighteen

As Emma waited for Riley to pick her up for school the next morning, she didn't know what to expect. When she left his house the previous night, things still seemed off between them. Was their fight over? Did they still need to talk? She'd spent half the night replaying the conversation and scolding herself for not handling things differently. She didn't want Riley to think she didn't care about him or wasn't invested in their future together, but he'd said some mean and hurtful things too.

When Riley pulled into the driveway, she climbed into his jeep, hoping for the radiant smile he always greeted her with before he leaned over to kiss her, but all she received was a forced tight-lipped smile.

"You okay?" she questioned him.

He rested his elbow on the interior ridge of his door and rested his head on his open palm. "Yeah, I just didn't sleep very well."

She bowed her head. "Riley, about last night—"

"Emma, stop." He reached over to squeeze her hand, but she had to look to make sure it was his hand on hers and not some stranger's. Void of its usual warmth and tenderness, his grip felt foreign. "Everything's fine. I promise."

Which meant everything *wasn't* fine and he'd just lied to her. She reclaimed possession of her hand, dragging it into her lap, and stared out the windshield. A barrier had formed between them. She felt like he was a ticking bomb and she was the one who had lit the fuse.

Knowing he wouldn't tell her anything until he was ready, she remained quiet the rest of the way to school. When they arrived at her locker, he muttered a goodbye before kissing her on the cheek and disappearing down the hall.

The day went downhill from there. Usually Riley engaged with her and the guys during lunch, but today he sat quiet, only talking when someone else asked him a direct question and even then, he only gave one or two word answers. She caught him staring at her in class a couple times, but he always diverted his eyes from her when she looked his way.

In the hallways between classes, he was more affectionate with her than usual but it was less playful, more serious. He was always holding her hand or wrapping his arm around her waist to hold her close to him, like their time was coming to an end and all he wanted to do was hold on until the last possible moment. When she questioned him on his behavior he would force a smile, kiss her hand or cheek, and reassure her that everything was fine. She was tempted to call him on his lies but school was the last place real life issues should be discussed. So she clung to patience and tried not to push him into engaging more than he wanted.

However, when she followed him up to his room after school, she couldn't hold back any longer. She dumped her bag on the floor just inside the door, determined to set things right. "I know you said everything was okay, but—"

Her words died when he took her hands in his and said, "We need to talk."

Emma froze. Everything was wrong. The softness of his tone, the way his eyes flickered from one spot to the next but never focused on her, the way his hands shook. "Why do I get the feeling I won't like this conversation?"

His fingers linked through hers, and he pulled her toward him.

"I've been thinking a lot about what you said yesterday, about us going to college together."

She swallowed, her throat dry.

He caught her eye for a split second before looking down at their entwined hands. It could have been her imagination, but she thought his eyes glistened more than usual. "You're right in that college is a big decision."

He was stalling. Classic Riley move right before he revealed news she wouldn't like. It was different when they were just friends, but for some reason, now that they were more than that, she felt she had more to lose. She wouldn't survive this conversation if he drew it out. "Riley, what is this a—"

"I-I need some space."

She glanced down at their clasped hands and how only a couple inches separated them. "Okay," she said, taking a step back.

"No." He shook his head and pulled her back to him. "You don't understand." He closed his eyes and took a deep unsteady breath, as if preparing for a life-changing moment. When he looked up at her, his eyes contrasted with the look of resolve on his face, a look that made her heart beat faster in fear. "I mean I need some space..."

She questioned the look in his eyes as he stared at her. It took her a minute to realize they were pleading with her to understand—to spare him the task of saying the words out loud to complete the sentence. She sucked in a breath, never taking her eyes off of him, waiting for him to take back his implication. An eternity passed, but he didn't finish his sentence, so she had to. "You mean time away from us...from me." Emma shook her head from side to side, trying to shake away the thought. She tried to align the

173

pieces in a variety of ways and look at them differently, but no matter how she looked at it, she always came to the same conclusion. "You're breaking up with me."

His eyes snapped up to hers, eyes wide and frantic. "No, Em, I'm not—"

"Not what? Not breaking up with me?" Did he think she was naive and stupid because she didn't have any experience with boys and relationships before him? Did he think he could sugarcoat it to disguise the truth behind his intent? "I know I've never been through a breakup before, but I'm pretty sure it feels a lot like this." Heart aching, room spinning, difficulty breathing.

His hands secured her head between them, forcing her to look at him. "I love you. I'm not going anywhere. Things are just really confusing right now and with graduation coming soon, I just need some time to figure some stuff out. That's it. That's all this is."

She knew he was trying to soften the blow, but it didn't help. In the past eight years they'd been friends, no matter how bad things got, Riley had never needed space—he had never needed time away—from her.

Never.

Until now.

His ridiculous response made no sense. He'd always been able to figure things out with her standing by his side, but she attempted to verbalize his rationale for herself to see if she could make more sense of it. "Space. That's it."

He swallowed, his eyes filling with tears, as he nodded and tried to smile. She searched for the truth in his eyes because they both knew he was lying. The pain etched in his face confirmed her suspicion: he was breaking up with her; he was just too chicken to admit it.

The reality of his words slammed into her full force, and she tried so hard not to break into pieces. Acid seared her chest, a cannonball swelled in her throat, and her eyes desperately needed water to quench the fire burning them.

Best friend or not, there was no way she would let Riley or anyone else see her lose it, especially not over a guy…not over him. She took a step back, causing Riley to drop his hands, and creating the distance she desperately needed, apparently the distance they both needed. She refused to beg and plead for him to reconsider or tell her what she'd done wrong; she refused to degrade herself by becoming a crying slobbering mess because some boy kicked her to the curb.

She shoved her emotions down and forced a smile. "Okay. I understand." The lie scorched her tongue. The look in Riley's eyes told her he would accept her words because he wanted to, because he needed to, not because they were true. It was about him right now, not her. "Take all the time you need," she choked out, using the last breath she had.

"Em," he pleaded. The back of his hand swiped across his cheek as a tear escaped.

His room no longer felt safe; he no longer felt like home. If she stayed any longer she would suffocate. "I should go," she mumbled, and before he could respond, she stumbled backward through the doorway.

"Emma."

Ignoring the urgency in his tone, she turned down the hallway and sprinted down the staircase. He called out to her again, but when she kept going, a loud BAM! sounded behind her. Had he punched the wall? She thought about stopping but forced herself to keep going, his words, *I need some space,* echoing in her head. She passed Tyler in the hallway and Mr. and Mrs. Ledger in the living room. Although she felt their eyes on her, she didn't stop. She couldn't face any of them.

She ran all the way home, burst through the front door and found herself gripping the edge of the kitchen counter, staring down at a sink full of dirty dishes, on the verge of hyperventilating. Part of her had known her and Riley would never last as anything more than friends, but the fact he needed space away from her for the first time in over eight years was what hurt the most.

Pressure built in her chest and she could no longer resist breathing. A choked sob escaped. Refusing to let another one seep out, she squeezed her eyes shut and held her breath. It only caused a tear to slip down her cheek. Breathing seemed to be a necessity, but she couldn't stand to hear her ragged breaths, so she turned the kitchen faucet on full blast and concentrated on the sound of rushing water. Her eyes snapped open. She brushed the tear away from her face with her sleeve. Never one to dwell on girlie emotions, Emma grabbed the under-used scrubber brush off the counter and a food-encrusted plate and started scrubbing. It brought a small amount of satisfaction to be in motion, so she slipped the plate into the empty dishwater and picked up another one, scrubbing the grime free and sending it down the drain.

She picked up another one.

Another one.

Another one.

The pile of dishes in front of her dwindled. When she came to the last dish, she knew she needed something else to keep her busy. She turned the dishwasher on and started on the counters, tossing empty food containers in the trash, putting away items left over from her brothers, and scrubbing the stains that clung to the counter as if their lives depended on it. From there, she swept and mopped the floor until the kitchen looked brand new. She had never seen it that clean before, but she didn't care about cleanliness, she only cared about staying busy.

Footsteps briefly broke her out of her trance. She stopped cleaning and glanced up. Lenny froze when his eyes met hers. What he saw caused him to raise his hands like someone was holding a gun to his chest.

"I—" His eyes widened as they scanned the spotless kitchen before reconnecting with Emma's. "Yeah," he muttered before spinning around and beelining it out of there.

The front door opened as Emma returned to her cleaning. She barely heard the exchange of words from her brothers.

"Whatever you do, do *not* go into the kitchen."

"Why?" Logan asked.

"Cuz I think our sister is possessed."

If circumstances were different, Emma would have laughed at one of her brothers claiming her as his sister.

With nothing left to clean, Emma frantically searched for something to do, anything to do, so her tears wouldn't leak out. Food. In a house full of boys, there was always food. Opening the refrigerator, Emma scanned the shelves and pulled out random items. She didn't know how to cook very much, and had no idea what ingredients she needed to make something halfway edible, but it didn't matter.

She grabbed a knife in one hand and a cutting board in the other and attacked an onion. She cut it in half and then proceeded to slice it, chop it, dice it. Her eyes burned, but she kept taking her anger out on the innocent vegetable until tears ran unchecked down her cheeks.

If Riley needed space, then fine, she'd give him space. At least he broke up with her rather than stay with her out of pity or out of fear that she wouldn't be able to live life without him. She'd prove to him, she'd prove to everyone, that she could stand on her own two feet without a boy by her side. She waited for the tears to ebb, for the pain in her chest to subside, for her heart to piece itself back together and heal, but nothing happened. Nothing could change the fact that she'd just lost her boyfriend and her best friend in the same second.

"Emma?"

The soft voice spoken with so much concern spoke louder than the thoughts in her head. She glanced up and saw a set of green eyes staring back at her, eyebrows raised in question. "Are you okay?"

Emma couldn't do anything but nod.

"Why are you crying?" Lucas asked.

"I'm not." She gestured to the liquefied mess in front of her. "It's this stupid onion."

He tilted his head as if needing a closer look to determine her sanity.

"Hey, what's going on?" her dad asked, stepping into the kitchen behind Lucas. Like Lenny, he scanned the room, his eyebrows rising in question.

For lack of a better response, she said, "I cleaned."

Her dad chuckled. "Apparently." He looked around the kitchen and took in the empty sink and clean counters. "Thank you."

Oh no. Now was not the time for her dad to express his gratitude for her. She wasn't strong enough to accept his compliment with her emotions in check. Her hands shook so she dropped the knife on the counter and backed away from the pile of mush.

Her dad set a bag of groceries on the counter and pulled out a couple of boxes. "I got pizza for dinner."

She wasn't in the mood to fight over food with her brothers; she doubted she could eat anyway. "I'm not hungry." She walked toward the garage door to escape to her room.

"Sweetheart."

That word, coming from her dad and directed at her, caused her feet to stop their retreat and made fresh tears pool in her eyes. He'd never called her sweetheart before. His hand settled on her shoulder and squeezed.

"Are you okay?" he asked.

When she didn't answer, he turned her around to face him. Emma couldn't remember the last time her dad had looked at her with such tenderness and concern; she couldn't remember a time when he looked in her eyes and searched their depth for understanding. The stupid cannonball was back in her throat, growing bigger by the second. Tears flooded her eyes at an impossible rate, so she nodded instead of speaking.

He brushed away a few traitorous tears from her cheeks before pulling her against his chest. It wasn't a one-armed hug or an awkward embrace. He hugged her like he was trying to make up for a lifetime of hugs lost. It was then, with her dad's arms securely around her, holding her together, that she broke. Sobs erupted from deep within her, and her arms wrapped around her dad's waist, clutching his shirt in her fists, finding comfort. She should've been embarrassed for acting like such a girl on a crying fest, especially hearing the footsteps enter the kitchen and knowing her brothers were witnessing her breakdown, but she wasn't. Instead, she found strength in her dad's embrace. He didn't say anything; he didn't ask what was wrong. He just held her.

After what felt like an eternity, he kissed the top of her head and released her, no more questions. Riley had always been the one to comfort her when life upended and left her clinging. Riley had always been the one to hold her together when she broke. It had always been Riley. She never thought she would need someone to catch her when Riley abandoned her. She never thought it would be her dad who caught her.

Nineteen

Sleep evaded her for hours as she tried to understand why Riley needed space from her. Had she done something wrong? Had he grown tired of her? Did he want to distance himself from her now before they went off to college? Did he really think she didn't care about him as much as he cared about her? She knew verbal communication and outward expressions of affection weren't her strong points, but he knew her better than anyone. He should know she would do anything for him. On and on the doubts came, but no answers accompanied them.

When sleep did come, she figured it would stick for a lot longer than it did. She woke up way too early the next morning and couldn't get back to sleep. Thankfully, it was Saturday, and she had a couple days until she had to face Riley again.

She threw an arm over her head, trying to block out the world around her—the world had other plans.

A high-pitched shriek caused Emma to bolt upright. Even she recognized the sound of a fire alarm. She knew she was supposed to find the nearest exit and call 911 and wait for the fire trucks and all that, but the Wrangtons didn't have the what-to-do-in-case-of-a-fire plan and she had two younger brothers she refused to leave behind. She sprinted through the garage, nearly tripping over boxes and weights with every step, fear and panic welling within her. She burst through the door into the house and peered through the haze. Inhaling smoke, she coughed. Lance flew into the kitchen from the other doorway across the room. They spotted Lucas at the stove at the same time, but Lance beat her to him.

"What the hell are you doing?" Lance shouted. He swept his arm to the side, pushing Lucas out of the way.

Lucas's eyes widened and he stumbled back, slamming into the adjacent counter. His arm caught the handle of a pan, causing the pan on the stove to crash to the floor and send charred pieces of food flying everywhere.

Lance spun around and grabbed Lucas by the shoulders. "What is wrong with you? Are you trying to burn the house down?"

"I-I'm s-ssorry," Lucas choked out, his voice breaking. "I didn't mean to—"

"Are you really this stupid?" Lance shook Lucas, causing the small boy's head to roll back and forth. "Why do you screw everything up?"

Lance's aggressiveness snapped Emma out of her frozen state. She crossed the kitchen in three strides. "Hey," she barked. "Leave him alone."

Lance's glare shifted from Lucas to her. "Stay out of this." His tone was low, threatening.

Speaking through clenched teeth, she matched it with a deadly tone of her own. "Let. Him. Go."

Lance let Lucas go, shoving him toward Emma. She wrapped her arm around her young brother and guided him behind her out of Lance's reach.

"This is your fault," Lance said, shoving a finger in her face. "You suddenly want to play Martha Stewart, and the stupid brat follows your lead."

"Lucas isn't stupid."

"No? You call nearly setting the house on fire the act of a genius?"

"What is wrong with you?" Emma glared at him, wondering if the guy even knew what the word compassion meant. "He was probably hungry. Did you think about helping him get something to eat for breakfast or were you brooding in your room like usual, caught up in yourself?"

"And where were you? Crying in your room like a little girl?" She opened her mouth to respond, but he cut her off. "You make me sick."

He kicked the pan, and it thudded against the bottom of the kitchen cupboards before flipping upside down and dumping the rest of its contents onto the floor. He spun around and stomped toward the hallway. "Clean this mess up."

Emma closed her eyes, willing her breathing to slow down. Interactions with her older brother seemed to grow worse with time. Taking a deep breath, she turned to Lucas. His eyebrows scrunched over his eyes as he glowered at the floor. Without acknowledging Emma, he turned to follow Lance out of the kitchen, but she grabbed the back of his shirt and yanked him back. "Where do you think you're going? You just gonna leave me here alone?"

He risked a glance at her but turned his head away quickly. Emma still saw the unshed tears in his eyes. She grabbed him by the waist and hoisted him up on the counter. She rested her hands on the counter on either side of him, trapping him there. "Hey," she said softly. "You okay?"

He continued to avoid her gaze.

"What were you making?"

He brushed his arm across his nose, snot and tears soaking into his shirt. "Scrambled eggs," he mumbled.

She'd made her brothers eggs for breakfast a few days ago, but Lucas refused to touch them. "I thought you hated scrambled eggs."

His glistening eyes peered up at her. "You don't."

She eased her head back to get a better look at his face. "You…" Her throat constricted and her voice cut off. She cleared her throat and tried again. "You made me breakfast?"

"I thought it might cheer you up."

Her eyes glistened, and the corner of her mouth tilted up. She threw her arms around his small frame and clutched him to her.

"Emma," he croaked. "Too. Tight."

She laughed and loosened her hold on him. "Sorry."

A small smile appeared on his lips. "S'okay."

"You hungry?"

He nodded.

"How about we clean up the kitchen and try again?"

"Okay." He hopped off the counter and pushed the sleeves of his sweatshirt up to his elbows. "Emma?"

"Yeah?"

"Sorry I ruined breakfast."

She tousled the hair on his head. "You didn't ruin anything. I'd rather cook with you than by myself anyway."

A feeling of being watched washed over Emma and she looked for the source. Partially hidden by the wall, Lenny stood beside the archway leading into the living room, peering in at them. The kid was quiet as a ninja, and his unannounced presence always took Emma by surprise.

"Hey," she said. "Do you want to help us make breakfast?"

Lenny turned his glare on Lucas whose arms were filled with various food items from the refrigerator. In the amount of time it took her to look at Lucas and back, Lenny had vanished.

"Guess not," she muttered.

◆◆◆

The weekend passed quicker than a thirty-second

timeout, and Emma found herself face-to-face with Monday. She had skipped the Saturday morning basketball game with the guys, in part to hang out with Lucas, but mostly to avoid Riley. Yes, she was a chicken, but she'd rather confront Riley for the first time post breakup at school where she could get lost in the flood of her peers and have a million distractions at her disposal than have to conjure the strength to appear normal in front of the guys. The truth was, she had no idea what to expect. Had the weekend given Riley the space he needed away from her or was this arrangement more of a long-term thing? Were they supposed to avoid each other or act like nothing had happened as they continued to hang out? Stepping out the front door and seeing him would tell her so much.

Taking a deep breath, she twisted the doorknob and stepped into the day. Her heart clenched in her chest and she held onto the door to steady herself. Instead of Riley's jeep, an older black Chevrolet Camaro was parked in the driveway with a cocky Tyler leaning against the hood. She didn't need any more evidence—things between her and Riley were done, over. She bit her tongue to redirect the tears from flooding her eyes.

"What are you doing here?" she growled.

Tyler's smile widened. "Good morning to you too, Princess."

"That doesn't answer my question."

"Your boyfriend asked me to give you a ride. Normally I would've said no, but since I know your day doesn't start until you see me, I figured I'd be charitable." She didn't care if Riley sent the limo service to take his place as her transportation to school; she didn't want his handouts. Especially not in the form of Tyler.

"Thanks, but I'll walk." She brushed past him on the way to the street, making her point clear that she'd rather miss first period than endure the commute with him.

He wrapped an arm around her waist and pulled her

against him.

His closeness fueled her anger. She pushed against his chest, trying to break free. "Let me go," she barked.

Leaning his face close to hers, so only a breath separated them, he said, "I never take no for an answer."

"You'd better start," she said through clenched teeth as she ground her elbow into his bicep.

He cursed and broke his hold on her. "Damn, girl. You don't have to get vicious."

Satisfaction warmed her as he massaged his arm, and she turned toward the street again.

"You know what?" he called after her. "Have it your way. I'm not the one who has to walk to school under the threat of rain. See you in first period...if you make it by then."

She looked up at the gray clouds hovering above, wondering if the rain would hold off long enough for her to walk the mile to school. It didn't look promising and she didn't want to sit through school in wet clothes.

"Come on, Princess." Tyler sighed. "You can thank me later."

Reluctantly, she turned on her heels and headed to the car. Sliding into the passenger seat, she caught sight of his smirk. "Shut up."

He threw the car in reverse and let out a throaty laugh. "As you wish, Princess."

"Don't call me that."

On the way to school, they fought over radio stations, the volume of the speakers, and the heat controls. The two-minute ride to school seemed more like two hours. When he pulled into the parking lot, she exhaled a sigh of relief.

She slammed the car door and headed into school. Despite hundreds of students, the hallways felt foreign and empty without Riley by her side. She didn't know if she was supposed to avoid him or seek him out. Usually when they fought they made up fairly quickly. But things were different now. She'd never been an ex-girlfriend before and didn't know the rules she was supposed to obey.

An arm slid across her shoulders, and she stiffened. "Well, look at us," Tyler said, squeezing her against him. "If you'd told me a month ago you and I would be sharing car rides to school and walking to class together, I never would've believed it."

She looked up at him, slapping on her best girlie girl smile. "Just because you gave me a ride to school doesn't mean we're friends or besties or any sort of civilized companions. You put your arm around me again, and I won't guarantee you'll get it back in one piece." She grabbed his arm and twisted, applying enough pressure to cause Tyler to grimace. Her smile widened.

"Got it?"

Not giving him the chance to respond, she released him and headed toward her locker with his low grumbled laughter following her.

She spun the combination on her lock, forcing herself to focus on the task at hand rather than search for Riley among the sea of people surrounding her.

"What's up, Wrangton?" At least Shiloh hadn't abandoned her.

Emma turned to greet her.

"What's with your tag-a-long?" Shiloh asked, nodding down the hallway behind Emma.

"My wh—" Emma turned to find what Shiloh was talking about and almost smacked her face into Tyler's chest. She groaned. "Seriously?"

"What?" Tyler said, holding his hands up in innocence. "We have first period together." He gestured down the hall. "I'm not going the long way around campus just because you can't deal with your feelings toward me."

His comment didn't elicit a response. Emma spun back around to talk to Shiloh, but was stopped mid-turn by a pair of blue eyes. Riley stood at his locker across the hall, Tom and Jerry engaged in conversation beside him. Riley's focus didn't sway from her, but anyone could feel the disconnect between them. Her breath caught in her throat. Riley wasn't looking away from her. What did that mean? He couldn't find it in his heart to pick her up for school like a friend, but he could stare unabashedly at her from across the hall without blinking an eye? And why couldn't she look away from him? He broke up with her and was making it apparent he didn't want her back. The last thing she was going to do was act like a desperate heartbroken ex-girlfriend and beg for him to come back to her. She forced herself to break the connection with Riley and turn back to Shiloh.

Shiloh's accusatory finger flipped between Emma and Riley. "What was that?"

Maybe Emma could feign stupidity or cluelessness. She opened her mouth to try, but Shiloh shook her finger and stepped closer to Emma. "Don't even think about it. What's going on with you and Riley?"

Emma bowed her head to avoid eye contact. "Nothing."

"It sure looks like something." When Emma didn't say anything, Shiloh turned to Tyler. "You." She jabbed her finger in his face. "Leave us." Something in her tone or look communicated clearly to Tyler that her command was nonnegotiable. He muttered a departure to Emma and took off down the hall without a fight. Why couldn't he do that when Emma told him to leave?

Shiloh waited until he was out of earshot before turning back to pry more. "I'll ask you again, what's going on with you and Riley? The truth."

Girls and their need for details! What if she didn't want to spill? What if she didn't want the world to know that she had failed as a girlfriend and now had no best friend?

"Nothing's going on." At least not anymore. "We just aren't, you know, together anymore."

"What!" Shiloh screeched. "Why in the world would you break up with him?"

A gasp sounded from behind Emma. "You broke up with Riley?"

Emma looked down at the freshman's face. Overheard conversations were not exactly the way she wanted news about her breakup to travel. "No, I didn't break up with him; he broke up with me."

"What?" Shiloh asked in disbelief. "Why?"

"I don't know," Emma said, trying to play it off. "But it's not a big deal."

"What's not a big deal?"

Lauren and Madison sidled up beside Shiloh, Madison's eyebrows arched in anticipation of an answer to her question.

"Nothing," Emma said as Shiloh blurted out, "Riley and Emma broke up."

Lauren's mouth dropped open. "What?"

Madison's eyes darkened. "I knew I never liked that jerk."

"You love Riley," Emma said.

Madison's scowl deepened. "Not anymore I don't. I always knew there was something off about him."

Four pairs of eyes glared at Riley from across the hall as if they wanted to combine their powers and shoot death lasers at him.

"I'll be back in a minute," Shiloh muttered before taking a step in his direction.

Emma snagged her arm and hissed, "What are you doing?"

"Nothing." Shiloh shook Emma's hand free.

Panic struck Emma when she realized her friend's intended path would take her right to Riley. "Shiloh," Emma called after her friend. "Shiloh!" Not even the desperation and fear in her voice made an impact on the girl striding across the hall, intent on a mission. Riley glanced at Emma as Shiloh stopped in front of him.

Emma couldn't hear what Shiloh said, but Riley bowed

his head before responding. Their conversation only lasted a couple minutes and all Emma could do was hold her breath and hope Riley didn't think she had anything to do with sending Shiloh over to talk to him.

Shiloh gave a short nod before spinning away from Riley and sauntering back over to the girls.

"What did you say?" Madison asked, her voice bordering on excitement at being on the forefront of a breaking story.

"What did *he* say?" Lauren chimed in.

"He claims you two didn't break up, just that you're taking some time apart."

Emma snorted, not believing it any more today than she did when she heard the words from his mouth a few days ago, but maybe she needed a professional's opinion, or four of them. "What would you believe if a guy told you he wasn't breaking up with you but that he just needed some space and then didn't talk to you for three days and sent someone else to pick you up for school?"

"That jerk!" Madison growled.

"When did this happen?" Lauren asked Emma.

Emma shrugged. "A few days ago."

"And you didn't say anything?" Shiloh backhanded Emma on the arm. "What's wrong with you?"

"Ow." Emma rubbed the sting from her bicep. "It was over the weekend."

"Ever heard of a phone?" Shiloh shot back.

"I told you," Emma said. "It's not a big deal."

"Uh, yeah, it is." Madison nudged Shiloh out of the way to take Emma on herself. "It's a huge deal. You can't go through your first breakup alone."

"Breakup party. Friday." Lauren's fingers flew across the screen of her cell phone. "My house. Who's in?"

Emma waved her arms in the air to ward off the craziness. "Whoa, whoa, whoa. I am not going to a breakup party, especially not my own." Not that she knew what a breakup party was, but the concept itself confused her. Was it a celebratory party in honor of the breakup or a pity party for getting dumped? Either way, it didn't sound fun.

"Yes, you are coming to your breakup party," Shiloh said. "It's mandatory."

"Look." Emma tried to gain control of the conversation. "The situation is complicated. I don't even know if it's an official breakup or..." she didn't want to go into details, "not."

The four girls looked at her like she was crazy. Considering who Emma was, did they not understand how confusing relationships and breakups were to her? They engaged in a five-way stare down until the warning bell rang.

"Good," Lauren said. "It's settled. My house. Friday. Five o'clock."

Emma looked up, surprised that Lauren offered up her house and that her tone was not filled with satisfaction or mocking over Emma's misery. Lauren shrugged one shoulder. "Pizza and basketball."

"And don't forget the whipped cream," Madison said.

Emma groaned, knowing she wouldn't be able to change their minds. So much for the week improving.

They waved their goodbyes and took off in various directions to their first period classes. Unable to resist, Emma looked over her shoulder for one last look at Riley. He gave her a nod as his hand swiped at his locker, slamming the door shut, before he turned the opposite direction and joined students heading toward the north end of the school.

No smile, no wink, no nothing except a nod that could've meant anything in the world. For all she knew, he could've been scaring a fly off his face.

Sighing, she watched his back retreat, a sight she rarely saw from him. She knew how to be his best friend, she sort of knew how to be his girlfriend, but what she didn't know how to do was be nothing at all to the person who meant everything to her.

♦♦♦

Emma entered the cafeteria, following the normal path toward her usual table. There was only one problem. Riley was at that table. He'd managed to avoid her all morning, but lunch was different. Lunch involved the two of them, plus all their mutual friends, staring at each other from across the table for a thirty-minute duration. If she joined them, would she be treated like normal or like an alien invader? She didn't want to be an alien invader.

As she tried to decide whether to advance or retreat, an arm landed across her shoulders. "Need a lunch buddy?"

She shouldn't have waited so long to determine her next move. "No."

Tyler chuckled. "Stop lying."

She glanced up at him, refusing to play his game.

"C'mon." He tightened his arm around her neck. "Just don't expect me to buy your lunch, engage in civilized conversation, or feed your ego because your BFF turned his back on you."

Emma tried to pull out of his grasp, but he wouldn't let her. Instead, he led her to a table on the opposite side of the cafeteria. She half expected him to sit with a group of his friends, but when he sat down alone Emma couldn't hide her surprise. "Don't you usually eat lunch with a posse?"

He pinned her with a glare. "What posse? This school, and everyone in it, is lame. I prefer my loner status to enduring precious out of class time listening to idiots complain about their lives."

"Wow. I can see why so many people gravitate toward you, begging for friendship. Your compassion is astounding."

"Oh, how sweet," he said with fake gratitude. "You're worried about my social status."

"Hardly."

"What? Am I not cool enough for you?"

Reality struck, and her shoulders sagged in defeat, knowing she had no room to talk. "Do you hear me complaining? I'm the one who can't sit with my friends because my boyfriend dumped me."

He swiped a fry from her lunch. "We make quite the pair, huh?"

As much as she hated to admit it, "Yeah. So if you don't have friends and you don't eat in the cafeteria, why are you here now?"

He shrugged. "I hoped I could make fun of you for sitting at the loser's table."

"Takes one to know one."

He slapped a hand to his chest. "We have so much in common."

Not wanting to talk about Riley, and not wanting to give Tyler an opportunity to focus the conversation on her, she decided to take advantage of the one-on-one time with him. "So what's your story?"

"My story?"

She nodded. "How did you end up as the Ledgers' houseguest?"

One stiff shoulder shrugged with seeming indifference, but his eyes turned to ice. "Not your story to know, Princess."

"Oh, come on. Given the state of my life right now, do you really think I'm going to judge you?"

He studied her for a minute before sighing and giving in to her request. "I got into some trouble that tarnished my parents' reputation, so they found the first person who would take me, and here I am. End of story."

Emma knew it was hardly the end of the story, that his wounds were still fresh, the betrayal of his parents too heavy on his mind. Compassion for him hit her, and she dropped her eyes to the food in front of her. "I'm sorry."

"Don't pity me, Princess."

His harsh tone surprised her.

One of his hands curled into a fist, while the other one covered it, almost like trying to hide his true feelings. "Family is stupid. I don't need them."

They embarked in a staring war. He tried to hold up his tough exterior, and he did a good job, but having spent years at odds with her family, Emma saw right through it. Maybe if she took time to truly see Tyler, she'd find he harbored a pain similar to hers.

His eyes flickered over her head before he cleared his throat and looked away.

"You know, if you needed a backup plan you had us." Emma looked over her shoulder to see Shiloh with her arms crossed, glaring down at Tyler. Madison and Lauren stood behind her.

Emma shrugged. "I needed someone to insult for the next thirty minutes and he volunteered."

Tyler threw his head back and laughed like their previous conversation had never happened.

"Want me to get rid of him for you?" Shiloh asked.

Tyler didn't look like he cared one way or the other but was curious as to how Emma would respond.

Madison nudged Shiloh in the ribs. "Leave him alone. If nothing else Tyler will make Riley jealous, and he'll come running back to Emma by the end of the day."

Emma rolled her eyes. "I'm not trying to make Riley jealous."

Lauren glanced up from her phone, her fingers still flying across the screen. "Judging by the look on Riley's face, you don't have to try. It's already happening."

Emma couldn't stop herself from whipping around to find Riley. True enough, he looked angry. Great. Looks like she just solidified their relationship into the enemy zone.

◆◆◆

Fourth period. A class she anticipated and dreaded in the same breath since it was the first class she had with Riley post breakup. The class didn't have assigned seating, so students could sit anywhere they wanted. Riley usually sat beside her in the back of the room so they could keep each other awake through the monotone history lectures and share a laugh when their teacher used outdated terms no one had heard in the past century.

Emma arrived to class early, taking the back corner seat like usual. Pulling out her AP World History book, she tried to nonchalantly scan every classmate entering the room. Riley's choice of where to sit was crucial. It would tell her everything she needed to know. The voice within tried to convince her not to worry, that there was no way he wouldn't sit beside her, because that's what he did, that's where he belonged. Everyone in class knew this, which was why the seat next to her remained empty after all the others filled. By the time Riley stepped through the doorway there were only two seats left—the one beside her and the one in the front row.

Against her will, Emma's head snapped up when he paused at the front of the room. Their eyes met, and then he glanced between the two empty seats as if deciding which one to claim. Maybe he just needed some reassurance that she still wanted him to sit next to her. Despite the plummet in their relationship, she allowed a smile to form on her lips to let him know he was welcome to take his seat beside her.

He took one step toward her, then another. Her smile grew. She brushed a stray hair behind her ear to disguise her sigh of relief. Everything was okay. *They* were okay, or at least they would be. But instead of meandering through the aisles of desks, Riley plopped down in the desk in front of him. The one in the front corner of the classroom; the one farthest away from her. Her breath caught. He hated sitting in the front. As in despised it with a passion.

I'm okay.

I'm okay.

I'm o—

She could only think it so many times before the words became more lie than truth.

When he turned his back on her and faced the front of the classroom, she felt like he'd slapped her. Her eyes burned, and she bit her tongue to prevent tears from escaping. With that small movement, he said everything he needed to say.

Anger and resolve washed over her and she sucked in a breath of determination. Fine. If space was what he wanted—what he needed—then fine. She was over him, over them. If he didn't care, neither did she.

Maybe if she kept telling herself that she'd eventually start to believe it.

Twenty

News of their breakup spread like a gasoline-induced wildfire in a dry summer. The rest of the week followed a pattern: Tyler picked her up for school, despite her protests; Riley stared at her from across the hall when he decided not to avoid her; and the rest of the student body started bets on whether their breakup was permanent or temporary and how long their separation would last. Emma just tried to keep her sanity. When Friday arrived, she found herself looking forward to a night with the girls.

She stood on the curb, staring up at Lauren's house. Brick stairs leading up to the front door, huge picture windows, wraparound porch, landscaped yard. She still had to laugh at the double pillars extending from the ground up to the roof, reminding her of some southern plantation house. It was monstrous, especially compared to the Wrangtons' one floor rambler, but it wasn't as scary as it had been the first time Emma had seen it.

At her last slumber party with the girls, she had spent most of the time feeling like the world's biggest reject as Lauren tried to humiliate her, and Riley crashed the party to rescue her.

Music blared from the house. It almost seemed like too

much for only eight girls, but the dancing figures in the living room didn't seem to mind as they bounced around and sang off-key lyrics at the top of their lungs. Emma shook her head and smiled again. If there was one thing she could count on from the girls, it was entertainment.

As soon as Emma entered the house, Lauren pulled her into the dance circle and together they reenacted some of the moves from the father-daughter dance. The two girls laughed way too hard as their friends tried and failed to mimic their movements. Who knew crazy dance moves could make a slumber party so enjoyable?

When they collapsed in a heap an hour later, sporadic giggles still bursting from them, Mr. Thompson arrived with the pizza. As Emma settled on the living room floor with three slices piled on her plate, she had to admit, the girls had done a great job of making her feel better and forgetting all about a certain someone.

Once everyone had pizza, they joined Emma, and the chatter fizzled out as their mouths filled with food.

In the attempt to satisfy her hunger pains, Emma took a huge bite of her pepperoni pizza, her taste buds sighing with content.

"Okay." Madison dropped her pizza on her plate and clapped. "It's breakup story time."

Emma almost choked on her food. What? This was a slumber party designed to make her feel better, not make her rehash the details.

When Emma swallowed, Shiloh thrust a can of whipped cream in her face. "Any time you feel like crying, spray this in your mouth. Trust me. It helps."

Seriously? Emma looked around the circle, waiting for someone to crack a smile or break out with giggles, but no. Each of the girls stared at her with expectant eyes, waiting for her to start story time.

Be cool, she told herself. Bite tongue, don't forget to breathe, and just be cool. "Riley and I were together, and now we're not. End of story."

"Come on, Emma," Madison cried. "We want details."

"What did Riley say?"

"What did *you* say?"

"Was he at least nice about it?"

"Did you cry?"

"Did you punch him?"

The questions piled on top of each other, making Emma's head spin.

"It's okay to cry," Madison said gently.

When Emma didn't say anything, Lauren spoke for the first time. "It's therapeutic to talk about it."

"I don't care if it's therapeutic or not. I'm not dishing out the details of my breakup with Riley. And even if I did, I certainly wouldn't cry." None of them needed to know about her sob fest on her dad's shoulder the day it happened. She had to hold on to at least some of her dignity.

"At least tell us why you broke up," Madison said.

Emma shrugged. Sure, she could repeat the excuse Riley had given her, but she still didn't understand any of it. Especially since his actions contradicted his words. "I guess we're better off as friends."

"So why aren't you two talking then?"

She swallowed. That was the real question. What believable excuse could she give? "We aren't not talking. We're just taking some space is all. We've both got college applications to finalize and meetings with coaches and stuff. It's a busy time for both of us, and we didn't want to distract each other."

Not bad for making up that excuse on the spot. At least she thought so until she realized everyone staring at her with pity in their eyes.

"Okay, that's enough of the third-degree," Shiloh said, waving the rest of the girls off. "I vote we throw on a stupid movie and eat until all the food is gone and pass out on sugar highs. Who's with me?"

Ashley's hand shot into the air, followed by everyone else's. Emma shared a look with Shiloh and hoped her gratitude was communicated with one of those nonverbal looks girls share.

Rising from the floor, Shiloh grabbed Emma's shoulder and gave it an extra squeeze, like she wanted to reassure Emma that she wasn't alone through this mess with Riley.

After the first chick-flick, the girls voted on the next movie. The one they chose featured a high school couple who fell in love and had to beat the odds to stay together and prove love knew no bounds. Hitting a little too close to home, Emma knew she would either cry or punch someone by the end, so she decided it best not to stick around. Waiting until the movie introduced the main characters and set up the central conflict, she snuck out of the room and slipped out the back door into the night.

She shivered in the cool spring air as she stepped off the back patio and onto the lawn. She had never had the luxury of sprawling out on such perfect grass, so she lowered herself to the ground and leaned back, the stars overhead capturing her attention.

Laughter from the girls seeped into the night. A soft smile graced her lips as she realized there was no other place she'd rather be than at this slumber party, even if the girls did want the juicy details of her life. At least they cared.

Sometime later, amidst the quiet of the night, she heard the patio door slide open and wondered who would be joining her.

"Told you she didn't leave."

Ashley. Emma should've known.

"Yeah, yeah." Without looking, Emma knew Shiloh playfully pushed the freshman as they crossed the grass toward her.

They plopped down on either side of her.

"Took you long enough," Emma said.

"The freshman said I needed to give you some space before I sought you out, whatever that's about."

As much as she thought she wanted to be alone, everything felt right when her two friends joined her. As much as she loved Riley and the guys, Emma could no longer think of her life complete without the girls, especially Ashley and Shiloh.

The three of them soaked up the night in silence. She thought maybe they had come out to hound her for more details about Riley, but neither of them said a word. Maybe that was why the words bubbled to the surface so easily.

"I don't know what happened," she admitted.

Ashley turned her head to look at Emma's profile.

Emma started to reveal more, but her throat clogged and her eyes burned at the memory. Shiloh offered her a can of whipped cream, and Emma didn't hesitate to grab it and fill her mouth with the rich foam.

Shiloh laughed. "Told you it would help."

"Shut up," Emma said with a laugh of her own.

When she was confident her voice wouldn't crack, Emma tried to make sense out of Riley's words verbally. Maybe having an audience would somehow click their meaning into place and help provide Emma with some clarity. Her voice was hardly more than a whisper. The stars in the sky had been so clear before, but now they blurred above her. "We had a fight about colleges and our futures. He said I didn't care about him as much as he cared about me because I didn't want him to sacrifice college ball to go to the same college as me. It's not like it was the worst fight we've ever had, but—" She took a deep breath to steady her emotions. "The next day he said he needed space. I saw in his eyes that it was his way of breaking up with me, even if he wouldn't say it."

Shiloh stole the can back and squirted whipped cream in her mouth. "Boys suck."

Emma refused to lump Riley in that category. Whatever

was happening, he'd always stuck by her, and she wasn't about to make him out to be a monster. "Not all of them."

Shiloh shook her head. "You're missing the point. It doesn't matter if they do or don't. You have to say it. It's part of the healing process."

"What is? Making Riley out to be some kind of jerk because he broke up with me?"

"Yes," Shiloh said at the same time Ashley said, "No," causing all of them to laugh.

When the renewed silence became too much, Emma once again voiced her thoughts. "I thought he was the one, you know? I mean we've known each other since we were kids and have always been there for each other. I thought we'd be able to survive anything together, and I don't understand why he would need space—" her voice hitched, so she paused to regain her composure before finishing, "space away from me."

She didn't expect her friends to give her answers; she was just grateful that they were here. That they weren't guys afraid to talk about their feelings or girls who craved drama, but that they were there to listen and support, without judgment or criticism.

"Hey, Emma?"

"Yeah?" she asked, rolling her head to the side only to discover Shiloh was already looking at her.

"You know it's not your fault, right?"

Afraid Shiloh could read her thoughts, Emma remained silent.

"Whatever is going on with Riley, whatever his reason for breaking up with you, it's not because you're a bad person or you're not worth it or because you did something wrong. Everyone knows he loves you, and you guys will find your way back to each other if it's right, and if not, then there's someone out there better for you."

How did Shiloh know that Emma felt like it was all her fault? That maybe if she had done something different or said something different then they wouldn't have broken up.

"Whatever. It doesn't matter." Emma turned her focus back to the sky above. "If he doesn't want to be with me, he doesn't want to be with me. I'm over it."

"Yeah," Shiloh said quietly. She handed over the can of whipped cream, and the only thing she said when Emma filled her mouth with its substance was, "I know."

Twenty-One

A week and a half later, the door to Emma's AP World History classroom opened and a girl stepped through the doorway. A pink slip hung from her fingers as she searched the room for the teacher. Mr. Goldstein paused his lecture. He grabbed the note from the girl's outstretched arm and his eyes scanned the message. Everyone watched him, wondering who the note was for. Was it for Bradley who got caught fighting during lunch? For Jessica who got caught making out with her college boyfriend under the football stadium bleachers? Or for Ryan who always seemed to get random notes from the office because his mom needed him to come straight home after school?

Mr. Goldstein glanced up and met Emma's eyes. Seven steps in her direction and Mr. Goldstein held the pink slip out to her. Confused, she hesitated before grasping the edge of the paper and pulling it down so she could read the note.

Lenny suspended from school for fighting. Needs you to pick him up now.

Clutching the note in her fingers, she wondered why it had been delivered to her. Schools usually contacted her dad or Logan when something happened.

She didn't have time to sit dazed as her mind tried to

conjure up all the possibilities for why the note about her brother was in her hand. Did something happen to her dad? She gathered her things and almost sprinted toward the front of the room. Mr. Goldstein must have read something in her eyes because before she could utter a word he nodded his head toward the door, dismissing her. Muttering a relieved, "Thank you," she bolted out of the classroom. She was so focused on getting to her brother, she didn't hear the classroom door open and close behind her.

"Emma."

She willed herself to continue walking, but her feet had been conditioned to stop and turn at the sound of his voice. Even after two weeks of silence his voice still sounded like home.

Riley closed the distance between them until he was standing less than a foot away. "What's wrong?"

It would have been too easy to tell him about the note, ask him for a ride, and tell him she needed him. "Nothing. Everything's fine."

He searched her eyes for the truth her lips refused to say. "Emma, please. Talk to me."

"There's nothing to talk about. I just…I have to go." She turned to leave, but his hand grabbed her forearm, turning her back to face him.

"Em." The emotion he put into the first syllable of her name punched her in the heart, and she almost forgave him for everything right then.

He bowed his head and seemed to struggle with his next words. "I know things between us have been…different lately," he raised his head, connecting his eyes to hers, "but we're still friends. I still lo—"

She yanked her arm out of his grasp, unable to hear the rest of his sentence. "Don't," she snapped. "You told me you weren't breaking up with me, promising me you just needed space but that we were still friends. Then you proceeded to ignore me for two weeks. Two weeks!" She shook her head and took a step back, not even trying to cover up the hurt and anger she felt. "Friends don't do that to each other."

He threw his arms out to the sides, his voice growing louder to match hers. "You think I like this? You think staying away from you is easy? Well, it's not. It's *killing* me."

The pain in his voice and the sadness reflected in his eyes surprised her.

I need some space.

He had used those exact words when he broke up with her—he had repeated them at least twice—and now he acted like it was the last thing he wanted. He wasn't making any sense. "You're the one who wanted this; you're the one who needed space from me."

His shoulders sagged, and his next words hung heavy with defeat. "I never wanted this, Em. I'm just trying to do what's best. For both of us. I just need time to figure stuff out."

"Why? We've always been able to figure stuff out together."

He shook his head, his eyes filling with pity. "Not this time."

"Why not?"

"Because."

"That's not an answer."

"It's all I have right now."

"Is it—" she cleared her throat, not knowing if she was ready for his answer, "because there's another girl?"

His head jerked back as if she'd punched him. "What? No! Of course not." Riley shook his head. "Do you not know me at all?"

"I thought I did, but now I'm not so sure." Her admission tasted bitter on her tongue, so she took a step forward, hoping to bridge the gap between them. She let some of her anger dissipate, hoping he'd give her a clue as to what he was thinking. "I just don't understand."

"I know," he whispered, closing his eyes. "I'm sorry."

His words hung in the air between them, not the words she wanted to hear, at least not unless they came with more of an explanation for why he'd abandoned her, but he didn't add to them. "You're sorry? That's it?"

"Emma, please." He brought his hands together as if to pray. "Just trust me. Please."

"Trust you? All I've ever done since the moment we met was trust you and look at what happened. The one person I never thought would let me down abandoned me."

"Emma." He took a step forward, reaching for her, his face desperate. "Please, it's not like that. I'm—"

She didn't have time to talk in circles with him, her brother needed her. "I have to go," she muttered. Before he could stop her, she spun around and sprinted down the hallway, leaving him to stare after her.

The middle school was a few miles away from the high school, and since she had no car and didn't have money for the city bus, walking was her best bet. Her increasing worry quickened her speed as she pushed open the door leading toward the student parking lot. She was so focused on her mission that she didn't register the sound of a car door slamming closed until a voice called out to her.

"You're not skipping, are you?"

She groaned as Tyler stepped in her path. What was it with boys getting in her way today? She tried to step around him, but he was too quick.

"Shouldn't you be in class?" she growled.

"Shouldn't you?"

He crossed his arms over his chest and smirked at her. "I never pictured you for a delinquent teen. I mean what would your perfect boyfriend and his parents think?"

He didn't deserve a response so she pushed past him again, ramming her shoulder into his. He laughed like she had fallen right into his trap, and she hated herself for it. His hand grabbed her bicep. With murder in her eyes, she looked at him and then down at his fingers circling her arm.

He got the message loud and clear. He released her and raised his hands in the air. "All right, all right. I'll keep my hands to myself."

"I don't have time for this."

"Where are you going?" he asked. "Need a ride?"

"No."

"Come on. You're obviously in a hurry, and my car's right here. Since neither one of us is going to class, it couldn't hurt, right?"

As much as she didn't want to ask him for help, she couldn't ignore the fact that the clock was ticking. Her thirty-minute walk would be reduced to five if she accepted his offer for a ride. She sighed. "Fine, but you don't ask questions."

He smiled. "Deal."

She followed him to his car and scoffed when he opened the passenger side door for her. "Really?" she asked.

"What? You didn't think I knew how to act like a gentleman and treat the ladies with respect?"

She slipped into the passenger seat without saying a word. Tyler came around the car and slid into the driver's seat. "Where to?"

"The middle school."

He opened his mouth to speak, but Emma cut him off. "Don't talk; just drive."

She could feel Tyler's eyes on her, but she refused to acknowledge his stare. Instead, she counted down the minutes until he dropped her off at her brother's school and left.

"You know," Tyler said.

Jeez, the guy seriously had issues with silence.

"I'm not as horrible as you think I am."

"Once I see evidence to the contrary, maybe I'll reconsider my opinions, but until then..."

He put on the blinker and turned the corner onto another

street. "You aren't what you appear to others either."

"Meaning?" She didn't care about what he thought about her, so why did she just invite him to continue talking?

"Meaning, even if you have everyone else fooled to think you don't care—don't care about basketball or college or what anyone thinks about you or Riley breaking up with you—inside it's killing you."

"How very astute of you. Are you looking for a gold star or perhaps a medal?"

Tyler shook his head. "There you go, always keeping people at a distance so they can't hurt you. Your family must be so proud."

And there it was. The button that swiped all joking aside and catapulted Emma into defense mode. "Don't you dare talk about my family. Just because you succeeded in getting kicked out of yours doesn't mean you're an expert on mine."

Stopping at an intersection, Tyler turned to look at her— to study her. For a second, his eyes lost humor and filled with understanding. "Fair enough."

He turned back to focus on the road, and Emma thought she'd be able to enjoy some peace and quiet.

"So, how are things with lover boy?"

She closed her eyes and took a deep breath, exhaling loudly. The last thing she wanted to talk about was Riley.

After a few seconds of silence Tyler laughed. "What, no comment? I thought girls loved talking about their boyfriends."

"*Ex*-boyfriend."

"Yeah, what's the deal with you two? I thought you were soul mates, besties for life, and all that, yet the first sign of trouble sends you both running in opposite directions." He slouched a bit lower in the driver's seat and flopped a wrist over the steering wheel like the world was his playground. "Must not have been true love after all."

She didn't engage; she forced her fists to remain in her

lap as she continued staring out the window, wondering why sometimes Tyler felt almost like a friend and other times he felt more like an enemy.

"I'm just saying, if he really cared about you, he wouldn't be keeping his distance. Maybe he doesn't love you as much as you think he does."

His words hit a little too close to home, causing a knot to form in her throat. *Do not engage!* she screamed at herself.

"If he's one of the good guys, maybe it wouldn't be so bad if you gave a guy like me a chance."

Her vow of silence shattered at his suggestion. "Keep dreaming. You're the last person I would ever think about being involved with."

"I didn't mean it like that. I meant give me a chance to be your friend."

That didn't sound any better. "And why would I do that?"

"Because it seems like both of us could use one right now."

She hated that he was right. Sure, she had formed bonds with the girls and they were great, but she missed her guy friends who had all seemed to choose Riley. Not that she had put much effort into hearing their take on the whole thing, but she couldn't handle flat out rejection, so she avoided them too.

Tyler pulled up to the curb in front of the middle school, sparing her from having to respond. As soon as the car stopped, she threw open the door. "Thanks for the ride. See you later."

"Hey," Tyler said, leaning over the middle console as she stepped out. "You want me to wait?"

She shook her head. "No, I've got it from here. Go home."

"But—"

She slammed the door shut, cutting off the rest of his refute, and went in search of her brother.

Twenty-Two

E mma tried to push aside the memories that assaulted her once she crossed the threshold into the middle school. Although her eyes focused on the path leading to the main office, they managed to pick up everything in her peripheral vision: the bench where Riley held her hand the first time they got called to the principal's office for skipping class to play basketball in the gym, the pillar they hid behind the day after her mom left and Riley held her to ward off a panic attack, the window where they made funny faces at the secretary because it looked like she needed to laugh. Too many memories surrounded her. It was like no matter where she went, Riley was always with her. She pushed the thoughts of him aside and refocused on finding her brother.

Pulling open the main office door, her eyes scanned the front desk, the hallway leading to the principal's office, and the waiting area with a row of seats backed up against the wall. Her brother sat with a tough guy slouch in a chair, one arm propped on the back of the chair beside him. He looked so much like Lance that she almost retreated, letting him face suspension with their older brother's attitude on his own. But when he looked up and saw her, he dropped his arm from the back of the chair, his shoulders slumped, and he bowed his head. Having never seen any of her brothers look ashamed, she didn't know which was an act—the tough guy or the one who had a conscience.

"Hey." Emma dropped into the chair beside him.

"Hey," he muttered.

"You okay?"

He nodded, keeping his head bowed.

Emma didn't know how to talk to any of her brothers. Sure, Lucas was the easiest, but he did most of the talking. She took a deep breath, hoping the words out of her mouth would be the right ones.

"Do you want to tell me what happened?"

"No."

"Will you tell me anyway?"

He leaned forward, elbows resting on his knees, his focus on the floor. She didn't know her brother well enough to know if he was avoiding the question or gathering the words to answer, so she waited.

"Who started the fight?" she eventually prompted.

"I punched him first."

"That's not what I asked. Sometimes fights start way before the first punch is thrown."

He looked at her over his shoulder, his eyes glimmering with what appeared to be confusion or hope or something in between.

Crossing his arms, he leaned back in his chair. "The guy hates me. He's always making comments about how stupid or poor I am, like he's so much better than me because his parents have all kinds of money to throw around. He's always trying to call me out in front of people for all kinds of stupid stuff."

It sounded like Lucas wasn't the only one who struggled with being bullied. "Is that what happened today?"

He shrugged one shoulder. "I was talking to this girl in the hallway. She's nice, you know? She always smiles at me and says hi, like she doesn't care what anyone thinks. Next thing I know, Broden shoves me against the lockers and tells me to stop talking to his girl. He starts calling me names and saying a bunch of stupid stuff. Usually I would just hit him, but I didn't want to do that in front of her." His cheeks turned red. "So I kissed her instead."

"What?" Emma exclaimed. "Why?"

"I figured it would shut him up...or piss him off."

"And he didn't hit you for that?"

Lenny shook his head. "No, but he called me trash and said she would never give a loser like me the time of day."

Emma's chest tightened. They reminded her too much of the words Lance threw her way not too long ago. "So you hit him," she said softly.

"So I hit him," Lenny confirmed. Truth be told, she probably would've hit the kid too.

Apparently, Lenny was out of words, and she didn't know what else to say, so they let silence settle between them. She replayed the conversation in her head. What stuck was not the angry exchange of words or fists, but what the girl must have felt. In Emma's head, the girl could've been someone like Shiloh or Madison...or Ashley.

"Hey, Lenny?" Emma said.

Her brother turned to look at her. "Yeah?"

"Don't use a girl for revenge against some jerk, okay?"

Lenny bowed his head and nodded. "She'll probably never speak to me again, but I guess I deserve that. I always screw everything up."

On impulse she grabbed his shoulder. "That's not true. You don't screw everything up, but you may want to think about others before you act next time." She paused, knowing she didn't know what his life or his peers were like. "And if she's as nice as you say she is, you could always apologize."

"You think that'd work?"

Emma shrugged. "It's worth a shot. Especially since you like her."

Lenny whirled toward her, his mouth opening to protest, but when he saw Emma's raised eyebrow daring him to lie to her, he shut it. "Doesn't matter anyway. She's got a boyfriend."

"So? It sounds like she could be a good friend. You don't have to date a girl to talk to her. Besides, you never know what might happen."

He settled back in his chair again and they watched the business of the office around them. People coming and going, phones ringing, voices hollering. She didn't know how long it would take for the vice principal to call them into his office, but she knew from experience it usually took an eternity and a day. She'd never met a vice principal who looked forward to talking to kids in trouble.

"Hey, Emma," Lenny said, breaking her concentration. "Thanks for coming."

"No problem." As Emma thought about it though, she wondered why it was her sitting beside Lenny and not their dad. "Why did you send for me? Why didn't you call dad or Logan?"

Lenny shrugged. "I don't know, I just…"

His voice trailed off, but she refused to let him off the hook that easily. "You just what?"

He took a deep breath. "You've been helping Lucas with his homework and stuff, so I figured maybe…maybe you'd care enough to help me too."

She stared at her brother, unable to speak over the lump that seemed all too ready to swell in her throat these days. "Of course I care," she whispered.

"And thanks for not yelling at me."

"Yeah, well, I figured that's Dad role."

He laughed. "At least he'll do it at home and not here this time."

The minutes collected into chunks of time. The end of school bell rang, and the office just kept getting busier and busier. A cute black-haired girl swept through the doors, her wide eyes buzzing around the office until they landed on Lenny. She pushed her way through the people standing in front of her and stopped in front of him.

"What happened?" she asked breathlessly.

Lenny stood. "What are you doing here?"

"I came to see if you were okay. Did you get suspended? Or did you get—" Her hand clutched Lenny's forearm as she squeezed her eyes closed. "Please tell me you didn't get expelled."

"No, I—" Lenny glanced at Emma. "We haven't talked to anyone yet."

Her eyes popped open. "Really?"

Lenny nodded.

"Oh, good." She pushed him down in his seat and took the one on the other side of him.

"What are you doing?" Lenny asked.

"Waiting with you."

"Why?"

"Because I'm not letting you get suspended. Broden deserved to get punched. There's no way I'm letting him weasel his way out of this while you get punished."

"Thanks, Tara." He glanced quickly in her direction. "And, hey, I'm sorry for kissing you. It wasn't right, and you didn't deserve for me to use you against Broden."

Tara bowed her head, her face growing red. "Oh, um, yeah. Well, if you kiss me again without permission, I'll be the one hitting you, but this time," she tucked hair behind her ears, "I guess I can let it slide."

Emma watched her brother's cheeks redden and bit back a smile. Who knew she'd get a glimpse of her brother's life when she got the pink slip at school?

After a minute, he cleared his throat. "By the way, this is Emma." He looked from Tara to Emma, a small smile lifting the corners of his mouth. "My sister." It was the first time she'd ever heard him claim her as his sister in public, and yeah, her heart melted a little.

From the corner of the office, the vice principal's door finally opened and a balding man stepped out. His eyes peered over his glasses and zeroed in on Lenny. "Mr. Wrangton. We meet again." Based on the man's tone, his run-ins with Lenny happened often. His pointer finger curled, indicating Lenny to step into his office. Before Emma and Lenny could even stand, Tara was across the room, words spewing from her mouth. "Mr. Hammock, the accusations made against Lenny Wrangton are completely unfounded."

"Ms. Winters, this situation has nothing to do with you."

"It has everything to do with me. I was a witness; therefore, my statement has a huge impact on the outcome."

"So, you're saying Mr. Wrangton didn't hit Mr. Lee?"

Tara swept her arm in Lenny's direction, her index finger pointing. "Whether Mr. Wrangton did or did not resort to violence is irrelevant. The fact of the matter is that bullying and harassment of any form are not tolerated in this school. So how is it fair that the one getting punished in this situation is the victim?"

All Emma could do was stare at the girl. With her shoulders squared to the vice principal and her head tilted upward, the girl resonated confidence. Everything about her made Emma feel like they were in court awaiting Lenny's conviction. Emma didn't know whether to be impressed or intimidated. How in the world did Lenny get this girl on his side?

Beside her, Lenny chuckled and turned toward Emma. "She's pretty awesome, isn't she?" he whispered.

Emma nodded. That was one way to describe his friend.

"Both her parents are lawyers."

Ah, that would explain it.

Mr. Hammock pinched the bridge of his nose, his glasses teetering on the edge of his knuckles. "Okay, Ms. Winters. I'll take your argument under advisement, now may I please see your client? Alone?"

"Only if you promise to treat him fairly and understand that he is not the criminal here. Broden is."

He huffed out a sigh. "Good day, Ms. Winters." He turned down the hallway again, raising his hand over his shoulder and flicking two fingers toward his office to indicate that Lenny should follow.

Lenny and Emma stood. Tara sidled up next to Lenny, whispering a mile a minute words Emma couldn't hear. When they got to Mr. Hammock's door, Tara gripped Lenny's shoulder.

"Good luck."

Lenny and Emma sat in the cushioned seats facing Mr. Hammock's desk as he shut the door behind them. When the vice principal joined them, he looked at Emma and asked Lenny, "Who's this?"

"My sister."

"Where is your father?"

Without missing a beat, Lenny answered. "He wasn't able to come."

"I don't know if your sister is qualified to talk in this situation."

Lenny looked over at her. "She is."

Mr. Hammock sighed and readjusted his glasses on his nose. "Very well. So, you and Mr. Lee are having issues again."

Lenny remained silent, neither denying nor confirming the accusation.

"How many fights does that make for you this year? Three? Four?"

Again, Lenny didn't respond. It looked like he had been through this drill before, and it didn't matter what he did or didn't say, the outcome would be the same.

Mr. Hammock sighed. "You know the drill. Three-day suspension, and—"

If her brother wasn't going to say anything, Emma sure as heck would. "Mr. Hammock, I don't want to say what

Lenny did was right, but there's got to be a better way to handle this than suspension. It seems to me like the rightful place for him to be is here at school where he will be in an adult-supervised environment and learning, rather than cast off to isolation for a given time period."

"I don't think you understand how this works—"

"I know exactly how this works. My brother is pegged for a troublemaker and without even hearing all the details you've already labeled him as the one at fault who deserves to be sentenced in a way that doesn't teach him anything and doesn't solve the problem."

Mr. Hammock took off his glasses and rubbed his eyes before placing the glasses back on his head with a sigh.

"I'm sorry, but your brother's actions can't go unpunished."

"I'm not saying they should. What I'm saying is that maybe there's an alternative. Maybe he stays after school and helps clean classrooms or helps plan the eighth-grade dance or does extra homework in classes under the supervision of teachers."

"Emma," Lenny hissed. "What are you doing?"

"Shush," she told him.

"You're making everything worse," her brother scolded. "I'm fine being suspended."

She mustered up a hard-nosed older sister look and threw it at him. "Then you shouldn't have called me, because I'm not letting you get suspended."

Mr. Hammock watched the exchange between them. He leaned back in his chair as if contemplating a whole new set of possibilities.

"Your father usually just goes along with whatever decisions we make."

"And our father is a good man, doing his highest sense of right. However, it doesn't seem like suspending Lenny again will do anything good for him or anyone else since he's already proven a suspension doesn't automatically mean no more fights."

"I see that," Mr. Hammock muttered, leaning forward to rest his elbows on his desk. "All right. Give me this evening to look into a few possibilities, and I'll let Lenny know his punishment tomorrow."

"Thank you, sir," Emma said. "And what about the other boy?"

"What other boy?"

"The one Lenny fought with."

"Technically, he didn't throw a punch so there's nothing we can do."

"With all due respect," Emma said, "Fists aren't the only weapons people use in a fight. Just because some kid knows how to use words to slice through a person's heart and avoid punches doesn't make him innocent."

"Now you sound like Ms. Winters." Mr. Hammock sighed again. "All right fine, I'll look into it."

"And?"

"And determine an equal punishment for the other boy too."

Emma nodded her approval. "Thank you."

"Now get out of my office before I end up giving you my car as part of some wacky reward system."

"But—"

Emma grabbed her brother's arm to prevent him from altering the course of action and hauled him to his feet. Grasping his shoulder, she gave him a small shove toward the door.

"Thank you for taking the time to talk to us, Mr. Hammock, and thank you for not suspending my brother."

Without looking away from his computer, Mr. Hammock waved them out of his office as if he could no longer stand the sight of them.

She latched the office door behind them. As soon as they were back in the main office, Lenny turned on her. "What did you do that for? I was fine getting suspended."

"Yeah, well, I wasn't fine with it. I don't like the idea of you sitting at home for three days doing nothing when you could be at school. Besides, you probably don't need to miss any more classes."

"Yeah, but plan the school dance or do extra homework? Did you have to suggest those? I'll be the biggest loser in school."

"Maybe next time you'll figure out a different way to solve problems than using your fists.

"Lenny!"

Tara's voice cut off his response, but it didn't prevent him from grumbling as he turned to face his friend.

"What happened?"

"Thanks to my sister, I didn't get suspended. I'll probably end up having to clean up litter or plan the stupid school dance."

Tara's eyes nearly bugged out of her head. "Really?" she squeaked, sounding like a junior high girl for the first time since Emma met her. "I'm on the dance committee, and we could use your help. It would be so much fun."

Emma elbowed Lenny in the shoulder and whispered, "You're welcome."

She returned to her seat near the door, giving Tara and her brother some privacy. She wondered how many times Lenny had been suspended, how many times some punk kid said the right words to set Lenny's fists flying.

Emma and Lenny exited the school, preparing to walk the three miles to their house, only to find Tyler's car still parked at the curb. Emma stopped walking, anger boiling to the surface. What would Tyler do if they ignored him and just kept going?

"What's wrong?" Lenny asked.

The passenger door on the car popped open and Tyler's head appeared. The side of his mouth tilted up, and he shrugged as if to say he couldn't just leave and she couldn't not accept his offer for a ride home.

"Nothing," she muttered, guiding him toward the car. She popped the seat forward to let her brother slide into the back.

"Who's this?" Lenny asked, gesturing to Tyler.

"You don't want to know," she mumbled.

Tyler spun around in his seat and held out his hand as Lenny scrambled into the back. "I'm Tyler."

"Lenny," her brother said with a head nod as he grasped Tyler's hand. "You're not dating my sister, are you?"

She spun around in her seat to glare at her brother. "Of course not!"

"Hey," Tyler said. "You make it sound like I have the plague or something."

"I'm not entirely sure you don't."

"Good," Lenny said. "Because I like Riley better."

"Yeah, well, Riley's the idiot who let your sister go."

"What?" Lenny said as he thrust his head between the front seats to stare openmouthed at his sister. "Since when?"

"What's it been now?" Tyler asked. "Two weeks?"

She didn't need Tyler's smugness to hit his point home. "Shut up."

"Two weeks? Oh," Lenny said, his voice trailing off.

Tyler glanced between the siblings. "Oh, what?"

Lenny remained focused on Emma as his face softened. "So, the night you cleaned the kitchen…"

She turned to stare out the passenger side window. "Yeah."

"What am I missing?" Tyler's tone bordered on desperate.

"Nothing," Emma and Lenny both responded.

"Just because you're not with Riley doesn't mean you have to go for this guy." Lenny flicked his thumb over his shoulder at Tyler.

"Don't worry," she assured him. "I'm not going for this guy."

"And why shouldn't she go for me?"

"Because you're a jerk and my sister deserves better."

"How do you know I'm a jerk? You just met me."

"Exactly," Lenny said, like he knew other kids like Tyler and could identify them as jerks in 2.5 seconds. "Plus, it's written all over your face and in the way you hold the steering wheel."

Emma laughed. "My brother has you pegged."

"Maybe I'm being a jerk because that's what guys like me do when they like a girl."

"That's no excuse, and you don't like my sister. She amuses you, there's a difference. And if you do anything to hurt her, you'll regret it."

"What are you going to do to me?"

Lenny smirked. "We have older brothers. And they have friends. And *they* have friends. And nobody messes with my sister."

Tyler's laughter filled the car. "I like your brother. You're lucky to have him."

Her eyes connected with Lenny's. "Yeah, I am." It didn't matter that his threat toward Tyler didn't carry much merit. After all, she couldn't imagine Lance ever sticking up on her behalf, and Logan had never been much of a fighter, but it didn't matter. The fact that Lenny would was enough for her.

♦♦♦

Tyler pulled into the Wrangtons' driveway and Lenny let out a growl from the backseat.

"What's wrong?" Tyler asked, turning in his seat to look at Lenny.

Emma didn't need to hear her brother's answer. "Our dad's home."

"So?"

"So he's early. He's never home before six, which means…" Emma looked over her shoulder at Lenny.

"He knows," Lenny finished for her.

"He knows what?" Tyler asked, switching his focus to Emma. "What happened?"

"Nothing," Emma said, unbuckling her seatbelt.

"Princess."

She ignored Tyler, popped open the door, and got out. Reaching down to scoot the seat forward, she waited for Lenny to climb out of the back before sliding the seat back into its normal position.

Tyler's hand lashed out and grabbed her wrist. "Princess," he breathed. She was surprised to find his eyes filled with worry. "You don't have to go into details, but just tell me, if you walk through that door," he nodded toward the front of her house, "are you going to be okay? Do I need to worry about you or your brother?"

She shook her head and gave him a small smile, touched by his concern. "No, we'll be fine." Sure, their dad would probably be angry that Lenny had gotten into another fight, and maybe yelling would pursue, but Emma knew that's as bad as it would get.

"Promise?"

"Yeah, I promise."

His fingers reluctantly released her.

"I'll see you tomorrow." She closed the door and raised her hand in goodbye as she followed Lenny up the front steps and into the house. Lenny stopped inside the door and looked up at her. He opened his mouth to speak, but she shook her head knowing what was coming. "There's no point in trying to hide it, so we may as well get it over with."

"You're coming with me?" Lenny asked surprised.

She placed a hand on her brother's shoulder. "Of course."

When they entered the kitchen, their dad looked up from his spot at the table, disappointment clouding his face. "Another fight, huh?"

Lenny threw up his arms and his head rolled from one shoulder to the other as he let out a growl. "How did you know?"

"Did you think the school wouldn't call me?" their dad asked. "No matter who comes to the school to get you, I'm your parent. They'll always call me."

Lenny grumbled something unintelligible.

Their dad scooted the chair out from under the table and stood. "Lenny, we've talked about this. You promised me no more fights."

"It wasn't my fault!"

"It never is." Their dad's controlled voice counteracted Lenny's boisterous one.

"Great. You don't believe me. You never believe me!"

Emma stayed quiet, refusing to take sides.

Their dad pinched the bridge of his nose, obviously tired of the same old conversation when discussing Lenny's latest fight. "How long did you get suspended for this time?"

Lenny crossed his arms over his chest and frowned at the ground. "I didn't."

Their dad looked up in surprise. "You didn't what? Get suspended?"

"No."

Emma met her dad's eyes and figured she should clarify. "I kind of convinced the vice principal to let Lenny stay in school."

"You did?" their dad asked in disbelief.

She shrugged. "I didn't think banning him from school was the best solution, so I asked for an alternative punishment."

"Meaning?"

Lenny threw up his arms again, clearly not having come to terms with Emma's tactics yet. "Meaning now I'll probably have to clean gum off of desks or plan the stupid dance at school with a whole bunch of girls."

His scrunched face communicated so much disgust,

Emma bowed her head to hide a smile, while their dad snorted and turned away, trying to hold back laughter.

Lenny glared up at her. "It's not funny!"

"I know," she said patting him on the shoulder and wiping the grin off her face. "But it won't be that bad. Besides, I thought you'd like spending time with Tara."

Lenny's cheeks tinted red as their dad asked. "Who's Tara?"

"No one." Lenny spun around like his pants were on fire and ran out of the room.

"I don't know whether you've made a friend or an enemy," her dad said.

Emma didn't know what the altercations from her actions with Lenny might be, but she hoped one day he'd understand why she couldn't let him get kicked out of school again. He deserved better and if he kept missing school, she hated to think how that would impact his future.

"I'm sorry he pulled you out of school to meet with the vice principal. I could've left work and gone myself if they'd called me earlier."

"Dad, it's fine. I'm glad I could help. I'm surprised he had them call me at all."

"Your little brother's an interesting one." Her dad looked in the direction of Lenny's escape as if putting the pieces of his son together. "He acts tough, like he doesn't care about anything, but I think deep down he cares a lot. He fights because he's trying to prove he's worth something and he doesn't know how else to show it. Like Lucas, I think Lenny just wants to be loved. I do my best, but..."

His voice trailed off and the wave of sadness almost brought Emma to her knees. She touched his arm. "Dad, you're doing great."

He forced out a smile and patted her hand, like he appreciated her attempt to make him feel better, but he didn't believe her words.

"I've got some work to do in the shed out back, but I'll

be back in to cook dinner."

In other words, he needed time alone. She let him go rather than try to make him feel better. Despite not knowing what to say, she sensed now was one of those times that the assurance of others wasn't enough to destroy the self-condemning thoughts of one's own convictions.

♦♦♦

The next night, Emma and Lucas finished their homework early and decided to play a game of cards. Lucas sat across the bed from her, his brows furrowed in concentration, a hand poised over the discarded cards between them.

She peeled the top card off the pile in her hand, and with the speed of a slug, lowered it to within inches of her mattress before flipping it over. In the time it took her to drop the card and get her hand ready, Lucas slapped her card. "Slapjack!"

"Ugh," she groaned flopping back onto her bed. "That's like ten in a row for you."

Lucas smirked as he gathered the cards and added them to the bottom of his growing pile. She looked to her own dwindling stack where only a handful of cards remained. If she had any hope of winning, she seriously needed to step up her game.

Suspended in the air over where his card was sure to land, her hand buzzed in anticipation. He laid down a four of hearts. She played a ten of spades. They switched turns, waiting for a jack to appear: a two of diamonds, a two of hearts, a king of clubs, an ace of diamonds. Waiting for Lucas to add his card to the pile, something made Emma's eyes flicker, not to the waiting pile, but to his fingertips. Instead of drawing the card on top of his pile, he slyly pulled from the bottom. Before she could say anything, he dropped the card. "Slapjack!"

"You little cheater," she exclaimed.

"What?" He looked up from his victory pile but failed to hide his smile or his laughter. "I'm not cheating."

"Yes, you are." No wonder she'd been losing!

"What do you mean? I didn't do anything." Yeah, she had to look away so his cuteness didn't work its magic. She tossed her cards aside and pounced. Her tickle fingers attacked his ribs. He squealed beneath her and tried to wiggle away, but she was bigger and stronger. His little legs kicked and caught her a few times, but they were both laughing so hard his defenses lacked any real punch.

"Help!" Lucas screamed, his arms stretching out to the side as if reaching for someone.

Emma took her eyes off of Lucas to acknowledge Lenny. "Hey," she said unable to hide her surprise at him being in her room. It seemed as if, one by one, her family members were breaking through the invisible barrier that had separated her from them for so long. Instead of feeling irritated at the lack of privacy, she welcomed their visits. It made her feel like her garage/bedroom was more of a haven than an outcast's cave. Their presence destroyed the feeling of isolation and made her feel like part of the family.

She paused her attack on Lucas to give him the chance to breathe. "What's up?"

Lenny smiled shyly. "They broke up."

"Really?" Emma didn't have to ask who. She jumped off of Lucas and gave her full attention to Lenny.

Lucas rolled away from her, seeking refuge in the corner of her bed, out of her reach, breathing hard.

Lenny nodded. "She saw him harassing a sixth grader and made a public display of breaking up with him."

"Good for her."

"Yeah," Lenny said as his cheeks turned red. "I wish it was Valentine's Day or something so I could do something nice for her."

"It doesn't have to be a holiday for you to do something

nice for a girl. Just do it."

Lenny's voice filled with doubt. "Won't that be weird?"

Emma had been around enough girls that she could answer this one honestly. "Nope. Girls love it when you surprise them, especially when it's not a holiday."

"But what should I do?" Lenny plopped down on the bed beside Lucas.

Emma shrugged. "How should I know?"

"Because you're a girl."

"Yeah, but that doesn't mean I know anything about them." Especially considering her one and only relationship had sunk like the Titanic. "Maybe you should talk to Lance or Logan about this. Or dad. I'm sure they have experience winning the hearts of girls and would know exactly what to do."

"Emma, come on." Lenny scooted closer to her. "You know they'll laugh at me and make me feel stupid. I'm asking you." She never thought she'd see the day when any of her brothers asked her advice, especially Lenny.

"What about flowers?" Lucas suggested

They turned and stared at him.

"All girls like flowers," Lucas defended his words.

"How would you know?" Lenny asked.

"Because they do. All the girls in my class are, like, flowers are *soooo* pretty. They smell *soooo* good. I *loooove* flowers. And they draw them all over. It's gross."

Emma and Lenny laughed at his high-pitched imitation of girls.

"There you go," Emma said. "Flowers it is."

Lenny turned back to Emma. "Do you like flowers?"

"Me?" His question caught her off guard since she'd never thought about it. "I, uh, I don't know. I guess."

"What do you mean you guess? You either do or you don't." Lenny waited in vain for her answer. "Would you like it if some guy gave you flowers?"

What she wouldn't give for their mom to be here so a

more experienced female could answer their questions. Moms always knew the right answers. Emma, on the other hand, had no clue. Too bad she couldn't freeze time and run over and ask Riley's mom. "I don't know. No one's ever gotten me flowers before."

"Really?" Lucas asked with a scrunched up face. "Not even Riley?"

"Nope."

"Do you want him to?" Lenny asked.

She never pegged herself for a romantic, but she had to admit, if Riley showed up out of the blue and presented her with flowers, she certainly wouldn't toss them. "Yeah. I mean no. No, I just..." she stopped and took a deep breath. "If Riley got me flowers, I'd love them."

Lenny nodded, satisfied with her answer. "Okay, so flowers it is. What kind?"

"Doesn't matter," Lucas said. "Just make sure they're not dead or filled with bugs. For some reason, girls hate that."

Twenty-Three

Drenched in sweat from her pick-up game with the girls, Emma walked home thinking about whether or not college was in her future. Over the past few weeks, one by one, colleges had dropped her from their radar. Not enough experience. They decided to go with someone else. Scholarship funds weren't available. She probably wouldn't see much playing time for the first two years. The endless reasons drove Emma crazy. Her hope diminished with every rejection. She didn't have many options to begin with considering her late start to the whole recruitment game.

The deadline for signing with a college loomed in the near future, and since she hadn't heard from Coach Krola in a while, Emma knew her chances weren't good for Oregon State either. They did have other recruits on their list with way more experience, so it made sense. Besides, Division I ball came with a lot of pressure and Emma didn't know if she was ready for that yet. A few Division II schools sounded promising and the site visits had gone well, but the radio silence did nothing for Emma's confidence.

A loud crash welcomed her as she stepped across the threshold into her house. She dropped her backpack on the floor and ran to the kitchen to determine the source. She certainly didn't want Lucas to have to fend for himself against the wrath of Lance again.

Logan whipped his head around. "Emma," he exhaled in relief. "Thank God you're home."

She took a step back, ready to run. Her last real interaction with Logan consisted of him telling her she wasn't worth much and that she should give up her dreams of playing college ball. "Why?"

"I'm trying to make this stupid casserole thing, but I keep messing everything up."

"Okay," she said slowly, not understanding why her brother thought she could help.

Speaking in a volume twice what he needed to, Logan provided background information.

"Lucas wouldn't shut up about wanting one of your meals for dinner. I didn't know where you were or if you were coming home, so I figured I'd give it a shot, but—"

Something on the stove sizzled and popped. Logan flinched and muttered a curse under his breath. "Ow! The stupid grease won't stop attacking me. What am I doing wrong?"

He turned to Emma, waiting for a response.

She leaned toward the stove trying to get a better look at what he was cooking. "Number one, how am I supposed to know and number two, since when do you cook?"

He stood beside her and watched the sauce in another pan bubble and hiss like he was afraid to stir it. "Number one, you've cooked before and number two, since when do you?"

"The things I've cooked before consisted of less than five ingredients or they were a matter of dumping cans into a pot and heating it up. Beyond that I'm clueless. And in terms of me cooking..." She let her words trail off, trying to decide if she should be honest or not.

Her brother turned toward her as if he sensed her holding something back. "What?"

If it wasn't for his genuine interest she probably wouldn't have said anything. "I wanted to do something nice for everyone, and I thought since we don't have many home-cooked meals it might be nice to cook for all of you."

"Oh."

That's all he said. Emma waited for more but apparently her brother was a guy of few words, except for when he was being attacked by burning grease.

Even if she could offer advice, she didn't know where to start. Dirty dishes, half chopped vegetables, and empty boxes littered the counters. So much for her cleaning job last night.

He waved his arms at the kitchen. "What am I supposed to do? I have all this food and I don't know how to cook any of it."

Laughter burst from Emma's mouth at the chaos of the situation. She clamped a hand over her mouth in the attempt to force it back down, but she couldn't contain it.

"It's not funny," Logan scolded her, but a smile fought its way through his scowl. Within seconds their laughter built until they could hardly stand and they gasped for breath. Something about kitchen catastrophes could really bond people.

Having never shared a moment like this with Logan, she committed every second of it to memory: how his deep laughter joined hers, how his eyes crinkled when he smiled, how his hand clutched his stomach as if trying to hold himself together. It was everything she had ever wanted—to share a happy moment with him, a moment untainted by the baggage they always seemed to carry that prevented them from being any sort of friends.

When their laughter subsided, she glanced around at the empty containers and dirty dishes piled on the counters. "I'm sure we can figure something out. Did you read the directions?"

"What directions?"

"The directions on the side of the package?" Emma skimmed the directions on the bacon wrapper, turned down the heat, and tossed the wooden spoon Logan was trying to flip the bacon with into the sink and chose a fork instead. She did her best to scrape the blackening pieces of bacon off the bottom of the pan and flip them. She opened the window above the sink to try and air out some of the smoke. "What are you making?"

"I don't know. Some casserole dish I saw on the cooking station that we had most of the ingredients for."

"You watched a cooking show?"

He shrugged and the muscle in his jaw twitched as if he was preparing for her to make fun of him.

"Maybe I should try that."

Her brother didn't respond, but she could tell her comment pleased him by the way his shoulders relaxed, realizing she wasn't criticizing him but complimenting him.

A cooking adventure among two amateurs. Great. They worked together: chopping, slicing, and mixing, debating over what to do with certain ingredients and how to cook them. They emptied their concoction into a pan and stuck in it the oven. Both of them stood in the middle of the kitchen staring at the closed oven door, Logan biting his nails while Emma crossed her arms over her chest.

"Think it will be edible?" Logan asked.

"I don't know. How high is your tolerance for bad food?" They looked at each other and laughed again.

The kitchen was a disaster. Emma didn't know if the meal they had prepared would be worth the mess. She started collecting dishes and dumping them into the sink. "I'll clean up."

"Not by yourself." Logan grabbed various spices and placed them back in the cupboard. "We made the mess together, we can clean the mess together."

Not the answer she expected, but no way would she turn down his help. "Fine, but whatever that gunk is plastered on the side of the refrigerator is all you. If it's lethal, I don't want to be the one to die because I touched it."

Logan gave her a playful shove as he headed toward the lethal substance. "Wimp."

♦♦♦

Lucas came bounding through the family artifacts that littered the garage and launched onto her bed, crumpling half of her homework in the process. "That wasn't one of your best meals," he declared.

Emma laughed. "And yet you cleared your plate and had seconds."

He sprawled across her bed on his back. "I liked it; it just wasn't my favorite."

Thankful her and Logan's concoction proved edible, she tousled his hair. "Then next time you can cook."

He made no motion to move, and as usual, she didn't have the heart to kick him off. Staring at the ceiling as if looking for stars, he seemed content to lie beside her, so she let him have his thoughts while she attempted to finish her homework.

"Do you think Mom will ever come back?" Lucas's words set Emma on edge. He didn't ask the question with longing or regret in his voice like Emma often did, and she had to remind herself that he had been a toddler when their mom left and he probably didn't remember her that well.

Emma frantically tried to find an answer to satisfy him, but she failed.

"Logan and Lenny say no, but I think Lance thinks she will. Someday." He seemed indifferent, but she wasn't sure of his exact feelings about the woman who had left him without a mom. What was Emma supposed to say when she'd asked herself the same question a million times? "What do you think?" he asked.

For lack of a better answer, all she could say was, "I

don't know. I wish I could tell you she will. I wish I could tell you that she loves you and is doing everything in her power to come back to us, but I don't know." She didn't want him dreaming of their mom's return; she'd rather spare him the potential disappointment if their mom never came back. "I'm sorry."

Lucas shrugged. "It's okay. At least we have you." His smile could heal the worst pain. "You're never gonna leave us, right?"

The poor kid wanted a mom, needed a mom, but all he had was an older sister who'd just started making up for lost time. The guilt swelled within her. Did going away to college count as leaving? She wanted to ask, but didn't want to disappoint him. She'd save that conversation for another day. Besides, even if college did work out, she wouldn't abandon her brothers. "Right," she assured him. "I'm not going anywhere. But I can't guarantee you won't get sick of me. Especially when…" She paused, waiting for her brother to question her. When he did, she pounced on him. "The tickle monster needs a victim!" He crumpled in a heap of giggles as she attacked his sides with her fingers, putting off potential heartbreak for another day.

Twenty-Four

After Lucas's question about their mom, Emma spent the following day feeling the loss, not of her own mom, but of Riley's. Unlike her brothers, Emma had been fortunate enough over the years to have Mrs. L as a designated mom, but for the past month, Emma had been momless too.

She stared at the pot resting on the kitchen counter. It didn't have eyes or anything resembling face-like features, but she could feel it staring at her anyway. Mrs. Ledger's pot. Emma knew she needed to return it, she'd had it way too long and Mrs. Ledger probably thought Emma had stolen it, but ever since Riley broke up with her, she'd avoided their house. Now, with Lucas's question about their mom hanging over her and an overwhelming desire to see Mrs. L, Emma knew she had to do the unthinkable.

Glancing at the clock, she saw that it was a little after two. Being Saturday, Riley should still be at the court playing basketball with the guys for another couple of hours. She should be safe to venture over to the Ledgers' for ten minutes without having a run-in with her ex-boyfriend. Her chest tightened at the thought of Riley being her ex anything.

Gathering courage, she grabbed the pot from the counter.

Every step toward the Ledgers' house was deliberate, forced. Hoping Riley's parents didn't forbid her entry into their house in some united front for their son, she begrudgingly ascended the front porch steps and raised her hand to knock.

Mr. Ledger answered the door. His face lit up when he saw her standing before him.

"Hi, Mr. Ledger," she said, barely able to meet his eyes.

He pulled her in for a hug. "Hi, sweetheart. How've you been?" No, he wouldn't elaborate, but they both knew his question centered around how she's been without Riley.

"Good, I guess." She held up the pot. "I came to return this."

He waved her into the house and motioned toward the hall. "Kate's in the kitchen."

"Thanks, Mr. L."

She sauntered through the house and peeked her head around the corner to look in the kitchen. Mrs. Ledger had her back to Emma, pulling a tray out of the oven. The smell of fresh chocolate chip cookies wafted toward Emma, and she couldn't help but smile.

"I hope you don't plan on eating all of those yourself, because I may have to steal a couple."

Mrs. Ledger glanced over her shoulder. "Emma!" She dropped the tray on the counter and held out her arms. "How are you?"

Emma laughed as she wrapped her arms around the only mom she knew. "I'm good. How are you?"

Mrs. Ledger's arms tightened around Emma's frame. "Better now." She pulled away, grasping Emma by the arms to look at her. "I've missed you."

Emma tried to keep the smile on her face, but she felt tears prick at her eyes at the woman's words. Riley, her best friend of eight years, had cast her aside, requesting space. In part, Emma figured his parents would automatically line up to support him and cast her aside too. The fact both his parents welcomed her with open arms, despite Riley's decision, made the situation all the more heartbreaking. Riley hadn't robbed her of just a best friend/boyfriend, but of two parents as well.

Mrs. Ledger never failed to notice anything. Her forehead crinkled as she observed Emma. "Sweetheart, what is it? What did I say?"

Emma shook her head, trying her best to clear the tears from her eyes with a fake smile. "Nothing. You didn't say anything. I just didn't know if you'd want to see me, since, you know, Riley doesn't—"

With a hand on her hip, Mrs. Ledger huffed. Yes, an actual huff. "That son of mine. I could disown him for breaking your heart like that."

Emma fell into a chair beside the kitchen table, propping her arms on the table. "I don't even know what I did," she said in little more than a whisper.

"Nothing." Mrs. Ledger's voice was quiet but firm as she gripped Emma's chin and held her gaze. "Whatever is going on with Riley, it is *not* your fault. You didn't do anything wrong."

Emma pulled at the string on her sweatshirt, her focus anywhere but on Mrs. Ledger. "How is he?"

"He misses you."

She dared to look up and meet Mrs. Ledger's eyes. "He said that?"

"Of course he hasn't said it," she said. "He's too proud for that. But a mother knows when her son's heart is hurting—when a piece of him isn't quite whole." She squeezed Emma's shoulder. "He'll find his way back to you. I promise."

"I wish that were true, but I think—" Emma paused to force back tears. "I think it's over between us. He hasn't talked to me in weeks, and he's acting like I don't exist...like I never did."

Mrs. Ledger flung her arms around Emma and pulled her into a hug. Her mothering gesture was too much. Emma's dam of tears broke, and she buried her head in Mrs. Ledger's shoulder. Her entire body shook as she freed the sobs that had welled up over the past month. Mrs. L let her cry as she rubbed Emma's back and whispered reassurances to her.

Emma was so caught up in her sob fest that she didn't hear the front door close or the approaching footsteps.

"Hey, Mom, I—"

Emma jerked her body from Mrs. Ledger's arms at the sound of Riley's voice, her eyes bulging at the prospect of facing him. He was supposed to be gone. He wasn't supposed to come home and see her falling to pieces in his mom's arms. Emma frantically swiped at the traitorous tears streaming down her cheeks, but they kept coming.

"Emma?" Riley's tone was filled with confusion, as if he didn't know why in the world she would be here. Since he wanted space, she guessed she had no right to be in his house.

Ignoring her son, Mrs. Ledger gripped Emma's arms in support, silently encouraging her to take deep breaths and not freak out. Emma felt more than heard Riley take another step closer.

She needed to escape. Now. Without it seeming like he was the reason she needed to bolt.

Be cool, she told herself. "Hey, Riley." Her greeting would've been great if her voice hadn't cracked on his name. "I was just leaving."

She stood, gathering courage and keeping her back to Riley so he couldn't see her face. "Thanks for the pot, Mrs. L." Despite her attempt to appear strong, her voice wobbled. Darn emotions. She gave Mrs. Ledger a smile of thanks.

"You're welcome," Mrs. Ledger said with a sympathetic smile of her own.

Emma spun around, desperate to be outside and away

from Riley, but she miscalculated her escape. Instead of spinning around Riley toward the open doorway, she slammed into his chest. Half expecting him to push her away, she was surprised when his arms clamped around her and squeezed her against him without hesitation. Great. It was bad enough he caught her crying her eyes out over him, but with the way she face-planted into his chest, he probably thought she had planned the whole thing to get his attention.

His head bowed, bringing his lips near her ear. "Emma."

How he could still fill her name with such tenderness and love she would never know, since his actions communicated something way different. She hated how being in his arms still felt like home. Oh how she wished things between them could go back to the way they were. Even if they could only be friends, she preferred anything over them being nothing at all.

Pulling back, she made the mistake of looking into his eyes. They were filled with regrets and apologies and sadness, and she waited for him to say something, to take it all back and tell her their break was over and that he no longer needed space away from her. His hands cradled her face, his thumbs lightly brushing her cheeks and freeing them from tears. "I'm sorry," he whispered.

Sorry? He was sorry? For what? For saying he needed space? For not talking to her for weeks? For breaking up her moment with his mom? What exactly was he sorry for?

"I think I messed up."

Understatement of the year!

She waited but he didn't elaborate, as if he expected her to read his mind and spare him from having to find the right words. Not this time. If he was truly sorry, he'd have to find a way to convince her using more than a few mumbled syllables.

"I should go," she whispered back. She broke free from his embrace and raced to the door.

"Emma," he called after her.

Her steps slowed as she reached the front door and realized Riley wasn't following her. Wiping tears from her eyes to clear her vision, she stepped onto the porch. Tyler leaned against the post, arms crossed over his chest, his eyes peered up at her from his downturned head. "You okay?"

Emma groaned. It was bad enough Riley caught her in the middle of a meltdown; she didn't need Tyler as a witness too. "Peachy," she spit out.

She could only imagine what she looked like—blotchy cheeks, bloodshot eyes, red nose.

He shrugged away from the wall and, wrapping his arms around her, pulled her against him. One hand splayed out against her back, smashing her to him, and his other hand sandwiched her head against his chest. Emma's arms remained limp at her sides.

"Why are you hugging me?"

"Because you're crying."

"So?"

"So, this is what guys do when girls cry."

"Since when do you classify me as a girl?"

"Since you started crying."

"That's stupid."

"I know," he mocked her, patting her head like she was a toddler. She tried to wiggle free from his embrace, but he held fast. "I'm trying to comfort you. Stop fighting it."

Forgetting her tears, Emma snorted out a laugh. "Since when do you care about comforting me?"

"I don't."

"Then why are you hugging me?"

Tyler sighed. "Because you're crying. We've been over this."

She was glad he couldn't see her face; glad he couldn't see her growing smile. "I guess we have."

"Besides, by the way you stormed out of the house, I figured I should hug you as a way to restrain you before you punched me."

She laughed. "Ah, the truth comes out. You're afraid of me."

"If that's what you need to believe to sleep at night." She felt him bow his head, hiding his face in her hair to hide his laughter, but his chest rumbled anyway.

For some unknown reason, she relaxed against him. Her hands grabbed the sides of his shirt. Not a full hug, but maybe a small gesture that she kinda maybe sorta appreciated him in that solitary moment.

"Are you really okay?" he murmured against her head.

If she hadn't known better, she would've thought he truly cared about her answer. Biting her tongue so she didn't say something hurtful, she nodded against his chest.

"You don't need me to punch him, do you?"

"Why do you always think someone should punch someone else? There are other ways to solve problems, you know." Not that she was one to talk. Growing up around the guys, she'd thrown her fair share of punches.

She expected him to come back with some smart aleck comment, but he didn't. He just held her tighter and murmured, "I know. Just not ways I'm good at."

Pulling back to look up at him, she asked, "Have you tried?"

He opened his mouth to respond, but something caught his attention. "If you don't want another face-to-face with lover boy, I suggest you go now."

She followed his line of sight. Sure enough, she could see Riley inside the house, heading their way. She didn't want a repeat of before. "Thanks for the warning. I'll see you later."

"Hey," he called after her. He rubbed the back of his neck as he peered up at her. "You wanna hang out later? Maybe catch a movie or play basketball or something?"

She always thought Tyler was hard and cold, cocky and conceited, but in that moment, the guy looked a little uncertain of himself. Maybe he was just like everyone else;

maybe even Tyler needed a friend. She shrugged, having nothing better to do. "Sure."

The horror of humiliating herself in front of Riley haunted Emma as she found refuge at home and refused to leave, in fear she'd run into him again. Sure, Tyler had brought a momentary smile to her face as he tried to comfort her, but her thoughts kept going back to Riley. She was over him, had been for a while, or at least she thought she'd been getting better, but running into him at his house made her question that fact. She didn't have the heart to analyze her feelings and admit guilt. What she needed was a distraction...a *big* one.

Since she'd managed to keep the kitchen at least partly clean, there wasn't much to distract her in terms of cleaning and no way was she going to play servant girl and pick up after her brothers throughout the rest of the house. Through the front window, she spotted weeds overtaking the front yard and the overgrown bushes crawling up the side of the house that she despised. The chaos drew her to it.

Twenty minutes later, covered in dirt, she smeared sweat across her forehead. She'd always hated these stupid bushes. Yanking from the base of the ferns, she tried pulling them out from the roots. They put up quite the fight. The more she pulled, the tighter they clung to the earth. Anger bubbled within her, determined to prove dominion over shrubbery. With one final tug, she pulled one free and grunted in victory as it showered her with dirt. "Take that," she said with satisfaction, throwing it across the yard. "Stupid plant," she muttered.

She set her sights on the next one as the front door opened and Lucas plopped down on the front steps to watch her. He didn't say anything and neither did she. He seemed to understand her need to work out her frustration, and she loved him for it. His presence, along with the lingering thoughts about Riley invading her consciousness, made her even more determined to gain victory over every last bush that didn't belong in the front yard.

Her anger didn't dissipate as she worked, but at least now she had an outlet and could mutter as many complaints about Riley and their failed relationship without worrying about the consequences of her unfiltered spouts. "Stupid boyfriend," she muttered, adjusting her grip on the fern's base. "Needing space from me." Yank. "It's *me* who needs space from *you*." Tug. "Never want to be friends again. Fine." Pull accompanied by a grunt. "Have a nice," one final heave, "*life!*"

Another bush taken down. She threw her latest victory into the slowly growing pile of shrubs and tackled the next one. Trying to gain an advantage, she dropped to her knees and dug out the dirt around the base of the next shrub, vaguely aware that Lucas was no longer alone.

"What is she doing?" Lenny asked.

"Pulling weeds," Lucas said.

"Why?"

Lucas shrugged. "Don't know."

"She looks mad."

"Yeah."

"It looks like she's digging a grave."

"Yeah," Lucas nodded. "Probably for Riley."

"Riley?" Logan appeared in the open doorway behind them. "Why would she want to bury Riley?"

Lenny dropped down next to Lucas. "He broke her heart."

"What do you mean he broke her heart?" Logan inquired, shrugging off the door frame.

Lucas swiveled his head to look up at Logan. "They were boyfriend-girlfriend."

"Since when?" Logan asked.

"Since a while ago."

"But they broke up?" Logan's voice was filled with confusion.

This time it was Lenny who answered. "Yep."

Emma heard her brothers, but refused to respond. It wasn't like any of the events in her life were secret. At least not anymore. Their talking ceased for a few minutes as they watched her attempt to displace another fern that proved to be obnoxiously strong.

"Is it true girls go crazy when they break up with a guy?" Lenny asked.

They were all silent again as they watched Emma plant one foot against the side of the house for leverage. She heaved, every muscle in her body bracing against the strain.

"Apparently," Logan said as Emma's effort dominated over the vegetation once again. She stumbled backward, almost losing her footing, as the fern broke at the base, leaving the root still intact.

"I can hear you, you know," she yelled, flinging the fern in their direction. "And if you don't all shut up, I'm going to dig a grave to fit all of you."

Lucas grinned at her. "Except me, right Em?"

Smiles of guilt grew on their faces. She'd spent so many years seeing their frowns and scowls that their smiles, no matter how guilty, made her forgive them on the spot. Lenny leaned over to Lucas and whispered something in his ear before they disappeared. Thinking they abided by her wish and left, she returned to her weeds, despite Logan's lingering presence on the porch.

The first spray of water hit her on the back and she screamed. The freezing water soaked into her shirt and there was nothing to stop it. The next squirt spun her around toward the source. Lucas and Lenny held the hose spray nozzle in their hands, aimed directly at her chest. Both of her little brothers laughed hysterically.

"Don't you dare," she warned.

Their mischievous grins alone told her she didn't stand a chance. She charged them as they squeezed the handle and fired an unrelenting stream of water at her. She screamed to ward off the cold, but it didn't help, nor did her lame attempt to shield her body with her hands. When she got within reach of her brothers, they dropped the hose and ran, their laughter carrying in their wake. She was all about retaliation. Grabbing the hose from the ground, she raced after them only to be shot in the head from the opposite direction. She froze in surprise as Logan's laughter accompanied the next shot toward her from his Super Soaker. From there it was an all-out war.

Within minutes, Emma was soaked. It seemed her brothers were all ganging up on her. *Bring it,* she thought. Given all she'd been through, a little water never hurt. She advanced on her younger brothers who had once again claimed possession of the hose, but she was determined to get it back. They retreated until their backs hit the house and they exchanged glances of fear. Emma wrestled the hose from their hands and turned the spray on them as they took off in opposite directions only to converge once they passed Emma. They grunted and squealed and sprinted toward the front of the house where Logan hit them with the spray from his Super Soaker. The two boys were caught between a water ambush. Drenching her younger brothers was fun and all, but Logan didn't look wet enough. She turned the hose on him, and he gasped in surprise before erupting in laughter.

The sound of tires crunching gravel announced Lance's arrival. He parked his CR-X and stepped out of the car. He glanced at his siblings and his scowl deepened as he headed toward the house. Emma thought maybe it was a great way to include him in their fun, and who didn't like a water fight? She aimed the hose at Lance and fired, the spray of water catching him in the back. Their brothers laughed, and Emma felt her smile join theirs, but Lance found no humor in the gesture. He barreled over to her, his glare unforgiving.

"What the hell was that for?" he yelled.

Okay, so maybe not all of her brothers viewed water wars as fun. Her brother towered over her, demanding answers.

"I'm sorry," she mumbled. "I didn't think you'd—"

"That's right. You didn't think, because you're incapable of doing anything except messing everything up!"

Logan stepped beside her. "Leave her alone, Lance."

Emma swiveled her head toward Logan. Since when did he stick up for her? Especially against Lance.

"She didn't mean—"

Lance shoved a finger in Logan's face and growled, "Stay out of this."

"No." This time it was Lenny's voice.

"What did you say?" Lance sneered, whipping around.

Lenny took a step toward Lance, undeterred by the height difference or the anger that distorted their older brother's face. Lenny puffed out his chest; he wasn't backing down. "I said no. We were just having fun. You should try it sometime; maybe then you wouldn't be such a jerk."

Emma stepped between them as Lance advanced toward Lenny. She reached her hand back, feeling for her little brother, and pushed him back a step. She appreciated her brothers sticking up for her, but she refused to let them put themselves in Lance's warpath. "I'm sorry," she said. "I didn't mean to make you mad. I just thought you might like to join us."

"You thought wrong."

Yeah, he'd made himself clear the first three times. "It won't happen again."

"It better not," he muttered. He gave each of his brother's a glare before stomping into the house.

Emma exhaled, feeling some of the tension leave her body.

Logan touched her arm. "You okay?"

The sincerity in his eyes made Emma's heart clench. She wasn't used to her brothers' concern for her. She managed to nod. "Yeah, I'm fine."

He squeezed her arm. "Good." And then, in a move so quick she had no time to react, he raised his gun and shot her in the chest. The cold water seeped through her already soaked shirt and she stumbled back, her mouth gaping open. Lenny and Lucas started laughing, and their water war resumed as if Lance had never interrupted it.

A few minutes later, their dad's truck rumbled into the driveway. He cut the engine and stepped out, taking in the scene before him. "What are you doing?"

"We're having a water fight," Lucas shouted between his giggles.

Their dad frowned. "It's not even warm outside. Shouldn't this wait for summer?"

Emma and her brothers exchanged shrugs. Sometimes you just couldn't plan the perfect day.

Their dad shook his head as he walked between his kids toward the house. When he passed Emma, he reached for the hose. She relinquished it to him without question, thinking he had final say of their behavior. Before any of them could react, he spun around like a kickboxer, shot Logan in the chest, and showered the rest of them with water. Emma stood frozen as her dad dropped the hose and picked up a laughing Lucas to use as a shield as Logan raised his gun to retaliate.

Lenny and Emma exchanged a look as if they couldn't understand what just happened. Did their dad seriously just join their water fight? The four of them united against their dad, surrounding him on all sides to attack him with water. The sound of her dad's laughter was all she needed to ward away the chill of the day. She never thought she'd hear it, thinking maybe he didn't have a laugh to share with the world, or that it had died out a long time ago. But he proved her wrong, and his laughter made everything she'd been through the last few months worth it.

Having had enough, their soaking dad surrendered, holding up his hands in defeat. "Okay, okay, I think that's enough for one day. Everybody inside. Change into something warm and meet in the kitchen. I'm sure we've got hot chocolate around somewhere."

Emma looked around at her family. The red smiling faces of her brothers mirrored her own. Soaked clothes, freezing temperature, and shivers that wouldn't stop accounted for a pretty perfect day in her book.

Feeling the need to shower, Emma grabbed her things and headed to the bathroom. Three open doors flooded the hallway with light, while one remained closed. She crept in front of the closed door, pausing just outside of it, listening. Silence. She'd thought for sure engaging Lance in some harmless fun would help break down his hatred of her, but it had only made it worse.

She left his door untouched and entered the bathroom, wondering what she would have to do to break through her brother's cloak of darkness and help him see the light, or if that was even possible.

◆◆◆

By the time Emma had showered, dressed, and returned to the kitchen, her brothers were already there. Her brothers, plus one.

"Tyler?" She stopped when she saw him sitting at the table opposite her brothers. "What are you doing here?"

"We had plans to hang out, but I think I'm getting interrogated by your brothers instead."

The protest of wood on wood snapped her attention to Logan who had pushed his chair away from the table and stood. His face was in stark contrast to what it was moments ago, when happiness softened his features. Not taking his eyes off Tyler, Logan said, "Emma, can I talk to you." His words were a command, not a request.

"Uh, sure?"

Logan ushered her into the living room; Lenny and Lucas

followed.

"Who is that guy?" Logan demanded.

"Yeah, I've never seen him before," Lucas piped up.

Emma had to hold back her laughter. Is this what having brothers was really like? "Relax, guys, Tyler's not the devil's spawn or anything, at least not most days. He's a houseguest of Riley's. He's been here for a few months and goes to my school."

"I thought you didn't like him," Lenny said.

"I don't, but he's kind of like an unwanted pet that grows on you."

"What about Riley?" Lenny asked.

"What about him? We broke up. End of story."

"So it's true," Logan mumbled.

Emma bowed her head, knowing he was referring to her relationship with Riley. "Yeah, it's true."

"And you're just going to replace him with that guy?" Lenny pointed in the direction of the kitchen. "No, I don't like it." He crossed his arms and jutted out his chin, challenging her to fight.

"I'm not replacing Riley with anyone. Tyler and I are just friends."

"Does Tyler know that?" Logan asked.

"He should. It's not like I've been leading him on or anything."

Before her brothers could decide whether to trust her or not, their dad interrupted their staring contest.

"Hey," their dad called from the hallway as he joined them. "What's going on, and who's the guy in the kitchen?"

"Yeah," Lenny smirked. "Let's see what Dad has to say about all this."

Before Emma could respond, Lenny spun around to address their dad. "Tyler is Riley's *houseguest.* Ever since Riley and Emma broke up, the guy's been hanging around Emma sporting a look of a wolf after his prey. Emma says he's harmless, but the guy doesn't give up. I'm telling you,

Dad, I don't like it."

Emma rolled her eyes. "Thank you for the debrief, Lenny."

Lucas stepped beside her and slipped his hand into hers. His wide green eyes looked at her and she gave him a smile, squeezing his hand.

"Emma," her dad said, after a thorough examination of the situation. "Let's talk. Boys go back into the kitchen and keep Tyler company. We'll be there in a minute."

Her dad waited until the boys had vacated the room, each of them casting looks over their shoulders as they left.

Facing her, her dad casually crossed his arms. "Seems like you've got three bodyguards in your corner."

"Yeah," she replied. "That's a recent development I wasn't expecting."

"So, what's the story with Tyler?"

"Oh, not you too," she groaned.

Her dad chuckled. "Is he okay? Do I need to play big scary dad for you?"

She laughed at the image, knowing her dad could pull it off. "He's just a friend. Been through some rough stuff, I guess, but I can hold my own with him."

"I don't doubt that for a second." Her dad paused. "How are things with Riley?"

She shrugged. "Same."

"All right, well, it looks like you've got bigger problems right now."

"Why?"

Her dad nodded toward the kitchen. "Your brothers are interrogating your friend, and it looks like your friend is losing."

Between the bodies of her brothers, she saw Tyler losing an arm wrestling match with Logan. She groaned and stalked to the table with the sound of her dad's laughter ringing in her ears. "What are you doing?"

"Nothing," Lenny said, though he sounded way too

250

excited. "Just a little test among men."

"Test among men." She shook her head and broke through her little brothers to pull Tyler and Logan's hands apart. When they didn't budge, she stopped trying. "Are you two seriously doing this?"

"Yep," they both breathed out, their voices and faces strained from the effort.

"Why?"

"If Tyler wins, he can stay and hang out with all of us," Lucas said, "If Logan wins, Tyler leaves."

She could tell he, too, was excited about the competition, but he didn't want to show too much enthusiasm if Emma opposed. She ignored him and turned back to the wrestlers. "And what happened to me making my own decision about whether or not I want to hang out with Tyler?"

"You're a girl; you're unable to make the right decision," Tyler managed to huff out between breaths.

Without hesitation, she grabbed his ear and pulled.

"Ow!" he cried, his focus now on the pain in his ear. "I was kidding."

Taking advantage of the distraction, Logan slammed Tyler's hand down on the table and stood with a victorious smile on his face. "Turns out she's not hanging out with you after all."

Emma cast him a look. He held up his hands in surrender. "Not that you needed me to tell you that."

She dragged a protesting Tyler into the living room, where she reluctantly let him go.

"Geez, woman." He rubbed his ear and glared at her. "What was that for?"

She tilted her head to look at him, raising an eyebrow and pursing her lips.

"It was a *joke*," he said, glancing over her shoulder and flinching a little.

Turning around to see what caught his attention, she muffled laughter when she saw the scowls on her brothers' faces and Lucas pounding a fist into his palm.

"I thought you said your brothers hated you," Tyler whispered into her ear, not taking his eyes off the three boys silently threatening him.

"Yeah, well, things changed."

Tyler grunted but didn't say anything more about her brothers. "You still want to hang out?"

She shrugged. "Sure, why not? What did you have in mind?"

"How about—"

"A movie!" Lenny hollered, striding into the room and heading toward the TV. He wasn't shy about shoving his way between Emma and Tyler, causing them to stumble apart.

"Yeah," Lucas joined in, snatching Emma's hand and pulling her to the couch. He pushed her down into the cushions and immediately hopped up beside her. Before Tyler could claim a seat next to her, Lenny dropped down in the vacant space instead, eyeing Tyler the whole time.

Tyler scratched the back of his head, and resorted to sitting in the armchair across the room. He cast Emma a look, but all she could do was shrug. Apparently, the boys had other plans for them.

Logan sauntered into the room, snatched the remote from the TV stand, and pushed play as he sat in the remaining chair, one that conveniently faced Tyler. Logan sat back in the chair and rested both of his outstretched arms on the armrests. She watched her oldest brother, surprised that he could look threatening when he wanted.

The TV came to life as the video started. Emma expected to see the beginning credits of some action movie but instead, it was a how-to video for home maintenance. It must have been their dad's.

Lenny fidgeted beside her. When she looked over at him and saw his cheeks burn, she got the impression that the 'movie' he chose was not intentional. She expected one of her brothers to balk at the video and waste no time changing it, but they all remained seated, their eyes flickering between each other in silent communication.

Why did it seem like they were all willing to spend their time watching a video none of them had any interest in just so she wouldn't leave the house with Tyler? Why did they act like they wanted to spend time with her? First the water fight, then Tyler's interrogation, and now this?

Her heart swelled with emotion and she blinked back the moisture in her eyes. It took her a minute to realize what she was feeling. After all this time, after everything they'd been through, love for her brothers hadn't died out, it had merely been dormant, waiting to be reactivated.

Knowing there was no other place she'd rather be, she settled back against the couch cushions between her brothers to learn about how to install drywall.

Twenty-Five

Emma missed Saturday games with the guys. Knowing she would miss yet another opportunity to see the guys and play ball, she failed to drag herself out of bed Saturday morning. She stared at the ceiling, wondering if her life would ever return to normal.

She heard shuffling from the other side of the garage. It was a sound she had gotten used to over the past few weeks as her room had suddenly become a high traffic zone for her dad and younger brothers. Having flown solo for so many years, the sound always brought a smile to her face.

"Give them to me," someone whispered.

"No."

"It was my idea."

"Nuh-uh, it was *my* idea. Besides, I'm the youngest."

"Exactly, so you have to do what I say because I'm older. Now, give them to me."

"No."

She held back her smile as she listened to her brothers bicker. "Do I need to intervene before you two start throwing punches?"

Their whispers ceased, as did their footsteps.

Her bed groaned as she rolled into a sitting position. "It's no use boys, I already know you're there. You may as well show yourselves."

The shuffling sounds made Emma think their verbal whispers turned into pushes and shoves. Lucas stumbled into view, glaring over his shoulder at Lenny, who tentatively stepped up behind him. Lenny put a hand on Lucas's shoulder and pushed him forward. She tried to figure out what they were up to, but they gave nothing away, until Lucas pulled his arms from around his back and offered her a handful of flowers. There was no rhyme or reason to their arrangement, just a clump of wildflowers, tulips, daffodils, and peonies.

The mere offering of flowers with their brilliant colors didn't distract Emma from taking in the bigger picture. As her eyes left the beauty of flower petals and traveled down Lenny's dirt covered hands to the straggle of roots at the bottom of the stems, something didn't add up.

"Where did you get these?"

Her brothers shared a look, eyes bulging, frantic shakes of their head as if agreeing to keep their mouths shut.

She stood from her bed and towered over Lucas, knowing he was the weak link...or at least hoping. "Lucas." His eyes snapped to hers. "Where did you get these?"

He shrugged. "Around."

"Around where?"

"What difference does it make? Do you like them?" His grin filled his entire face.

She smiled, unable to resist his enthusiasm and the fact that her little brothers had brought her flowers—no one had ever given her flowers before.

It took her a minute to realize she'd seen the radiant colors before. Separating the curtains over the small dingy garage window, she peered out at their neighbor's yard. Even from across the street she could see the same purple and pink flowers that she held in her hand.

She whipped back around to face her brothers. "You dug

these up from Mr. Farly's yard, didn't you?"

The boys looked at each other again. Lucas's shoulders shrugged, scrunching his face. "Not all of them."

Lenny elbowed him.

"Did you ask him if you could pick his flowers?"

Again, her brothers looked at each other.

"Guys! You can't go around picking flowers from people's yards."

Lenny rolled his eyes. "Who cares? He has plenty, and he never uses them. He just lets them sit there and die."

"That's kind of what flowers do."

"Well, it's stupid," Lucas exclaimed without hesitation. "People should enjoy them."

Emma squeezed her eyes closed, at a loss for how to get her brothers to understand flower thievery. Especially since most of their neighbors already saw the Wrangtons as a family full of troublemakers. She didn't want to give their neighbors any more reason to resent them.

"Aw, c'mon, Emma. You're not really mad at us, are you?" Lenny fingered one of the petals in her hand. "We are the first ones to get you flowers, after all."

Their twin smiles melted her anxiety. She shook her head. Who knew she'd be a sucker for her brothers' puppy dog looks. "I guess I can't be, can I?"

They shook their heads.

"Just promise me you won't steal flowers from people's yards next time, okay?"

Lucas nodded his head, eager to agree as long as she liked the flowers, while Lenny just shrugged.

"Come on," she said. "Let's get these flowers in water so they'll have a life longer than five minutes."

After years of watching Mrs. Ledger cut the stems off flowers and fill vases with her own collection of flowers, Emma sort of had a concept of what to do as she pulled a large cup from the cupboard and cut the roots off the flowers in her hand. Lucas rested his elbows on the counter beside her as he watched.

"What do you want to do today?"

"I don't know," she said. "What do you want to do today?"

He stared up at the ceiling thinking. "Don't you usually play basketball on Saturdays?"

"How did you know that?"

He shrugged. "Lenny and I used to follow you."

She turned to see if Lenny agreed, but he'd already left them to find Saturday morning cartoons on TV. "Yes, I do, but I haven't felt like it lately."

"Why not?"

He already knew about her breakup with Riley, so she didn't feel the need to lie. "Riley's there, and I don't want to ruin it for him by forcing him to deal with me."

"That's stupid."

Emma laughed.

"The other guys are your friends too, right?"

"Yeah."

"Then you should go."

"You think so?"

"Yep."

Something about her brother's confidence weakened her resolution not to go. Maybe it wouldn't be so bad to go, just this once. Even after her breakdown at the Ledgers' a couple days ago, Riley had made no indication he'd wanted to repair their relationship. If her presence didn't affect him, his shouldn't affect her. And it wasn't like she'd have to guard him or talk to him or anything. Besides, she did feel like playing basketball. She glanced down at Lucas. "You wanna come?"

He bounced upright, his eyes growing wide with excitement. "Really?"

"Sure. If I need someone to run interference between me and Riley, you'd be there."

"Let's go!"

The closer they got to the park, the more Emma regretted her decision to invade the guys' basketball games. She didn't want her drama with Riley to ruin the day for anyone. As soon as she saw some of the guys shooting hoops, she grabbed Lucas' shirt to tug him back to the house.

"Well look who it is," Tom called out to her. "You finally decided to come out of hiding and grace us with your presence, huh?"

She smiled, her opportunity to escape lost. "Something like that. Can't have you getting sloppy in your ball skills, can I?"

Tom ignored her jab and nodded toward her brother. "Who's this?"

Emma put her hands on Lucas's shoulders. It was weird that after so many years knowing the guys, they'd never met any of her brothers. "This is my brother, Lucas." The guys nodded greetings. She glanced around the court, searching for Riley, but he had yet to arrive. She breathed a sigh of relief. Maybe he decided not to come today. The guys returned to the hoop to shoot, but Jerry broke free from the group and approached her.

"Hey, Jerry."

He launched himself at her, his arms encircling her neck and squeezing her into a hug. She would've laughed if he wasn't blocking her air supply. Apparently, Jerry had grown stronger in the time she'd been away. "It's good to see you, Em," he whispered in her ear. "I'm glad you came."

She patted him on the back. "Me too."

"Saturday games haven't been the same without you and Riley."

"What do you mean?"

Jerry shrugged. "You haven't been here at all, and Riley only comes for maybe an hour. He doesn't talk to anyone and plays like the game is a complete waste of time. He spends most of his time glancing over his shoulder as if looking for you, and when you don't show, he grunts, shuffles off the court, and leaves without explanation. He's miserable without you."

She certainly hadn't seen that side of Riley. Ever since he broke it off with her, he seemed to be doing just fine. "Yeah, well, it's his own fault."

"Probably, but maybe everything will change now that you're here."

He squeezed her shoulder and joined the rest of the guys near the basket, while she snagged her brother and headed to the other side of the court so he could shoot without having to dodge a dozen balls. She didn't know how much he played basketball, so she tried to give him a few pointers. He took some of them seriously, but mostly he liked dancing in front of her like a monkey to see how many shots she could make over his waving arms. She missed half her shots due to laughing. The boy sure did bring fun into her life. After a couple minutes, he stepped close to her and shielded his mouth with his hands. When she bent over, he whispered in her ear. "Riley keeps looking at you."

Her head swiveled to look over her shoulder, surprised she hadn't noticed him arrive. Sure enough, his blue eyes were locked on her. Unlike other times over the past month, they didn't look away. All she could think about was him finding her a crying mess in the arms of his mom last week. "He's probably wishing I wasn't here." *I wish I wasn't here,* she thought.

Lucas shook his head. "No, it looks like he wants to come over and talk to you."

"What do you think I should do?" Who knew she'd be seeking relationship advice from her eight-year-old brother?

"Let him suffer."

Emma laughed and passed him the ball.

Her brother threw up a one-armed baseball shot that missed the backboard and went flying through the hole in the chain-link fence and into the park. "Good one," she muttered. "Stay here." She jogged toward the ball, trying to ignore the fact that as soon as she left, Riley made his way over to Lucas. *He's probably just trying to be nice,* she thought.

Even though they weren't together, Riley was still Riley. He was still a nice guy who was probably keeping Lucas company while she retrieved the ball. She glanced over her shoulder to check on her brother. Arms crossed, sneer in place. Emma may not have known her brother very well, but she knew enough about him now that he had learned that offensive stance from their brothers, and he was in protective mode. "Not again," she muttered. She snatched the ball from the ground and tried not to appear frantic as she trekked back across the park before her brother said something she'd regret.

Even from a distance she saw the glare on her brother's face harden as he puffed up to his full height.

"Lucas!" she called out, trying to distract him from confronting Riley.

Lucas ignored her. "You hurt my sister."

"Lucas," she warned. "Don't."

Riley glanced over Lucas's head and connected his eyes with hers. Even from a distance she heard him say, "I know."

His admittance caused Emma to freeze.

Lucas stomped his foot when Riley didn't say anything else. "Aren't you going to apologize?"

The corner of Riley's mouth twitched as he tried to hide a smile. "How big of an apology do you think I need to give?"

Lenny looked into the sky thinking, his finger tapping against his chin. "Big," he said. "She deserves a big apology. And flowers."

"Flowers?"

"Yes," Lucas emphasized. "Flowers."

"I didn't think your sister liked flowers."

"Well, she does," Lucas said, pointing a finger at Riley.

"And you should get them for her."

"What kind of flowers?"

"Pretty ones. Just make sure you don't dig them out of Mr. Farly's yard. She doesn't like that very much."

Their talk about flowers snapped Emma back into action. She crossed the distance between her and the boys and slapped a hand across her brother's mouth to prevent him from embarrassing her further. Trying to cover up her nerves, she forced out a laugh, but it came out like she was choking. "Sorry about him."

Lucas yanked her hand away from his mouth. "Lots of 'em. Don't skimp out on my sister."

Riley chuckled as Emma spun Lucas around to face her. "You know what? Go bug Tom. Tell him he can't make five three-pointers in a row." Knowing Tom would be up for the challenge, she gently pushed Lucas in Tom's direction.

Lucas pointed at Riley. "Don't forget. Flowers."

"Go!" Emma shouted, her face flaming. Over the past few weeks she'd been fooled. Little brothers had an evil streak and when least expected, they launched a full-blown attack. Never trust them. "Sorry about him."

Riley shoved his hands in the front pocket of his hoodie. "So, flowers, huh?"

"Inside joke."

"You'll have to tell me about it sometime."

She would've laughed but she didn't know if they really would talk later. "Yeah, maybe."

Talk about awkward. In all the time they'd been friends they'd had their share of awkward moments, but nothing like this. Not moments when they had no clue about what to say to each other.

"I'm glad you came," Riley said.

"You are?" She didn't even try to hide her surprise.

"Yeah," he said simply. "I am."

She nodded, not knowing whether or not to believe him. "How have you been?"

"Fine," she said with a shrug. "And you?" Man, she hated small talk.

He took a step closer and bowed his head. "I've missed you."

She wanted to appear indifferent, like the way he'd been treating her over the past month hadn't crushed her. Yes, she had so many things she could've said to reinforce that it was his fault they were no longer friends, but instead, all she could focus on was how much she'd missed the sound of his voice, his crooked smile...him. She scolded herself. Now was not the time to melt under his gaze.

Needing to regain her composure, she glanced away. Lucas jumped for the ball that Tom held out of his reach, Ashley chatted with a small group of guys, and Tyler stood across the court, twirling a ball in his hands and watching Emma and Riley.

"There's a cold front moving in tonight, along with a big storm," Riley said, causing her to shift her focus back to him. "The temperatures are supposed to drop."

Emma had heard whispers of the change in weather. Not that she followed the weather closely, but when everyone expected the cold weather to give way to sunshine and they were met with potential record low temperatures for May, it became a buzzing topic.

"Do me a favor?" Riley asked.

"What?"

"Sleep with extra blankets tonight so you don't freeze, and keep a flashlight by your bed in case the power goes out."

"Riley, I'll be fine."

"Then do it for me, so I don't worry about you. Please?"

Not wanting to talk in circles and knowing he wouldn't give up until she agreed, she nodded. "Okay."

He leaned toward her and kissed her cheek. "Thanks."

Instead of softening her, his little show of affection fueled frustration as she watched him walk away and join the guys. She didn't even know where to start to make sense out of the encounter. How dare he waltz over to her and pretend he hadn't ignored her for the past month and then kiss her on the cheek like all was well. No apology. No explanation. Not okay!

"What was that about?"

Emma scowled at the excitement in Shiloh's voice. "I have no idea."

"Seriously?" Shiloh rolled her eyes. "Even you should be able to figure this one out, Wrangton."

"What's that supposed to mean?"

"It means the guy is still crazy about you."

"I don't care." Even though she might have cared. A little.

"Sure you do." Shiloh nudged Emma with her elbow and raised and lowered her eyebrows a few times like they hid some secret message. Emma wasn't falling for it.

"So what? He suddenly decides to talk to me again and I should automatically thank the lucky stars and pretend like nothing happened? I don't think so."

"Then what's your game plan?"

"I don't know." Was Riley talking to her now or was this just a blip in his silent treatment and he'd go back to ignoring her tomorrow? She hated not knowing where she stood with him. She looked to Shiloh who had gone through this whole breakup thing before. "Any advice?"

Shiloh shrugged. "Depends on what you want. The way I see it, you've got two options. One, you could quit being so stubborn and cold and let the boy grovel for forgiveness."

Emma raised her eyebrows in question. "What happened to all boys suck?"

Shiloh waved her comment away. "The guy has been your best friend forever. He's always been there for you; he loves you for who you are; and aside from the whole breakup incident, he's been the best boyfriend a girl could ask for. Yes, he's a great guy, but even he can make mistakes. Besides, I know you miss him like crazy, so if you decide to give him another chance, the world won't crash down on you."

"What's the second option?"

"Cut him loose and possibly lose him forever."

Neither one sounded optimal. "And the third option?"

"There is no third option."

"There has to be."

"Sorry, there's not."

"Then make one up."

Shiloh opened her mouth, but no words came out. When she realized Emma was serious, she threw up her arms in frustration. "I don't know. Um, option number three." She looked to the sky for answers. "You walk over to him right now and kiss him."

Emma glared at her friend. "You're no help."

"You asked for a third option. It was the best I could come up with under pressure."

"I knew getting together with him was a bad idea," Emma muttered. "We could've saved ourselves the drama and just stayed friends."

"Emma," Shiloh asked gently. "Do you miss the guy?"

"No." Even though they both knew she did.

"Is there any possible way you could forgive him?"

"No." Even though they both knew it was probably inevitable.

"Then it sounds to me like it's only a matter of time before you're besties again."

"Not likely."

Shiloh laughed and grabbed Emma's cheeks, squeezing them together, and directing her focus across the court. "Tell me that's not the face of someone who wants to make up with you."

Emma tried to slap Shiloh's hand away, but the girl held strong. Despite her attempt to free herself from Shiloh's grasp, Emma couldn't help but see what Shiloh wanted her to see.

Riley stood talking to Tom and Jerry, but he kept glancing her way, eyes sad but hopeful, an apologetic smile tugging at his lips. It contrasted the looks he'd been giving her for weeks, ones of anger and jealousy. Geez, the guy was like a pendulum, swinging back and forth, and she didn't know what to believe. All she wanted was to play basketball!

She was half tempted to congratulate herself for showing up at the court and leave before the game started, but Lucas dragged her toward the guys when they started picking teams. Seconds later, Jerry called her name to be on his team and the pull of basketball with the guys proved too strong to resist.

Twenty-Six

The other team won possession of the ball first. By the time Emma realized it, the only person on the opposing team left unguarded was Riley. No way did she want to defend him. They were hardly on speaking terms, and the few words they'd exchanged before the game didn't count. Even though she thought about forgiving him, that didn't mean she was ready to do it now. Without trying to be obvious about it, she walked over to Jerry and whispered in his ear.

"Switch with me, will you?" She couldn't hide the pleading in her voice. "Please?"

Jerry leaned around her to look over at Riley, then back at her. "No way. Not a chance."

"Jerry, come on." She knew he was the weak link, and if she pushed him enough he'd cave. "Please?"

For a second it looked like her pleading worked. He looked over her shoulder at Riley again, as if trying to decide whose side to take, but then he shook his head. "You know I can't keep up with Riley, and I'm not going to lose this game just because you two are having issues."

"Jerry—"

"What's going on?" Tom intervened, stepping between

them. "Why aren't we playing?"

"She doesn't want to guard Riley," Jerry said.

"What? Why?" Tom demanded.

She looked at him with bulging eyes and a pinched mouth, figuring even he was smart enough to know the reason without her having to spell it out.

"Is this because you two broke up?" He flicked his hand in front of him as if to say that monumental detail was too insignificant to acknowledge. "That's stupid. You two have been friends forever. Deal with it."

"I don't want to deal with it," she said through clenched teeth, growing angry that neither one of the guys would help her out. "How about you guard him instead?"

"I'm not guarding him," Tom pointed at her face, "*you* are. Now go, so we can get this game started."

"I'll guard him." Emma's heart soared as Tyler joined their huddle. Words of a true friend. "I just need someone to switch teams with me."

Tom stepped in front of Tyler, blocking him from the conversation. "Nope, sorry. Can't. Teams have already been chosen."

"Tom, come on," Emma pleaded. "We change teams up all the time."

"Rules changed while you were gone. Teams stay as they are."

Tom pointed across the court. "Emma, go guard Riley."

She glared at Tom and Jerry. "Thanks for nothing, *boys*."

Jerry gave her a guilty shrug, while Tom tried to throw an inconspicuous head nod to someone behind her. She whipped her head around, meeting Riley's eyes for a split second before he snapped his head in the other direction.

"What was that about?" she demanded, feeling like she was being set up.

Tom threw his guilty hands up way too quickly, his tough authoritative manner gone. "Nothing. I swear." Which only made him look guiltier.

She popped his personal bubble when she stepped closer to him, their chests nearly touching. "Did Riley say something to you?"

"No?"

She should've known the cat and mouse would be loyal to Riley, but what did Riley care if she guarded him or not?

"You two," she pointed at Tom and Jerry, "are both dead to me."

"Emma, come on," Jerry pleaded. "We're only trying to help you two figure things out."

"Doesn't matter." She started walking backward to her place opposite Riley, knowing none of the guys would help her out if Riley had set it up so she'd have to guard him. "Dead."

Jerry punched Tom in the arm. "See? I told you this was a bad idea."

She sucked in a breath, knowing she'd have to suck down her pride and broken heart if she was going to last the day with Riley and her traitorous friends.

"Princess, if you want me to—"

She held up her hand to hold Tyler off as he fell into step beside her. "It's fine," she snapped, even though it wasn't. "Just...be ready if I need to yell at someone. It might have to be you."

Tyler nodded. "I'm here for you."

She matched up opposite Riley as everyone else fell into their respective positions. Looking everywhere except at Riley, she settled into a defensive stance, ready for the game to begin.

"Don't be mad at them," Riley said.

"Don't tell me what to do."

He ignored her comment. "I maybe sorta kinda asked them to help me out."

Basketball forgotten, Emma straightened up out of her stance. "Why? Why would you care if I guarded you or someone else?"

"Because if you guard someone else, it would ruin my mission."

She huffed out a breath, knowing he was playing with her. "What mission is that?"

He threw her a smile, like he was all cute and clever and had her exactly where he wanted her. "My mission to get you back." Leaving her with her jaw on the ground, he brushed by her, caught the pass from Ashley, and drove to the basket. With no defender, he scored easily for his team.

Unable to recover in time to join her team on offense, she set up on defense again opposite Riley after Shiloh scored.

Ashley dribbled the ball across half court. Riley jabbed left before holding his hands up for the ball. Emma didn't even try to steal it, nor did she intend to play tight defense, preferring to remain at a distance.

Riley squared up with her, the ball tucked at his hip in triple-threat position as they stared each other down. A smile graced his lips. "Em, what are you doing?"

"Knitting a sweater," she growled. "What does it look like I'm doing?"

He looked at the three feet of space separating them. "It looks like you're giving me an open shot."

"Why don't you worry about your game and I'll worry about mine, okay?"

"Come on. Guard me for real. I won't bite. I promise."

"You'll have to excuse me if I don't believe you."

"Fine," he said before putting up a three-pointer. She didn't have to get a visual to know the ball swished the net.

They switched positions with Emma now on offense and Riley defending her. Whereas, Emma gave him plenty of space, Riley wasn't playing the same game. He guarded her like he usually did, close and in her face so she couldn't take the long shot. Jerry snapped her the ball, and she surveyed the court, trying to decide whether to drive or shoot. When Riley put a hand on her hip to ensure he'd stick with her whatever direction she moved, his touch caused her to get rid of the ball as soon as possible. Cy intercepted her imperfect pass, and Riley's team scored another shot...because of her.

When Riley got the ball next, Emma still gave him space, even though she knew he would take advantage of it. "Come on, Em," he said. "You know you won't be able to play like this all day. You can't stand to lose."

If it meant she didn't have to get close to him? "Watch me."

"Suit yourself." Riley put up another three. Yeah, that one hurt too.

The next time down the court, Emma tried to drive to the basket, but when her shoulder rammed into Riley, she dribbled off her foot and the ball rolled out of bounds. Ugh! It was like she'd forgotten how to play. And she thought college coaches would want to take a chance on her when she choked under the pressure? And over a guy no less!

Shiloh's arm caught Emma around the neck. "Deep breath, Wrangton."

"This was a bad idea," Emma muttered. "Me coming here."

Her friend laughed. "Welcome to the world of breakup awkwardville."

"What am I supposed to do?"

"For starters, relax and stop giving that boy power over you. Play your game and make him realize that you are just as good without him as you were with him."

She hated feeling weak in Riley's presence, and Shiloh's words struck home. "Good point. I can do that." *I think.*

"Then let's do this."

They pounded fists and resumed play with Riley's team having the ball.

"Go, Emma!" Lucas shouted from the sidelines. His little hands clapped for her, and when she turned to acknowledge his support, he waved at her. It was all the encouragement she needed.

She held her position on the opposite end of the court while Riley brought the ball downcourt. Taking a deep breath, she shook out the tension in her arms, and as Riley crossed half-court, she focused on the ball. *Time to play.* Expecting her to play loose defense, Riley set up for another three-pointer, but before he could get the shot off, Emma lunged toward him and her fingertips caught the edge of the ball, sending it off course. Shiloh rebounded the ball and passed to Jerry on the sideline. Emma raced toward their basket and caught the overhand pass from Jerry. Riley crossed over from the opposite side of the court to defend her, but with her momentum carrying her forward, she initiated a spin move toward the basket only to pull the ball back and shoot from the outer edge of the key, giving her team its next two points.

Basketball always had a way of bringing Emma and Riley together and forcing them to deal with their issues with one another. This time was no different. They grew quiet and focused as they played, their actions on the court communicating their feelings better than words ever could. Hesitation moves, spin moves, drives, and shots weren't merely ploys to score, but a way to express their feelings and beg for understanding and forgiveness and second chances. Some steps were confident, others cautious, as the game became more about them and less about the sport.

As if sensing the game no longer required more than two people to play, one by one their friends drifted off the court, congregating at the sidelines to watch as Emma and Riley battled over their pride, regret, and fear. Their friends could've complained, but they probably knew Emma and Riley needed this moment with each other.

She pushed the ball forward, ramming her shoulder into Riley's, but he stood strong, forcing her to find a new path to the basket. She pulled back and, keeping the ball low, executed a double crossover to bring the ball right. The second he realized her change in direction, she dribbled between her legs left and blew past him to the basket, making a clean shot.

He caught the ball as it bounced off the ground and glanced at her over his shoulder. She tried to avoid his gaze, but his half smile telling her he was proud of her caused her stomach to do weird things. She scowled in return.

They matched each other shot for shot. A drive to the basket, a jump shot from the baseline, a three-pointer here, a three-pointer there. Back and forth they played, neither one gaining an edge over the other. Riley had the height advantage, while Emma excelled at speed. He preferred the hesitation moves to throw off her timing, while she favored various speeds to catch him off guard. It reminded her of all the years they'd learned this sport together, side by side, shot for shot. The scraped knees, the air balls, the celebratory moments when they conquered a new skill. Their trust, respect, and love for each other had blossomed and strengthened on the court through the years, and Emma felt her resolve to stay mad at him weakening. Playing basketball against him felt too familiar, too personal, and their month of separation hit her hard as she realized she didn't want to lose Riley forever. She didn't want to throw away their friendship and everything they'd been through together, but she couldn't ignore the past month either.

When tears threatened to overcome her and all she wanted to do was surrender the victory and beg for what they once had, she ground her teeth together and fought harder for every basket. She wondered if Riley felt the same way, as he seemed to find reasons to touch her between plays. A brush of the hand here, a shoulder tap there, only to turn around and dominate the next play. She had a feeling that while she played to prove he didn't have power over her, he played to prove how sorry he was for everything. So why didn't he talk to her? Confused, hurt, angry, she rebounded one of her own shots and took a minute to calm down before resuming play.

Before her minute was up, she felt his body press into her from behind, felt his hands rest on her hips.

"Deep breath, Em," he whispered as if sensing she was two seconds away from losing it. "We'll get through this. I promise."

She turned toward him, her eyes glistening with unshed tears as she tried not to yell at him. One minute he was ignoring her and the next it was like nothing had changed between them. But everything had changed, and no basketball game could resolve their issues.

"Em," he whispered, his eyes pleading for something she couldn't acknowledge but so desperately wanted to. "I—"

"Next basket wins," Tom hollered from the sidelines, cutting off Riley's next words and reminding Emma of their spectators.

She took a deep breath and handed Riley the ball. "If you let me win, I swear, I'll hate you forever."

A faint smile slid across his lips. "You mean you don't already hate me forever?"

Neither his tone nor his eyes held any indication of teasing, but she had no words to answer his question, so she took a step back from him for some much needed distance.

He placed his hand on her back, guiding her to the top of the key, and she'd be lying if she said the gesture didn't make her knees wobble and her heart stutter.

Riley had one of the best head fakes Emma had ever seen, and after years of playing against him, she still couldn't tell the difference a lot of the time between the fake and the real deal. Riley knew this. He didn't overuse it, knowing exactly when to pull out his secret weapon, and now would probably be one of those times.

She crouched down in a defensive position as Riley initiated play. A hesitation move, followed by a low triple crossover, before he pulled up. His head fake sold the shot too well, and she exploded in the air to cause a distraction. An unnecessary one. Riley waited until her feet returned to the ground before he jumped up and released the ball.

Spinning toward the basket, she saw the ball finish its perfect descent down and through the hoop. Half of their spectators cheered, half of them groaned. Riley beat her. He beat her! How in the world did she let that happen? He reached his hand out to her as if to congratulate her on losing. In times like these, being a sore loser was an understatement. The one game she needed to win, and Riley proved to be better. Disgusted with him, disgusted with herself, she slapped his hand away and stalked to the bleachers, unable to look at him for another second.

She needed to walk it off. Alone. When Shiloh and Ashley attempted to join her, she held up her hand and shook her head to keep them away. She laced her fingers through the chain link fence, disappointment over her loss weighing her down. Not that she couldn't lose with dignity against him, but this time was different. This time mattered more than all the rest.

Twenty-Seven

When Emma got home later that afternoon, two folded blankets and a flashlight sat on her bed, but the item that caused her breath to catch in her throat was the white crane nestled on top. All she could do was look at the white paper bird—the promise of Riley's commitment to her. He had said he'd never let her go, that no matter what happened they'd never lose their friendship.

Lies.

Still upset over the game, she snatched the crane off the blankets, crumpled it in her hand, and threw it aside like it was just a folded piece of paper. No way was she going to succumb to Riley's charity, at least not for herself. She picked up the blankets and carried them into the house. The dark hallway swallowed her in its shadows as she walked toward the last door on the left and pushed it open.

Lenny and Lucas watched her without a word as she draped one blanket over Lenny's bed and the other one over Lucas's. She turned to exit and caught the stares from her brothers. "In case it gets cold tonight," she said, before closing the door behind her.

By the time Emma climbed under the covers for bed, she was already freezing. The large space of the garage, plus the freezing temperature, would be too much for her little sometimes working space heater to make any difference. Her body shook as she clung to the blankets, closing off any air holes that invited in the cold air. As she shivered beneath the covers, her eyes adjusted to the dark. She saw the outline of her bedside table and the outline of the wrinkled paper crane standing watch over her. Only then did sleep find her.

Emma didn't know what woke her a couple hours later. The wind howled outside and rain pelted against the roof of the garage, but she didn't think the intensity of the storm was to blame for her abrupt awakening.

The crash of falling boxes caused her to jerk upright, fully awake. Her heart pounded at the sight of a silhouette cursing in the dark and making its way toward her.

"Sorry," the shadow whispered.

"Dad?" Her dad had never come in here at night, so she knew immediately something was wrong. "What is it? What's wrong?" she questioned him, her voice filled with panic.

"Emma—"

"Is it one of the boys?" Ignoring the cold, she flung off her blankets and lunged for her shoes so she could assist as needed. "What happened? Do we need to call someone?"

"Emma," her dad practically shouted, stumbling forward to grip her arm and turn on the side lamp near her bed. Light flooded the dark space, and her dad guided her back to bed.

"Calm down. Nothing's wrong." He pushed her shoulder back so she fell against her pillows and he pulled the blankets around her again like she was five years old and he was tucking her in. Sitting on the edge of her bed he started to laugh. "But at least I know who to come wake if the house is burning down."

"If nothing's wrong then what are you doing?"

He cleared his throat and looked away. "I couldn't sleep, and with the storm raging outside, I wanted to come check on you. The power went out, and I realized you didn't have any heat in here." He held up a blanket. "I brought you an extra blanket."

"You did?" she whispered, touched by his concern for her. Emma looked at the material he clutched in his hand. The vibrant stripes of greens and purples and yellows stood in contrast to each other, but were somehow the perfect blend. She reached out her hand to feel the edge of the blanket. The material felt like furry silk. "I've never seen that blanket before."

"It was your mom's favorite. I was keeping it safe in case she—" He cleared his throat. "Well, just in case, but I thought you could use it tonight."

"Thanks, Dad."

His smile was a mixture of sadness and happiness as he unfolded the blanket and spread it over her. "Goodnight, Emma."

Even though her mom had left him to raise five kids on his own, Emma sensed how much her dad still loved his wife and how much pain Emma caused him.

"I'm sorry I remind you of Mom." Emma's voice was soft, almost a whisper, but it reached across the vastness between them, causing her dad to look over his shoulder at her. It had been something she had wanted to apologize for since Lance accused her of it months ago.

Her dad frowned. "Why would you say that?"

She looked to the ceiling, her eyes burning with unshed tears. "Because you don't deserve to be reminded of all the bad stuff with her every time you look at me."

Her dad turned back around to face her, his head cocked to the side. "Is that what you think?"

She couldn't find the words to answer him, and she didn't want to risk tears escaping her eyes if she shook her head, so she didn't say anything. Her dad returned to her side and sat on the edge of her bed. He closed his eyes and dragged a hand down his face, exhaling deeply. "I sure have made a mess of things, haven't I?"

"Dad, I didn't mean—"

He held up his hand to silence her. "You don't remind me of all the bad stuff, sweetheart. Yes, you look like your mom, but that's where the similarities end. You have a fire in your eyes that your mom never had. You walk with a confident athletic stride and dare to take on anyone who stands in your way. You're a fighter; your mom…wasn't."

"I'm sorry she left you."

He nodded. "I'm sorry she left us. Your mom made her choice. Although I don't agree with it and it pains me every day knowing how much she hurt you and your brothers, I hope someday you'll be able to forgive her so her choices don't drag you down."

"You told me once that you didn't give her what she needed. What did she need?"

He exhaled a deep sigh. "Your mom and I got married right out of high school with so many plans. We thought marrying young would enable us to do everything together. We planned to go to college, get fancy jobs, buy a big house, and have two or three kids several years down the road. Of course, I think the kids were more my dream than hers, now that I think about it. Not long after we were married, we found out we were pregnant with Logan; Lance came close behind. When we learned about you, I thought your mom would be excited for a girl, and I think she was, but parenting was taking its toll on her. By the time Lenny and Lucas came, your mom's love for me turned into resentment. Five kids are a lot for anyone, but it was too much for her. She still wanted the big house and fancy things that I couldn't afford." He gave her a sad smile and shrugged. "So she left."

The words echoed in her head. *So she left.* Simple as that. "Do you ever hear from her?"

His nod surprised her. She assumed that when her mom left, she had disappeared without a trace. Emma never imagined she'd stayed in touch.

"Every once in a while, she'll call and let me know where she's at and what she's doing." ◦

As much as Emma didn't want to bring her dad sadness, there was one question she needed to ask, one question her and her brothers needed to have answered. "Do you think she'll ever come back?"

He closed his eyes and looked away. Emma thought maybe she had pushed him too far, but then he turned back to her, shaking his head. "No. She's not coming back."

"How can you be sure? Maybe she just needs more time. Maybe she's working to find her way back to us. Maybe—"

"She married someone else," her dad blurted out.

Emma didn't know what to say. Married? To someone else? "But that would mean..."

"Yes, sweetheart. Your mom and I divorced a few years ago."

A jolt of shock rushed through her. Divorced. It made sense, of course. Why stay married when you've left your family forever? Still, the news surprised her. She figured her dad was just waiting around with hope that his wife would return someday, that he was still locked . into the relationship, but she was wrong. "Why didn't you say something before? Or am I the only one who doesn't know?"

He winced. "The older boys know. Maybe Lenny does too. I'm not sure." A smile flickered across her dad's face. "He always seems to know more than he's told. Lucas doesn't know. I know I'll have to tell him one day, but..." He ended his sentence with a shrug.

"Is she happy?" The bitterness in her tone was unmistakable. Who cared if the woman was happy? She had abandoned her family for stupid, shallow, selfish reasons. She didn't deserve to be happy.

Her dad shrugged. "Honestly?"

She nodded. More than anything she needed him to be honest with her. "She married some guy who buys her everything she's ever wanted and who never wants kids. So yeah, I think she's happy."

Anger and hatred toward her mom rushed through Emma. How dare she leave her family and make a new life—what she considered to be a better life—without them?

"Does she at least pay child support?" Emma bit out.

Her dad shook his head. "No, and I don't want her money."

She knew her dad worked two, and sometimes three, jobs just to provide for the family, while her mom bathed in riches without caring about the five kids she broke by fleeing from them. The disgust she had for her mom was so strong she could taste it. All she wanted was to punch something. But then she looked at her dad, the man who remained with his five children, beaten down over the years due to the relentless storms of parenthood, yet he never complained or left to spend time alone. The love and respect she had for her dad dissolved the hatred toward her mom. Taking a deep breath, she said, "Then I'm glad she's gone. You deserve better than her, we all do."

"Emma, don't say that. She's still your mom."

"Maybe, but that doesn't mean I have to love or respect her. I refuse to respect a woman who leaves her husband to raise five kids alone and trades her kids in for material possessions. She's shallow and she's a coward."

Her dad broke out in laughter. "And here I thought you were going to blame me."

Her jaw dropped. "Why would I do that?"

"Your mom did. She said I drove her away."

"Yeah well, I'm not her."

He smiled. "I know."

Her dad leaned over and picked something up off her bedside table. His fingers pinched the tossed aside paper crane. Yeah, a part of her flinched that she had crumpled up Riley's attempt to be thoughtful and kind. "Crane?"

When she nodded, he unfolded the sorry looking bird and

used his thigh to flatten the paper. He paused, focused on the center of the paper. The tip of his mouth tilted up with a knowing grin as he showed her the message:

Stay Warm

Love, R

Then, without a word, he set to work, refolding the lines and bringing life back into the paper. His gentle fingers worked purposefully, rebuilding what she had destroyed. The features of his face softened and a smile graced his lips as if caught in a happy memory. A couple minutes later, what he presented her with, after the final fold, was a bird of absolute perfection. No bent tail or imbalanced wings, but a figure of grace and beauty.

"Did you know the crane is a symbol of motherly love?"

She shook her head.

He twirled it in circles between his fingers before passing it to her. "It's perfect for you. You're a good sister, but over the last month I've seen you express so many beautiful mothering qualities to Lenny and Lucas. More than your mom ever did." He cleared his throat and looked up at her. "It makes me so happy to know you're going to make a great mom someday. Strong and fierce, yet gentle, loving, and kind."

Yeah, it was just a piece of paper, but her dad had somehow transformed the crane into something better than it could ever be on its own.

He looked around the garage. The small circle of light only reached so far and cast the rest of the space in shadows. "I know you're probably going off to college soon, but maybe we can clear out some of this junk and figure out some ways to spruce this space up for you."

"It's fine the way it is, Dad."

"No, it's not. You deserve better."

His shoulders sagged, and she knew he was probably thinking about all the times he'd failed her over the years. If she could take away his pain, she would have. With no words to say, she threw her arms around him. "I love you, Dad."

Tense arms, stiff back. Her hug had taken him by surprise, but it only took him a second to relax into her embrace and return it, whispering words she never thought she'd hear from him. "I love you too, Ems."

Twenty-Eight

The final bell screamed through the school, releasing students from their academic prison for the day. Emma fought through the crowded hallways to her locker and stumbled to a stop when she saw Riley leaning against the wall with his legs crossed at the ankles, like he didn't have a care in the world. Seeing him at her locker reminded her of how they used to be, when he used to wait for her after classes and greet her with a smile as he pulled her in for a hug, scanned the hallways, and snuck a kiss.

While Emma contemplated whether or not to skip her locker visit and head home, Riley looked up and spotted her. He straightened and raised his hand in greeting. Now any attempt she made to turn and run would look stupid.

One side of his mouth tilted into a smile, and she scolded the butterflies for taking flight in her stomach. They should've died weeks ago. Taking a deep breath, she forced her feet forward toward her locker...toward him.

"Hey," Riley said as she approached.

"Come to gloat?" His victory against her on Saturday still made her want to poke her eyes out. Of all times she'd played one-on-one, he proved to be her most difficult opponent, and she really wanted that victory that he had claimed.

"No." He bowed his head to hide a chuckle. "Not when you look on the verge of hitting me."

She spun the lock, stopping and changing direction with each number, but when she tried to open her locker it remained locked. "Then what do you want?"

"To drive you home."

Spin, spin, spin. Attempt number two at her combination. "I already have a ride. You know, with the guy you sent in your place when you ditched me a month ago."

"I deserve that."

"Yeah, you do."

"And everything else you throw my way."

When her combination failed a second and third time, she slammed her hand against the door, blaming the metal for its incompetence.

Riley wrapped an arm around her waist and smoothly moved her out of the way so he could spin the combination of her locker and pop open the door to show her how easy it was to get it right the first time. She felt like growling or grunting or drop-kicking him out of her way, but she didn't. She couldn't. Not when he was being so...nice.

Needing a minute, she opened her locker door wider, concealing his face from her view. He didn't take the hint. Instead, he moved to the opposite side to maintain a visual and invade her personal bubble. Placing his hand on her lower back, he drew his body closer to hers.

"Em, I know I don't deserve your forgiveness, but I hope you'll let me beg for it anyway."

She stepped out of his embrace and crossed her arms over her chest, as if they could protect her from him. "And why would I do that?"

"Because you, of all people, know that sometimes even an idiot like me needs a second chance."

Why did his self-inflicted insult sting her? Maybe it was the sincerity of his tone or the regret pooling in his eyes or the scrunched lines of his forehead speaking to each of the ways he planned to make up for all he had put her through over the last month.

Her resolve to hate him started to melt. "You're not an idiot," she mumbled, looking down at the ground.

"Yeah, I am. I let you go, didn't I?"

She didn't know what to say. With her cheeks reddening, all she could do was meet his gaze and stare back at the boy who'd been her best friend for half of her life, trying to figure out whether or not she should forgive him and what that would say about her. Would it make her weak, like he could treat her however he felt and she would just take it? Or would it be a sign of strength that she could forgive his past mistakes and not let them sever what was good and true?

He reached out to put a hand on her hip, pulling her closer against him again. "Listen, I have some stuff I have to do for my mom, but let me take you home first. I'll pick you up around six and take you out to dinner. My treat."

Could it be this easy for them to go back to normal? She bowed her head, not able to look at him as she questioned what to do. "Riley, I—"

"Emma, please." His hands cradled her face, tilting her head up so he could look at her. "I know I've been an idiot, I know I don't deserve a second chance, especially after pushing you away and not talking to you for weeks, but I'm begging you. Please. I just want to talk, and then you can tell me to get lost."

His blue eyes always had a way of breaking her down. Maybe it wouldn't be too horrible to hear him out. "Fine. I'll let you take me home on one condition."

"Anything."

"If you say anything stupid and I tell you to pull over to let me out, you will."

He nodded. "Deal."

"I mean it. No apologies, no negotiations. You pull over

or I jump from the moving vehicle. I'm not kidding."

He beamed at her. What about her response propelled him to smile? Before she could stop him or voice a protest, he nearly tackled her in a hug. "I've missed you."

He always was the hugging type. She allowed him the hug, patting him on the back like a buddy, before taking a step back. "Let me get my stuff."

She pulled the remaining books from her locker and shoved them into her backpack, hoping she wouldn't hate herself later for letting him talk her into this.

"Ready?" he asked.

She nodded, propelling Riley to close her locker door and lead her toward the direction of the parking lot. She paused at the sight of Tyler leaning against the opposite wall of lockers. He caught her staring and bowed his head, taking a step in the opposite direction.

"Give me a minute, Riley."

She left Riley to wait for her while she followed Tyler. "Tyler, wait up."

Surprisingly, he stopped and let her catch up. Tyler may have been a bit cold at first, but even she could admit that he'd been there for her over the past month when she needed a friend, and she refused to cast him away just because Riley decided to talk to her again.

He refused to meet her eyes, but he spoke before she could. "So, you and lover boy are back together again, huh?"

"Hardly," she said. "He just wants to talk, but it looks like I won't need a ride home from you today."

He nodded, his disappointment clear.

"Hey," she said, slugging him in the arm, "At least this way you won't have me cramping your style when you go prowling for girls."

Tyler chuckled and looked at her. She figured he'd respond with some sarcastic comment, but he didn't. Instead, he took a step forward and enveloped her in his arms.

"Why are you hugging me?" she mumbled into his chest, remembering the last time he hugged her. "I'm not crying."

He pressed his face into her hair and chuckled. "Shut up, this time you're comforting me."

"Oh," she said, wrapping her arms around him and returning his squeeze. "Let me know when I'm done." With a smile on her face, she counted to ten. When he didn't release her, the smile slipped from her face as she realized the seriousness of his statement. Maybe he felt that their forged friendship was going to dissolve now that Riley wanted to talk with her. Her hug turned sincere as she tilted her head up to gauge Tyler's face. "You okay?"

He patted her head and brought it back to his chest. "Yeah, Princess, I'm okay. You can go back to your boyfriend now." Despite his words, he didn't let her go. "But if he makes you cry, I *will* punch him this time. I'm just giving you fair warning."

She didn't exactly know what his feelings were for her, but she could tell he was doing his best to protect her, and she couldn't fault him for that. "Thanks, Tyler."

He released her, but when she turned to leave, he held onto her hand and brought her back to him. "Do me a favor?"

She nodded.

"I know he's your bestie and all, but protect your heart. No matter what happens, you're not lost without him. Got it?"

She smiled at her friend and squeezed his hand. "Yeah, I got it."

With a final nod, Tyler hitched his bag up on his shoulder and sauntered down the hall ahead of her. She returned to Riley's side.

"You two seem pretty close nowadays." It was Riley's way of asking for information he didn't know if she would tell him or not.

"Yeah." She kept her answer short, but as they exited the school she pondered over Tyler's parting words.

At first, she did feel lost without Riley by her side. After all, they'd been friends for so long and had been practically inseparable over the years that his request for space had crushed her. But when she thought about how far she'd come with her dad and brothers to heal their broken family, she wondered if any of that would've happened if she had continued to spend all her time with Riley. Maybe the space Riley needed was the best for both of them.

◆◆◆

The ride to her house took place in silence. Emma couldn't help but sneak glances at Riley as he drove. He seemed relaxed, happy even. His left arm was slung across the steering wheel, while his other wrist rested on the gearshift between them. The faint hint of a smile graced his lips, especially when his eyes flickered her way. When he stopped his jeep in front of her house, she thanked him for the ride, not sure what else to say.

He reached over to squeeze her hand before she got out of the car. "I'll see you at six."

"Okay, see you then," she mumbled, giving him a short smile.

After crossing the threshold, she closed the front door of her house and leaned against it, the full impact of her impending meeting with Riley slamming into her. The prospect of talking to him after weeks of silence caused asteroids to take up residence in her stomach. What did he want to talk about? She couldn't spend the next three hours sitting around the house obsessing about it…about him. It would drive her insane. She had to do something—anything—to distract herself. The house was clean thanks to her brothers' help, her dad had told her he would take care of dinner tonight, and none of her brothers were home except...

She stopped pacing the living room, an idea coming to her. It was so absurd and ridiculous, but maybe, just maybe, it was exactly what she needed, what her family needed. Dropping her bag, she picked up the basketball by the pile of shoes near the front door and ventured into her dad and brothers' domain—the hallway. The overhead light was off, the hallway settled in darkness. It seemed ten times longer than usual as she made her way, one step at a time, toward her brother's door. The few deep breaths she took did nothing to calm her fears.

Lance's door was closed. She stood before it, reminding herself to breath as she raised her fist to knock. Was she really going to do this? One breath, two breaths. Squeezing her eyes shut, she tapped her knuckles against the wood and took a half step back.

"What?" Lance hollered from the other side. Taking his response as an invitation to turn the knob and peek inside, she pushed the door open just enough for her head to poke through. He was sprawled across his bed reading a magazine, past issues of *Sports Illustrated* scattered around him.

"Hey," she said, assessing whether or not it was safe to cross enemy lines and negotiate a peace treaty.

He took a moment to stop time and glare at her. "What do you want?"

Pushing the door open wider, she twirled the basketball in her hands, taking one more second to decide if she should ask her question or bolt in the other direction. Taking a deep breath, she said, "You wanna go shoot around?"

The look of disgust on his scowling face was enough to send even the most fearless soldiers running. "Why would I want to shoot around with you?"

Forcing herself not to cower, she plunged ahead. "Because you've got nothing better to do?"

"I've got plenty of better things to do than hang out with

you."

"Okaaaay," she drawled out, unsure of what direction to go from here, but figuring she needed another tactic. "You know what? Forget about it. I know it's been a while for you and you don't want to be embarrassed when I show you up on the court. I shouldn't have asked."

She turned to leave, but her brother's snort of contempt stopped her.

"Is that how you want to play this?" He slapped the magazine down on his bed and jumped up. "Fine. Let's do this. Maybe you'll stop acting like the queen of basketball when I put you in your place on the court."

She tried to hide her smile and swallow the surge of competitiveness fueling inside her. Ever since she started playing basketball in fourth grade, she had wanted to play against Lance, had always questioned how she would measure up to him on the court. In her mind, based on how good of a player he used to be, he would be one of her biggest competitors, maybe even better than Riley. She was ready for this challenge. "Bring it on."

◆◆◆

To Lance, the neighborhood basketball court was probably just that—a basketball court nestled between trees and houses—but to Emma, the neighborhood court where she'd spent so many weekends competing against the guys and improving her talent was sacred ground.

Inviting her brother to engage in a competition on her court meant more to her than it probably should. Basketball could be the thing that brought them together and bridged the divide between them.

Offering Lance the ball first, she set up on defense. Unlike the other guys she'd played against over the years, who took their time at the top of the key to figure out how to proceed against a girl, as soon as Lance's hands touched the ball, he plowed through her like a football player going for a touchdown. His shoulder led his charge, ramming into hers with enough force to knock her off balance and out of his way. His drive to the basket was clear, and he made the shot easily. Emma didn't bother calling the foul. The arrogant gleam in his eye when he turned to look at her, to mock her, said it all. Fairness wasn't part of this game, and he dared her to call him on it. If she did, he would probably call her weak and walk off the court; if she didn't call him on it, well, that's what would make things interesting. Her brother didn't think she could play with the big boys. He was wrong.

Lance flipped her the ball as he settled into a defensive stance to force her left. Despite how poor of a player he thought she was, Lance didn't leave her any room to prove her shooting ability from the three-point line, nor did he give her a path to drive to the basket. She would have to fight for every basket.

Her assumptions about him being a fierce competitor proved true as she dribbled the ball around the three-point line, assessing how he moved and looking for weaknesses. He was cocky, that was for sure, but his overconfidence didn't prove detrimental to his play, at least not yet. He was quick and knew how to read her movements, reducing her ability to fake him out, and he stuck with her as she tried various moves to test him. When she was ready, she drove to the basket, but instead of trying to power her way through him, she executed a series of hesitation moves before catching him off guard and blowing by him, tying the score at two.

With Lance's second possession of the ball, he tried to power his way through her again, but she hadn't played for years with the guys and not learned anything. Rather than standing firm, she relaxed her stance so when Lance rammed into her, his momentum spun her around just enough that she was in the perfect position to stay with him as he drove to the basket, preventing him from making an easy shot. He set up at the top of the key to try again as they battled for dominion on the court.

Lance made a jump shot from the side of the key; Emma followed with a jump shot from the top of the key.

He sank a three-pointer; she answered with one of her own.

He outmuscled her for a layup; she outsmarted him with a reverse hook shot.

And they played on, matching each other shot for shot, point for point.

As they played, Emma got the feeling their game of one-on-one was more than just a time passer—it was a test of her worth in the eyes of her brother. He was looking for a way to prove her incompetence, but she refused to give him the evidence he sought. If she managed to prove herself to him on the court, maybe she would finally be able to win him over.

She was wrong.

Twenty-Nine

E mma should've known they weren't ready for a friendly game of sibling basketball. The hatred between them sliced way too deep to be cast aside in a truce. Lance probably thought she would weaken after the first few plays, but she held her own, and his frustration built as they played for the final point.

He took possession of the ball at the top of the three-point line. Dribbling toward the basket, he faked one way then changed direction by bouncing the ball between his legs to switch hands. When he couldn't get around her, he attempted a few moves before boxing her out beneath the basket. Rather than admit defeat, she slipped behind him. When he jumped to shoot, she jumped with him. Extending her arm, she caught the ball with her fingertips as he raised it above his head. The ball tipped out of his hands into the air and fell into her possession, granting her the possibility of proving to her brother that she was more than a worthless little sister—that her talent, hard work, and dedication to the sport they both loved wasn't a farce, but a gift. One that he could respect her for.

Since the ball hadn't touched the rim, she didn't need to take it all the way back to the top of the key, but due to her brother's quick recovery she couldn't put up an immediate shot and give him the opportunity to block it. She did the only thing she could. She pushed off the ground to shoot, but rather than forcing her momentum upward, she jumped backwards, throwing up a fadeaway shot so he couldn't deflect the ball. Praying it would find its way through the net, Emma held her breath as the ball travelled through the air, reaching the peak of its arch and starting its descent. The ball fell through the hoop. Two points Emma.

Her face split into a smile. She'd done it; she'd beaten Lance. Surely that counted for something in his eyes.

When her brother turned around, her smile wilted at the murderous look on his face.

"What's wrong?" she asked, hoping her teasing tone would ease the tension. "Didn't think your little sister had any game?"

He took the ball and threw it at the basket with enough force to crack the backboard.

What had started as a friendly game of basketball turned into something so much more as fear crept in, and she stumbled back a few steps away from him. The muscles in his arms bulged, each of his fists clenched in a death grip, and his face scrunched in a look so evil Emma was tempted to turn and run, but her legs wouldn't move. Her brother was a loose cannon, she knew this, so why did she think being alone with him and proving herself on the court was a good idea? Stupid!

"Lance, I'm sorry. I—"

He stalked over to her, his face pulling up inches from hers. "You think you winning this stupid game proves anything?" he roared. "Well, it doesn't. You're still just as worthless as I am!"

Whatever was happening, she got the feeling it was more than just her beating him. She'd been on the receiving end of his temper before, but never anything like this. His eyes looked crazed, the muscle in his jaw throbbed, the rest of his body coiled with rage.

"You think you're better than me because you got some stupid college coaches looking at you for a scholarship? Well, you're not. They're going to eat you up and spit you out. You'll come crawling back home like the loser you are." He paused in his rant to smile with such viciousness her breath caught in her throat. "And I can't wait for that to happen."

Emma felt her fear turn to anger and disgust. How could her own brother find so much joy at the prospect of her failing? Did he hate her that much?

She could feel the venom radiating from him and took a step back.

He matched it, coming forward. "Don't think for a second I don't know what you're doing. Cooking dinner, making nice with our idiot brothers, pretending like Dad doesn't hate you. Being their slave will never make them love you." He towered over her, the scowl on his face deepening. "You're *pathetic*."

"Yeah, you've said that before," she responded bitterly, remembering all too well the times he'd torn her down with his words, and all the times she'd let him. Thinking of Lucas and Lenny, she knew their feelings toward her were genuine. How Lucas's face lit up whenever he saw her, how Lenny sought her out for advice because he knew she wouldn't laugh at him. No matter what Lance said, he couldn't make her believe all those tender moments with her younger brothers were lies, and she was tired of allowing him to have power over her. "But you know what? I don't care what you think. Not anymore."

"You say that, but I can see in your eyes that you do. You know what I'm saying is true because we're all from the same family," he spit out. "And nothing you do will ever make you better than us. You're just like me. A nobody."

His comparison made her temper snap. She shoved her open palms against his chest, forcing him back a step. "I'm *nothing* like you! You're the one who's pathetic. You're the one wasting your life away. I'd rather fail a thousand times than be a screw-up like you." Her voice got stronger, her anger building with it. It felt good not to let him dominate her into submission. She pushed him again. "You always say Mom left because of me, well, maybe she left because of *you*. Maybe the world would be a better place if you were never born!"

The realization and regret of what she'd said hit her at the same time as Lance's fist. His knuckles slammed against her face. Her head exploded in pain. The impact of his hit sent her sprawling to the ground.

Her eyes struggled to focus on the concrete beneath her, while her thoughts tried to grasp what just happened. Lance hit her. He *hit* her! It wasn't a slap or a half-meant jab. He full-on hit her. Gaining some balance, she thrust herself off the ground and spun toward her brother, ignoring how the pain in her face screamed in protest. She looked into his eyes, but she couldn't register the shock on his face.

He took a step forward, his arm slightly extended as if reaching for her. "Emma, I—"

She swatted his hand away before shoving him back with both hands. "Do you feel better now?" She pushed him again, her hands slamming against his chest. "Do you want to hit me again? Do you feel like a man now because you put me in my place?" She shoved him a third time and he did nothing to stop her. "Huh?"

He'd done it. Months—years—she'd endured his hatred, and she'd never cracked. This time it was different. This time it mattered. He was no longer a twelve or fifteen-year-old boy ragging on his sister, he was practically a grown man, and after everything she'd done to try and make amends with him, he had still hit her with everything he had. She knew then that nothing she did would ever make things right between them.

She went to shove him again, but the fight left her. Her

fists slammed against his chest and clenched the fabric of his shirt, but instead of pushing him away, her eyes pleaded with him to help her understand as her shoulders sagged in defeat. "What do you want from me? I've tried to show you that I care, to show you that I don't hate you and I don't think I'm better than you. I'm sorry Mom left you. But she left me too. She left all of us. And I know what it feels like to be in so much pain and to feel so worthless you can hardly breathe, but you have to find a way past it, because it's eating you alive."

She didn't feel the tears sliding down her cheeks or the pounding of her face from where he had hit her. All she could feel was herself drowning in guilt. "I'm sorry I failed you," she choked out. "I've tried to make it right, but I don't know what else to do. What do you want me to do?" she pleaded, staring into his eyes, desperate for answers.

"Emma," he croaked out. She didn't recognize the pain in his eyes or the desperation of his tone. Despite her need for answers, she shook her head, unable to listen to anymore of his hateful words. She unclenched her fists from his shirt and her arms fell to her sides.

The space between them suddenly became too close—too much—so she took a step back, and then another and another. She didn't want to look at him, but she couldn't force her eyes away. His hunched shoulders, his unwillingness to meet her gaze. The growing distance between them still wasn't enough, so Emma turned and fled. She hit the sidewalk and kept going, taking a left instead of turning right toward home. She couldn't go home; she couldn't go to Riley's, so she took to the streets, meandering between houses and cars and shadows, letting her feet guide her.

She thought distance would free her from Lance, but with every step, she replayed the scene at the court: their one-on-one basketball battle, Lance's escalating anger, his words, her words, the hit, the hit, the hit. Pain registered in her face making it all the more real. Her breath caught. She didn't want to see the hatred in his eyes that was now burned in her memory, she didn't want to hear her hateful words on constant replay in her head, and she didn't want to feel the impact of his fist connecting with her face over and over and over again.

Her steps weren't fast enough so she picked up her pace. Her feet slapped against the pavement and her arms pumped faster and faster as she ran through the streets. The hatred in his eyes, the anger in his voice, and the strength behind his punch propelled her forward to an unforeseen destination.

The clouds overhead broke open and rain poured to the ground. The raindrops fell faster and harder, but Emma was immune to them. Her feet guided her to the woods and to the trail that led down to the water's edge where her and Riley always went when they snuck out of their houses at night and wanted to be alone. Maybe all the happy memories with him would dispel a teaspoon of the darkness within her so she could breathe again without feeling like she would explode. The night surrounded her. It held her captive just like her brother's voice as it echoed in her head. She hated him. Hated him for making her care about him even though he clearly didn't feel the same. Hated him for bringing out the worst in her.

How could she have said the world would be better off without him? Despite all that he had done and how much he hated her, she had never once felt that way. But she had said it. What kind of person said that, especially to her own brother? She was just as bad, if not worse, than Lance was, and she hated herself for it.

No matter how fast she ran, she couldn't outrun the shame she felt, but that didn't stop her from trying. She couldn't breathe, she couldn't think, she couldn't free herself from the pressure building within her.

Bursting free from the woods, she ran down the beach. Raindrops splattered the ground around her and soaked her clothes. She always thought her heart would break over some boyfriend; she didn't know her brother would have enough power to shatter it.

The sand and rocks proved to be too much for her trembling legs. She stumbled to a stop.

The lack of motion only caused the pressure within her to build faster. It hurt. Everything hurt. She grabbed fistfuls of her hair and pressed her knuckles against her head trying to ease the tension, but it didn't help. Lance was right. She was worthless and pathetic and mean. She didn't deserve a college scholarship or a family that cared about her or a best friend who would sacrifice everything for her.

She gasped for breath, desperate to gain control, but the pressure in her head, in her chest, in her heart kept building and building until she couldn't take it anymore. Straightening up, she threw her arms out wide and tilted her head back to the infinite sky above.

The scream that ripped from her throat shot into the night, filled with desperation and pain and failure. It broke the silence and filled the cracks of time with heartache and loss. She screamed until her bleeding heart had nothing left to bleed.

Her throat raw, her energy spent, she fell to her knees, and her body collapsed onto the sand. Sobs fought to escape and she let them rack her body as tears carved paths down her face. Pulling her knees to her chest, she waited for Riley to come—he always came when she needed him most. He always seemed to know where to find her and what she needed. She didn't even care if he had beaten her in basketball or had ignored her for the past month or disagreed with every decision she made. She just needed him. But he never came. She was alone, so utterly alone, and she didn't know if she had the strength to make it through any of this.

The rain continued to pelt the earth as thunder roared in the distance. The pressure within her had eased, leaving a bottomless void in its place as she stared unseeing at the water lapping the shore, letting the rain soak her clothes.

She didn't know how long she lay there, maybe minutes, maybe hours. The tears stopped eventually, leaving both of her eyes nearly swollen shut and the hole in her heart still aching to be filled. Somehow, she found strength to stand. Her legs wobbled, but she forced them to hold her weight, and then they slowly carried her home.

Thirty

E mma moved through the shadows around her house. She made her way to the side of the garage and reached up to retrieve the key to the exterior door of her garage/bedroom. Her fingers ran along the thin edge of the door frame, but they came up empty. Only then did she remember her decision to hide the key.

It had started out as a spare key. Then the only way in when her family locked the doors before she returned home. Then a way to enter her private space while escaping interaction with her dad and brothers. It was often her way of avoiding them. But she realized months ago that if she wanted to mend the relationships with her dad and brothers, she couldn't have a crutch—an excuse to escape when things got hard.

She closed her eyes and let her forehead fall against the door. Exhaustion like none she'd ever known washed over her. The one night she needed to hide and she was forced to go through the house, unless she wanted to sleep outside. She contemplated it, but cold temperatures still owned the nights and she was still soaked from the rain.

Walking to the front of the house, she saw the illuminated windows and had to force her feet to keep moving, knowing someone was still awake. Maybe her dad and brothers would be enthralled with a game on TV or something and her entry would go unnoticed.

Hoping the door was unlocked, she took an eternity to turn the doorknob, trying to prevent it from squeaking and alerting anyone to her presence. Opening the door just enough to creep through, she kept her head down. If she didn't look in the living room, maybe she'd remain invisible. She took two steps before his voice stopped her.

"Emma." Riley sighed with relief as he stood from the couch and turned toward her.

His presence did nothing to calm her, but her body went on high alert. "What are you doing here?" Her tone was cold, detached. Riley must have heard it too because he didn't approach her. Good. She didn't want him to see her like this.

"We were supposed to meet."

They were supposed to meet. She had forgotten all about having dinner with him. The day he started talking to her, and she couldn't face him.

For once she was grateful for the shadows in the living room. Not much light came from the single floor lamp in the corner. No way could Riley or her dad see the state of her eye if she kept it away from them, showing them only the profile of the unharmed side of her face.

Her injured eye had swollen shut a while ago, so she stared straight ahead with her good eye rather than sideways at Riley, not trusting herself to make eye contact with him. If anyone could see right through her, it was Riley. Maybe the best approach would be to walk straight to her room and lock herself in, rather than risk an interrogation from Riley and her dad. The less time she spent with them the better.

Taking a step in the direction of her escape route, she looked up and froze.

The silhouette of a person stood just out of view of everyone but her.

Lance.

She forced back a sob, and it took everything she had not to turn and run. She couldn't walk past him and act like nothing had happened. She was stuck. Stuck with Lance ahead of her, Riley and her dad to the side, and a storm behind her. What should she do?

"Where've you been?" Her dad's voice brought her back to the present.

Her fear and desperation came out as anger. "Out."

"Out where?" The tenderness she'd gotten used to hearing in her dad's voice over the past couple of months was gone.

"What do you care? You've never cared about anything I do, so why start now?"

"Emma," Riley scolded.

Her dad stood from his chair. "Riley's been waiting for you for over three hours." She heard the anger and confusion in his voice, probably questioning why she would treat him like this.

"So? Let him wait. I'm sure he'll survive."

Riley took a step toward her. She responded by taking a step away from him, maintaining the distance between them. She wanted him to be mad—she needed him to be mad—so he would leave, but even after their time of separation, he knew her too well. Instead of anger, his words only filled with more concern and caution. "Emma," he said as if approaching a wild animal in need of help. "What happened? What's wrong?"

"Go home, Riley. You broke up with me, which means I'm not your problem anymore."

"Emma, look at me."

When she didn't—when she couldn't—he bridged the gap between them. As he stepped in front of her, she turned her face to the side, ensuring that the left side of her face remained out of Riley's view.

He wouldn't let her hide.

She felt him study her, trying to put the pieces together to explain her hostility.

He touched her shoulder. "You're soaked. Have you been outside this entire time?"

The concern in his voice almost brought another round of tears to her eyes.

She stared at the wall, hoping, wishing, praying he would leave, but he didn't. His thumb and forefinger caught her chin and turned her head slowly toward him, despite her resistance. His eyes scanned her face and she knew the instant he saw her secret. He sucked in a breath between his teeth. "What happened?" he demanded.

"Nothing. I fell."

"Don't lie to me, Emma," he growled. "You didn't fall."

Knowing he wouldn't let it drop without an explanation, but not wanting to have that conversation in front of her dad, she gripped Riley's forearms, her eye meeting his. Her anger melted into desperation. "Riley, please," she whispered, begging him not to question her, pleading with him to let it slide until they were out of her house and away from her dad and brother.

His jaw clenched and his nostrils flared as he looked her in the eye. "Who did this to you? Was it Tyler?"

She shook her head.

"Then who?"

"Nobody," she said, but her good eye inadvertently flickered toward Lance. It was less than a second, but it was the only confession Riley needed. His head snapped in the direction she had looked. He glanced between the two siblings before taking a step back and turning his focus on Lance. "You did this?" he accused.

Emma grabbed his arm and tried to pull him back. "Riley, don't."

He twisted out of her grasp and bolted toward Lance. Grabbing the front of Lance's shirt, Riley slammed Lance against the wall. "You hit Emma?"

She caught Riley a second later, grabbing his arm again. "Riley, stop. Please. It was an accident. We were playing basketball and—"

"And he hit you."

"It was an accident."

"Like Tyler's elbow was an accident?" he roared, casting her a look.

She flinched.

"Riley," her dad said, putting a hand on Riley's shoulder. "It's okay. I'll take it from here."

Her dad's voice was low and even, but it held a level of superiority that no one could refuse. She turned to look at him, surprised at the anger pooling in his eyes. His glare was focused on Lance, and she realized her dad could do more damage than Riley ever could. It didn't escape her attention that Lance wasn't fighting back, wasn't bracing himself for an attack, wasn't trying to justify his actions or blame her like he usually did. Instead, he remained silent.

Riley maintained his hold on Lance, seemingly struggling at the thought of not finishing Lance off himself. He slammed Lance against the wall once more before releasing his hold and turning toward Emma. He wrapped an arm around her waist and pulled her against him, turning them so he was between her and Lance.

She clung to Riley, but her focus was on her dad. "Dad, it was an accident. He didn't mean it."

Her words sounded false even to her.

"Riley, take Emma out of here, please." Her dad's voice rang with controlled fury. "I need some time alone with my son."

What did that mean? Was it too much to think they would solve this with a heart-to-heart chat? Or was her dad going to choose fists as his way of communication? She always expected Lance to push their dad too far and give their dad no choice but to use his fists, but she never thought she'd be the cause of it. She also never wanted to be anywhere in the vicinity if it ever went down between them, but now, she didn't want to leave.

Struggling against Riley, she tried to shift her dad's focus off Lance. "Dad, please. It was my fault. I said some things I shouldn't have. Things got out of hand."

Her dad turned to look at Riley, but his eyes stopped on her, giving him a close-up view of Lance's damage. He flinched at the sight of it. Raising his hand, her dad gently brushed her cheek with his knuckle, his face scrunched in pain. "I'm sorry."

His broken voice caused her to stop struggling.

"Riley. Please." Her dad's voice was no more than a whisper, but it held so much pain and guilt that she almost collapsed against Riley. She couldn't leave, not like this.

Riley's arm tightened around her waist, and he practically carried her to the door as she fought against him. His vice-like hold prevented her from gaining any ground. "Riley, let me go."

He got her through the front door and closed it behind him before he loosened his grip around her waist. "Em." The tenderness and regret of his tone made her stop fighting. His hands gripped her face, asking her to look at him, so she did. The love, the protection, the admiration he'd always had for her shimmered in his eyes and brought tears to hers. "Come home with me. Please. Let your dad and Lance work this out, and then I'll bring you back. I promise. For now though, just…come home with me."

Several tears dripped from her eyes and she bowed her head. Resting her forehead against his chest, she nodded.

His arms wrapped around her, crushing her against him. He kissed the top of her head before leading her home.

They stepped over the threshold of Riley's house. It felt safe and warm like it always had, everything that a home should be. But she didn't belong there. A growing sense of angst consumed her, propelling her back to her family. Imagining the worst, she couldn't just sit back, not knowing what repercussions unfolded due to her confrontation with Lance. Her brother wasn't the only one to blame for what happened, so he shouldn't be the only one punished.

She spun toward the door, but Riley blocked her way, his arms securing her against him. "Riley, I have to go back. I don't know what my dad will do to him."

"I'm not letting you go back there."

"Riley, please. I'll be fine."

"I can't. I'm sorry."

"Then will you go?" She saw the hesitation in his eyes, so she grasped his arms to take advantage of his potential weakness. "Please. Don't intervene, just go make sure my dad doesn't hurt Lance. Make sure they're all okay."

"Emma, they'll be fine. I promise." His hands cupped her cheeks. "My priority right now is you. Only you."

"Emma? Riley?" Mr. Ledger and Tyler joined them in the entryway. "What's going on?"

Riley may not fulfill her wish, but Mr. Ledger might. She pulled free from Riley's arms and spun toward Mr. L. "Mr. Ledger, please. You have to go to my house; you have to make sure they're okay."

Mr. Ledger grasped her upper arms, his eyes searching her face like Riley's had earlier, and when he spoke his tone was one of urgency. "Emma, what happened?"

She didn't want to answer his question; she didn't want her answer to sway the results of her request.

"Lance hit her," Riley said from behind her.

Father and son shared a look, communicating without words.

"Please, Mr. Ledger. You have to go to them. Please."

He nodded once. "Okay." He transferred her back into Riley's arms. "Riley, tell your mom where I went."

Riley only nodded.

"And Tyler?" Mr. Ledger turned to look at him.

"I'll be here," Tyler said, his focus on Emma.

They watched Mr. Ledger leave and then Riley pulled

her into a hug. "Come on. We need to get you out of these wet clothes and get you warmed up."

She caught Tyler's glance, filled with concern. Not knowing what to say, she followed Riley, but as she passed Tyler, he reached toward her.

"You okay?"

Not trusting herself to speak, she nodded, but it wasn't enough for him. He pulled her out of Riley's grip and enveloped her in his arms. She wrapped her arms around his waist, but couldn't help questioning his motive. "Why are you hugging me? I'm not crying."

Tyler chuckled. "No, but you have been, so stop fighting it."

Their private joke brought a smile to her face. He pressed his lips to her temple, and then released her, going to stand guard near the front door.

Riley reclaimed her hand and guided her to his room. Halfway up the stairs she started shivering and couldn't stop, the events of the evening catching up to her.

He rummaged through his clothes before producing a pair of sweats and a thermal shirt. He pulled her to the bathroom and turned on the shower. All Emma could do was shiver.

She didn't realize Riley was talking to her until he tilted her head up. "Hey," he said softly. "You're going to be okay. Everything is going to be fine. Take a hot shower and come find me when you're done, okay?"

Emma nodded. The door clicked shut, and she turned toward the mirror. It wasn't her swollen and bruised eye that drew her attention, but the haunted look that consumed her face. She looked lost, scared, vulnerable. Maybe she wasn't very good at hiding her emotions after all.

Unable to face the stranger in the mirror, she turned toward the shower and didn't hesitate to immerse herself beneath the stream of water. The hot water thawed her body and she soaked longer than she probably should have, but she wasn't in a hurry to face the rest of the world.

After she dragged herself out of the shower and dressed, she went in search of Riley and found him in his room.

He sat on the edge of his bed, his elbows resting on his knees and his focus on the ground. His face scrunched in what appeared to be anger. She'd faced enough anger tonight; she couldn't deal with more. "Riley?" she said hesitantly.

His head snapped up and he stood, the anger sliding from his features. "Hey. How are you doing?"

"Better," she said, rubbing her arms. "Warmer."

He nodded. "Good."

After weeks of no talking, she wondered why silence settled between them now. After everything that had happened, she couldn't handle his silence. She had to say something, anything, to fill the gap between them.

"I'm sorry," they said at the same time, each taking a step toward the other.

"What are you sorry for?" they responded together.

Riley ran his hands through his hair and laughed.

"You first," she said.

He took her hand in his and led her to the bed. They perched on the edge, facing each other. "I'm sorry I wasn't there. I'm sorry this happened to you."

"You don't have anything to be sorry for."

"Yes, I do. If I wasn't so stupid and told you I needed space, this wouldn't have happened. You would've been with me, not Lance."

"You don't know that. And besides, it doesn't matter. What's done is done. I don't want to rehash the past and what did and didn't lead up to this. How my brother feels about me...you couldn't change that." She looked down at their joined hands and whispered, "I couldn't change that."

"Em—" The sound of the front door closing jerked Emma upright and Riley stood beside her. "Let's go," he said, tugging on her hand to lead her back downstairs.

Mr. Ledger was hanging up his coat as they reached the front door. Emma bombarded him with questions, not giving him time to answer.

He held up his hands to ward her off. "Whoa, Emma, slow down. Everything is fine. Let's go sit down, and I'll fill you in." He ushered her and Riley into the living room, directing them to the couch. Tyler was already there, and Mrs. Ledger joined them and stood in the doorway.

Mr. Ledger perched on the coffee table directly in front of Emma. "Both your dad and brother are fine. When I got there, they were just talking."

"Talking," Emma said, not sure she believed him. "Another word for yelling and screaming, right?"

"No, just regular old talking."

Since when did Lance and her dad ever just talk? Especially to each other. "Were either of them bleeding?"

He shook his head. "No."

"Any bruising? Ripped clothes? Broken windows or dishes?"

"No, no, and no. I promise, they were just talking. Your dad will tell you the same thing when he gets here."

"He's coming here?"

Mr. Ledger nodded. "When he's through talking with Lance."

She nodded. "Okay." Now all she had to do was wait.

◆◆◆

Someone knocked on the front door. Mr. Ledger crossed the entryway from the kitchen to answer it.

"Hello, John," Mr. Ledger said, holding out his hand.

"Robert." Her dad nodded as he accepted the handshake and stepped across the threshold. "Is my daughter here?"

Mr. Ledger nodded to where Emma stood in the living room. All she wanted to do was run to her dad and ask him what had happened, but she held back. Her throat constricted at the memory of the things she'd said to him an hour ago when she returned home and her attitude when she had tried to hide her eye. Their relationship was still so fragile, almost like a dream, and it could shatter at any second. Maybe she didn't deserve her dad's forgiveness, but she so desperately needed it.

"Ems." He took a step toward her, his arms starting to rise to the sides.

It was all the sign she needed. She stumbled forward into his outstretched arms, and slammed against his chest.

"I'm sorry," she mumbled into his chest. "The things I said to you, I didn't mean—"

"I know," he soothed her. "Shh, it's okay."

She felt his lips kiss the top of her head before he stepped away. His hands still gripped her biceps as he held her at arm's length. His eyes searched her face, lingering on her eye. "Are you okay?"

Unable to speak, she nodded.

His fingers gently touched her bruised cheekbone. "I'm sorry, sweetheart. I never thought Lance would…"

His voice trailed off and she shook her head. "It was my fault. I said some terrible things. I—"

"It's all right," her dad said, gripping her shoulders. "We can discuss the details about what happened later."

"What about Lance? Is he…" she couldn't finish her question.

"He's fine," her dad reassured. "I do think it would be best if you stayed here tonight though, if that's all right?" He directed his question to Mr. Ledger.

"Of course," Riley's dad replied.

Upon seeing the hurt look on her face, her dad reassured her. "He just needs some time to cool off. You can come home first thing tomorrow after you've gotten a good rest."

She raised her head, searching her dad's face. The question on her mind needed his honest answer. "Why does he hate me?" she whispered.

"He doesn't." Her dad dragged a hand down his face, exhaling loudly as he looked at the floor. "He looks at you and sees everything he's ever wanted but wasn't strong enough to fight for. You've overcome so much to be where you are right now, and he never fought for anything. He just let it all slip through his fingers."

"I don't understand."

"Jealousy is a funny beast. If left unhandled, it grows stronger until it obtains the power to consume a person whole."

"This is all about jealousy?" She couldn't wrap her head around that thought. It would be different if he began hating her these past few months when she started playing basketball, but his issues with her ran deeper and darker than that.

"Let's not talk about it anymore tonight. It's been a long day, so let's all get some rest and tackle it in the morning." He squeezed her shoulder. "Okay?"

She nodded, still unsettled by her dad's rationale.

Mr. Ledger invited her dad in to sit, and Mrs. Ledger brought him a cup of coffee. They settled into lighthearted conversation, steering clear of the night's events.

Emma rested her head against Riley's shoulder as she sat beside him on the couch. She didn't know if tomorrow would bring back their friendship or if they would go their separate ways, but for the moment she found peace being with Riley, acting like all was well. His arm wrapped around her shoulders and it felt like old times.

She tried to stay invested in the conversation, but now that she was safe and warm, her eyelids drooped closed, and she felt her body grow limp. A few seconds later, Riley's chest rumbled with laughter. "We should get you to bed."

He helped her stand, but before she took a step on her own, Riley flipped her world upside down as he secured her over his shoulder. She laughed. "Aren't guys supposed to be all romantic and carry their girlfriends bridal style rather than flung over their shoulder like dead prey?" Girlfriend? Why did she say that? She didn't know what they were at the moment. "That only happens in books and movies. In real life, most guys aren't strong enough. You, my dear," he said, slapping her on the back of the thigh, "are pure muscle and weigh a ton. If I tried to carry you bridal style, we'd pull a Jack and Jill down the stairs."

"You calling yourself a wimp?"

"You better believe I am. Besides, it was either this or the old fashioned piggyback ride."

"And I didn't get to choose?"

He shrugged. "I made an executive decision."

Their audience laughed and wished her a good night.

Having made it upstairs in one piece, Riley carried her to his bedroom, rather than to the downstairs guestroom she usually stayed in. Even with her hanging over his shoulder, he still managed to pull back the sheets on his bed and smoothly lay her down. She didn't resist him tucking her in. Snuggling with his pillow, encompassed in the smell that was all Riley, her eyelids floated closed and the exhaustion she'd felt down by the water consumed her again.

She felt the bed dip as he sat beside her. His lips pressed against her forehead and she anticipated his departure, but it never came. Instead, she felt his fingertips brush hair away from her face, felt his hand encircle hers, and heard the melody of a familiar lullaby as he started to hum. Sleep pulled her under.

Thirty-One

D espite the late night, Emma woke early the next morning. Since she didn't have any clothes of her own, she sauntered downstairs in Riley's shirt and sweats. The house was quiet, but the sun flooded the house with light. The creak from the bottom stair ricocheted throughout the house like a bomb. She was certain it would wake everyone, but no one stirred as she slipped out the backdoor onto the patio.

She took a deep breath of the chilled morning air and listened to the birds fill the day with their song. Such a contrast from yesterday's storm clouds and rain. With a sigh, she sat on the steps and leaned her head against the stair railing, her eyes captured by the lush grass and flower garden Mrs. Ledger had diligently worked on throughout the year. If Lenny and Lucas ever snuck into the Ledgers' yard to pick flowers, they would have their pick of roses, lilies, daisies, sunflowers, and a bunch of other flowers Emma couldn't identify.

The glass door slid open behind her.

"What are you doing up so early?" Tyler asked, not completely finished with his full body yawn.

"I couldn't sleep any longer."

He tapped her shoulder. "Mind if I sit?"

She shook her head.

"Sooo," he said, after a few minutes of silence. "Last night was...interesting."

"Yeah," she said with a snort. "That's one word for it."

Her head still rested on the railing and she had yet to turn her head in his direction, but that didn't prevent her from seeing him glance her way several times before gaining the courage to speak again. "Are things really that bad for you at home?"

She wrapped her arms around her legs and brought her chin to rest on her bent knee. "Sometimes."

He let out a breath. "Families suck."

Since she didn't know anything about his family and she couldn't contest his statement after last night's events, she chose to remain silent.

He rested his elbows on his knees, bowing his head to look at the ground between his legs. "I'm sorry about that day at the park." His voice was quiet, filled with a remorse she didn't know he was capable of feeling. "You know, when—"

"When you hit me?"

He scratched the back of his head, his discomfort speaking volumes. "Yeah. I'm sorry I hit you."

She studied his profile. It seemed like a lifetime ago when he'd shown up at the park and battled Emma and the guys on the court. "Why'd you do it?" Maybe if she understood Tyler's reasoning, she'd be one step closer to understanding Lance's. Did he just lose his temper and have a momentary lapse of control? Was it intentional? Was there even a possibility that he regretted it?

"Because I'm jerk?" Tyler chanced a look at her, but she wasn't buying his lame excuse. There had to be a deeper reason, and he knew it. "I don't know, I guess because I was mad that, once again, I was some place I wasn't wanted."

The sadness in his voice threw her. "What does that

mean?"

Taking a deep breath, he looked to the sky. "Growing up, my older brother was in and out of juvey." He picked up a pebble from the porch and ran his fingers across the surface. "Bad seed or what not. He was always getting into fights or stealing or whatever else he did to build his reputation as a bad boy. Kids hated him, and teachers were afraid of him. By the time I got to high school everyone only saw me as Hunter's little brother. They expected me to follow in his footsteps and cowered anytime I stepped into a room. Teachers hated me from day one and before I knew what was happening I was being blamed for all kinds of things I didn't do. No matter how much I denied them, no one believed me. After a while I figured if I was going to get punished for things anyway, why not do them?" He tossed the stone across the yard and clasped his hands together. "I've been expelled from two schools, so my parents decided to send me here as a last-ditch effort to save me or something stupid like that." Tyler blew out a deep breath. "I hate them."

"Why?"

"Because they look at me like I'm everything they despise in the world. My parents are afraid of me for no reason. They don't see me, they don't know me, and they don't want to. They don't care about me, so why should I care about them?"

The conversation hit too close to her heart, but Emma could never find it in her heart to truly hate her family, even if she did think they spent the majority of their lives hating her.

"Tell me you don't hate your family," he challenged her.

"I don't ha—"

He waved away her response. "I know I don't know much about you and your family, but I know enough. I know they've treated you like scum. So after all they've done to you, after *that*," he said, pointing to her black eye, "how could you not hate them? Why do you care what they think?"

It was a great question. Why did she care? "I'm not saying family isn't difficult, but for me, family should be everything. They see you at your best and at your worst, but they love you and support you anyway. At least they should. And you're right, my family hasn't treated me very well. I've spent most of my life thinking they wanted me to disappear and never come back. A few months ago, I was ready to walk away from them forever, but then I realized I kept looking at them and seeing their faults and expecting them to make the first move to bring our family together. But they didn't, none of them did, not even me. When college became a possibility for me, I realized I didn't want to leave and become estranged from my family. It was my last chance to fix things with my dad and brothers. Mrs. Ledger suggested I make them dinner. It was such a small insignificant gesture to try and let them know I cared about them. I never thought it would work, but you know what happened?"

Tyler shook his head.

"My youngest brother sought me out for the first time in his life. We ended up doing homework together, and the next thing I know he's following me around like a puppy. Without even knowing how it happened, my family started rebuilding itself, and I got three brothers and a dad out of it. Turns out there's not much to hate about them after all."

"What about Lance?"

She bowed her head, last night's events still too fresh. "I learned that sometimes you can't help them all." The admission hit her hard. She refused to let the tears reappear, especially in Tyler's presence, but when he put his arm around her shoulders, it was a good indication he suspected the girlie emotions were close enough to touch.

"At least you have me."

His confident cheesy grin made her laugh and roll her

eyes. "Yeah, Tyler, at least I have you."

"I know things between us started out rough and you had every reason to hate me, but thanks for not totally ditching me these past few months. It's only been halfway bearable because of you."

Her head tilted upward, needing to see with her own eyes how serious he was in his admission. A look passed over Tyler's face as he leaned infinitesimally closer, watching her, studying her. She had seen the same look on Riley's face enough times to recognize it. Sure, her and Tyler were friends and had just shared a heart-to-heart chat and all that, but that didn't mean she was ready to pucker up and kiss the guy. "Tyler?" she whispered, their faces only a couple inches apart.

"Yeah?" he said softly, his eyes intent on her mouth.

"You come any closer and I'll give you a black eye to match mine."

His gaze flickered from her mouth to her eyes before he chuckled and pulled back. "You can't blame a guy for trying."

"Sure I can."

"Okay, fine, be that way." He squeezed her shoulders and smiled, but didn't pursue her any further. "So, are you and lover boy back together again or what?"

She shrugged. "I don't know. We didn't get to talk yesterday. I don't even know if he wants to get back together."

"Oh please. That boy is so in love with you it's disgusting."

"Oh yeah? Then tell me what went wrong. Tell me why, after eight years of friendship, he needed space away from me." Despite Riley taking care of her the previous night, she still didn't know if she could forge ahead with their relationship without knowing what had happened. She didn't want to brush everything under the rug and pretend it wasn't there, eating away at them. "That's not love. At least not in my book."

Tyler dropped his arm from around her shoulders. "Yeah. About that."

"What?"

When he didn't answer, she looked at him more closely. Tense shoulders, anxious hands that couldn't find a comfortable place to rest, eyes looking anywhere but at her. "Tyler." Her stomach dropped. "What do you know?"

He cleared his throat, trying to choke out a laugh. "See, Princess, it's kind of a funny story."

She knew from his posture that whatever he had to say didn't elicit jokes to lighten the mood. "Spill it."

His eyes flickered in her direction as his face wilted. "My parents couldn't deal with me."

"You've told me this already."

"They sent me here to live with some other family."

"Again, old news."

"They sent me to live with the rich golden boy who has it all: parents who care about him, true friends, money. You. It was like a punch in the face. I couldn't live with that. Few people in my situation could."

"And?"

Tyler studied her before turning away and rubbing his hands down his face. "You're going to hate me for this."

"Tyler," she warned.

"You know how they say misery loves company?"

"Yeah," she said slowly.

"Well, see, it's like…how do I say this?"

Emma grabbed his arm in a death grip. "Spit it out already."

He covered her hand with his as he turned to face her, his eyes pleading for forgiveness. "You have to understand. When I got here I was so mad. I was mad at my parents for dropping me off and fleeing, and I was mad at myself for getting into this mess. Living with Riley only made me feel worse."

She swallowed the building lump in her throat. "Go on."

"So I took my anger out on Riley, and I hit him where it would hurt the most." He paused, waiting for her to catch on.

Her eyelids slid closed. "Me."

"I figured if I could make him as miserable as me, I'd feel better. So when I overheard you talking to him about not attending the same college, I used it to my advantage."

She looked to the blue sky, already knowing the end of the story, but needing to hear the details. "What did you say to him?"

"Emma, I'm sorry. I—"

"What did you say," she growled through clenched teeth.

"I told him he was suffocating you but that you'd never admit it. You telling him to go to a different college was your way of telling him to back off. I said if he didn't give you space now he'd only end up hurting you later and causing the end of your relationship. It didn't matter that none of it was true. The guy is so in love with you that the tiniest doubt would cause him to sacrifice everything for you...even if it meant losing you."

"Why in the world would he believe you?"

His guilt-ridden face broke into a smirk. "I can be very persuasive when I want to be."

Now was not the time for his jokes. "How could you?" She jumped up and whirled on him. "You cost me my best friend."

He stood, arms raised and palms out to ward off a fight. "I know, and I'm sorry. If I could take it back—"

"You can't." She shook her head, knowing the damage was done. She should've known Tyler was involved somehow. Riley never would've treated her this way on his own.

Tyler stepped in the way of her pacing and placed his hands on her shoulders. "I know, and I'm sorry. Consider me indebted to you forever."

Needing to talk to Riley to settle all this once and for all, she pointed a finger at Tyler's face in warning. "You and me? We *will* continue this conversation later, but I can't guarantee you'll survive it without bruises."

"There are other ways to solve problems without throwing fists, you know," he said, using the words she'd used on him a while ago.

"Not with you there's not," she growled.

Despite the fact he had earned himself a one-way ticket into the doghouse, he threw his head back and laughed as his arms enveloped her. "I look forward to it."

She pushed away from him and took the porch steps two at a time. As she flung open the door to reenter the house, Tyler called out to her. "For the record, Princess, I can carry you bridal style anytime you want me to."

She recoiled at his claim. "Like I'll ever give you the chance to prove it."

Slamming the door behind her, she weaved through the house and down the stairs to the guestroom, where she assumed Riley had slept. Since he had given up his room for her and it was still early, she figured he would still be asleep. She cracked open the door to look in on him. While he was still in bed, sprawled on his back, his eyes were open and alert, like he'd been awake for hours.

"Hey," she said.

He smiled and reached out a hand for her. "Hey."

She approached the bed and took his hand. With a tug, he pulled her down beside him.

"How are you this morning?" he asked.

She knew he was referring to her family, but her conversation with Tyler caused her relationship with Riley to be on the forefront of her thoughts. Riley's hand found hers in the space between them, and he laced their fingers together while his thumb caressed circles on the back of her hand. Given everything that had happened the previous night, it would be all too easy to fall back in with Riley and forget the past month, but she knew they couldn't avoid their issues forever.

"Tyler told me what he said to you." She turned her head to look at Riley's profile as he stared up at the ceiling. "He said you broke up with me because of him."

Riley drew her hand to his mouth and kissed it before emitting a sigh. "While I'd love to blame Tyler, he didn't say anything that I wasn't already thinking."

"What happened to us?" she whispered.

"You wandered by my house for the first time when we were nine. You were tough as nails and ready to take on the world." He smiled at the memory. "I wanted nothing more than to be your friend. It wasn't long before I saw the frightened, lonely girl you kept hidden on the inside. As soon as I saw her, I promised myself I would do whatever it took to make you happy and to protect you. I never expected you to do the same for me.

"Ever since we were kids, our lives have been intertwined. Sometimes it's easy to forget that we're two different people living different lives and making our own decisions, because all I've ever wanted was to be with you. When you went out for the girls' basketball team, I started planning what it would be like to go to the same college together—the late night study sessions, hanging out in our dorm rooms together, coming home together on weekends and holidays. I had our entire lives planned, yet I never considered the possibility of us going to different colleges." He sighed and turned his head to look at her. "So when you told me OSU wasn't the right choice for me, I panicked. I thought you didn't want to be with me, that we didn't want the same thing. The idea of you having this entire life I wasn't a part of—new guys for you to choose from, not being there for you if you needed me—scared me. That's when I realized that what I was truly afraid of was that you'd realize you didn't need me anymore."

"Riley." Her pained whisper encapsulated the depth of

sorrow for her best friend who always seemed so confident about himself and life. He never let on that he had insecurities, especially about them.

He returned his focus back to the ceiling. "The night we fought, after you left, I realized that I'd been holding onto you, onto us, so tightly, not wanting you to be able to survive without me. I kept seeing you as the weak little girl that needed me by her side, not the strong, capable, self-sufficient girl you've proven to be. I was so blinded by the idea of possibly losing you that I based all my decisions on how to keep you close, not what was best for you or me. I don't want that kind of relationship for us, the kind where we're afraid and are so dependent on one another that we aren't free to do what's right for us. So I did what I thought I had to do."

"You broke up with me."

"I didn't mean to, nor did I mean to be such a jerk. It was just so hard to be near you and keep the distance I felt we needed."

"Why didn't you tell me?"

"Because I knew you could talk me out of it." He took a deep breath. "I couldn't do as you asked and make the right decisions for me in terms of college and next steps without gaining the clarity I needed. And the more I felt myself holding onto us, the more I felt us breaking. I felt me breaking us, and I didn't know what else to do. I figured if we took some time apart we could sort out what we needed to without interfering with each other. I knew if we didn't, we'd end up making mistakes and possibly hating each other later, and I couldn't let that happen."

His words made sense, and she found that she couldn't be mad at him for doing what he felt was right, despite the fact he'd left her in the dark through it all. "So what made you decide to talk to me again?"

"The day I came home and saw you with my mom."

She groaned and covered her face with her hands. "You

mean my embarrassing sob fest that no one was supposed to see?"

He rolled onto his side and pulled her hands away from her face. "Whenever I saw you at school you looked so happy, like you didn't care one way or another whether I was with you or not, and that hurt. A lot. When I saw you crying, my heart broke all over again because I didn't know what was happening in your life, and I didn't know how to help you. When I asked my mom what was wrong after you left, the glare she gave me said it all. Your tears were because of me. It was the first time I realized you were hurting as much as me, and I knew I had to get you back. By the way, after you left, my mom yelled at me for almost an hour about how she raised me better and she didn't understand how I could be so thoughtless and unkind to you. She didn't talk to me for two days. I even had to make my own breakfast."

"You poor baby."

"You mock me, but having the two most important women in my life mad at me ripped me to shreds." He bent his arm and propped his head up on his hand so he could look down at her. "Em, I am so, *so* sorry. I know I've been horrible to you and made tons of mistakes, but you're still the most important person in my life, so I have to ask. Do you think there's any way we can give us another try?"

Maybe she should've made him grovel or put him on probation rather than forgive him so quickly, but after everything that had transpired over the past 12 hours, she didn't want to put anyone through any more pain. They'd been best friends for too long just to throw it all away over insecurities and uncertainty about the future. They were both new at the whole relationship thing and combining that with life changes that were soon coming their way, was it so bad to learn from their mistakes and move forward together?

"Riley, I've never needed you to solve my problems for me or protect me from the world. What I've needed is for you to be my friend. To stand by me when things get tough, to make me laugh when I feel like crying, to support me so I can regain my footing when I fall. And you've never let me down. Ever. Even if we go to different colleges, that won't change anything. College will be new and different for both of us, but I'll still need you just as much as I always have. You're irreplaceable in my life."

His head bowed, and he exhaled in relief. "I'm so glad you said that because there's one more thing I need to tell you."

Everything stopped when his eyes begged for forgiveness for some act he'd committed. *Here it comes,* she thought. *He's ripped up all our childhood pictures. He wrote hate messages about me and posted them on the Internet.* She sucked in a breath. *He fooled around with some girl who wasn't me during our time apart.*

He brushed a hand through his hair and took a deep breath before racing through his confession. "I accepted an offer from the University of Oregon to play basketball next year. If I work hard, it's possible I could have a starting position as a freshman, and they've got great architecture and business programs, which might be careers I'm interested in pursuing. Please don't be mad. I gave it a lot of thought, and I think we can still make things work between us."

"What?" Excitement won out over the string of fears. "Riley, that's fantastic!" She flew off the bed and tackled him in a hug, crushing him beneath her.

His face broke into a smile. "You think so?"

Looking down at him, she couldn't hide her smile. "I know so. I'm so proud of you."

Without hesitation, he pulled her face to his, crushing his lips against hers.

She thought he would deepen the kiss in the attempt to make up for the last month, but he surprised her. He didn't need anything more than reassurance that they were okay.

The kiss remained soft and gentle, fueled with regret for mistakes made, relief of being back together again, and a love that they'd always shared. He rolled them over so he was on top and with a final kiss he pulled back. "We should stop before my mom finds us and grounds us both."

She laughed but pulled his lips back to hers, grateful they'd found their way back to each other. Seconds passed before they heard footsteps coming down the stairs. They broke away from each other, and in the attempt to put space between them, Riley accidentally shoved her off the bed. She landed on her hip with a thud. "Ow," she moaned into the carpet.

His head popped over the side of the bed. "Em, I'm so sorry. Are you o—"

The door swung open and Mrs. Ledger appeared with a hand on her hip. "What is going on in here?"

Riley and Emma both looked up, but neither of them could contain their laughter.

"We were just talking?" Emma said as if trying the words on for size at the same time Riley said, "She's breaking the rules again, Mom."

"I am n—"

Riley's hand slapped against her mouth, preventing her from finishing her sentence.

"She lies," Riley shout-whispered. "I had to shove her off of me to preserve my innocence."

Emma twisted away from his hold, swiped a pillow off the bed, and beat him with it. "You are such a liar."

Laughing too hard to defend himself, he wrapped his arms around her and brought her crashing down onto the bed beside him.

Mrs. L cleared her throat. "I came to tell you breakfast is ready, but I'm glad to see things are back to normal around here."

With a wink, she left them to their wrestling match, making sure to leave the door propped open as she retreated.

Thirty-Two

E mma left Riley to venture home and check on her family. Aside from the tick-tick-ticking of a clock, silence engulfed her when she entered the house. The living room was dark, but light from the kitchen beckoned her.

Lucas's voice broke the silence. "Emma!"

A smile broke out on her face. She didn't think she'd ever get tired of hearing his joy at seeing her. "Hey, you."

He jumped up from the table and bounded toward her. When he caught sight of her bruised eye, he froze, his eyes widening. "What happened to your face?"

She pointed to her eye. "What, this?" She waved it aside. "It's nothing. You should've seen the other guy."

A smile spread across his face as his hands made fists like a boxer and he bounced around the kitchen on his toes. "Did you give him the old one-two?"

She laughed and tousled his hair. "Yeah, something like that."

Everything was fine. Her youngest brother was role-playing her supposed stellar boxing skills with pride. He didn't need to know the truth, at least not right now. Everything could've gone back to normal, but nothing in the Wrangton house ever did.

"Lance hit you, didn't he?"

She glanced up, surprised to see Lenny standing in the doorway. The smile fell from her face. She wanted to protect her younger brothers from the truth, but what could she say? She couldn't lie to them. "Lenny—"

Lenny's face hardened as he crossed his arms, looking too much like Lance. "I heard him and Dad talking last night."

Emma silently scolded herself. Riley and her dad had convinced her to stay the night at the Ledgers', but she should've been here to make sure Lenny's prying ears didn't learn the truth.

She took a step toward her brother. "Lenny, he didn't—"

"It's okay." Lance's voice came from the living room before his body appeared in the doorway behind Lenny. "He deserves to know the truth; they both do."

"Lance," she warned.

"Yeah, it was me."

Lucas whipped around, his eyes flashing hurt and anger. "You did this? You hit Emma?"

Even Emma flinched at the power of his accusatory tone.

Lance bowed his head. "Yeah," he said quietly. "I did."

"Why?" Lenny asked. No thirteen-year-old should've ever owned so much pain.

Lance's eyes shifted to Emma as if he was addressing her rather than answering Lenny's question. "I was mad, and I guess...I lost control."

Was that his way of trying to apologize? She knew there was more to the story than just losing control. Years of hurt and hatred fueled his actions, but she wasn't about to have that conversation with Lenny and Lucas as witnesses.

"That's a lousy excuse," Lenny spit out.

She didn't miss how Lance's advancing step into the kitchen caused Lenny to step in front of her, almost in a protective stance. The kid was a head shorter than Emma and no match for Lance, yet his hands fisted at his sides and he puffed up his chest as if ready to fight...for her.

When Lenny spoke, his voice was like ice. "You don't go near her."

Emma placed a hand on Lenny's shoulder. "Hey, it's okay. I'm—"

Her reassurances were cut off when Lucas charged past Lenny and shoved Lance with as much power as his little body could muster. Even though Lucas was half his size, Lance stumbled backward.

"I hate you!" Lucas screamed. "How could you?"

"Hey," Emma said, rushing forward. She'd never seen Lucas react like this before, and it scared her. Her body moved automatically to crouch in front of her littlest brother, not caring that she turned her back on Lance—the biggest threat to them all. She gripped Lucas's arms to steady him, feeling his small body shake with fury. "It's okay," she whispered.

"No, it's not. It's not okay," he yelled. Tears formed in his eyes and slid down his cheeks as sobs broke from his chest. "Now you hate us, and you're gonna leave, just like Mom did."

His words hit her like a punch in the stomach. "Lucas," she said softly, trying to calm him down.

"All because of him!" he screamed, pointing at Lance.

Emma exchanged a look with Lance. For once he looked like he actually cared, like the words of an eight-year-old mattered.

Lucas threw his arms around her and sobbed into her neck. "Please don't go," he pleaded. "Please don't leave us; please don't hate us."

She wrapped her arms around him and hugged him tight, rubbing his back. When she thought she could speak without her voice cracking, she attempted to reassure him. "Shh, it's okay. I'm not going anywhere. I'm staying right here."

Lucas hiccupped, his sobs not quite gone. "Promise?"

"Yeah, buddy," she said, tightening her hold on him. "I promise. After all, I only have one homework buddy."

He didn't say anything in response, but his arms tightened around her neck. The scene remained frozen— Lucas clinging to Emma, Emma doing her best to console him, while Lance and Lenny watched in silence, stealing glances at each other. Movement caused her eyes to shift toward the living room. Her breath caught when she saw Riley and Tyler standing outside the kitchen archway, witnessing the Wrangton saga. She didn't know how long they'd been standing there or how much they'd heard.

Taking her look as an invitation, Riley strolled into the kitchen. "Hey." He delivered his greeting friendly enough, but his body stiffened as he looked between Emma and Lance, last night not forgotten. "Everything okay?"

Lucas pulled away from her, and she knew he didn't want Riley to see him cry. "Yeah," he said, wiping his sleeve down his face to remove all traces of tears. "Everything's good. Right, Em?"

His eyes sought confirmation for so much. Confirmation that she wouldn't leave and scar the family like their mom had, confirmation that she didn't hate him, confirmation that they were, beyond anything, a family and weren't beyond hope. She nodded at his question before standing up, kissing his head, and slinging an arm around his shoulders. "Yep, everything's good."

Lance slipped out of the kitchen. Riley turned to follow him, which caused Emma to step forward, her hand reaching out to stop him. She didn't want another encounter like last night. Before words formulated on her tongue, Riley reappeared a few feet in front of her. Lucas brushed past Emma, his entire face lighting up as he saw what Riley held in his hand. "You brought Emma flowers!"

A blush accompanied Riley's smile. "Yeah," he said, stepping toward her and extending his arm. "Some kid told me you might like them." He gave Lucas a wink, which only caused the smile on her younger brother's face to widen.

Taking the massive bouquet of assorted flowers with trembling hands, she couldn't explain why her throat closed up and her heart thumped in her chest like it was preparing for a championship game. Her eyes focused on the bright red roses, purple carnations, and pink stargazer lilies that combined in the most perfect bouquet Emma had ever seen. She was grateful she didn't find any roots from the neighbor's yard. As she turned the flowers in her hand, her eyes found the white crane nestled among the petals. She picked out the bird that now held so much meaning to her. Unable to wait, she unfolded the paper to reveal a perfectly drawn heart in the center of the page.

"I didn't know what ones were your favorite," Riley said.

"They're perfect," she whispered. It turned out she did like flowers.

Lucas patted Riley on the arm and beamed at him. "You done good, buddy."

Riley and Emma burst into laughter, and Lenny, Lucas, and Tyler joined them.

Riley tousled Lucas's hair. "Thanks for the advice."

Emma wished she had a 'get out of school free' pass. Sure, she could skip, like 75 percent of her classmates did when the idea of going to class was too much to bear, but she doubted college coaches would overlook the mark on her record when considering her for a scholarship, if they were still interested. She hadn't heard anything from colleges in weeks. Out of the handful of colleges that had contacted her and expressed interest in her as a player, only two hadn't confirmed their decision. She didn't want to do anything to jeopardize what small chance she may still have to earn a spot on one of their teams.

As Riley pulled into the parking lot, the school loomed before her. A building where thousands of teens swarmed the hallways, sat brooding in classes, and waited for the latest gossip to entertain their days. She didn't want to be the topic of conversation, but how could she avoid it when part of her face served as evidence of her altercation with Lance? How could anyone not notice?

Riley squeezed her hand. "You could always say you fell."

She couldn't help but laugh. "Yeah, because that excuse worked so well on you."

He kissed the back of her hand. "I can't help that I'm incredibly astute. But everyone else?" He shrugged. "They might believe you."

"Doubtful," she muttered. If anything, it would bring her more attention, considering she didn't have a reputation as a klutz.

"You can blame me."

Emma turned around to look at Tyler. With his broad body and long legs, he filled the backseat.

He shifted under the weight of her gaze, and his eyes filled with sadness. "They'd probably believe it."

Which was exactly why she wouldn't throw him under the bus. Yes, he had been a real thorn in her side over the past few months, but he'd also been her pillar of support when Riley ditched her, and she couldn't overlook his kindness for selfish reasons. "Thanks, but I'll figure out something else."

Even though they had arrived at school later than usual, they still had time before the bell. Both Riley and Tyler walked her to her locker. She wondered how they had reconciled their differences to be able to stand side by side in the hallway without killing each other.

Emma did her best to shield her face from wandering eyes by turning her head into Riley's chest as he tucked her into his side, but when the bell rang they'd have to go their separate ways. She couldn't hide behind him all day.

At her locker, she switched out books and was about to close the door when the girls showed up.

"What's up, Wrangton?" Shiloh said, causing Emma to flinch. She didn't want to start her day off confronting the girls, knowing they would ask way too many questions.

Shiloh nodded at Riley and Tyler. "Boys."

Emma felt the guys both tense beside her, but they managed to nod back. Knowing there was no way to get out of it, she took a deep breath and turned to her friends. Shiloh, Ashley, Madison, and Lauren. One collective gasp escaped them at the same time, and Emma almost found it humorous.

They converged around her, having the decency not to gain the attention of others passing by. "What happened to you?" Shiloh whispered.

Ashley looked on the verge of crying, Madison's mouth had popped open as she stared, and Lauren's face collapsed in an angry scowl.

"It's a long story," Emma tried.

"Did Tyler hit you again?" Shiloh asked loud enough for Tyler to hear.

Emma hated how Shiloh and Riley had both jumped to that conclusion first. "No, he didn't." She made sure her voice left no room for doubt.

Fingers wrapped around her bicep. "Told you," Tyler whispered in her ear. "See you in class." She watched him weave through the hallway, then disappear when he turned the corner.

Riley placed his hand at the small of her back and took a half-step closer as if asking whether or not she wanted him to save her from the girls. She glanced over her shoulder, not knowing what answer to give, when Lauren grabbed her arm and dragged her around the corner. She pushed open the bathroom door and dragged Emma behind her, the rest of the girls following.

"I'm sorry, but I can't let you walk around school like this. It's ugly."

Lauren set her backpack on the counter and retrieved a small bag from inside it. She whipped open the zipper and emptied the contents on the bathroom counter. Various sized tubes and containers spilled over the counter.

"What are you doing?" Emma asked, her eyes growing wide at all the makeup. She took a step back and bumped into Shiloh, who held Emma in place. "Now is not the time to make me into one of your Barbie dolls."

Lauren ignored her, pushing Emma against the counter while looking at Shiloh and Madison, communicating without words to close their ranks on Emma and hold her still. "Close your eyes."

"Lauren—"

"Do it!"

Outnumbered, Emma did as she was told. Emma kept her eyes closed, afraid to see what transpired. She felt several different textures brush over her skin. Something wet, something dry. The smell of powder invaded her nose, causing her to sneeze. Aside from a huff, Lauren didn't say anything. Lauren blew on her face, and Emma flinched with surprise. What the heck was this girl doing? Emma imagined white face paint, purple eyebrows, a painted-on tear, and big red lips drooping in a frown. When Lauren declared, "Done!" a few minutes later, Emma knew she'd be in need of a big round nose and a wig of orange curly hair to complete her role as a clown.

Peering out from one squinting eye at a time, she saw her reflection in the mirror. She looked like...herself. Emma Wrangton. Blonde untamed hair, pale complexion, green eyes, void of the bruising that she had sported moments ago. "What did you do?" she asked, not even trying to hide the shock in her voice. Her black eye had disappeared.

Lauren shrugged. "Not much."

"Stellar work, isn't it?" Madison asked, her arms crossed

over her chest in a smug way as if it satisfied her to be the best friend of the blonde-haired makeup artist.

Ashley looked from Emma to the mirror as if trying to find the trick glass.

Shiloh just kept nodding. "You look good, Wrangton."

The best part was that it didn't look like Emma had any makeup on. She saw herself smile in the mirror at the idea she wouldn't have to field people's incessant questions about what had happened. "Lauren, you're a genius."

"I know." Lauren swiped the contents on the counter back into her bag and zipped it closed before tossing it in her backpack. Flipping her hair over her shoulder, she headed toward the door as the first bell rang, a grinning Madison in her wake.

"Hey, Lauren?" Emma called before she could leave.

Lauren turned back to her.

"Thank you."

Lauren's smugness gave way to the sincerest smile Emma had ever seen from her. "You're welcome. What are friends for?"

Thirty-Three

E mma should've gotten up a while ago, but the events of the past week had exhausted her. It had been six days since Lance hit her, and she hadn't talked to him since. The only time she ever saw him was at breakfast and, unlike before when he would lash out at her over every little thing and make her feel like the world's most useless person, he never spoke anymore, to her or anyone else. He hid behind his newspapers and kept to himself. She didn't know what to do. As the days passed, she grew more and more anxious about all that was unresolved between them.

After her encounter with Lance and her brothers earlier in the week, she had hung out with Tyler and Riley every afternoon, shooting hoops and watching movies at Riley's house. Aside from school, Lucas had refused to leave her side, and she was grateful Riley and Tyler didn't mind including him. Half the time, her little brother fell asleep before the movie ended, and Riley carried him home. Poor kid. He was so worried she'd leave him because of what Lance had done that he exhausted himself looking out for her.

Sometimes Lenny would join them, but other times he'd stay at home, and she had the suspicion he was watching

Lance and making sure he didn't come anywhere near her. Whenever she returned home, Lenny would greet her with a smile and corral her in the path least likely to cross with Lance's. As a result, it was difficult for her to catch a look at Lance's face to see what he was thinking.

The door leading into the house creaked open. Expecting Lucas or Lenny, she sat up in surprise when Logan stepped into view from between the aisle of boxes.

"Hey," he said.

"Hey." Her simple answer gave no indication to how curious she was about her older brother's presence.

"I didn't wake you, did I?"

She shook her head. "I've been awake."

Logan took a tentative step toward her. "I was thinking about making something new for breakfast." He massaged the back of his neck as if it was tight with tension. "Want to come burn some food with me?"

She laughed and tossed her blankets aside. Not exactly the question she'd thought he'd ask. "Sure."

Of course Logan had to pick another recipe that neither one of them knew how to cook, nor did either one of them have the skills and cooking expertise to attempt, but who could turn down another cooking adventure?

They stood side by side at the counter, Logan dicing an onion and Emma grating cheese.

Knowing Logan wasn't much of a talker, a comfortable silence had settled between them. Every once in a while, they'd compare thoughts about the recipe or what a word meant, otherwise, they remained quiet. But then Logan stopped dicing and dropped his knife on the counter. "I'm sorry."

"Sorry for what?" She scanned the recipe, thinking he'd missed a step. Wouldn't have been the first time for either of them.

"For not being there."

She remained focused on the grater to make sure she

didn't slip and grate her finger instead of the block of cheese. "For not being where?"

When he didn't respond, she paused in her work to look at him. He nodded at her, his eyes flickering to her fading black eye. For the past week, Lauren had worked her magic on Emma's eyes before school each day, but now that it was Saturday, the lingering bruise stood out on her pale skin.

Attempting a smile, she shrugged. "It's okay."

"No. It's not," he argued. "The ridicule, the names," he stood up straight and turned his body toward hers, "the blame. I witnessed Lance treat you badly so many times, but I never did anything about it. I just watched. As the oldest, I should've said something, I should've done something to get him to stop, but I didn't."

His anger slid into anguish as he slumped against the counter, breakfast forgotten. She leaned against the counter beside him. "So why didn't you?"

His eyes slid closed as he dragged his thumb and forefinger across his closed eyelids. "Because I'm a coward."

Knowing they weren't the hugging type of family, but wanting to show some sort of affection to let him know she didn't blame him, she took a half step sideways so their shoulders rested against each other. "I don't believe that."

His bloodshot eyes looked at her and a laugh erupted from him. "It's true."

She crossed her arms, hoping he'd continue. He didn't disappoint.

"I was a book nerd in high school, everyone knows that. I had a few friends, but I was far from popular. That was Lance's crowd, and I was fine with that. But one day, Corinna Meyers talked to me. Pretty girl, a cheerleader, half the guys in school wouldn't have been sorry for her to set her eyes on them, and she was interested in me. I didn't believe it at first. I mean it wasn't like I was taking an active role in finding a girlfriend or anything, and aside from a few hellos, I'd never talked to her before. We hooked up one night at a party." He laughed a heart-wrenching laugh. "I fell, and I fell hard." He shook his head. "I was an idiot."

She didn't know if she wanted to hear the rest, sensing his story wasn't heading toward a happily ever after.

"We talked every day and went out a few times. I thought we had something good. A few weeks later, I took her to a party and introduced her to Lance as my girlfriend. Two hours later, she left me to go to the bathroom. When she didn't come back after a half hour, I went to find her."

He looked at Emma then looked away. "I found her in a corner of the basement...making out with Lance."

She gasped. "What?"

He shrugged. "I should've known she was only using me to get to him; it's not like her interest in me made any sense from the start."

"What did you do?"

"I confronted them. I sort of expected her to feel guilty, you know? But she didn't. She only laughed and said, 'Why would I want to be with you, when I could have someone better?'"

Emma's eyes slid closed as her heart broke for Logan. All this pain her brothers had experienced, and she'd been clueless. She was afraid to ask the question burning on her tongue. "What did Lance do?"

Logan exhaled a sigh, one indicating he wasn't completely over the incident. "He laughed and said, 'Sorry, bro,' before dragging a giggling Corina away."

"I'm so sorry, Logan," Emma whispered.

He turned back to his onion. "It doesn't matter. He was in it for the conquest of hooking up with another girl. Maybe he didn't know how I felt about her."

For the first time all evening, anger sparked within her. "Why do you do that?"

"Do what?"

"Defend him." The number of times she'd defended

Lance wasn't lost on her, but for some reason it felt different when Logan did. "After everything he's done, how can you possibly have so much compassion for him?"

"Mom," he said simply.

"Mom," she repeated the word, but it didn't bring her any clarity. "What about Mom? Because she left?" She shook her head. "That's no excuse. She left all of us; that's no reason for him to treat us all horribly."

Logan abandoned his onion again to face her. "You don't understand. Mom and Lance were really close. She went to all of his games, bragged about him to anyone who would listen, and she gave him anything he wanted. Lance loved her attention. For some reason, Lance and Dad never got along. Whenever Mom and Dad fought, Lance told Mom to leave him, telling her she deserved to live a better life without Dad holding her back. I don't think Lance was ever surprised that Mom left; he just thought she would take him with her. Lance held out for so long thinking she would come back to get him, that after she got settled into her new place she would send for him, but when she didn't, he blamed Dad and started hating him and the rest of us on a whole new level. Yeah, Mom left and we've all had to deal with that, but I don't think Lance ever recovered. I think Mom broke him."

The words alone couldn't have made Emma understand the depth of pain Lance must have felt, but the look in Logan's eyes did. The anguish for his brother's loss screamed from every line in Logan's face and pity filled his eyes, giving her a glimpse of the compassion her oldest brother had for others, despite how they treated him. How had she not seen it before? How had she not known?

Thinking about Logan's explanation for Lance's behavior brought her much needed clarity, and she started to see every interaction with Lance in a whole new light. Everything made so much more sense now. Every time Lance told her she was pathetic and worthless and a loser, he was voicing the thoughts he was thinking about himself because Mom must not have deemed him good enough to take with her. When he said Emma reminded Dad of their mom, it wasn't their dad she reminded, but Lance. It was Lance, not Dad, who hated Emma by association for all the pain their mom had caused him.

A tear slipped down Emma's cheek. For so many years everyone in her family had suffered in silence, at war with each other as they failed to find healing from one woman's selfishness. Emma wanted so badly to hate her mom, to hate her for all the pain she caused while she lived her dream life, but Emma didn't want to harbor hatred. Not for her mom or for Lance. She didn't want to sink into its depths and let it take hold of her, not when she could put the energy from hating into forgiving, into loving, into healing. Her dad and brothers deserved that much from her.

"After Mom left, I tried talking to Lance, to tell him to get his anger under control, but that only made me the target of his tirades. I hate conflict, I hated fighting with him...I hated him." Logan closed his eyes and exhaled a laugh. "I don't do hatred well." His eyes pleaded with her to understand, to not resent him for doing what he had to do to stay sane. "It was the last time I ever tried to stand up to him, the last time I put myself in his warpath. So whenever he needed a target for his anger, I let..." Logan paused and swallowed. "You're stronger than me, Em. Hell, you're stronger than all of us."

Emma laughed. "Why? Because I do hatred well?"

"No, I don't mean it like that. It's just—" His eyes scanned the kitchen as if searching for answers. "You're not afraid to face the fire. When things get bad, I hide, I stay quiet, I do whatever I have to do to not draw attention to myself. You rear back like a cobra, willing to strike if that's what's needed. No matter what Lance has said to you, you always come back stronger, and you haven't let him define you."

"That's not true." She thought about how Lance's words had been embedded in her consciousness for so many years, being the voice that told her she wasn't worthy of Riley's friendship or affection, that she didn't deserve to be part of a basketball team, that she wasn't accepted by her own family. She had suffered like the rest of her family. In so many ways, she attributed Riley and the girls on the team as her saving grace, the ones who helped her see her worth and made her feel she had good to give the world. "It's been hard for me too."

His shoulders slumped forward. "I just wish we could move past all this crap and be happy."

She nudged his arm with hers. "I think we're getting there."

He smiled down at her, the strain around his eyes lessening. "I hope so."

Pushing away from the counter, he returned to breakfast preparations, glancing her way every once in a while to share a smile.

Feeling like they'd gained a new level of trust for each other, she threw out a question, hoping to get an honest answer. "I don't know if I'll go to college, but if by some crazy miracle I do, do you think me going off to school is the same as Mom leaving?"

He stopped chopping and faced her again. "What? No. Of course not. Why?"

She dragged the cheese slowly over the grater. "Because I'm afraid Lucas will see it that way, and I don't want to disappoint him. I don't want him to think I'm leaving like Mom did." She thought of their littlest brother and wondered how her future decision would affect him and if he'd be okay if she went off and left him with their brothers. "I feel like we're all just starting to be a family, and I don't want to jeopardize that."

"You won't."

"How do you know?"

"Because OSU isn't that far away, and I know we'd all love to come see you play. I'm sorry for what I said before about college not being the right place for you; I was wrong. I think you going to college would be amazing. Plus, you can come home on weekends and during holidays. It'll be okay," he reassured her. "I promise."

Knowing Logan supported her like their Dad did brought her a sense of peace. Maybe they could help Lucas understand.

"Now I have a question for you," Logan said.

"Okay."

"What would you say if..."

She sensed his nervousness so she nodded in encouragement, telling him to continue.

Taking a deep breath, he set his knife on the counter, bracing himself with both hands against the counter. "What would you say if I told you I was thinking about taking some cooking classes?"

Her face broke into a smile. "Seriously?"

His head bobbed and his cheeks turned red. "I have some money saved and thought it would be fun."

"I think that would be great."

His head snapped up. "Really? You don't think it's stupid?"

She watched as he looked to her, almost as if seeking her approval. "Of course not."

"I was thinking maybe if I got good enough, I could get a job at some restaurant. Maybe I could earn more than I do now and help Dad with some of the bills and stuff, so he wouldn't have to work so hard. Who knows? Maybe we can go camping next summer as a family." He shrugged. "Or something like that."

She punched his arm. Who knew her brother had dreams of his own beyond the books he read? "I think it's great. It all sounds perfect." It sounded like she wasn't the only one who wanted a family. "But I expect home-cooked meals every time I come home. And cookies to take back with me. And full holiday meals, and—"

He cut off her list of food demands with a laugh and pulled her into a hug, their first hug. "Consider it done."

She would've thought a hug from Logan would be all stiff and awkward, but like Lucas, Logan seemed to need someone in his corner just as much as the rest of them did. His hug reflected his gratitude and relief, and maybe there was a little bit of love mixed in there too.

◆◆◆

An hour later, only crumbs remained from Emma and Logan's breakfast casserole, cinnamon rolls, and fruit salad. It turned out the Wrangtons liked breakfast just as much as dinner. Even Lance joined them, although he sat silently at the end of the table as the rest of them laughed and joked and stuffed themselves full.

The doorbell rang and Lucas jumped up to answer it as everyone else cleared the table. When Emma took her plate to the sink and returned for additional dishes, she saw Riley step into the kitchen.

She smacked her palm against her forehead. "I'm so sorry, I totally forgot!" Before their breakup, Riley and Emma would meet at the neighborhood park as soon as the sun rose to practice before everyone else showed up, but with everything going on, she'd forgotten.

Riley chuckled. "I see how it is. One little fight and we have to start from scratch again."

"That's not what I meant, and you know it." She crossed the kitchen and kissed him on the cheek. I'll be ready in a few minutes. Can you wait?"

"Sure," he said. "Take as much time as you need."

"I get to come too, right?" Lucas asked.

She tousled his hair. "You can if you want."

"Can I come?" Lenny spoke so quietly she almost didn't

hear him. He looked as if he was afraid she'd say no.

"Of course you can. We'd love to have you."

She turned back to finish cleaning when her dad stepped in her path. "Go."

"What?"

"Go." He pointed to the door. "Take your brothers and have fun. Logan and I can clean up."

She glanced to her oldest brother. "You sure?"

"Yep," Logan said. "It'll take five minutes."

Since they had cleaned while the casserole cooked, it was just the eating dishes that needed cleaning. It would only take five minutes with two people working, which helped ease some of her guilt. "Okay," she said. "Thank you. I owe you."

She herded Lucas and Lenny through the front door, with Riley trailing behind.

◆◆◆

More players showed up at the park to play than usual, so Shiloh, Emma, and Ashley took a break and let the guys play.

"It's crazy to think we'll be at college in a few months," Shiloh said. She had received an offer from Western Washington University. No scholarship, but she would have the option to try out for the team and see what happened.

"Maybe," Emma said. She couldn't deny the possibility that her next step may not be college. Since she still hadn't heard from Coach Krola, Emma figured Oregon State had decided to go with another girl, especially since the deadline to sign was only a week away, but her conversation with Logan made her think college might still be an option even if she didn't get a scholarship. She could get a job, save money, and maybe start out at a community college. It might be fun to go to the same school as Logan, and she'd be able to live at home and be there for her dad and brothers. Besides, community colleges had basketball programs too, didn't they?

Ashley covered her face with both her hands. "Please, please, don't talk about college."

Shiloh leaned toward the freshman. "College, college, *college*," she taunted.

"Stop it!" Ashley screeched.

"What's wrong, freshman?" Emma asked.

The kid pulled her hands away from her face and when she looked at Emma, her eyes glistened with unshed tears. "You two are my best friends and you're leaving. I'll be all alone next year."

"Aw, freshman," Shiloh rested a hand over her heart, "You gonna miss us?"

Emma reached out her hand to Ashley. When the kid took it, Emma pulled Ashley onto the bench between her and Shiloh. "We get it, kid. We do. It's going to be hard on all of us."

"Not me," Shiloh said. "I am *so* ready to bust out of high school."

Emma cast her a look over Ashley's head and attempted the whole silent communication thing with her scolding eyes and head nods toward the freshman.

"What?" Shiloh mouthed.

Emma shook her head and looked to the sky. When did she become the compassionate one?

Ashley looked between Shiloh and Emma, her face crumpling. "I'm going to miss you so much." The freshman buried her head in Emma's shoulder and cried.

Emma looked over Ashley's head at Shiloh. The girl who always had a comeback, who always knew the right words to say, was speechless, her eyes sad. As seniors they looked to the future and knew their entire world would change—college, new friends, work, and whatever else came with the decisions they made. But they hadn't stopped to think about those left behind and what challenges they would face. Sure,

Emma had thought about that with her family, but not once had she thought about Ashley. She was a sweet kid, and Emma had to admit she had grown a soft spot for the freshman, but she hadn't realized how much the kid relied on her and Shiloh this year, how maybe Ashley hadn't felt like a person worth much until they had taken her under their wings.

Shiloh palmed Ashley's head and then Emma's and pulled them into her arms. "You're all going to make me cry, and I am *not* a crier."

Emma laughed. She couldn't help it. "I'm not a crier either, yet after the gallons I've cried in the past two months, tears keep coming."

"Stupid girlie emotions," Ashley muttered against Emma's shoulder. The fact she sounded just like Emma made them all laugh.

"What are you girls crying about over there?" Tom shouted. They looked up to see half the guys watching them.

"We never realized how horrible you all are at basketball," Shiloh hollered back. "It's a disgrace to the game and just so sad; it brought us all to tears. No wonder you need us girls."

"Oh yeah?" Tom threw his arms out. "Bring it."

"With pleasure." Shiloh broke free from the embrace and hopped down the bleachers. "Sorry, girls, but I believe we have a game to win."

◆◆◆

After a couple hours at the court, Lucas and Lenny had found friends at the park and waved goodbye to Emma, so when the game was over, she returned home alone. She paused before ascending the steps to the front door. Lance's car was the only one in the driveway. It didn't necessarily mean anything, considering his car only worked half the time and he sometimes hitched rides with friends or took the bus, but still. If Lance was the only one home, was it wise for her to go inside? Her dad had warned her to stay away from her brother, or at least keep her distance unless other people were around, but she couldn't avoid Lance forever. Did he scare her? Yes, but she refused to spend the next four months in hiding.

A week ago she had resolved to give up on ever reconciling things with her brother, deemed to have him hate her forever, but could she really do that? The words she had yelled at him haunted her, holding her captive, and she knew she couldn't live with herself until she did everything she could to find peace with Lance.

She entered the house and closed the door quietly behind her, listening for sounds that would indicate who was home. Aside from the neighbor's lawnmower and a barking dog, she didn't hear anything.

Her bedroom called to her, begged for her to seek refuge among the hidden artifacts of her family, but her feet led her to the mouth of the hallway instead. Aside from the crack of light coming from Lucas and Lenny's room, the hall was dark. Her eyes narrowed on Lance's door. She took a step forward and felt the shadows converge around her, but she didn't let them push her back. Instead, she stood among them, trying to decide what to do. Proceed or retreat. She took one step forward and stopped. Her heartbeat quickened. Another two steps forward. Mouth dry. Another step and it felt like a heat lamp had been turned on overhead. Her breath came out in puffs as her nerves escalated, and she tried in vain to calm down. Standing outside Lance's door, she raised her hand in case she got the courage to knock.

This is a bad idea. No one else is home. Dad told me to stay away from him. There would most certainly be yelling. He could hit me again. Now's not the time. I already tried to settle our differences. No matter what I do, he's going to hate me forever. What in the world will I even say to him?

She lowered her hand as the excuses flooded in, trying to lure her away.

I think Mom broke him.

Logan's words sounded so clearly in her head. Closing her eyes, she took a deep breath and tapped her knuckles against the wood of Lance's door.

Thirty-Four

"**W**hat?" Lance called from the other side of the door. Emma pushed the door open, but didn't cross the threshold into his room. Her eyes scanned his room. One of the sliding closet doors leaned against the wall, the wood cracked. Contents spilled out of the closet, inching toward the middle of the room. A collapsing pile of clothes occupied the opposite corner. Old pictures and trophies were strewn across the top of the dresser and bookshelf. Fast food cartons overflowed the small plastic garbage container, littering the floor surrounding it. She didn't even want to guess the source of the toxic smell invading her nostrils.

Lance reclined on his bed, a rumpled quilt beneath him. He glanced up, and his mouth curved into a sneer. "You shouldn't be here."

I know.

"Dad told you to stay away from me. If he catches you, I'm not taking the fall for you."

Guilt for disobeying her dad paled in comparison to the guilt she felt over failing her brother. Their dad didn't know that the pain that lingered from their fight wasn't going to disappear until she talked to Lance. So yeah, she was willing to risk her safety and her dad's wrath to find some sort of peace with her brother.

With Emma's continued silence, Lance raised his eyebrows. "You come in here for a reason or just to stare at me like I'm some caged zoo animal?"

Against her better judgment, she took a small step forward, crossing the threshold into his room, coming into his territory. One step; no farther. She raised her eyes to meet his, holding her chin high to feign confidence. "I'm sorry." Her voice was barely more than a whisper, but her words seemed to shout into the near silence of the room.

Lance flinched as if she'd slapped him. "What?"

Taking a deep breath, it took everything in her to stand her ground. Ten feet still separated them. As long as she maintained that distance, his arms couldn't reach her, his fists couldn't punch her. "I'm sorry for the things I said to you." Shame and guilt washed over her, and she dropped her eyes to the bedspread. "About you being the reason Mom left and how..." She couldn't even bring herself to repeat the words that had fled so freely from her mouth a week ago.

Before she collected herself enough to speak, Lance finished for her. "And how the world would be a better place if I was never born?"

Emma winced, feeling the tension between them build. Maybe it was the punch he put behind every syllable or the murderous look in his eyes, but the words sounded a hundred times more horrible when he repeated them. She didn't know she could be so cruel. Lance, however, did. "You're not sorry," he spit out, rising into a sitting position. "You meant every word."

"That's not—"

"True?" he challenged her. "Sure, it is. So why don't you just be honest? Why don't you tell me what a horrible monster I am!"

She flinched at the power behind his words, knowing he had every reason to be mad at her. "You're not a monster," she whispered.

"How can you say that?" he shouted. He snatched the baseball from his bedside table and threw it across the room with enough force to crack the plaster of the wall. Her body shuddered, grateful he hadn't thrown it at her. Nevertheless, his action caused her to shift almost entirely into flight mode. She took a step back and bumped against the doorframe. "Life is hard—"

"Don't do that," he growled.

Before Emma could execute the flight part of her plan, Lance flew across the room toward her. The four inches he had on her seemed like four feet as he towered over her, his accusing finger in her face. She cowered beneath his rage. So much for the carefully conserved space she'd kept between them, thinking it would keep her safe.

His glare hardened. "*Don't* make excuses for me or try to make any of this okay because it's *not.*"

"Lance—"

"I hit you!"

The volume of his words, released with such force, reverberated through her. She screamed at herself to run before things got violent, but her feet refused to move.

"I lost control and I hit my sister." His voice broke on the last few words. The fight left him as he stumbled backward into the adjacent wall and slid to the floor. Pain and anguish flooded his face. "That's not something I can take back. Ever."

Stunned into silence, she stared at her brother. His elbows rested on his bent knees as he grabbed fistfuls of his hair, his face shielded by his forearms.

What just happened? Did her brother just fall to his knees? No. Not possible because that would mean her brother's armor could crack and he could bleed and feel pain and sorrow and Emma didn't know how to deal with that. Was Logan right? Had Lance been broken all this time, while desperately trying to appear whole?

The answer came so clearly to her. She had spent years thinking her dad and brothers were so consumed with hatred for her and the world that nothing could ever change, but when she pulled back the layers of hurt and pain and fear, she saw the root of it all. They were signs of grieving. Grieving over the loss of a woman who had abandoned her husband and children and left nothing but suffering in her wake. How were any of them supposed to think highly of themselves when the woman who was supposed to love them unconditionally had left them all behind in search of something better?

Forgetting her dad's warnings and Lance's tendency toward violence, Emma crossed the distance between her and her brother, then lowered herself to the floor in front of him so they were on the same level. Hands shaking, she reached out to her brother, her fingers closing around his forearms. His shoulders shook, and her eyes burned like fire.

"Lance," she choked out. "Lance, I'm sorry." For her words, for their mom leaving him behind, for the years of pain and hurt that had built up within him, for the loneliness he'd been drowning in. Essentially, for everything. "I'm so sorry."

Closing her eyes, she lowered her forehead to his bowed head, hoping he could feel the sincerity in her words.

A breath later, his hand covered hers. Strong fingers squeezed a desperate grip. A grip that begged for forgiveness, for strength, for a do-over for all the years wasted.

"I'm sorry too," he whispered. His fingers tightened around hers. "God, Emma, I'm so sorry."

That was all it took to unleash the tears stacking up in her eyes. The initial ones broke free and led the charge down her face. When she looked up a moment later to wipe her face dry, she met Lance's eyes. His own tears carved paths down his cheeks, and with each one, Emma saw the regret, the pain, the desperation. They stared at each other for a moment, neither of them saying anything until Lance growled. He dragged a hand down his face to erase the moisture lingering on his skin, his tongue swiping the ones that had traveled down his lips. "You're turning us all into a bunch of girls around here."

A couple months ago she would've been horrified at the mere thought, but when she thought about Ashley, Shiloh, and the rest of the girls, she couldn't help but laugh. "There's nothing wrong with getting in touch with your emotions."

"Shut up," he said, the hint of a smile on his lips.

Not knowing what else to do, she scooted beside him to rest her back against the wall and wait. She would take her lead from him, but as the seconds stretched into minutes and the minutes expanded into too much silence, she couldn't help but apologize...again.

"Lance, about the horrible things I said to you, I really don't believe them. I was mad and..." She swallowed the lump in her throat. "And I was trying to hurt you the way you've hurt me. I was wrong."

Her body tensed. However he reacted, she would deal with it. She just wanted this nightmare behind them.

He closed his eyes and leaned his head back against the wall. "I saw you play against Evergreen."

"What?" The change of topic was so unexpected and his admission so absurd, she must have misheard him.

He turned his head to look at her, confirming his words with a simple nod. "I've seen you play."

"How?" No, that wasn't the right question. "Why?"

His focus shifted to the ceiling and hers stayed on him.

"Every time Dad saw you play, he'd come home and talk about how good you were. He kept telling me I needed to see you play, that you took after me, but I refused every time." Lance's laugh surprised her. "The last thing I wanted to do was watch some stupid girls' basketball game, but I figured if I got to see you get shown up on the court by a bunch of girls, it would've been worth it." He shook his head and breathed out a sigh. "Man, I was an idiot."

"What do you mean?" she asked.

"You were amazing." Her heart swelled at his compliment, but the feeling was short-lived. He dropped his eyes and turned his face away from her. "And I hated you for it."

Her eyes burned again as his disgust for her surged in his tone. Knowing the truth and hearing him speak it were two different things. "Why?" she whispered.

He dragged his hands down his face, exhaling as he let the back of his head thud against the wall behind him again. "Basketball meant the world to me in high school. I lived for every game. I loved to face my defender and see fear flicker in his eyes at the prospect of having to guard me. I loved the feel of the ball in my hand. I loved the roar of the crowd cheering me on. People would always tell me how great I was and how I could go all the way, and I thrived for the spotlight. But then I faced off against Graham Conway. There was a lot of hype about us playing against each other. I thought I was unstoppable, and when we competed against each other at the state playoffs, I was convinced I could beat him—I was wrong. I got cocky. We started out even, but as the game continued, he kept the pressure on me. I made my first turnover in the first half of the third quarter, and he took advantage of it. It didn't take long for his taunts to crack me. A missed shot here, a sloppy pass there. He owned me in the fourth quarter. The more I faltered, the more he excelled, and by the end of the game he proved to be the better player."

His story brought back memories of her facing off against Morgan Quinn at the state tournament. Emma, too, had been unexpectedly beaten by an opponent.

"People thought I just had an off game and told me to shake it off, but I couldn't. I learned the hard way that no

S A M A N T H A G U D G E R

matter how good I was, there would always be someone better, and I couldn't stand to be humiliated like that ever again. The pressure, the expectations, everyone looking to me to be some sort of basketball hero. I knew I would fail every time, and I couldn't live with that."

"So what happened?" she asked quietly.

"I panicked. I didn't want to be known as a quitter, so I let my grades drop, little by little, until I became ineligible to play. Coach was pissed. He tried to set me up with tutors, but like you said, I played the big dumb jock card."

When she'd said the words months ago, she'd been grasping at straws. He had told her she was wasting time playing basketball. His words had dripped with loathing as he told her she was worthless and that their dad hated her. It was the conversation that had changed everything.

"By the time I realized what an idiot I'd been, it was my senior year and I barely had enough time to get my grades up to graduate, much less play ball."

"Oh, Lance," Emma whispered, her heart breaking for her brother as he stared off into space, lost in the memories of his own demise.

After a few minutes he shook his head, returning to the present. "The second I saw you on that court, I knew you were different than me. In your game against Evergreen, you didn't cave under pressure; you rose to it and all of your teammates followed. That is something I would never be able to do."

"That's not true."

"Yeah, Emma." His look left no room for her to refute.

"It is. Which proves how much better you are than me."

"No, I'm not."

"But you are." Sincerity lit a fire in his eyes. "We both have the skills, but unlike me, you gained the respect of your teammates. They look up to you and trust you, and you didn't let them down."

"I'm sure your teammates respected you too."

He shook his head. "No, mine feared me. I was all about myself. I did everything I could to get my hands on the ball and shoot, whether I had an open shot or not. For me, the team was only there to make me look good. But you—" He shook his head. "They'd follow you to the ends of the earth."

It was no use fighting with him. She could've told him that the girls had started out the season hating her and would've loved nothing more than to kick her off the team. Or how it had taken half the season for any of them to treat her as an equal. She ended up coaching the team in the Evergreen game because the girls had basically guilted her into it, not because they had respectfully reached a decision and consulted her expertise.

Nevertheless, her and Lance's differences on the court didn't matter. "We're not in competition with one another, Lance. And for what it's worth, I think you would've been great."

"Yeah, well, there's nothing I can do about it now."

The green eyes of Lucas and Lenny came to thought. "Maybe not with your high school team, but you've got a dad, three brothers, and a sister who need you now."

Lance shook his head, glaring at the ground. "You don't need me. You're all better off without me."

"Of course we need you," she protested. "You don't think Dad could use your help to look after Lenny and Lucas to make sure they do their homework and stay out of trouble? You don't think Logan needs you as his brother, as his friend, someone to rely on? You think I don't need you to help me prepare for college ball?"

"No," he said honestly. "I don't."

Emma thought about the email she'd received from Coach Krola a few weeks ago. At Mr. Ledger's suggestion, Emma had contacted the coach to ask if she had any suggestions on how Emma could stay in shape and work on her basketball skills over the summer. It was a way to stay on Coach Krola's radar and show Emma's commitment. "I've got a summer training program a mile long and I don't even know how to do half of the exercises." Yeah, she was definitely going to need a workout buddy. "Geez, Lance, open up your eyes and look. We all need you."

"I know what you're trying to do, but it's not going to work. After everything I've done, after how I've treated everyone, they all hate me. I can't go back from that."

"I don't hate you." Even as she said the words, she knew they were true. Yes, they had a history a mile long filled with hateful words and ill will, but she couldn't conjure any hatred toward her brother now.

"You should."

"Maybe. But just because I should doesn't mean I do."

"And just because you don't, doesn't mean you shouldn't."

She rolled her eyes. It was like the guy wanted to be hated. "You really need to get over yourself, stop making excuses, and be part of this family. Yeah, you've got some groveling to do, but if you stopped running, I'd bet winning people's trust would be easier than you'd think."

"Why do you even care?"

Her voice hitched as she tried to decide how honest to be. Might as well put it all out there. "Logan told me about Mom and how you thought she'd come back for you when she left, but she never did."

"How did he—"

She shrugged. "I guess you're not as unreadable as you thought."

"Lance," she said, interrupting his silent cursing. "You deserve to be free of your hatred. Mom's not coming back, but we've got a pretty good family here if you want to be a part of it."

The corner of his mouth tugged up into an almost smile. "I don't know how you do it."

"Do what?"

"See any good in me when all I've ever been is cruel to you and everyone else."

Emma shrugged. "You're my brother. Going through life hating you isn't really the top on my priority list."

Lance took a deep breath and exhaled. "So where do we go from here?"

"Where do you want to go from here?"

"I don't know. What if I..." He unclenched his fisted hands and stared at them as if they were weapons he feared.

"You won't."

He looked up at her, his eyes flaming. "How do you know?"

"I don't, I just—"

"Get away from her." Lenny's growl could've punched a hole in the wall.

Emma flinched at her younger brother's intrusion. She'd almost forgotten that she was forbidden to be in Lance's presence without supervision. Despite what had transpired between her and Lance over the past half hour, Lenny didn't know about it. Of course he would be hostile at finding her beside Lance, especially since Lenny had taken his role as one of her protectors seriously.

"Lenny, it's okay," she tried to reassure him. Her attempt did nothing to prevent him from barging into the room.

"It's not okay." His voice twisted in disgust as he pointed at Lance. "He's not allowed to be anywhere near you."

"I know, but I needed to talk to him. We needed to make things right between us."

"Nothing will ever be right as long as he's here."

"And you think he'll trust me again?" Lance muttered beside her.

"Shut up," she ordered him.

"I'm just saying."

"Fine." If Lance wanted things to be better, now was as good a time as any for him to prove it. No sense in her having to do all the work. She waved her arm in Lenny's

359

direction, ushering Lance to take over. "He's all yours."

Lenny took advantage of the pause to voice his opinion. "You hit her," he said through clenched teeth, staring at Lance but pointing at Emma. "I'll never forgive you for that."

Lance looked at Emma, his eyes squinting as if questioning whether or not he could trust her when she said their brothers were capable of forgiving him for all the wrong he had done. Her heart swelled when he rose to the challenge.

"You shouldn't," Lance said.

Lenny's eyes flickered between Lance and Emma, his forehead scrunched in confusion.

"I don't deserve your forgiveness, but I could use your help." For the first time, Lance didn't try to act superior to Lenny. His voice remained calm, his hands limp at his sides rather than fisted in anger.

"Why should I help you?" Lenny spit out.

"Because you'll be helping her," Lance said with a nod toward Emma. When Lance knew he had Lenny's attention he continued. "I'm not going to lie, sometimes I get mad and lose control, and that scares me. But I don't ever want to hit Emma again, so I could use your help to keep her safe."

"How am I supposed to do that?" Lenny asked.

"Be a good brother to both of us. Don't let her be alone with me. If I get mad, get everyone away from me and get Dad. Deal?"

Lance held his hand out to Lenny, asking for a truce. Lenny looked down at his brother's hand, unsure how to respond. Instead of slipping his hand into Lance's to forge an agreement, Lenny held his hand out to Emma. When she took it, he pulled her to her feet. As he led her back across the room to the open door leading out of Lance's bedroom, he glanced back at Lance who had resumed his position on the floor. "I'll think about it."

Before Lenny pulled her out of Lance's line of sight, she

looked back over her shoulder at the brother she'd been convinced she'd failed. She gave him a smile as if to say, "Good chat, big brother, but now the ball is in your court."

He gave her a half smile in return, and for the first time in forever, she caught a glimpse of the brother she hoped he'd become.

Thirty-Five

I t took less than an hour for everyone in the family to know that Emma had disobeyed orders. The previously quiet house buzzed with the voices from her dad and all her brothers. After sending everyone but Lance and Emma to their rooms, her dad pointed to two chairs on opposite sides of the kitchen table, silently ordering Emma and Lance to sit. Their dad stood at the head of the table, his hands gripping the back of the chair as he stared them down.

"Lenny told me he came home and found you two talking after I specifically told you not to be alone with each other."

He may have been talking to both of them, but he only had eyes for Emma.

She bowed her head not even trying to justify her actions.

"Thanks a lot," Lance called out over his shoulder.

Considering Lenny's history of hiding in shadows, they all knew he stood just beyond the kitchen, trying to remain hidden as he eavesdropped on their conversation. Emma threw a look at Lance, telling him to back off.

"What?" Lance whispered to her, as if asking how calling out their little brother was wrong.

"I'm glad he told me," their dad said. "It made me realize

362

we should talk about stuff. So let's talk."

Lance and Emma exchanged a look. What were they supposed to say?

"Why don't you start by telling me what you two talked about."

Emma swallowed, searching for the right words that would convey her motive for seeking out Lance. "I wanted to apologize to Lance for the things I said to him on the court that made him hit me." Shame and guilt still glazed her words.

"Stop, right there." Her dad's voice commanded her to listen. When she looked up, his eyes burned with an intensity she had never seen from him. "I don't care what you said to him, nothing, and I do mean *nothing*, gives him or anyone else the right to hit you. This is not your fault. Do you understand?"

She bowed her head but couldn't tear her eyes away from him. "Not even if I told him the world would be a better place without him in it?"

Her dad stared at her for a second before collapsing in the chair at the head of the table. He exhaled a defeated breath and dropped his hand to cover hers. "No, sweetheart, not even then." He looked between his two children, his eyes tightening. "How did we get here? Why are we exchanging hateful words and punches rather than jokes and high fives?"

Neither Lance nor Emma had an answer for him.

"Okay, listen." Their dad leaned forward to rest his elbows on the edge of the table and clasp his hands together. "No, you shouldn't have said that to your brother, but there are a lot of things he shouldn't have said to you either, and nothing gives him the right to hit you." He threw a look at Lance, and Lance bowed his head. It was the first sign of submission Emma had ever seen Lance express to their dad.

"If we are going to make this right, what do we need to do?"

Emma and Lance looked at each other.

"I'll move out."

"What?" Emma questioned Lance's suggestion.

Their dad seemed just as surprised.

"I'm not doing anyone any good by staying here, and I don't want a repeat of what happened." Lance shrugged. "So I'll move out."

A resounding groan echoed from the hallway. "That means I'll have to move out too."

Emma and Lance snorted laughter as their dad shook his head.

"All right, boys," their dad hollered. "Come on out."

For a second nothing happened, but then Lucas stumbled into view as if someone had pushed him. With a closed-mouthed grin, he raised a hand in greeting.

"All of you," their dad ordered.

Logan and Lenny stepped into the kitchen, and their dad waved a hand at the vacant chairs around the table. "Have a seat."

Lucas hopped into the seat next to Emma, giving her a smile, while Logan and Lenny stared at the vacant seat beside Lance. Neither one seemed to want to sit next to him, but Logan pushed Lenny into the seat at the end of the table before claiming the one beside Lance.

"So, about this moving out thing," Logan started.

Their dad held up his hands. "Relax. We're not deciding anything right now."

"Why not?" Lenny asked. "I think Lance should leave."

"No one's going anywhere," their dad said.

When everyone started talking at once, their dad scratched the back of his neck in frustration. "Enough. Let's take things one at a time. First off, I want to know what happened between the two of you." His eyes shifted between Lance and Emma. Since she had initiated the interaction with Lance, she figured she should be the one to start. Between the two of them, they recounted the conversation in general terms, neither one describing the more personal details for the rest of their brothers.

When they were done, their dad looked at each of his children in turn. "I think we should talk more. We need to start solving our issues rather than burying them, so I'm instigating weekly family meetings, and you are all required to attend. No excuses. Do you all agree?"

Emma exchanged looks with her brothers as they came to an agreement and nodded.

"Good," their dad said. "I know this won't solve everything, but I hope it will be a start."

He started to say something else, but the phone rang. All eyes turned to their dad, asking for permission to answer it. Their dad looked at Logan and nodded his head toward the wall.

Logan pushed away from the table and answered the phone. "Hello?" There was a pause as he listened to whoever was on the other side of the conversation. "May I ask who's calling?" Another pause. "Okay, can you hold for a minute?" He covered the receiver with his hand. "Emma, it's for you."

She waved away the offered phone. "Take a message." No way would she put some phone call ahead of her family.

"Emma."

She couldn't ignore the demand in Logan's voice, so she scooted her chair back to stand. "Who is it?"

As he handed her the phone, his face remained stoic except for the crease of concern in his eyebrows.

She braced herself for something bad. "Hello?" she asked tentatively.

"Emma, hi. This is Coach Krola. Do you have a minute to talk?"

Emma's heart raced as she glanced at her dad and brothers. *This is it,* she thought. She swallowed. "Sure."

"Great. I'm sorry I haven't been in touch in a while. There's been a lot going on, and we wanted to make sure we made the right decision for our team."

Emma nodded in understanding even though Coach Krola couldn't see her. Closing her eyes and bowing her head, Emma sucked up her pride and came to terms with the rejection. "I understand. Thank you for calling."

"Emma."

"And thank you for considering me to be part of your team, it was an honor just to be considered."

"Emma."

"I'm sure you'll choose the right person, and I wish you all the best."

"Emma!" Coach Krola laughed. "How would you like to be a beaver?"

Emma was confused. Why would Coach ask her if she wanted to be a buck-toothed critter that sawed wood with its teeth? Yes, the beaver was the mascot for Oregon State, but the question would only make sense if... "Wait. What?"

"My coaching staff and I talked about it, and we would like to offer you a scholarship to play for us next year."

Her legs failed to keep her upright so she fell to her knees, tears pooling in her eyes. "What?"

For some reason she couldn't think of any other word to say.

"Congratulations. We have high hopes for you and look forward to you joining our team. That is, if you accept our offer?"

Emma sucked in a breath. Was this really happening?

"What?" She seriously wanted to slap herself. "I mean, yes! Yes, I would love to."

Coach Krola laughed again. "Great. I'll send you a packet in the mail with all the details, but I wanted you to hear it from me first. Good job, kiddo."

Emma practically shouted into the phone. "Thank you! Thank you so much."

"I'll be in touch."

The phone went dead, and Emma let it fall from her hand

to the floor.

Her dad stepped beside her. "Who was it?"

"What did she say?" Logan asked.

Emma took a minute to compose herself and then found the strength to stand and replace the phone back in its holder. She turned toward her family. Five sets of eyes stared back at her. Talking through the emotion clogging her throat, she said, "I'm going to be a beaver."

A half second later, her dad's arms wrapped around her in a death hold and smashed her against his chest, as her brothers whooped and hollered.

"What do you mean you're going to be a beaver?" Lucas asked.

Her dad's hug loosened as they laughed.

"It means she's going to college." Lenny grinned up at her.

"When do you leave?" Logan asked.

"You're leaving?" The pain and hurt in Lucas's voice cracked Emma's heart, and the celebratory moment shattered. His eyes sought the truth from her, but she didn't know what to say.

"You didn't tell him?" Lance asked.

"No." Emma kicked herself. She should've taken the time to prepare Lucas for the possibility of her going to college, but as time passed she didn't think she'd have to.

"Oh," Lenny muttered.

Lucas jumped from his chair. "You promised you wouldn't leave." Lucas's voice broke on the last word.

"It's not what you think." She reached for him, but he slapped her hand away.

Their dad knelt down to Lucas's level and curled an arm around his waist. "Emma got a scholarship to go to college and play basketball, buddy." Their dad's voice held the right amount of patience and reassurance. "This is really good news, and we're all happy for her."

"I'm not leaving, not really," she said, desperate to

downplay what going off to college meant. "I'm just going to school, but I'll only be a few hours away, and I'll be back for holidays and weekends."

"And summers," Lance added.

Emma nodded. "See? I'll be home so much you'll hardly miss me." *Please help him understand.*

Lucas stopped crying and thought about their words. He sniffed and wiped his sleeve across his nose as he leaned against their dad. "Promise?"

Sighing with relief, she held her hand out to her littlest brother. "I promise."

He jumped into her arms and squeezed her tight as if wanting to believe her but not knowing if he should.

Crisis averted, she made to return to the table with her brothers, but her dad blocked her way. "I believe there's a boy down the street who'd love to hear the news."

She looked to the table. "But—"

"Meeting adjourned," her dad called over his shoulder before turning back to her and giving her a knowing smile. "But family meeting same time next week, and family movie night tonight to celebrate."

She stood on her tiptoes to kiss her dad's cheek. "Okay, I'll just be a few minutes." Jogging through the house, she realized she couldn't make that promise. "An hour tops." She pulled open the door, but before she shut it behind her, she turned back once more. "Maybe two."

Her dad waved her away, and Emma sprinted down the street to tell Riley that all their hard work and dreaming had finally paid off.

◆◆◆

The next afternoon, Emma lounged on the couch as Lance entered the room and kicked her foot off the armrest. "Come on."

"Where are we going?"

"You want to get ready for college ball, don't you?" He picked up the basketball by the front door. "We better start now."

She rolled into a sitting position, unable to hide her smile, and reached for her shoes.

"You want to come with us?" Lance asked.

She glanced up and shifted her gaze to see Lenny standing in the doorway of the kitchen, arms crossed over his chest.

Lance's invitation threw Lenny off balance. His arms dropped to his sides.

"Come with us." Lance propped his foot up on the edge of the coffee table to tie his shoelaces. "We could use your help. If it makes you feel better, we can invite Logan and Lucas too. We'll pick up Emma's boyfriends along the way."

Emma stopped on her way to the door. "Boyfriends? As in plural?"

"Yeah," Lance said, not looking up from his shoes. "Riley and Tyler."

"Riley, yes. Tyler, no." How did he even know about Tyler? Or Riley for that matter.

"Whatever. Like anyone can keep your love life straight."

A few minutes later, Emma knocked on the Ledgers' door as her four brothers waited on the sidewalk. The door flew open.

"What's up, Princess?"

Would he ever give up that stupid nickname? "You interested in playing some ball?"

He shrugged. "Maybe."

She rolled her eyes. "It's a yes or a no question, Tyler."

"Did someone say basketball?" Riley popped up behind Tyler, his face split into a smile.

She returned his smile with one of her own. "Maybe."

"I thought it was a yes or no question," Tyler muttered.

"Shut up," she muttered through gritted teeth, smacking him in the abs.

Riley pushed past Tyler and joined her out on the front porch. "I'm game. Anyone else coming?"

"Yeah." She looked toward the sidewalk. "My brothers."

Tyler's nonchalant attitude vanished as he followed her gaze. "Which ones?"

"All of them."

"Which one hit you?"

"Tyler—"

Riley cut her off. "The one with the basketball."

Since when did they become buddy-buddy? She positioned herself in front of both of them, placing a hand on each of their chests. The last thing she wanted was anyone throwing punches or seeking revenge on Lance. She sensed her brother was trying to change. After all, he'd invited her to play ball and invited others along, so there was no way they would have a repeat of the other night. "Guys, relax. Everything's good." She waited until they both looked down at her. "I promise."

Tyler closed the door and stepped outside, shaking tension out of his shoulders. "Let's go."

◆◆◆

Despite the years of training she'd received from Mr. Ledger, Lance had a few pieces of valuable advice as they played four-on-four, with Lucas playing both teams. With everyone in a good mood, the play was less instructional and more fun. No punches were thrown; no angry words exchanged. Just good old-fashioned basketball fun.

A couple hours later, entering the house with all of her brothers felt surreal. When was the last time they had all hung out together? Never. "I don't know about the rest of you, but I'm starving." She headed toward the kitchen with Riley in tow to figure out dinner options.

Lenny popped up in front of Emma. "Can we order pizza?"

Pizza sounded amazing, but as much as she didn't want to stifle his hope, pizza wasn't a likely option, considering she didn't have any money. "I wish we could, but—"

"Pizza sounds perfect." Riley leaned toward her, his lips brushing her cheek in a kiss before whispering in her ear, "I'll pay."

Emma was about to protest, when Lance spoke up. "No. I'll pay." He exchanged a look with Riley and for the first time, it didn't seem like he was resentful of the rich boy down the street. "But you're welcome to stay and eat with us."

Riley glanced at Emma, unsure how to take Lance's invitation. Great strides had been made in her relationship with Lance, but that didn't mean she knew him any better or had any insight into his intent. She shrugged a shoulder. Riley nodded. "Sounds good."

With a nod, Lance disappeared to order pizza.

Pizza boxes littered the coffee table. Light from the TV flickered across the darkened room. Riley, Emma, Tyler, and her brothers, sprawled across the old couch and rickety rocking chairs, immersed in a mystery movie. They each had their own theories as to whodunit; all that was left was figuring out who was right.

Riley's arm tightened around Emma's shoulders and his head rested against hers. On her other side, Lucas had his head resting on a pillow in her lap. He was two seconds away from falling asleep when the front door opened.

She looked toward the door. "Hey, Dad."

"Hi." His lopsided smile screamed exhaustion, telling Emma everything she needed to know about his day.

"You hungry?"

"Starving."

Emma started to get up, but Lance beat her to it. "Here, Dad, have my seat. I'll get you some pizza."

The coat fell from their dad's hand as he stared after Lance's retreating form. Apparently, a selfless gesture on Lance's part was too much for her dad to take after his long day. His eyes found Emma, searching her for answers.

"It's okay, Dad. You didn't transport to an alternate universe or anything."

"Are you sure?"

Refusing to look away from the screen, Logan answered for her. "We're sure. Turns out the big guy has a heart after all."

"I heard that," Lance said, handing a plate of pizza and a can of root beer to their dad.

Logan chuckled. "Good."

Lance picked up a pillow from beside the chair he vacated and threw it across the room, hitting Logan in the chest. Logan stuffed the pillow behind his head and snuggled against it. "Thanks."

Lance rolled his eyes and turned his attention to their dad. "Dad, seriously. Stop staring at me like I just arrived from another planet. All I did was get you food." He crossed the living room and sat on the floor, resting his back against Lenny's chair.

Their dad dropped into the empty chair and placed the pizza on his lap. While Emma and the boys watched the movie, Emma could tell her dad was more interested in watching them. He studied Riley, Tyler, and each of his children, trying to figure out what had happened to change things so dramatically. They'd had one family meeting, but surely that couldn't have made that much of an impact.

Rather than call her dad out on his staring and assessing, Emma pretended she didn't notice and instead, relished in the idea that for the first time in forever she was surrounded by her entire family and felt included.

Thirty-Six

B efore getting the official offer to attend Oregon State
University, everything had been subjective, but now
reality hit. She was leaving. No longer would she sleep in
the garage, get the wind knocked out of her when Lucas ran
from between the boxes to jump on her, discover too late
that Lenny eavesdropped on one of her private
conversations, have a cooking fiasco with Logan, or wonder
what kinds of thoughts Lance harbored toward her from
across the kitchen table.

As the day of her departure drew closer, Emma felt a
sense of panic grow within her. Was she doing the right
thing? By going to college, was she putting school and
herself before her family? When she left, there was no
telling how things would change, for better or worse, with
her dad and brothers. Maybe the college path really was the
wrong one for her or maybe it was the wrong time. So many
of her previous doubts about college still lingered. Despite
Mr. Ledger telling her to talk to her dad months ago about
her insecurities, she had avoided the conversation, but it
didn't feel right to put it off any longer.

After days and weeks of panicking, she caught her dad
alone in the kitchen. He held a steaming mug of coffee in

one hand and a section of the paper in the other.

"Dad."

He peered at her over the edge of the page.

As much as her feet wanted to pace a hole in the floor, she forced herself to remain still. "You know me going to school has nothing to do with me wanting something more or something better than you and our family, right? I mean, I know I won't be living here, but I'll come back. I promise. I'll be back so much you'll be sick of me in no time." She tried to force a smile, but her eyes filled with tears. She needed her dad to understand, she needed him to know she wasn't leaving him and the boys. When he didn't respond right away, a tear slipped down her cheek. "Dad," she whispered. "Please don't hate me."

He moved so fast, she didn't have time to react. He grabbed her arm and tugged her to him, crushing her to his chest. "I could never hate you," he spoke into her hair. "Ever."

Her fists clutched the back of his shirt, needing to hold onto his words, needing his reassurance that she had a home to come back to no matter what.

"I don't have to go," she said. "I can stay here and get a job and help around the house and—"

Her dad backed away. His hands gripped her arms and he stared deep in her eyes. "You'll do no such thing. You are going to go to college and make all of us so proud. Sweetheart, you deserve this opportunity. Take it and don't let anyone take it from you. Not even your own family. Okay?"

She waited for a forced smile, a tightening around his eyes, a flash of regret across his face, but none of it came. No matter how long the seconds stretched, she saw nothing but the sincerity of his love for her.

"You're sure?" The caution in her voice was unmistakable.

"Absolutely."

"And you'll come to one of my games?"

"I'll come to as many as I can. I may even be able to get your brothers to come with me."

Her lips grew into a smile, knowing he especially meant Lance. "And you won't hide, right? You'll let me know you're coming and we can hang out while you're in town?"

He smiled. "Right. No more hiding from you."

"I'm going to hold you to that."

The chuckle started deep in his chest before he delivered it to her. "I'm counting on it."

She looked around her room, trying to make sure she had everything. She didn't have much; she didn't need much. Even though it was the garage, she would miss it. Over the past few months it had become less like a hole she'd been exiled to and more like a haven. Images of Riley sneaking in to lead her down to their spot on the water, Lucas hunched over his homework, Lenny's shy grin as he admitted Tara broke up with her boyfriend, her two younger brothers bringing her flowers, Logan's invite to burn breakfast, the much-needed conversation with her dad about the woman who'd left them, and the place where a small paper crane became more than a promise—it became a symbol of the mothering love her dad recognized in her.

This is it, she thought. Knowing there was nothing left to take, but so much to come back to, she snatched her backpack off the bed and turned toward the door. She wasn't expecting to see Riley holding a present for her.

"Hey," he said. "I have something for you before you head out on your new adventure."

Smiling at him, she took the gift and released it from its wrapping paper. In her hands sat a new basketball with the message: "To Emma. With love always, Riley."

"Sorry it took me so long to replace it." Unable to look at

the carcass of the ball Lance had stabbed months ago, she had tossed the ball under her bed until she was able to repair it. Now, as she looked at the addition to the original message—*always*—she thought she liked this one better anyway.

Girlie emotions flooded her eyes. "Thank you."

"I thought you could use something to remember me by."

She laughed. "As if I'd need it."

Her life had changed so much in the past six months and fear flooded her at the thought of entering the next chapter in her life alone when so much of it would be different. "We're going to be okay, right?"

Riley wrapped her in a hug. "We're going to be perfect."

Unable to speak, she nodded against him.

"I'm scared too, Em," he whispered in her ear. "But I promise we'll get through this together. I'll only be an hour away. You call anytime you need me, and I'll be there. And when I need you, you'll find me crying outside your door, knocking until you let me in."

She laughed at the image, her arms tightening around his waist in gratitude for him. "I love you, Riley."

"I love you too, Em."

He slipped her backpack off her arm and slung it over his shoulder, while his other hand encompassed hers, and he guided her through the garage and out to the driveway where her dad and brothers waited.

Her dad's truck was packed with her belongings, and Riley added her backpack to the pile as she turned toward her family. "I guess this is it."

She hated goodbyes. Kneeling down to Lucas's height, she opened her arms for a hug. He didn't hesitate to return it. "I'll call you when I get there and tell you all about it, okay?"

He nodded and retrieved something from his back pocket. "I got you these, so you can do your homework."

She took the pile of pencils from him and failed to hold

back her laugh. It looked like he had scoured the house for whatever pencils he could find. Ones with teeth marks, ones with and without erasers, ones with designs. All of them used, most of them with some life left, and then she realized all of them were sharpened and ready to use.

His gift was perfect. "You saved some for yourself too, right?"

He nodded

Lenny was next. Before she could sneak in a hug, he held out his gift for her. "For old time's sake."

The most perfect orange stargazer lily rested in his hand, complete with the long stem...and roots.

"Lenny." She tried to scold him, but couldn't muster up the right tone. He flashed her a mischievous smile before flinging his arms around her waist and squeezing tight. How could she be mad at him now?

She shook her head at his plastered-on smile as she made her way to Logan.

"Your gift is in the truck. I hope you like chocolate chip cookies because I made them to last you a while."

"Yes!" she exclaimed as she received a hug from him. "I expect you to tell me all about your cooking classes and every piece of food you burn while I'm gone."

He bowed his head and smiled, probably hoping there wouldn't be too much. "You got it."

Lance was the last one in line, aside from her dad. She expected a short goodbye, possibly in nod and grunt form, but Lance surprised her by giving her a manila envelope with her name written across the front. "What's this?" she asked, unfastening the clip and pulling open the flap.

He reached out to try and stop her. "Don't open it..."

She pulled out a stack of newspaper clippings.

"Now," he finished, his cheeks turning red.

Her eyes scanned the first article, and then the second. She shuffled through the ones in her hand. They were all about her.

Lance shoved his hands deep into his pockets and stared at the ground, while she looked. It was like he had kept every article and every stat published in the paper about her, like he used to do for himself when he played. She never searched the paper for her name or game recaps, so she hadn't seen most of the articles he'd collected.

Words couldn't describe how she felt, so she didn't even try to vocalize her feelings. She didn't need to see her name in print or count how many times her name appeared in the paper, but the thought that Lance had tracked her performance through the season when she thought he'd hated her, meant everything to her. Not caring that they weren't a hugging family, she flung her arms around his neck and squeezed. He tensed. His arms remained in his pockets, but she still held on. "Thank you." Just before she pulled away, she felt his arms slide around her waist and hold her to him.

"Make us proud," he whispered.

Too filled with emotions, all she could do was nod. She released him and looked at her brothers. She felt bad leaving them, but she knew she had to give college a shot or she'd regret it for the rest of her life. Besides, she was determined to continue building relationships with her brothers, even if it had to be from a distance.

With a deep, shaky breath, she turned to the idling truck where her dad waited to make the almost four-hour drive down to Oregon State University.

Riley held open the passenger door for her, and she gave him one final hug.

He held her close against him for an extra minute before pulling back and brushing hair from her face. "I'll see you in week."

She nodded as he kissed her. It was only a week, but even that seemed like a lifetime at the moment. She climbed in the truck beside her dad, and as they pulled out of the driveway, she waved to Riley and her brothers until she could no longer see them.

Armed with piles of junk food, drinks, and oldies rock stations to ward off boredom, the time in the car with her dad passed too slowly and too quickly all at the same time. They talked more than they ever had, making plans for breaks and talking about basketball and family and life issues still hovering overhead. But when conversation ceased, Emma turned her focus out the windshield thinking about the friends she left behind.

Up until six months ago, she thought the only people she would miss if she left was Riley and the guys, but a lot had changed since then. Her family, the girls, Tyler. She felt a piece of her splinter for each of them as she traveled the miles from home to a new destination where she would be forced to survive on her own. Sure, Riley would be an hour away, but it wouldn't be the same.

Tyler had called his parents to ask about coming home. Apparently, he had mumbled his way through an apology and impressed his parents so much they made plans to go on vacation before he started college to rebuild what they had lost over the past year. Tyler had flown home a couple weeks ago, promising to come visit when time permitted. Him and Riley had managed to become something resembling friends and surprised everyone with a send-off bro hug at the airport.

A week ago, the girls had one last slumber party to say their goodbyes. Emma would never admit the number of tears shed and the number of addresses swapped to stay in contact with each other as the world changed around them.

Taking a deep breath, she leaned her head against the headrest and watched the highway steal away the miles.

They arrived at campus and the next two hours swept by in a blur. Unpacking the truck, moving her belongings into the dorm room she would share with some unknown individual, dinner. Now, as she stood beside her dad, she wanted to beg him to stay. She didn't want to be left alone on this foreign campus where she didn't know anyone. Sure, she had basketball, but she didn't know any of the players, and they didn't start team workouts for another few days. Her thoughts buzzed with fear and doubt and concern. Had she made the right decision in coming here?

Her dad cleared his throat. "I almost forgot." He reached into the cab of the truck and withdrew a plain paper bag. He handed it to her and she pulled out a cell phone. "Dad—" she started to say, but he held up his hand to stop her. "I know it's not one of those fancy iPhones kids your age have, and it's an older refurbished model, but it should work just fine."

She'd never had her own cell phone before, and she knew it probably wasn't an expense her family needed. "But, Dad—"

"No buts. I want you to be able to call me or your brothers from wherever you are, whether from here or when you're playing on the road. I want to be able to get in touch with you without having to remember which hotel your team is staying in. So, I guess you could say it's more for me than for you."

She gave a small smile before switching to the contacts on the phone to enter her home number, but there were already two numbers listed. "I suppose Riley's number was part of your plan too?"

He shrugged. "I figured my daughter should have a backup."

"Thanks, Dad," she said, wrapping her arms around his waist.

They stood beside each other staring around the campus in silence. She knew he had to go, but she wouldn't be the one to tell him.

"I have to admit, I never thought it would feel like this." Her dad's voice broke on the last few words, and she turned to him.

"What?" she whispered.

He looked down at his hands before clearing his throat and returning his gaze to her. "Having one of my kids go to college."

She opened her mouth to speak, but no words came out. Instead, a few tears slipped down her cheeks.

His arms wrapped around her and pulled her close, once again holding her together as she tried not to break. "You're going to be great, Ems."

"I love you, Dad," she said, squeezing him tighter.

He held on for a minute longer, then kissed the top of her head and held her at arm's length. "I love you too. Now go get that room of yours set up and call your brothers to let them know you arrived and that I'm on my way home."

She nodded. "Drive safe."

"Play hard."

One more hug and her dad climbed into the truck. The engine roared to life, and she wanted so badly to hop in the passenger seat and travel back home with him, but she didn't. She waved and watched him drive away until he turned the corner and disappeared.

Turning back to the building she would call home for the next year, she took a deep breath and ventured back inside her dorm.

College, here I come.

Acknowledgments

A huge thank you to everyone who made this book possible:

Verity Hiskey and Darcie Sherrick for taking time out of your busy schedules to read *A Shot Worth Taking* in its infantile stage and for your instrumental feedback.

Michelle Preast for capturing the essence of the story in the book cover.

My family and friends who continue to support me in my dream of writing.

My readers. With the infinite number of books in the world today, thank you for taking the time to read mine. Your patience and anticipation for this sequel propelled me forward in the writing process, even when I didn't think it would be possible to finish.

To my husband who never let me take the easy way out. His invaluable feedback made me think and rethink characters and scenes until all I wanted to do was throw the story out the window, but through his love, he made me realize that all the hard work only made this story stronger.

Lastly, to my daughter, who helps me gain a deeper understanding of love and family each and every day.

About the Author

A former three-sport athlete in high school, Samantha grew up with a ball in one hand and a book in the other. From the moment her first-grade teacher asked her what she wanted to be when she grew up, Samantha knew she wanted to be an author.

Samantha currently resides in Michigan with her family. When she's not writing, she can be found chasing after her two children. Books, writing, sports, and music top her list of favorite activities.

For more information about her and her books, visit her at www.samanthagudger.com or contact her at author@samanthagudger.com